BRIAN TRENT

REDSPACE RISING

Book Two in the
Ten Thousand Thunders Series

This is a **FLAME TREE PRESS** book

Text copyright © 2022 Brian Trent

FLAME TREE PRESS
6 Melbray Mews, London, SW6 3NS, UK
flametreepress.com

US sales, distribution and warehouse:
Simon & Schuster
simonandschuster.biz

UK distribution and warehouse:
marston Book Services Ltd
marston.co.uk

Publisher's Note: This is a work of fiction. Names, characters, places, and incidents are a product of the author's imagination. Locales and public names are sometimes used for atmospheric purposes. Any resemblance to actual people, living or dead, or to businesses, companies, events, institutions, or locales is completely coincidental.

Thanks to the Flame Tree Press team.

The cover is created by Flame Tree Studio with thanks to Nik Keevil and Shutterstock.com.
The font families used are Avenir and Bembo.

Flame Tree Press is an imprint of Flame Tree Publishing Ltd

flametreepublishing.com

A copy of the CIP data for this book is available from the British Library and the Library of Congress.

HB ISBN: 978-1-78758-658-1
PB ISBN: 978-1-78758-656-7
ebook ISBN: 978-1-78758-659-8

Printed and bound in Great Britain by Clays Ltd, Elcograf S.p.A

BRIAN TRENT

REDSPACE RISING

Book Two in the
Ten Thousand Thunders Series

FLAME TREE PRESS
London & New York

This one is dedicated to Donna –
the star in my solar system

PART ONE
PARTISAN

Year 348 of the New Enlightenment
Hellas, Mars
Redspace Jurisdiction

I still don't understand how a guy in IPC custody can escape, and then evade the biggest manhunt in history for the next twenty years. I've seen his dossier; I know he's clever. I know he has experience with strategy. And I see that he has friends in strange places. But still, twenty fucking years???

It's also aggravating that whenever I ask why he pulled his vanishing act, I get the bureaucratic runaround. As if his motivation is a kind of contagion that would convince others to break with the IPC, too. I'd really like to know why a high-ranking special investigator with the InterPlanetary Council decided to commit multiple counts of sabotage and murder, if only because his motivations might've helped me locate him for you sooner.

Those gripes aside, I'm happy to give you the news: we've received actionable intel on the location of Gethin Bryce.

He fled to Mars.

No idea how long he's been there, or what he's been doing. But your fugitive is presently hiding out on the redworld.

Of course, Mars did secede from IPCnet, breaking off all diplomatic and commercial contact, so we can't legally drop in and grab him. And since they're in the middle of the worst civil war since the collapse of the United States, there's that to deal with, too.

But hey, I did my job. Gethin Bryce is on Mars. Now, about my finder's fee....

—*Operative Mithridates, Listening Post 417*

CHAPTER ONE

Casualty of War

"We killed you," the unknown woman was saying as she squatted beside me. "We had to. You weren't responding to the reactivation protocols. Left us no choice but to take you down manually. I need you to sit up slowly. Breathe deep. Get your bearings."

There was a chalky texture in my mouth, as if I'd been eating dirt. My vision cleared and I considered the person before me. Pale eyes in a lean face. Cheekbones that looked like they could cut glass. Spiked hair. She was Martian-tall and ensconced in beetle-black armor. On her left breastplate, a military insignia depicted two dots flanking a large circle – Mars and her moons.

The insignia of the Order of Stone.

The enemy.

"We don't have a lot of time," the woman insisted. "But I can't send you back into the field until we've determined the upload has taken."

"What upload?"

"Sit *up*, soldier."

I didn't have the vaguest idea what she was talking about, but there was no harm in complying with her demand. For some reason, I'd been lying on the floor. Mouth still gritty with Martian dust – that shit gets into everything, like talcum powder. My back felt like it had been knifed just under the left shoulder blade. I rubbed my eyes and took stock of my surroundings.

We were in an airy building that had apparently come down on our heads: slabs of masonry lay scattered like giants' teeth. Twisted I-beams snaked through the debris. The green of an algae-lamp reflected in crumbled glass. That solitary glow steeped everything in a swampish, sickly hue, providing just enough light for me to read the placard on a nearby wall: **BAGGAGE CLAIM – GATES D, E, F.**

Beneath that was a large poster, red background and stylized silhouette of a Partisan soldier, accompanied by the words:

TRUE MARTIANS STAND TOGETHER. REPORT ANY SUSPICIOUS ACTIVITY, PEOPLE, OR CONVERSATIONS TO THE TIP LINE.
YOUR ANONYMITY IS GUARANTEED.

"Look at me, soldier," the woman commanded.

My gaze flicked from the poster to her stare.

"Tell me your name, rank, and current mission."

"My name?" Memories shuffled like mah-jongg tiles. Despite the rubble, I recognized that I was in Bradbury Shuttleport in the city of Hellas, Mars. I remembered being in a dropship, skimming the city's medinas and ziggurats. Remembered seeing sandclaws roaming the streets like the oversized metallic crabs they were, striding over makeshift barricades as easily as I might step over a rolled-up towel. Hellas was a war zone.

Mars was a war zone.

At war with itself.

I remembered the thrum of the dropship beneath my boots. Remembered it hovering above the shuttleport like a dragonfly over a pond.

The feel of a rappel cord in my hands. My heartbeat pounds in my temples. The excitement and fear of fast-roping out of a dropship never ebbs. The airport tarmac is deserted – the sitrep is that civilian air-traffic in Hellas is grounded. But that didn't mean the enemy wasn't already here.

My six-man squad clutches their rappel cords alongside me. We slide out together like spiders on silk tethers. Hit the tarmac. Spread out, advancing three-by-three formation, into the empty shuttleport. The dropship tilts away and vanishes over the building, keeping mobile until we signal for evac.

I remembered all this.

But my name? It was a blank spot in my mind. Like a sun-bleached corner of brocade.

"Soldier!" the woman snapped. "Your name, rank, and current mission. Report!"

"I don't know my name," I breathed, astonished to be saying the words. "But I know *yours*: Lieutenant-Commander Natalia Argos, First Sentinel with the Order of Stone."

The woman nodded. I abruptly sensed tension pouring off her. Her fingers whitened around the trigger of her multigun.

Following this one bright thread through faded tapestry, I continued. "You're Number Eight on the Partisans' Most Wanted list. Dead or alive."

Alive was the preference, because the Partisans employed uniquely skilled interrogators against enemies of the state. They would strip out Natalia Argos's neurals and plumb them for every scrap of information she had. Mars had been embroiled in a civil war for twenty years. The legally elected Partisan government had been increasingly challenged by a loose grouping of insurrectionists who, as the years rolled by, had coalesced into a formidable opposition: the so-called Order of Stone.

The Partisans therefore needed to know the enemy's battle plans, supply lines, covert operatives, sympathizers, intelligence cells. Needed to pinpoint the locations of their underground factories where they printed weapons of war. We especially sought to ascertain the names and locations of their leadership... the shadowy, ever-secret commanders of their resistance. And Natalia Argos would have that intel. She probably had a killswitch – an implanted bomb to blend her brain into useless soup. But a skilled interrogator could render her unconscious before she could activate it....

Natalia abruptly shoved the muzzle of her multigun into my neck. A standard-issue Greely model with default 3.33 millimeter unjacketed lead-alloy haze-release fleschettes, five additional magazines in the ammo wheel, and an EMP carriage beneath it.

"Last chance, soldier. What is your—"

"Harris," I blurted, the name seeming to outpace my conscious thoughts. "My name is...Harris Alexander Pope."

"Rank?"

Another blind spot. I was wearing the rust-red armor of a Partisan soldier, but I suddenly realized it was just a costume. Like one of Prospero's guests at his ill-fated masquerade.

And then the knowledge welled up within me, and I said, "I'm Special Operations for the Order of Stone."

"Very good," she muttered, a bead of sweat rolling down her neck.

Squinting in the algae-light, I considered further details of my environment. Martian dust had invaded the facility. It formed a granular residue on my tongue. It was also hazardous – prolonged exposure killed lung and brain tissue alike. Yet I wasn't wearing a dust-mask. Neither was Natalia. And I didn't remember my six-man squad from the dropship wearing them....

Which suggested that the terminal had been intact not so long ago.

I finally noticed a third person in the ruined chamber with us. He was an imposing, tank-like figure, framed in the algae-lamp's backsplash. Like Natalia, he carried a multigun. His armor, however, was bone-white and packed with ablative, tortoise-style layering. Nestled in shadow as he was, I couldn't make out his face.

Other details of the terminal collected in my sphere of awareness. Bullet holes and needle-spray perforated the rubble. Dead bodies lay scattered in the dust: a mix of Partisan and Order corpses.

"Looks like I missed quite the party," I muttered.

"The hell you did," Natalia snapped. "You were the guest of honor, you just didn't realize it." She glanced to her sole compatriot and nodded. The mysterious fellow moved off, making a patrol through the debris.

"Where are my weapons?" I asked, realizing how defenseless I was.

"In safekeeping for now. Get your bearings, Harris. Let the upload take."

"What upload?"

"You've been undercover with the Partisans for a long time. I need

you to remember who you truly are. Take all the time you need, but be quick about it."

"Yeah, sure." I shook my head. My thoughts coalesced like proto-planets wheeling around a newborn star.

My name is Harris Alexander Pope.

Having a name seemed to make things easier. It was attracting other memories.

I'd grown up in the coastal town of Lighthouse Point, where meltwater from the Amazon Sea was pumped into Canal Penthisilea and, from there, to the branching watercourses nourishing the cantons. In terms of human habitation, Mars was barely two centuries old, a child compared to the storied layer cake of Brother Blue and her moon. I remembered scampering along weedy shores as a kid, the velvet-soft, rust-hued sand between my toes. Remembered the sea's muddy, thick consistency, the polar caps melted by heating coils to return a long-extinct ocean to life after a billion-year slumber. Remembered, too, how sandstorms continually choked the canals and turned the water as red as an Egyptian plague. My first dust-mask was painted with vampire teeth.

More puzzle pieces clicked into place. I had a younger brother, three years my junior. Together, we'd scamper along the shore looking for oddly shaped rocks to pretend they were alien fossils. We'd buy pastries from kindly Mrs. King's bakery stall. On weekdays, we'd run to the seaport to meet Dad coming off his shift; Dad worked the sandships. My brother and I, sitting on the boardwalk, legs swinging over the water, eating our pastries and watching Dad's dragon-shaped vessel dock.

My brother! His name was....

"Dave!" I cried. "Where is David?"

Natalia frowned. "The exact location of *General* David Julius Pope is classified. But he authorized this operation himself. When we received word that you were back in Hellas, he acted immediately. Sent my squad to intercept you."

Life in the Partisan ranks fell away. The battles fought, late-night patrols of bombed-out cities. Years of memory unspooling as some grisly scroll in a dusky necropolis. Years of undercover operation. Years of battle....

Years?

"How – how long was I under?" I stammered.

"We're reactivating you for an important mission," Natalia said, breezing past my inquiry. "We embedded its details with the upload, so you should know it. Your orders are—"

"To infiltrate and destroy Partisan High Command and everyone with them." It was like someone else speaking for me, or having the words of an unfamiliar script appearing on my optics. Appreciating what I'd just said, I raised an eyebrow. "Infiltrate and destroy Partisan High Command? On fucking *Phobos*? How the fuck am I supposed to pull that off?"

Natalia bristled at my tone. "You've been undercover with the Partisans, Harris. As far as they're concerned, you're one of their most trusted operators. You've been working as a shadowman in their employ."

"That doesn't mean I spend my shore leave on a goddam moon!"

Partisan High Command was nestled deep within Mars's largest natural satellite. Decades earlier, Phobos had been a waystation and trading post, launching and receiving shipments to and from the rest of the solar system. Back when we were the ruby in the InterPlanetary Council's crown.

The election of 325 had changed that. The Partisans captured executive and legislative control of Martian government, and immediately made good on their campaign promise to secede from IPCnet. Mars broke off diplomatic and commercial relations with the rest of Sol society. Kicked out the IPC. Kicked out that planet-spanning corporate juggernaut known as Prometheus Industries. Kicked out the foreigners, the offworlders, the parasites on Martian society....

Mars was free.

For two years, the Partisans enjoyed control of the planet. They consolidated power in every canton. Took control of planetary media to free it of Earth influence. Arrested Earth loyalists...as well as those *suspected* of being Earth loyalists. Dissolved political opposition under the auspices of emergency powers.

And converted Phobos Base into a secure military bunker to keep a watchful eye on the planet below. Gods above Olympus itself.

How the hell was I going to infiltrate there?

"How the hell am I going to infiltrate there?" I demanded.

"You've been there before," Natalia informed me. "According to our intel, as a Partisan shadowman, you've been to Phobos several times."

I hesitated, sifting memories for the truth of this. Something ugly swam in my thoughts. I suddenly wasn't sure I *wanted* to remember Phobos.

"How many years was I undercover?" I asked again.

"Twenty."

Her words hit me like a grenade blast. "Twenty *years*!? I've been undercover for *twenty goddam years*?"

"We encountered unexpected circumstances."

"For *two decades*?" A sick feeling uncoiled in my stomach. "The plan was never for me to stay undercover that long! David would never have allowed—"

"I don't have time to explain it all to you."

"Make the fucking time!"

Natalia flushed angrily at my tone, but I could see her struggling to control her response. She needed me, that much was obvious. And it gave me a measure of power.

"Harris, you've been undercover as a shadowman. No one's *ever* been able to do that. The plan was to keep you embedded as a sleeper cell until needed."

"And I wasn't needed for twenty years?"

Natalia was sweating again, as if worried I might revert. "We couldn't find you, soldier. Shadowmen operate all over the planet. They're the best at what they do – infiltration, assassination, and straight-up combat. As one of their operators, you dropped off the ladar. It was only a week ago that your presence triggered a patmatch to local resistance cells. That's when the general – your brother – hatched this plan."

I was still reeling from the shock of it all. "My brother rose to the rank of Order of Stone general?"

"When General Pope realized you were back in Hellas, he devised an operation to end the goddam war. You don't want these twenty years to be for nothing, do you?"

I shook my head.

"Then listen up. You are to infiltrate Phobos Base and plant a bomb at the fusion core."

"But how do I get to Phobos? I doubt I can just dial up the brass and request a pickup!"

"High-value suspects are sent to Phobos for interrogation," Natalia said. "You're about to get your hands on a suspect as high-value as they come. An offworlder who many, *many* people have been searching for. We let it slip to Partisan intelligence that he was in our possession, that he's been a part of the Order since its founding, and that he was being moved to a safehouse." She pointed a finger at me. "Twelve minutes ago, your team shot down his transport. All you have to do now is go fetch him."

"And that's why the Partisans sent me and my squad here," I said, remembering. "We were to intercept and grab the target. We splashed his shuttle and were moving to retrieve him when—"

"When *my* squad hit yours. All for the purpose of reactivating you."

"Where's the target?"

"Exactly where you shot him down: Hellas Market. He's your ticket to the moon."

I stood on shaky legs, taking stock of the scattered corpses. Grisly halos of blood-spatter and viscera. Ropy brains, spent casings, empty magazines. The detritus of combat. A final chapter of life expressed in red footprints.

The shuttle is a blip on our dropship's ladar, flying low over Hellas. A dust storm rages, reducing visibility to only a few meters. We open fire and splash the vessel, knocking it out of the caramel sky like a duck clipped by birdshot. It comes down hard through the market dome.

Rappelling out from the dropship. Hitting the tarmac.

My squad enters the shuttleport. Beresha, Hammill, Conway, Shea, and Cuddy. Three-by-three formation. Zeroing in on our navpoint, numbers ticking down.

The ambush hits us near baggage claim.

Invisible attackers strike from all sides. Conway goes down first, then Hammill. Beresha and I leap into hyperacceleration and return fire. Needle-spray whispers by my face in slow motion. Trajectories burn in red arrows across my HUD. I thumb the switch on my multigun, selecting phopshire, and spray it in a glowing arc across the terminal. Invisible assailants are splashed as bright targets. Another thumbing of my rifle, selecting armor-piercing rounds. I fired center-mass, double-tap. One hostile goes down. Beresha is pulped three meters from me and I fall back to the cover of a column and—

Nothing.

The memory spool ends.

Natalia seemed to read my thoughts. "Like I said, we had to kill you. You fought like a fucking demon, Harris. You wrecked the goddam place. We killed you and healed you before you could become a permanent corpse like the others here." She indicated the bodies with a disgusted sweep of her hand.

"Who killed me?" I demanded. "You?"

Sighing impatiently, she pointed.

I turned to see that the mysterious third man had returned from his patrol. This time he stood in the full glow of the algae-lamp. His face was the stuff of nightmares, festooned with piercings and a web of chains. His flesh was scarred in tribal rows and glyphs. His teeth were fangs and his eyes were a rich violet. Tattoos glowed at his neck like neon gills. His hair was a lion's mane, dyed red.

A trog.

A goddam trog!

One of Mars's homegrown barbarians. Criminals, murderers, thieves, and pillagers, mostly hailing from the original and long-abandoned shipyards in Ybarra District. The Order of Stone must have been desperate indeed to have recruited one of *them* into the fold.

I met the trog's fiery stare. "Can I know the name of my murderer?"

The man was fully a head taller than me. Tall even by Martian standards. As massive and muscular a specimen as I'd ever seen.

"Not that it matters," he growled. "But my name is Eric."

"You don't look like an Eric."

"And thanks to me, you don't look like a corpse. I killed you clean."

"Um, thanks?"

The shuttleport thundered, spilling dust from the partial cave-in above. A marsquake maybe, or (more likely) an Order-versus-Partisan battle in our vicinity. Maybe the sandclaws in the streets were encountering resistance.

Natalia regarded the rubble as if ascertaining the likelihood of it collapsing on our heads. "Get to the transport, grab the asset, and complete your mission, Harris. This is the homestretch of the war if you do this right."

"No pressure."

Natalia smiled. It was a cold, cruel expression, and for a moment my memories clashed so vigorously they nearly gave off sparks. I was Harris Alexander Pope, soldier in the Order of Stone resistance, and in that capacity, Natalia Argos was my commanding officer. She was fearless, a tough taskmaster, an experienced combat veteran, and a key figure in their ranks. Her name and face were constantly parading around Partisan-controlled media.

But residual impulses from the past twenty years rang out like klaxons. Natalia Argos was the enemy. The Partisans wanted her alive or dead.

Preferably alive.

"Harris?"

"I understand my orders," I said.

"Then good luck, soldier." She gave me a brisk salute, but it seemed there was something mocking in the movement.

It was Eric who returned my weapons to me. I hefted my multigun, slid my shieldfist gauntlet over my left hand. Then I glanced back to Natalia.

"How am I supposed to blow up the most secure bunker in redspace?"

Natalia said, "We've given you something special. Outfitted your multigun with two very unique rounds."

I checked my weapon's ammo menu. The display pinwheeled open to show available ammunitions. Sure enough, there was a new tab there.

And whoever had installed it wasn't bothering with clever codewords.

ANTIMATTER ROUNDS (2) – OPTION SELECT

I blinked. "Holy fuck."

"Two is all we could give you. Don't waste them. You can set them for instant or delayed detonation. You need one at least to puncture the fusion core on Phobos."

"How is David?"

"He's the best hope we have. With your help, he's going to end this war."

"The Pope brothers save the planet, huh?"

Natalia was one of those rare people who can grin and glower at the same time, like a double-exposed Janus. "That remains to be seen. Get going, soldier."

I pivoted and fled into the darkness, setting my navpoint to Hellas Market. A hundred meters south, I turned down an inactive escalator and found a tram station. The trams weren't running. The shuttleport was a ghost town.

I hopped down onto the tracks, jogging along the black tunnel towards a distant point of light.

CHAPTER TWO

The Man in the Shuttle

The distant point of light was Hellas Market, the shuttleport's colorful central hub. I reached the station platform and hoisted myself into a jungle of high-nutrition plants – beets, spinach, red peppers, watercress, cauliflower, lemons, strawberries, pink grapefruit, white grapefruit, and sweet potatoes. The produce sprouted along floor-to-ceiling trellises, interrupted by placards showing the way to terminals, baggage claim, ground transportation, and the high-speed rails that crisscross Mars like radials of a spiderweb.

I hesitated, memories stirring.

Hellas Market!

It had been a monthly pilgrimage for my family – a jaunt my mother made with Dave and me as her helpful shopping assistants. Hellas was the premier supplier of fresh food, shipping its goods to every canton. But Mom liked to go straight to the source on the monthly Ides. I recalled the joy of those sojourns. The way our shopping carriage would gradually transform into a veritable arboretum.

The memory faded as I saw the shattered ceiling dome. Spokes of metal bent inward. The dust storm whipped across this breach, making a hollow sound like breath over the top of a beer bottle.

A message spiked into my audio:

Harris! You're alive?

Instinctively, I took cover behind a support column. At the same time, I plucked an airhound from my utility belt and flung it into the air. A 360-degree view of the market bloomed in my HUD.

Two hundred meters southeast of my position, Hellas Market had become ground zero for a shuttle crash. The vehicle was indeed the one my Partisan squad had blasted out of the sky. It had crashed through the dome, skidded across the agora, and lay sideways against a tangle of market stalls, splattered vegetables, and the sudsy foam of fire suppression systems.

A woman crouched by the shuttle, blowtorch in hand, cutting into the hull. She wore a flight suit and mirrored visor. As I gazed through the airhound, her blowtorch cut out and she turned in my general direction.

Harris? she repeated. *Are you receiving this? I've got eyes on your position. Respond please!*

"I'm here," I said carefully, sifting memories for the correct protocol. "What's your status?"

The woman laughed bitterly. *Relieved that you're not dead, that's my status! I've got airhounds all over the market but I'm alone here!* A hesitation. *Where's everyone else?*

"Dead."

What happened?

The woman's voice was instantly, intimately familiar. A rich, throaty voice that I could feel as well as hear. Watching through the airhound feed, I couldn't make anything of her face behind that reflective visor; the market's colors warped on its surface. Yet her voice was bringing memories into orbit.

"We were ambushed," I said, skirting parallel to the truth. "An Order patrol hit us in the terminal."

Fuck.

Committing to my course, I emerged from cover and advanced, vision split between immediate and overhead perspective. The woman slid up her visor.

I saw a lovely face, brown-skinned, with playful eyes that suggested mischief. Black curls peeking out from her helmet. She was of medium height, with features indicative of Persian or Pakistani genotype; her beauty was obvious even at a distance of fifty meters. Seeing me, she flashed a high-watt grin that made my heart skip.

Umerah.

Her name is—

"Umerah," I breathed.

"Your comlink went dead," she said, breathing hard. "I was circling overhead when I lost contact with the squad." Her grin grew larger. "Together again, huh?"

"Never apart for long," I said automatically.

The words leapt out of me spring-loaded, propelled by some autonomic function of wired-together neurons. And as I beheld her grin, a memory crawled to conscious light.

I ascend the stairwell of a burnt-out office building, climbing to the ninth floor. The Martian dusk is crushed velvet through the windows. At the ninth landing, I step into an empty corridor, watching my navpoint diminish to a pre-established rendezvous point. Rifle out, vision shifted to thermal. Ready for trouble. I don't know who my local contact is, and it's possible this is a trap: the Order of Stone has cyberwarfare specialists who can hackcast false breadcrumb trails, leading soldiers straight into an ambush. I watch the navpoint tick down in rhythm to my heartbeat.

There's a doorway ahead spilling faint light. I creep closer, peek inside.

Umerah Javed sits against a wall. She's laid a blanket out on the floor as if for a picnic. An MRE – chicken-and-broccoli by the smell of it – steams in her lap. A small lamp glows in the corner.

"U-Umerah?" I stammer.

She looks up from her ration, grins marvelously. "Harris! Together again, huh?"

"Never apart for long."

The memory pulled at me like mud at a boot. With difficulty, I brushed it aside. "Where's the dropship?"

Umerah pointed to the ceiling gash.

"You parked it on the roof?" I cried. "In a *storm*?"

"I'm something, aren't I?"

"And you came down here without support?"

"I thought you were all dead. What was I supposed to do, bug out? Our target was sitting here, prize inside…though I don't know if he's alive or dead." She wiped her dusty brow and her grin returned. "Stars, it's good to see you, Harris!"

I glanced skyward, saw her thin rappel line dangling there. "You have any idea how dangerous it is, what you did?"

She shrugged. "And yet here I am, without a scratch."

"Umerah...."

"Cover me while I finish cutting, okay?"

She snapped down her visor, and I saw my own scowling reflection on its surface. Then she resumed her blowtorch work. I scanned Hellas Market and tried to remember more. Tried to remember....

Everything. About this woman, about the war. Memories were there, but without reference. Like being dropped into someone else's VR photo album. Where do you start? Sifting twenty years of undercover life – *twenty fucking years!* – I found my only anchor to be the market itself. Being a little boy, wandering the aisles of produce and pretending I was some Old Calendar pulp adventurer like Doc Savage, pushing my way through a Congolese jungle towards a lost temple.

My attention slid back to Umerah. Sparks rained and danced around her handiwork. At last, a slab of metal dropped away like a fallen scab.

Beige crash-foam spilled from the breach. A shape moved, coughing and stumbling forward.

"Hold fast!" I yelled, snapping open my shieldfist and drawing my multigun over the transparent rim. "Let me see your hands!"

The shape hesitated. My optics auto-outlined him in the gloom. He was a man. An Earther, judging by that dense body.

He held out his hands.

"Come out slowly," I ordered.

"I'm unarmed," he said.

"For your sake, that better be true."

The shuttle's occupant emerged into the market's light. He was black-haired, handsome in a rough way, and sinewy. His eyes were as green as heated emeralds. My patmatch scanner read his face and threw a name onto my HUD.

I blinked, hardly believing what I was reading. Umerah must have been receiving the same data, because she gasped in surprise.

The man gazed directly at me and seemed to gauge my disbelieving expression. "Gethin Bryce," he said. "At your service."

The most wanted man in the universe! Holy shit!

Umerah's shocked expression mirrored my feelings. Awkwardly, she said, "Mister Bryce? Partisan High Command would like to have a few words with you."

His green eyes glinted in amusement. "Yeah? They're just the latest in a long line." He considered the state of his shuttle and sighed. "I really don't have good luck with these things, do I?"

★　　★　　★

We dashed through the market, following signs for the space elevator. Umerah had cuffed our quarry's hands, and she steered him along while I stalked ahead as vanguard, scanning for signs of ambush.

But there won't be an ambush, I realized. If we ran into Partisans, they'd think I'm one of them, as surely as Umerah still thought I was one of them. And the Order wasn't going to trouble us, because they needed me to reach Phobos intact.

We're safe.

The shuttleport concourse opened into the S-E tram's departure gate. I steeped myself in securing the premises. The western wall was a colossal sloping window, and Martian daylight – filtered through the dust storm – flooded the waiting area. My airhound was still with me, so I sent it to affix to the ceiling; its view took up a small corner of my own.

Umerah went straight to the empty reception desk and punched up tram controls. "Car is on the way, three minutes," she said.

I pushed Gethin Bryce into one of the waiting area's plastic seats. Then I viewed the scene through the window.

Beyond the tarmac and grounded shuttles, the tramline ran straight to the S-E for a half-mile. I felt my pulse quicken, much as when I was a kid, at the sight of the space elevator. Even through the dust storm, it ascended into a bruise-hued heaven like a mythical world tree. The sandstorm momentarily parted like a smoke-colored curtain; I saw two immense dust-devils chasing each other, hundreds of meters tall. They skittered in and out of each other's trail, and then the storm snapped shut over them.

A Martian sandstorm was deadly business. Its hurricane gales claimed dozens of people annually.

Umerah leaned against the reception desk. "So, what happened back there, Harris? I was sightjacked with the squad for about twelve seconds before the feed cut."

"Like I said, an Order squad hit us."

"You eliminated them?"

"Right down to the last." The lie came as smoothly as chilled wine.

"Whoever they were, they were a crack team." She looked thoughtful. "I only had a glimpse, but if I didn't know any better, I'd swear one of them was a trog!"

"Imagine that."

She looked sidelong at me. "You okay?"

I touched my fingers to the window. "I'm surprised the S-E is still standing."

"You kidding me? If either side lobbed so much as a spitball against it, the IPC would have pretext to 'protect their interests'." There was a sharp, bitter edge to her words – a pulse of emotion like a supernova lighting up an otherwise serene quadrant of space.

I glanced to Bryce. He sat obediently, hands cuffed in his lap.

Did he realize the Order was using him? Had he volunteered to help me get to Phobos? Or was he an innocent, sacrificial lamb?

I turned back to Umerah. Knowledge spooled from buried wellsprings.

Umerah Javed, pilot in Partisan employ. And a superb pilot at that. Taking a dropship into a hot zone was one of the most dangerous jobs in war. She handled her ship as if it was an extension of her body; she'd have been a Flying Ace in the Old Calendar's first big war. A *nachthexen* in its second. She'd even been with me at….

"The Siege of Noctis," I gasped.

Umerah raised an eyebrow. "Excuse me?"

"Sorry. Was taking a walk down memory lane."

"Tell you what, when we get to Phobos I'll buy you a drink and we can walk that lane together." She pursed her lips. "Do they have alcohol up there?"

"They're stocked with enough supplies to get through half a century." I spoke so automatically that I wondered if it was truth or pure bullshit. Natalia had said I'd been there before. I tried to remember.

It was a cramped place, set deep in Stickney Crater. I remembered the scene of its hangar from which craft darted off like falcons. Remembered how HubCentral sat within a network of corridors leading to the dormitories, supply caves, com array, and prisoner cellblocks. Ugly memories stirred, and I thought: *I don't like Phobos Base. I've been there several times over the past twenty years, and it's a place of fear.*

"I'm looking forward to seeing it," Umerah said. "Not for nothing, but Mars is a small planet. All this fighting? It's like microbes duking it out on a holiday ornament."

My attention flicked to our prisoner.

Umerah followed my line of sight. "Do we know why the brass wants him?"

"He's the most wanted man in the solar system."

"I know that, babe. But the IPC has been after him. Why do the Partisans give a shit?"

I shrugged and glanced to the tram display board. 1 MINUTE, 40 SECONDS to arrival. Squinting through the window and storm, I observed the covered track and pictured the car propelling towards us.

Umerah's hand brushed against mine. Instinctively, my fingers parted to allow the interlace. I remembered—

—*being in a CAMO tent in the foggy basin of Noctis Labyrinthus. The sight of Umerah skinning out of her flight-suit. Her tawny thighs straddling me. Her hips rolling in steady, relentless circles. Our hips and lips sealed together.*

The tent is unlit – we can't afford to betray our position to enemy snipers. My hands skate along the smooth geometry of her body. Her spine is a string of pearls....

Heat bloomed in my cheeks. Beyond the window, the dust storm was a tempest. It had swallowed not only the shuttleport, but the city as well – maybe the entire canton. Hellas appeared like some sunken Atlantis: an intricate warren of classical Greek-style structures set in concentric circles.

Still holding my hand, Umerah gave a toneless whistle. "Earlier this year, Hellas was firmly in our control. Now it's a goddam death trap."

"The entire planet is a goddam death trap."

She looked at me curiously. "You're usually more optimistic than that."

Thinking quickly, trying to choose the right words and not sure I'd find them, I was opening my mouth to reply when an explosion took out ten meters of track.

The blast made the window tremble in its molding. An instant later, the high-speed tram burst from the wreckage and went careening across the runway like an oversized tumbleweed.

Umerah's eyes went wide. "What the hell?"

"That was a missile strike," I gasped. "Somebody fired a missile at the—"

And then several things happened at once.

Gethin Bryce leapt up and spun towards the window, his previous calm replaced by instant, visible dread. Hands shackled, he strained to see the destruction that – even now – was being engulfed by the storm.

The airhound feed remained in the corner of my HUD; it suddenly switched to full overlay as it detected movement.

From the balcony overlooking us.

A narrow shadow had appeared there. A long thin shape suggestive of a rifle's stock, taking aim at Gethin Bryce.

I activated my blurmod. Umerah seemed to freeze in place, lips poised in mid-speech.

I rushed towards Bryce, shieldfist flowering open on my left hand, when a bullet whined through the ultrasonic and streaked towards his head.

★   ★   ★

My shield flared scarlet from impact. I grabbed Bryce – to my hyperaccelerated state he was as easy to move as a polystyrene dummy.

Another round splashed against my shield. I pushed Bryce away from the balcony's view towards a maintenance door. Then I looked back to Umerah. My blurmod shrieked as the charge timed out.

One second left....

I dropped from hyperacceleration.

Umerah was where I'd left her, blinking at my unexpected vanishing act. Her eyes found me thirty meters from where I'd been standing.

"Get down!" I screamed.

It was clear she didn't know what was happening, but neither did she hesitate. She leapt over the reception counter as rounds flattened against the window where she'd been standing.

The balcony! I transmitted to her. *The attacker's on the—*

In mid-transmission, an invisible shape leapt down to the waiting area directly in front of me.

I'd faced CAMOed soldiers before, the real-time optic camouflage and heat-sink capabilities turning such engagements into a deadly contest. Hell, Natalia Argos's team had been CAMOed when I'd faced them not twenty minutes earlier. Yet the technology had limitations: there was pixilation, battery power depleted rapidly, environmental conditions like rain or dust storms betrayed your position, and you had to vent heat before you literally cooked inside your armor.

The invisible attacker before me was wearing CAMO so perfect that I only knew he was there by the blocky shadow he cast. He was colossal in stature, far larger than the trog I'd met.

"Get behind me!" I shouted to Bryce, and expanded my shield's circumference.

A fusillade of rounds exploded off the nanofilament barrier, whining and ricocheting into the wall and floor. I fired back over my shield-rim.

And then I got my next surprise.

In response to my attack, green light sprouted over my attacker's invisible body. It was like he had transformed into a jade suit of armor. Shielding – not coming from a wrist-gauntlet but from his armor itself! He was encased head-to-boots.

The sight staggered me.

Who the hell had tech like that?

Behind me, Bryce was fumbling uselessly at the maintenance door controls. Security doors could only be opened by biometric profile, so he had a better chance of eating his way through.

Umerah popped up from the reception desk and returned fire. The shielded enemy fired back. My compatriot ducked as the counter erupted into chaff.

Behind me, Bryce shouted, "Let's go!"

"What?" I cried. "Door's open!"

Hardly daring to look away from my assailant, I rotated just slightly, amazed, to see that the maintenance door had indeed slid aside.

"How the hell did...never mind! Get in there and wait for me and... oh shit!"

My attacker's body-length shield vanished and he was invisible again. There was barely time for Bryce to slip through the doorway when I was struck as if with a battering ram.

I strained in opposition, amping my leg muscles. The would-be assassin shoved hard, pushing me backwards through the door. I expanded my shield so it was several inches wider than the doorway, snagging some leverage.

Not much leverage, as it turned out. The door's framing began to deform beneath the pressure. I amped my muscles to full power, trying to plant myself like a goddam tree.

Then I saw something *through* my attacker. The terminal window darkened as a shape hovered into view.

Umerah's dropship.

She must have called it by remote. Under her control, the vessel floated just outside the window. It opened up with a pair of fifty-calibers.

The glasstic window sheared away in seconds. My attacker grunted – a man's grunt – as he came under fire and sprouted his jade shielding anew. No defense I'd ever heard of could withstand a sustained barrage; to my relief, his was no exception. He bolted from the doorway and was lost to sight.

Umerah's head rose warily from the counter. Somehow, she managed to hoist her famous grin.

A window of opportunity has just opened, she transmitted.

I turned to Bryce. In the corridor behind me, he wore a haunted look.

"Our ride is here," I told him. "We're going to sprint to the ship and—"

The dropship exploded. The detonation was so near that it flung the desk Umerah had been using for cover and sent her flopping across the carpet.

Another missile strike.

But from where, goddam it?

Umerah recovered from the blast, lurched drunkenly to her feet, and blurred – transforming into something like a dust-devil to my eyes. My own mod automatically kicked in as its sensors detected her approach, the signal pinging back to my augmentation's receiver. The dust-devil coalesced back into my companion, while everything else became a slow-motion dream: the sandstorm a languid Ferris wheel, fiery debris from the dropship drawing incandescent trails through its eddies. Umerah had crossed twenty meters of terminal when a barrage of bullets streaked towards her. I leapt out, shield extended, to provide cover. Her face set in tight determination, eyes fierce, legs stretching in an Olympic sprint to attain the maintenance doorway.

In nearly the same movement, I thumbed my ammo switch, selected phosphire, and sprayed the waiting room.

It hit everything: plastic seats, floor, and walls were drenched in bright fluid. Some of the splash had caught a humanoid shape. Left leg, flank, shoulder, and part of a helmet. It looked like some transdimensional monster stepping into our reality.

My HUD auto-outlined the rest, extrapolating from what was revealed. The mysterious opponent was unlike anything I'd ever seen. His armor was an eccentric landscape of plating. The helmet sported diamond patterning. There was no visor.

Umerah and I retreated through the doorway. Bryce palmed the lock and the security door slid shut.

"Whoever's out there won't be stopped by a door," I said.

Umerah scowled. "And they've got a ship, too. Probably as CAMOed as he is."

"You saw it?"

"No, but that missile strike was close range." She jerked a thumb at Bryce. "They're trying to *kill* him! Why is the Order trying to *kill* him?"

She was right – it didn't make sense. Gethin Bryce should have been one of the safest people on a planet embroiled in war. Safer even than the neutral cantons, who were still susceptible to errant bombs or waspbot swarms with corroded IFFs. The Partisans wanted him alive. The Order *needed* him alive.

"It's not the Order," I guessed. "It can't be."

My compatriot stared at me, uncomprehending. "Why can't it be? What are you talking about?"

My gaze drifted to Bryce. He looked scared.

"The important thing is getting to the S-E," I said.

Umerah shook her head bitterly. "How? We've got no tram, no ship...."

"We can use the maintenance tunnels. Thing is, the blueprints would be encrypted—"

Bradbury Shuttleport's blueprints swiftly appeared on my HUD.

Umerah frowned, the movement of her eyes telling me she had received the same data. "How in the hell...?"

I looked hard at our quarry. "Did you do that?"

"You needed them," he replied.

"There are lots of security doors on the way to the S-E."

"I can override them."

"All of them?"

Bryce nodded.

I ejected my multigun's spent, steaming phosphire cartridge and loaded a fresh one. "Swell. Let's get the hell out of here."

CHAPTER THREE

Sacrifice Play

At the end of the maintenance corridor another door courteously slid aside for us. I went through first, followed by our quarry, as Umerah covered our six. On the other side, a short platform and staircase overlooked the Martian underdark.

My breath caught in my throat.

Most of the cantons had a subterranean dimension, a remnant of Old Calendar colonization attempts. In the New Enlightenment (with its successful marsforming projects) the ancient burrows had been expanded into fully functioning underground cities, ideal for when sandstorms went on their weeks-long rampages.

And sure enough, a portion of Hellas citizenry was gathered below us. Seeking refuge from the storm. From the war. From the upper world that had become a deadly game of *Go* between Partisan and Order forces.

I studied the narrow alley. Algae-lamps dotted the gloom, and people shuffled past these swampy constellations to gather at benches or underdark storefronts. I even spotted the indigo pyramid of a Brockhouse coffee shop; a few early risers were huddled at the patio there, sipping coffee and watching news holos. Mount Olympus appeared in a blazing hologram – verdant foothills, red midsection, and icy cone summit – while celebrity newswoman Victoria Nightfire of *The War Word* reported live from the volcanic battlefront.

I reviewed my available options. Always hated claustrophobic environments like this.

Umerah pointed. "We could try losing our attacker down there."

I jerked a thumb at Bryce. "*He'll* stand out like the Earther he is."

"Throw a shawl over him. Pretend he's our kid."

I considered that. It wasn't the worst idea. The problem was that the crowd would restrict our mobility, and if a gunfight erupted it would turn into a stampede. Besides, whoever the hell was pursuing us would almost certainly have airhounds – they were probably watching us right now. Our silhouettes would be tagged and flagged. Grimly, I remembered an old story from the Abraham's Flock cult – a bizarre tome called *The Bible*. In it, people had painted goat's blood on their doors as a sort of IFF signal to the Angel of Death, who spared them on its way to slaughter the first-born of Egypt.

I pulled a fleece from my backpack, tossed it to Bryce.

"Here's your shawl," I snapped. "Wrap it over your mouth and nose. There are multiple routes to the S-E and I don't want your face triggering any—"

Red spikes shot through my HUD. Hostile indicators from the northwest, above the Brockhouse.

My blurmod kicked in again.

I grabbed Bryce and jumped into the crowd below as a bullet whistled past and missed his head by two inches.

Landing hard, I expanded my shield until it was dangerously thin. Then I manually dropped back to real-time.

"Stay behind me!" I cried, positioning myself between the sniper and Bryce. Above, Umerah laid down covering fire at a catwalk above the coffeehouse. An instant later, she too dove off her perch as the bastard returned fire.

The crowd screamed, scattering in all directions.

Umerah crouched behind my shield and pointed to a boarded-up store façade reading PHARMACY. "How's that for cover?"

We shouldered our way to the store. The door had a manual lock; I amped my leg muscles and kicked it off its hinges. Then I shoved Bryce through the doorway and followed. The pharmacy's interior was a pillaged, ramshackle space. It was the doppelgänger of the shuttleport's pharmacy on the main level, aping the general look and floorplan of its topside outlet. The shelves had been looted, however. Several young men and women lay against the walls, legs sprawled out, their heads ensconced in VR rigs. They were alive, if the occasional twitch of their bodies was any indication. But by the body odor, they had been here a while. Hiding out in virtual playgrounds.

Umerah propped the door back in place. "Think it'll dissuade?"

"Maybe we could paint it with goat blood," I suggested.

"What?"

"Never mind." I regarded Bryce. "You seem to be taking this very well."

The green-eyed man shrugged. "This isn't the first time I've been hunted."

"Do you know who's trying to kill you?"

"No, but I can guess." He sighed in a kind of resignation. "It's the IPC."

Umerah darkened. "Bullshit!"

"There are no bulls on Mars."

"The IPC can't be operating here!"

Bryce raised an eyebrow in surprise. "Oh no? Just because you kicked them offworld doesn't mean they've gone quietly into the night. They've got special operators for this sort of thing."

But my companion was adamant. "That's ridiculous! That *has* to be the Order of Stone out there!" When he said nothing, she looked at me. "It *has* to be, right?"

I pursed my lips. "This *is* Gethin Bryce. The IPC has been after him for...."

"More than two decades." He said it with a certain pride.

"*Why?*"

"Maybe because I'm so likable."

Umerah and I exchanged a look. The legend of Gethin Bryce had been infamous when I was a kid; I recalled seeing his name and face on the newsfeeds. A hero-turned-criminal, a celebrity-turned-fugitive, and Sol's Most Wanted. The expression *hiding out with Bryce* spread like a dust storm from school playgrounds to my own college campus at Edlund.

And now...here he was.

In the flesh.

In *my* custody.

Back in 322, there had been some kind of incident on Earth. The blueworld found itself on the brink of war between the IPC and the corporate monstrosity known as Prometheus Industries. Ships from both sides had deployed. People had died. After three hundred years of peace, Earth was poised to collapse into Armageddon, threatening to take half the solar system with it.

Except in the end, the IPC and Prometheus stepped back from the brink. Peace was brokered…and it had been a special investigator in the IPC's employ by the name of Gethin Bryce who, along with a small group of comrades, had helped broker it.

Yet it's a reality of all decadent cultures that major events must pass through the filter of conspiracy theory. The newsfeeds entertained a parade of witnesses and experts who insisted that both the IPC and Prometheus Industries had been manipulated into the conflict by some mysterious third party. As to *who* or *what* that third party had been, gossip ranged from the mundane (blueworld terrorists) to the outrageous (alien terrorists).

As it turned out, a third party *was* officially blamed for the conflict. In January 323, the IPC and Prometheus Industries issued a joint statement regarding the mysterious Incident of the previous year. Together, they claimed that malevolent artificial intelligences had been responsible for the near-brush with destruction.

It wasn't so far-fetched. After all, for three hundred years Earth had been home to a single AI city – a place known as Avalon. The strange intelligences behind its walls seemed neither beneficial nor hostile; rather, they kept strictly to themselves. People warily studied them from afar, and maintained a policy of non-interference.

With the joint statement, that policy ended. Orbital bombardment commenced, scorching Avalon off the planet. Earth was once again home to a single intelligence. Human intelligence.

And as for Gethin Bryce?

He vanished.

Rumors arose that he'd opposed the AI genocide. What was known for certain was that in 323, Gethin Bryce sabotaged a research facility, killed everyone working there, and went AWOL.

The IPC scoured Earth for him. Planetary governments were deputized into the hunt. Twenty years passed and he'd managed to stay hidden from the biggest manhunt in history. Had managed to smuggle himself to Mars. Had kept his head down as the redworld seceded from IPCnet and erupted in civil war.

Until now, I thought with a chill. *And here I am, the latest link in that tale. Hiding out with Bryce.*

Umerah strode to the back of the pharmacy. A spiraling stairwell led up to a ceiling hatch – the topside pharmacy above us. She craned her neck. "This way! Let's get up there, take our chances in the storm."

"There's an IPC ship out there," I reminded her.

"Then we exit through—"

The north side of the store exploded. The force threw Umerah like a rag doll, showering me, Bryce, and the VR zombies at our feet with debris. One young woman was crushed beneath a portion of wall, a length of rebar spearing her chest. Her mouth was slimed with blood, but she kept smiling at some virtual fantasy…even as she died.

In the breach, I caught sight of an armored body leaping from one catwalk to another. I jerked my multigun, but the guy vanished.

Umerah crawled out from a sheaf of wall, coughing and spitting. "Hey babe? Time to leave, yes?"

I snapped open my shield as I crossed to her. To my amazement, a diagnostic warning flashed across my HUD:

SHIELD MALFUNCTION IMMINENT

"*What!?*" I erupted.

Umerah's eyes grew wide. "I said we should leave. Do you…not like that idea?"

I tapped my wrist-gauntlet's readout. Impact-data crawled. I stared, stunned, at the mount of conclusions.

My shield's nanofilaments were being *dissolved*. Already, the shield warped and withered in the store's dim lighting.

Hurriedly, I ejected the diseased cartridge and inserted my only spare.

But how deep was the infection? Would it rot the new cartridge too? I'd never heard of such a thing, and it was screwing with my assessment of an already deteriorating tactical situation.

Gethin stared at the breach. He was covered in dust, his eyes like two holes in a mask of grime. "That was an IPC praetorian," he muttered.

"A praetorian?!" I cried.

"Yep."

The top-line defense from the Interplanetary Council. Jacked to the eyes with the latest tech. The archangels in Heaven's army....

Umerah brushed chalk dust from her uniform. "I've got an idea, if anyone's— Harris! Look out!"

A black cloud swarmed at the breach.

Waspbots.

I fired an EMP cannister. There was an electrical burst, and the 'cloud' collapsed into a rain of dead machines, circuits fried, bodies jackknifing as they peppered the floor.

To Umerah, I said, "You were saying?"

She didn't reply in voice, but through subvocal transmission:

★Our attacker thinks we're trying to get to the S-E.★

★We *are* trying to get to the S-E!★

★We're trying to get to *Phobos*. The S-E isn't the only option for doing that.★

I was watching the breach for signs of another waspbot swarm. But at her words, I gaped at her. ★You mean...but...are you serious?★

★As the star. You take Bryce and head to the loading docks. I'll lead our attacker away on a goose chase.★

★What the hell is a goose chase?★

Umerah closed the distance between us and kissed my cheek. "Download a slang app, babe. Your life will never be the same."

"Wait! Don't do this!"

She squatted and examined the VR-addled people below us. Working swiftly, she pulled the dead woman free of rebar. Then she tore the shawl from Gethin's head and wrapped it around the corpse's face. Umerah hefted the body over her shoulder and gave me a final grin.

I blinked, heart pounding. I tried reminding myself that I – Harris Alexander Pope – had only known this woman for a half hour. She was expendable.

And she was handing me the opportunity I needed, to escort the asset to Phobos.

"We should stay together," I heard myself say.

Umerah shook her head, black curls dancing. *Just get to the loading docks. And when you're safe on Phobos, raise a toast to me.*

"Umerah—"

It makes sense for me to go out against the IPC.

Why?

Long story, babe. She kissed me on the lips. Her mouth lingered there. I kissed her back.

"Please don't do this," I whispered.

She cradled my face. "I'm not afraid, Harris."

And then she ducked through the doorway, body over her shoulder, and was gone in a literal blur.

*   *   *

I activated the CAMO functionality on my armor, slapped down my visor to complete the concealment, and buried my anguish. It was a live burial, however; kicking and muffled screams within the coffin of my mind.

I shepherded Bryce towards the spiraling staircase and we climbed to the ceiling hatch. Some forgotten engineer had screwed a brass placard into it, faded and scratched over the centuries, with an ancient coin – a United States of America New Hampshire quarter from 2061 Old Calendar. The words on the placard read: **LIFE IS A COIN FOR YOU TO SPEND ANY WAY YOU WISH, BUT YOU CAN ONLY SPEND IT ONCE.**

I lifted the hatch and pushed Bryce into the topside pharmacy. It was a brighter, cleaner replica of its Stygian shade. The shelves here were not looted, and there were no VR addicts present. The entrance was protected by a steel mesh like a castle portcullis; as with the rest of

Bradbury Shuttleport, it would take specific decryption and biometric keys to lift it.

I glared at my quarry. "Open it."

The man nodded. In seconds, the mesh rattled and retracted into the ceiling.

"That's quite a talent you've got," I said. "The shuttleport uses military-grade encryption." He said nothing.

We stepped into the corridor and hurried along its length, passing other topside shops that had sealed up during the storm and conflict. Following the blueprints, we pivoted towards a dead escalator and raced up its stairs.

"Where are we going?" Bryce asked, breathless ahead of me.

"The loading zone."

"Why?"

"Quiet!"

The way ahead was deserted. I tried not to think of what was occurring beneath us: Umerah, without any support, being pursued by an IPC praetorian through the congested bowels of the underworld. *Was she already dead? Covered in waspbots? Screaming in agony, alone?* Memories of a thousand deaths I'd witnessed during the war paraded through my mind.

I needed to get to Phobos.

For the orders I'd been given. For the sake of my brother's grand strategy.

For Umerah's sacrifice.

Please, I thought, *don't let these twenty years be for nothing.*

★   ★   ★

The loading zone of Bradbury.

It looked like a scene from a machine-dominated future on pause. The inclinator ran supplies to the roof for drone pickup and Lofstrom launch. Bots, cranes, and loaders were frozen halfway through packing an expansive inclinator with steel shipping crates, piling them into careful geometries like Mayan pyramids.

Gethin Bryce frowned at the fix-in-place machinery. "What the hell are we doing here?"

Ignoring him, I went to the control station and powered on the dashboard. Unlike the rest of the shuttleport, my admin rights would work here; the Partisans had appropriated all Lofstrom launchers on the planet. Partly, to have the option of getting emergency care packages to Phobos when other options were unavailable. Partly, too, to prevent anyone *else* from sending us care packages – namely, the explosive kind.

"Get onto the inclinator," I told Bryce.

My quarry blinked. "We're riding it to the roof?"

"Yes."

"As in, outside? We both know there's an enemy ship flying around there!"

"We'll have to chance it. The S-E tram was destroyed, and it's too far to make it on foot."

"So your solution is to cannonball us like in a Jules Verne—"

I seized him, threw him against the control station. "My job is to take you to Phobos, *by any means necessary*. Got that, Bryce?"

He met my gaze with a cryptic, dispassionate stare. The guy was cool under fire, I had to admit. Immortals tended to be that way; when you live long enough, you don't react the way younger generations do. You've seen so much, for so long, that it reshapes your emotional parameters.

At least, that's what I'd heard; I was only forty-five years old, whereas Bryce hailed from Earth arcologies. Those people tended to run long in the tooth....

Releasing him, I punched up the inclinator's warm-up cycle. Yellow lights dappled the shadows. "So how old are you, anyway?" I asked.

"Eighty-four."

I gave a sidelong look. He looked slightly older than me, which is to say, in our late twenties. Still, I didn't exactly hobnob with the ancients. We might all look in the prime of life, but there were people in the solar system closing in on their three hundredth birthdays.

"Made a lot of enemies in that time, huh?" I asked.

Bryce shrugged. "Must be my charming personality."

"Get your charming personality on the inclinator."

He complied, heading towards the crate-filled platform.

I set the inclinator timer for ninety seconds. Then I departed the control station, and managed to take a single step in Bryce's direction when my blurmod kicked in. A jagged arrow, like an angry lightning bolt, sprang to my eyes.

Something was rushing at me from the left.

In the microseconds it took for me to turn, my reflexive thought was that it was another bullet. Snapping open my shield, I twisted to face the attack.

It wasn't a bullet.

What was rushing towards me, like a derailed train-car, was the praetorian himself. Still invisible, though partly revealed by phosphire. He seemed a manic, vengeful phantom charging headlong at me.

Holy.

Shit.

There was no time to wonder how he had gotten back on our tail. No time to grieve for Umerah.

He struck my shield like a mass driver. The force was stunning, nearly shattering my shield-arm – my strength servos locked up. Energy exploded off the barrier.

The collision knocked me through the control station, shattering glass and support columns. Dazed, stunned into imbecility, I stared helplessly through my cracked shield, waiting for the follow-up assault.

It didn't come. A ghostly half-shape flew past me.

He was going after Gethin Bryce.

I drew myself up, blurmod screeching out its last bit of juice. And I saw Bryce, moving at the molasses crawl of normal speed. He was hoisting himself onto the inclinator.

I sent him a databurst, knowing it was useless, that his brain would never be able to process it in time. Yet I sent it anyway:

Get behind the crates! Now!

Antimatter is the most illegal weapon in the universe. It had decimated entire swaths of Earth during the Warlord Age. It was *the* doomsday weapon, an awful specter arising from the dust of a failed civilization. Since the New Enlightenment, the IPC had worked to dispose of any ancient storage facilities housing the stuff. Only the IPC was allowed to legally possess it.

Natalia Argos had outfitted my multigun with two capsules, each containing antimatter in a miniaturized Penning-Malmberg trap.

I didn't have to be accurate with it. The praetorian rushed towards the platform at normal velocity, his blurmod recharging.

I aimed five meters in front of his trajectory and fired a single capsule. It hit the floor at twice the speed of sound.

CHAPTER FOUR

Moonshot

The explosion still rang in my bones when, to my amazement, a familiar female voice pierced my comlink. "Harris! What the fuck was that? Are you okay?"

I rose unsteadily, grappling with the fact that I was still alive. The capsule's display had advertised as 'low-yield', complete with a ballooning diagram of the detonation's projected radius. Nonetheless, it still amounted to firing off an untested weapon. They don't teach antimatter munitions in any branch of the Partisan military. Exactly how the Order of Stone (and by extension, Natalia) had gotten hands on the stuff was anyone's guess.

The blast radius had gouged a perfect concavity in the floor. Everything within that blast zone had disintegrated. Including the praetorian. My armor was plastered with the chalky patina of what had been floor, crates, and several hundred tons of metal.

"Harris?"

"You're alive," I said stupidly.

Umerah Javed laughed across an unknown distance. "I'd love to say it's because I'm so totally amazing, but the truth is our opponent didn't fall for the splitting up routine." A hesitation. "How are *you*?"

"The praetorian is dead."

"Serious?"

"As the star." I felt tears welling in my eyes. "Umerah, I'm glad you're okay. I...."

"Where's Bryce?" It was a good question; I looked dubiously at the Mayan pyramid of shipping crates. They had toppled like building blocks, flung clear of the explosion. Bryce had been outside the blast zone, but that didn't mean he hadn't been crushed into a gooey pile. Like the VR addicts in the pharmacy.

Umerah's voice sounded: "Harris? Do you have eyes on Bryce?"

I was just about to tell her that no, I didn't have eyes on the asset, that the best I could hope for was to stumble upon the Earther's carcass in the rubble, when I found him. Caked in debris, curled up beneath the small space afforded by collapsed crates. Coughing, sputtering, looking as dazed as I felt...

...but alive.

"You're – you're alive," I stammered.

Bryce nodded. "Either that, or the afterlife is an awfully pedestrian place. Got your message. Dove for the nearest cover I could find."

I stared at him. "You *got my message*? You read it, processed it, at hyperaccelerated speed?"

The cool, measured expression was back on his face. "I'm a fast reader."

Umerah was still listening through my audio. She made a scoffing sound that tickled my ear, sending a pleasant shiver down my neck. "Stars, Harris. Glad you're both okay. Meet you on the roof."

As if responding to her cue, the inclinator completed its countdown and thrummed to life.

★   ★   ★

I had my doubts whether the thing would still work, considering the low-yield antimatter detonation. Yet the ninety-second command was nestled in the lift's computer, and whatever else had been obliterated, the lift itself proved functional. Dust shook loose as I paced anxiously, the inclinator crawling up the shaft. I could see the caramel sky. Could hear the banshee cry of the storm.

"We won't have much time," I said to Bryce. "Remember, that praetorian had air support."

He nodded. Dust powdered his face and hair, making him appear as his true age. "Even the IPC isn't immune to a Martian sandstorm.

They've probably landed somewhere, waiting for their ground team's evac signal."

The howling grew louder. The inclinator completed its ascent and we hopped off, watching the storm shriek across the wind levees.

Umerah sprinted to us, looking absolutely stunning in her form-fitting battle armor. Her face reminded me of a warrior-queen from a *Mahabharata* tapestry I'd once seen.

"Together again, huh?" she teased.

"Never apart for long," I said, and almost kissed her right there.

Her eyes flicked over my body. "What the hell was that explosion?"

"Something the praetorian had," I lied. "He must have been wired with a suicide bomb." I glanced around the rooftop. Helipads were painted in neat quadrants. The main attraction, however, was what appeared to be a comically massive cannon.

And, of course, that's precisely what it was.

Bryce blinked. "That's a Loftstrom!"

"That's our way offworld," I countered.

Umerah stole a glance skyward, as if expecting to find the enemy ship hovering there. "All aboard," she said. "Next stop, Phobos."

Bryce swallowed, visibly unnerved by the sight of the Lofstrom. They didn't have Lofstroms on Earth; the blueworld's gravity-well was too steep to make them feasible. But on Luna and Mars, they were the fast and convenient way of pitching materials into space. Far speedier than the slow crawl up an S-E.

I grasped Bryce's arm, dragged him to the launch pod. "It's not so bad," I told him.

"You've used these before?"

"No," I said, "but I've heard they're not so bad."

Growing up in Lighthouse Point, we were visited each autumn by the Dark Carnival. For the month of October, it unfolded its rides, funhouses, Arcadium stalls, food kiosks, and sensoramics. One of its contraptions was a reverse bungee ride unimaginatively named The Rocket. It was a test of manhood in my young life. You strap into the chair between two gantry towers, and then you wait, heart pounding, for the electromagnetic release of the bungee cords that sends you whipping skyward to a morbid height of almost three hundred meters. The Rocket. *Memento mori machina.*

The Lofstrom reminded me of that ride. Its cylinder curled upwards, supported by gigantic concrete pylons, aiming for heaven.

Umerah was at the control station, punching up a secure channel to Phobos Base. Across my cranked audio, I heard her say, "This is Umerah Javed, service number 77831-D-Talon. Prepare to receive supply shipment. Code Red. I repeat, Code Red."

The radio crackled. "Code confirmed. We are ready to receive."

She hit a final sequence of buttons and hopped into the pod, drawing the door shut. Pressurization hissed around us.

Bryce gripped his seat harness, adjusting it to his terrestrial form.

Umerah watched him for a time. There was curiosity in her gaze, and a tinge of sympathy. Again, I wondered how much Bryce knew of my brother's plan. When the Order packed him into that transport and sent him off to be captured by my team, did he have any notion of what was going to happen? Had he volunteered to be bait, or had he been thrown like chum into the water, ignorant of what awaited him?

And what *did* await him?

Fear squirmed in my thoughts.

I don't like Phobos. True to its mythological namesake, I'm afraid of it. Why? What the hell is up there?

Sitting beside me, secure in her harness, Umerah nudged me with her boot. "You okay?"

"Never better."

She gave a small smile. "For what it's worth, something big is happening at Olympus. Radio chatter is that General Monteiro is mobilizing her sandclaws for a massive offensive. Looks like the Order is about to be boxed in and cut to pieces."

"Terrific."

She touched my hand in the darkness. Our fingers brushed, interlaced, locked. I thought of other times we'd shared this gentle intimacy. Her fingers linking with mine in the shadow-rich privacy of pitched encampments, CAMO tents, dugout bunkers, and dropships. Closing my eyes, I focused on the rough quality to her fingertips. The creamy softness of her palms. The intimate space between her fingers.

"Launch in ten seconds," the Lofstrom VI spoke over the intercom. "Nine, eight, seven...."

Umerah whispered in my ear, "I want this war over as much as you do. Maybe we're on the cusp of good things."

I said nothing in response to this. I kept my eyes shut, held her hand, and read Natalia's embedded orders in my private blackness:

Infiltrate and destroy Partisan High Command on Phobos...

...and kill everyone up there.

The Lofstrom shot us off the surface of Mars, like a cannonball aiming for the moon in a flatfilm from another time and place.

CHAPTER FIVE

The Vampire Heart of Phobos

Phobos Base sat deep in Stickney Crater like a mythic abbey, sunken and forgotten. As the ugly moon filled our view through the crate's slot, Umerah and I pressed to the glasstic. We had sailed past Mars's orbital defense arrays – half-convinced they were going to blast us to smithereens despite the communication we'd sent. Now we were falling into Phobos's gravity-well, Stickney looking for all the world like a circular black lake ringed by the moon's elaborate point-defense network. As we plummeted into the crater, it looked less like a lake and more like some disease, a livid pustule festering on a plague victim.

I've been here before, I reminded myself. I sifted my memories, felt a convulsive shudder, and withdrew the attempt.

"Hey," Umerah said, prodding me again with her boot. She was strapped into place beside me, legs dangling. "You feeling all right?"

"The gravity," I lied.

She stared hard at me. Strapped across from her, Gethin Bryce looked as calm as a goddam monk.

Because he doesn't know what's up here, I thought. *He comes from Earth, and he's been living on Mars. But all he knows of Phobos is that it appears in the sky and careens like a hurried celestial rabbit to the eastern horizon. Might even know something of its history, geology, and orbital mechanics. But he doesn't know what's become of it.*

Sickness bubbled in my stomach. I tried remembering the last thing I'd eaten, and when.

The answer came to me: earlier that morning, in the Partisan-occupied corner of Hellas. My squad and I had woken at 0400 and cracked open an MRE breakfast consisting of vat-grown bison meat, lemon rice, and spinach. That had been many hours ago. There couldn't be so much as a rice grain left in my digestive tract.

The crater swallowed us. Everything went dark.

As if I'd been killed again.

Moments later, the clang of pitons thumped our pod, grabbing it and arresting our descent. Reeling us into anchor. And then an unusual, steady thrumming sound, like some chintzy sci-fi sound effect....

Umerah stiffened in the blackness. "What the hell's that sound? That pulsing...."

"Ultrasonics," I explained.

"Ultrasonics?"

"They're scanning us. Your message aside, they want to make sure we're not a Trojan Horse of explosives." I tried not to think of the remaining antimatter capsule in my multigun.

The multigun!

All visitors to Phobos had to relinquish their weapons. Heart pounding furiously, I shifted my vision to infrared. Umerah and Bryce appeared like glowing-eyed arboreal creatures in their harnesses. Quietly, I hefted my weapon and ejected the capsule Natalia had given me, tucked it into my palm, and slid it into a thigh compartment of my armor.

Our launch pod docked in an airlock. Clamps snapped around us.

I felt Bryce's eyes on me in the darkness.

Does he know what I'm here to do?

I couldn't believe the Order would have told him. It wasn't merely plausible deniability, but *actual* deniability that counted in an age when neurals could be ripped out and pasted into an interrogation box. The Partisans would scour every dendrite, shake loose every quantum of data from his cerebral matrix.

I stole a glance to Umerah. She had overcome her initial anxiety and was smiling now, a happy girl who had gone into space.

The pod door slid aside. We squinted at a transparent corridor leading across the hangar to the base proper. Several ships were clamped into moorings – small, nimble transports designed for planetfall drops. There were rows of colorful shipping crates, too, supplying the brass with what they couldn't make or grow or print on the moon.

"I feel like the blood is pooling in my head," Umerah muttered, walking beside me.

"The low-G here takes a while to adjust to."

"How many times have you been here?"

"Enough times to know you'll get used to it." My evasive answer felt like truth; the corridor was familiar, and my body was attuning to the gravity in a way not dissimilar to an experienced mariner's sea legs. The conduits of my brain hummed with knowledge of Phobos's floor plans, dormitory, mess hall, and...other, shadowy chambers.

Another pressure door opened. There was a blast of recycled air. Just beyond the threshold, picosurv scanners ringed the chamber like the ribs of a whale.

"Please discard all weapons and stand with your arms and feet apart," a woman's voice said from the intercom. Scanners appeared on the ceiling like clusters of radioactive blisters.

I nodded to Umerah. "You first, sweetheart."

She had her mirrored visor tucked under one arm like a fencer after a match; now she placed it on a sliding rack and proceeded to shed her service pistol, multigun, and grenades. Then she stood, arms out, legs slightly spread, as the scanning arc passed over her. Cold and clinical, it proceeded to sniff her biochemistry, measure the tilt of every motion, pressing an invisible ear to her speech and breathing patterns.

"Please state your name and service number," the voice commanded.

"Umerah Javed, service number 77831-D-Talon," she said.

A wall light flushed green, inviting her to proceed through the hatchway. Umerah passed out of sight with a wondering expression on her face that made her look like a child. I tried to remember the last time I'd felt awe like that.

Bryce went through next; the scanning arc seemed to pay extra attention to him.

"Please state your name and service number."

"Gethin Bryce, prisoner number 24601." He glanced back to me. "Fugitive first class."

He studied the scanning equipment even as it studied him, and when the light flushed green it matched his eyes.

It took me three full minutes to shed all my weapons: multigun, shieldfist gauntlet, service pistol, grenades, stiletto knife, ammo wheels, EMP charges, waspbot cannisters, and a diverse array of spare ammo clips. Then I edged forward and listened to the arc actuators as they spun. My heartbeat tapped at my wrists. An imp of the perverse rang in my thoughts, dwelling on the antimatter capsule in my thigh compartment.

"Please state your name and service number."

"Harris Alexander Pope. Service number 29491-T-Scythe."

The machine whirred over me.

Don't think of the capsule. Don't think of the capsule. Don't think—

The light turned green.

*   *   *

HubCentral was the vampire heart of Partisan command. It was an octagonal *sanctum sanctorum* ringed by individual broadcast podiums, not so different from a newsroom chamber and fulfilling a similar role. Partisan generals stood at each podium like conductors playing to unseen orchestras – receiving and relaying orders to planetside battalions in multicolored holography. It was a who's who of the besieged Martian military government – Generals Eileen Monteiro, Sabrina Potts (wearing a goddam eye-patch), Wesam Mujahid, Seraphim Pronovost, Kazafumi Ortiz, and Andrey Popova…but upon entry my attention was entirely arrested by the massive hologram of Olympus Mons at the room's center.

I stared, transfixed.

The volcano's three-dimensional display was like some alien artifact, divided into zones of control and zones of resistance and zones that had been lost wholly to Order forces. Lights crawled in tune to real-time tactical updates like competing colonies of luminescent ants: ruby ants for Partisan forces, blue ants for the Order of Stone. There were also indigo ants showing the march of sandclaw units – even now scuttling up the volcanic foothills to the contested mid-range – and orange ants for mobile, ground-based enemy turrets laying down covering fire. There was an exposed inner layer to the volcano, showing the miles upon miles of known lava tubes where troops were fighting and dying like fumigated termites.

I'd conducted shadowman operations in those forested foothills. Twice, I'd been sent to rescue the crew of downed Partisan craft on the barren mid-range above the cyanobacterial grids. As for the frozen cone summit, I'd seen it from afar throughout my life but had never ventured up that slope except in scholastic holo-tours, where my classmates and I viewed the Martian horizon bending like a frown.

Now, I saw the volcano as I'd never seen it – a marvel of billion-year-old geological happenstance under siege from the species of a neighboring planet. *War of the Worlds* in reverse.

Someone slapped my shoulder.

I thought it was Umerah, but when I turned I saw a man's face.

The other people in HubCentral – the generals and their assistants – looked harried and sickly – Phobos's weak gravity required constant physical and nanite maintenance, resulting in a disturbingly ghoulish pallor, their bodies wasting away to scarecrow reductions. Somehow, the man I now beheld had managed to preserve a sense of vitality. His sandy-blond hair and pale blue eyes accentuated a boyish face, a prankster, a player, a charismatic socialite. Teeth as white as alabaster. Eyes like some polar opposite of Gethin Bryce's – blue as winter ice. He wore a black uniform with the Partisan flag on one breast pocket.

"Harris!" he said, grinning broadly.

My heart spasmed in my chest. I raised my hand in salute, sifting memories.

Minister Peznowski.

"Minister Peznowski," I said.

The Partisans had appointed a host of political positions beyond those designated by the Martian Constitution, in effect creating a separate wing of government that directly supported the executive branch. These 'ministers' represented a broad cross section of political, social, cultural, and legal life. Ultimately, they were charged with rooting out all blueworld influence.

What Caleb Gradivus Peznowski had done before the war wasn't widely known. He had been an early supporter, I knew that much, having seen footage of his attendance at planetside rallies back when they were only a fringe group known as MarsAlone. After the election of 325, he was swiftly inducted into the political fold and appointed Minister of Media Intelligence.

He was in charge of interrogating the prisoners I brought here.

Umerah and I saluted him.

He cheerfully saluted us back, but clearly had eyes for our quarry. "Gethin Bryce! The most wanted man in the universe! Welcome to Phobos!"

Gethin shrugged. "I'll take what accommodations I can get."

Peznowski grinned. "We have our share of VIP criminals here, but no one of your status! Don't worry, sir. No extradition requests will ever be honored for *you*." His smile was radiant. "Fact is, no one will know you're here. Ever."

He nodded, and guards took Bryce towards a hatch marked CELLBLOCK.

"The IPC might already know he's here," I said when they were gone.

Peznowski raised an eyebrow. "Oh?"

"They sent an assassin after him."

"An assassin?"

"An IPC praetorian, by the look of the tech I saw."

He considered this. "Yet you managed to survive?"

I forged a grin. "My orders were to survive."

Peznowski glanced to Umerah. His eyes quivered and sharpened in a way that told me he was reading her dossier in augmented overlay. "Welcome to Phobos, Sergeant Javed."

"It's my honor to meet you, sir."

"You look pretty banged up. Why don't you visit one of the

doctors we've got staffed in the cellblock. A real doctor, not one of my sock puppets."

Umerah saluted again, and went through the same hatch as Bryce.

Peznowski watched her go. "How long have you been fucking her, Harris?"

"There rules against fraternization now?"

"How long?"

Memories shuffled as I tried to remember. "Since the Siege of Noctis."

Peznowski turned to me, eyes glinting. "Now, why would you lie about that?"

I stiffened. HubCentral was wired with surveillance; the smallest deception would trigger warning displays through the system. Up here, Peznowski acted as eyes of the regime, extracting information from prisoners when he wasn't sifting planetside intel, collating it to inform special operations.

"I don't see how my love life is any of your business," I countered, thinking fast. "But Noctis is where she and I got...." I swallowed hard. Downshifted my eyes in discomfort.

Common wisdom is to tether a falsehood to a truth, but in an era of constant surveillance that wasn't always the tactically sound option. Even for seasoned liars, there are physiological reactions that can't be controlled. So the most effective lies are interlaced with extant deceptions, spun around vulnerable, emotional cores. The fact was that human beings lied constantly. It wasn't just a matter of sifting fact from fiction, but of probing *layers* of fiction for what you needed.

Peznowski studied me. "Where you two got...serious?" He laughed in astonishment. A sharp, barking laugh that caused some of the generals to scowl at him from their podiums.

Lowering his voice, he chuckled. "Her cunt must be a velvet glove. I really do want the details, *compadre*, but for the moment, I'm more interested in something else."

"Yeah? What?"

"About what went on down there at Hellas. How you handled an IPC praetorian, if that's really what the hell it was. What caused that weird explosion we detected from orbit." He placed his hand on my shoulder. "And why you have a bullet hole in your chest-plate."

★　★　★

I kept my face neutral as I related certain details of the battle in Bradbury Shuttleport, aware that HubCentral's surveillance systems were breathing down my neck. Shadowman training had taught me to lock down my face as much as possible. Wear a manufactured expression, like donning an Athenian theater mask over the limbic troposphere of my psyche.

A troposphere I still didn't fully understand since Natalia had reactivated me.

Peznowski listened, eyes focusing and unfocusing in silent toggles between me and his HUD.

"The whole squad was wiped out?" he demanded.

"Beresha, Hammill, Shea, Conway, and Cuddy," I said, thinking of my dead squadmates, who were probably being downloaded into freshly printed bodies in a Partisan regen clinic. "The Order hit us hard."

"They knew you were coming."

"I don't see how. One of them was a trog, if that matters."

"Go on."

I gave him an edited version of the fight with Natalia's commandos, leaving out her name and the moments that immediately followed. Glossed to Hellas Market, where I had rejoined Umerah and acquired Gethin Bryce.

"It was good that she'd gone on ahead," I said. "With that IPC thug hunting Bryce, her presence was...."

"Yes?"

"Appreciated."

Peznowski watched me for a time. "*Appreciated*," he echoed, and then a rich smile spread across his face. "Like I said. Must be a velvet glove."

"Like *I* said, none of your damned—"

"You skipped over the part where you got shot."

I blinked. "It happened in the firefight." I inserted two fingers into the hole in my armor, sightjacking with the sensors there so I could see the path of the bullet. Eric the trog had hit me with a high-power, armor-piercing round that had gone straight through every layer and hit my heart. That alone wouldn't have been enough to stop me – nature's stinginess in giving human beings a single pump (while seeing fit to double up on kidneys and lungs) had been addressed by the Partisan military with nanite seedclusters and an implanted medcenter to immediately regenerate tissue, reroute blood vessels and arteries, and keep the soldier going.

So Eric's bullet must have contained an EMP charge. Detonated within my chest, where armor couldn't deflect or soak an electromagnetic pulse. The tissue in and around my heart must be littered with fried nanites like canal flotsam.

It was then they had resurrected me, injecting my skull with the upload while restarting my pump with fresh nanites.

"Bullet stopped a couple inches in," I lied. "Lucky me."

I withdrew my fingers and beckoned for Peznowski's hand. "Come here, Doubting Thomas."

His forehead creased. "What? Who's Thomas?"

"Download a slang app, Peznowski. Your life will never be the—"

A horrified cry rang out behind us.

We spun around to the command podiums, where one of the generals was roaring into her comlink, "Jacobs-1, report! Say again!"

I recognized the general at once: Eileen Monteiro, in charge of the planet's sandclaw units. She was an unsettlingly tall figure even for a Martian, with stooped shoulders and a hawkish face. Monteiro wore her shock of lustrous white hair in a flaring, brushed-back fashion like a Pharaoh's royal hood. Her eyes were hardboiled eggs in their sockets. The low-G hadn't been any kinder to her than her own genetics.

The holo of Olympus Mons glittered with representations of the sandclaws she had brought to bear on entrenched Order forces. They moved in large groups, scuttling like awkward crabs up the cone volcano's slope. Their piston-driven legs made them slower than sandtanks, though more flexible and adaptable. Order turrets strafed them as they came, and between the fusillade and sandstorm whipping the foothills, the metal monsters were forced to squat low, legs fanned out as they made the protective side-shuffle that is the domain of their biological inspiration.

But something was wrong.

"Jacobs-1!" Monteiro cried. "What the hell is going on down there?"

Her fingers brushed a holopanel link, and suddenly a wild, animal screeching flooded the audio channels.

"They're inside! *They're inside! Ahhhh! Get them off me! Get them OFF me! Hit the EMP! Ahhh!*"

Monteiro's lips trembled.

"*They're chewing into my eyes! Help me!*"

The other generals glanced at the commotion. The sandclaw advance collapsed in place.

"Son of a bitch," I whispered, realizing what must be happening on the redworld surface.

Sandclaw armor was thick and nearly impenetrable. They could shrug off missiles and electrical attacks. Ammunition bounced off their glasstic-and-titanium resin hulls. Attack them, batter them, set them ablaze, and for all your hard work you would only achieve tiny fissures in their carapaces.

For waspbots, tiny fissures were enough.

I suddenly realized – as General Monteiro surely did – what had been happening. The Order had been shelling her sandclaws with what seemed like futility, emptying millions of rounds. The mechanized units had tacked against the hail of bullets with stony defiance, working their way into the fight.

Now it was apparent that the shelling had *not* been a futile gesture, but rather a means to an end: cracking their armor for waspbots to infiltrate. The flying terrors had swept downwind, peppering the sandclaw hulls, swarming inside. The soldiers within were being stung to death, injected with doses of necrotic fluid that would liquify them. We had seen it before. Pry open a tank, and the crew pours out like raspberry pulp onto the sand.

Monteiro faltered at her podium. She moved her hand across several ID screens, hoping to find someone coherent enough to answer. Each sweep of her fingers brought a new scream, a new agony, as if she was playing a ghastly synthesizer.

A sheen of perspiration formed on her face. She whispered, "Override Command Bushido. Authorization Monteiro, five-five-six. Initiate."

"Not good," Peznowski muttered.

"What's a five-five-six?" I asked.

"VI override."

I felt my breath catch. If the sandclaw divisions flipped to VI command, they could continue to fight, marching onward despite the gory corpses in their metal bellies. They would shoot or spare whatever their IFFs told them to. The problem was that VI-controlled machines were poor tacticians indeed; they couldn't adjust to ever-changing and asymmetrical tactics. An actual AI would be a different story, but actual AIs had been exterminated by the IPC years earlier and no one – not even an independent Mars – was going to defy that rule.

Peznowski gave another of his barking laughs.

I gaped at him. "What the hell is so funny?"

He gave me an incredulous look. "Six months ago, we had Olympus as our playground. Now we're all stuffed in a fucking space rock, and our defensive strategy rests on zombified crab robots. You've got to laugh at that, Harris!"

"You seem awfully calm about the world falling apart, *sir*."

"Our strategy doesn't rest on a volcano. This is only a battle, *compadre*."

"Wars are lost, battle by battle."

"They're won the same way, especially when you're playing the long game." He slapped me on the shoulder. "You look like shit, Harris. Go see the doctor and get yourself patched—"

Monteiro gave another cry. Every pair of eyes in the chamber stared in amazement at the volcano holo.

Her VI-controlled sandclaw division was *supposed* to be continuing uphill to where the Order waited. Instead, they had all jerked northeast, changing direction in unison.

"Override Command Bushido!" she shouted. "Authorization Monteiro…."

The sandclaws scuttled towards a defensive line, stepping over the walls and bunkers and mobile units. Their twin railguns – one at the center of each claw – sputtered wildly, laying waste to every living thing in that quadrant.

Problem was, the living things in that quadrant were Partisans.

"Son of a bitch," I whispered again.

The Order of Stone hadn't just invaded the monsters with stinging death. They must have gotten something else inside to hijack the controls and flip the IFF. Partisan weapons killing Partisan troops....

Monteiro's eyes grew hideously wide.

"Bake the mountain," a new voice said.

The room went silent.

Heads twisted towards the lone figure who lingered in the background.

The legendary General Lanier Bishons. Shogun of Martian military.

Bishons lurked behind the holo, obscured like a moray eel in an inky crevasse. Now he edged into the holographic light. He was about my height, compact and solid. Pug-like face, close-cropped features. A sword at his belt, nestled in a jeweled scabbard.

Monteiro protested. "But...the air support...."

Bishons spread his hands, harnessing all Olympian forces. The audio channels blossomed.

"Trigger EMPs, all points," he commanded. "Bake the mountain."

Olympus Mons began to wink out like strands of dead Solstice lights. Monteiro slumped at her podium.

Peznowski was at my ear. "Poor Eileen. You know she likes to be tied up and ass-fucked by bots, don't you? She does it so often they've had to grow her a new rectum more than once. Gotta release your tensions somehow, you know?"

I couldn't tell if he was kidding or not. But the image he'd implanted of Eileen Monteiro, eyes bulging as machines pumped away in mirthless industry, was enough to turn my stomach.

I stepped away from my commanding officer, heading towards the dim light of Phobos's prisoner cellblock.

CHAPTER SIX

The Realm of Tortured Souls

The first thing that hit me was the smell. A stench of unwashed humanity that, upon first whiff, was like having fingers jabbed down my throat. My eyes watered, nose wrinkled. Sweat, old piss, the zoo odor of fecal matter and body oils. It was the stench of a refugee camp with a hint of iron and the chemical traces of fear.

The smell is what brought it all back to me. It banished the mental resistance that had been playing keep-away with my recollection of Paradise Row – that's how Peznowski playfully referred to the cellblocks. A kind of afterlife for our high-profile POWs.

Religion wasn't a feature of the New Enlightenment, having perished along with the Old Calendar's ashes. In the terrestrial outlands there were tribes clinging to some theological bastardizations, and I'd heard of deepworld outposts that had developed weird spiritual cults. The main selling point of organized faith had always been the promise of eternal life…something which technology ultimately bequeathed. In college, I'd taken an elective on Old Calendar folklore, and it had proved a bizarre sampler platter of belief systems.

Yet none of those religions had ever posited an afterlife like the one I now moved through. Paradise Row was a grid of standalone, twelve-by-twelve-foot cells. Smooth, featureless walls – no prison bars. At the flick of a master switch, those walls could be made opaque like milk-white cubes, or as transparent as polished glass; as I regarded them, most were opaque. Each cube contained a POW, with a single name and date of internment printed on the door. I read them as I passed.

The former governor of Evermist, who had publicly opposed the

Partisan election. A former secretary of education. A former journalist. A former general.

They were all former people now.

Reduced to vessels of eternal torment.

The milk-white cubes were not completely soundproof. Neither were they entirely sight-proof. This, I'd come to realize, was by design. Passing the cubes, I listened to shrieks of agony on either side of my path. Gangly shadows moved inside the cubes, freakish and inhuman.

My mouth went dry. A faceless thing walked by me, looking for all the world like a life-sized wooden marionette. Modular limbs, head smooth as a chess pawn. No visible eyes – no features of any kind – and yet the head rotated towards me, and a multijointed wooden arm raised to offer me a salute.

"Fuck," I whispered, remembering.

"Fuck!" the sock-puppet guard echoed in my own voice, speaking from a tiny cluster of dots in the center of the face. "Fuck! Fuck! Fuck!" It marched away, the mimicry fading as it did.

Phobos Base needed to use its personnel wisely. Assigning live guards to patrol Paradise Row would be a waste of resources; therefore, these lifeless automatons had been created to fit the bill. As I watched, another sock puppet marched through an intersection, wooden feet clacking on the floor in a maddening, percussive rhythm.

How many were there? It was difficult to tell. Each could be switched to a number of modes: Patrol, Pause…

…Interrogation.

These were the gangly shadows I witnessed behind the frosted glass cells. 'Interrogating' the prisoners without mercy, without anesthesia, without questions. The prisoners screeched and listened to their own screeching echo back from their faceless torturers.

Of course, questions *could* be piped through the sock puppets. Peznowski could, at the touch of a switch, say anything he wanted through any sock puppet he chose. I'd seen this. I'd watched as he interrogated—

—journalist Vanessa Jamison. She'd been a spunky investigative reporter who came to prominence while covering the trog riots of 235.

Vanessa 'Van' Jamison was – for many years – as much a face of Mars as anything in Cydonia. Asked the hard questions. Fearless, witty, and an exemplar of her trade. For six years she'd been Peznowski's favorite guest of Paradise Row, after she exposed the horrors of Sabrina Potts's death camps. I'd never seen the death camps. I couldn't imagine – refused to imagine – that they could be worse than what was happening here. One sock puppet would arrive at her cell at precisely the same time each day. Jamison was sick and howling wordlessly in the minutes leading up to its inevitable appearance. Insane, gibbering, and incapable of thought except the instinctive hope for it all to end.

I tried not to look at her cell. At the bloody smears visible on the transparent wall there. Tried not to think about how—

—*her face stretched into a howl as the sock puppet whistled merrily while skinning her alive*—

And that was one of the drawbacks of immortality. Every time she died, Peznowski would revive her. Each time, she'd come back as a sobbing, broken wreck.

And then I did pass her cell.

And I looked.

She was alone, curled on the floor. Shaking all over. She panicked at the sight of me, wondering if Peznowski was changing up the routine. I hurried past, not able to stand the look in those eyes.

How they pleaded for death.

I thought of the antimatter capsule in my thigh compartment.

At the end of the row, two people stood before an open cell. One was Gethin Bryce, hands still cuffed. The other was Umerah.

"Hey," I called to her.

She didn't react right away. She stood unusually stiff, one hand gripping Bryce by the arm. At my approach, she shoved him into the cell.

But she still didn't look at me.

"Hey," I repeated. "You okay?"

★Am I *okay?*★ Her voice hissed across my audio's subvoc channel. Even as a strained whisper, I could hear the outrage. ★**Are you fucking kidding me?** Am I *okay?*★

I tried to touch her hand. She violently jerked it away.

Don't you dare fucking touch me!

Umerah, you need to calm down! I messaged. *This station is under constant surveillance. Those sock puppets—*

She glared at me. *I need to calm down? Is that what you said? This – all this here – is not what I've been fighting for!*

I recognized the strangled pitch in her whisper.

Don't do anything, I pleaded with her. *Please!*

That was Vanessa Jamison back there. They said she died in prison.

Please—

Why are they keeping her? There's no reason to keep any of these people here! Umerah's throat bobbed as she swallowed. *They could copy her neurals and sift the data! So why keep her? It doesn't make sense!*

Umerah—

They're torturing these people!

A sock puppet marched past. Her outburst, barely constrained behind her teeth, caused it to look at us and issue a string of indecipherable whispers, like steam escaping from a valve.

Umerah watched it go. *Even POWs have human rights, goddam it. They're protected by the Geneva Convention!*

That's an Earther law, Umerah. This isn't Earth.

The words shot out of me spring-loaded, without any conscious formation or summoning. And they did something to my compatriot. Her posture changed. Her face went blank. It was what we called an aspect change in the field.

I broke into a cold sweat.

Umerah, I pleaded, *I'm not saying I agree with any of this. I'm only saying that blueworld legislation doesn't apply to Mars.* Panic thudded at my wrists. *Please don't do anything!*

My companion turned her lovely eyes to me, and they filled with as cold an expression as anything I'd ever seen. When her message arrived it was spoken in flat, dull tonalities.

I thought this was all Order propaganda. Stories of how Partisans treated prisoners. Propaganda. It had to be, right? Our enemies were merely trying to slander us. Her gaze was glacial. *Yet it was true. You've been up here before, Harris. You knew what they were doing. Knew it for *years*. And yet...you did... nothing.*

I looked at her helplessly.

Yes, I realized. *The Harris Alexander Pope who had gone undercover with the Partisans knew what was going on here. Knew that the POW camp had been transformed into a house of horrors.*

I couldn't imagine that lack of empathy, even for an undercover agent. Yet the memories were there – accompanying prisoners to cellblocks, passing by agonized stares and inhuman cries.

"It's war," I said softly.

Umerah walked off to the medical bay.

From within the cell, Gethin Bryce watched her go. "I think you just lost an ally."

"Shut up," I grunted.

"Too bad. You seemed a good couple."

I stood motionless, unable to conjure strength or will. The antimatter capsule filled my thoughts. Natalia's orders burned like a theater marquee.

Infiltrate and destroy Partisan High Command on Phobos. And kill everyone up there.

Another sock puppet passed by. Then another. The march of wooden feet on steel flooring.

Bryce cleared his throat. "Um, don't you have something to do?"

I realized I hadn't closed the door to his cell. It took a Herculean effort to reach for the knob, wrap my fingers around it, and pull it shut.

Bryce lodged his foot in the way before I could complete the action. He stared at me, eyes bright.

"Your mission, Harris," he said. "The reason I let you take me here."

*   *   *

Exiting the cell, he brushed past me with an air of authority I was unprepared for. Part of me nearly shoved him back inside – my commitment to an old set of orders screamed to gain control of this enemy combatant. My more recent orders clashed with these instincts, and Bryce slipped through that hesitation.

"We're safe for the moment," he whispered, eyes closed and hands slightly apart. "I just hacked into the surveillance here. Systems are receiving a visual loop but we won't have much time."

I gaped at him. "You hacked into...*how*?"

"Charm."

I thought of the doors he'd overridden at Bradbury. "No," I said, "you've got an AI in your head. That's it, isn't it? When you fled Earth, you rescued an AI from the purges." The theory gained traction as I mulled it over. "*That's* why the IPC wants you!"

Bryce wrinkled his nose unhappily. "They want me for more reasons than that."

"But—"

"You have a mission to complete, right? Get to it, soldier."

I had no idea how long he – or the thing in his head – could keep a false feed going. Amid warring instincts and a sense that every second counted, I fell back on my training. The patrol of the faceless sock puppets, the route to the fusion core, the realization that my cover would be blown the microsecond systems came back online and detected my prisoner and myself gone in a puff of edit.

I darted towards the westward doors, hesitated. "Are you coming with me?"

"I'm staying here."

"Do you know what I'm about to do?"

"Sure."

"So you can't stay here."

"I have a mission of my own, and it doesn't involve you."

Another sock puppet was approaching us. I readied the *jamadhar* harpoon that lay coiled in my left hand, wondering how effective it would be against a creature with no organs. Bryce motioned for silence, and I held my breath, watching as it strode past like a windup nutcracker. Taking no notice, apparently, that a prisoner was out of his cell.

"Umerah," I muttered.

"She's not part of your mission."

"You could get her to the shuttleport. Neither of you can be here when I—"

"*Follow your fucking orders!*"

A soldier's training runs deep. Before I realized what I was consciously doing, I was off and running, threading the route through Phobos Base.

Taking the quickest path to the fusion core.

★   ★   ★

There were two security guards at the entrance to the core. Two men in Partisan reds, weapons holstered, sitting at a table and playing Benoit Coast. The brightly colored chits were several spirals into the game.

When they saw me enter, they grinned and rose to greet me. I remembered them from previous visits. Friendly chaps. Humberto and Clinton. Eager to interact with someone outside of Phobos. Anxious to hear firsthand reports of the war. All toothy grins, merrily twinkling eyes.

I blurred and struck Humberto in the throat. He was dead on his feet, neck bent over his collapsed windpipe like a monk's polite bow. I speared Clinton's face with my *jamadhar* and killed him instantly, the weapon piercing his skull and detonating a small charge that turned his brain to slop.

Then I dropped from hyperacceleration. Humberto's body slumped to the floor, the life gone out of him, brain still firing along synapses. He would never know who killed him…would never realize he had been killed. Clinton slumped back into his seat, mouth slack.

In seven steps I was in front of the fusion core. I withdrew my concealed antimatter capsule and shivered.

The fusion core wasn't the glowing, humming tower often featured in old flatfilms. It hearkened more to some ancient, industrial-sized stove: encased in thick metal plating, as smooth and unremarkable as basalt. My earlier consideration of HubCentral as the heart of Phobos was wrong; it was the brain, but here – the fusion core – was the beast's heart.

Hey!

Umerah's transmission hit me so unexpectedly that I nearly jumped out of my skin. The antimatter capsule tumbled from my hand and skittered along the floor.

Hi, I transmitted back as I snatched the capsule. My fingertips linked to its circuits. A simple menu appeared on my optics:

TIMER SET?

00:00

I need to talk with you, Umerah said.

Now? I asked.

Now is what we own, Harris. It's all we ever own.

I set the timer to five minutes, and affixed the capsule's magfiber backing to the core. I backed away, beholding my handiwork in dread.

And then I ran.

There was time to reach her.

Where are you? I asked, dashing back to the cellblock.

The dormitory.

I'm coming to get you! The dormitory was three chambers deep from the cellblock. At a flat-out run and factoring in blurred movement, I could make it, grab her, and reach the shuttlebay. It was then I realized that Natalia's orders had not included an exit strategy.

I'd have to make my own. In thirty seconds I reached the cellblock and twisted towards medical and—

Something slammed into me sidelong. The impact pitched me off my feet, and I rolled, tangled up with my attacker. Managing to straddle it, I pinned its arms with my knees. Stared down into a smooth, wooden face.

Peznowski's voice issued from the little dots of its mouth:

"You fucking traitor! You fucking traitor!"

I clambered off the thing. It grabbed for my leg and I screamed as razor fingers pierced my thigh. It was all I could do to pull myself along the floor, the automaton clinging to me. My boots slid in blood sliming the floor around us.

Umerah's voice sounded in my comlink. *What the hell are you doing?*

I cut the link, hammering at the thing's head and arms, wildly trying to shake it loose. Rapid footsteps thudded the floor – numerous sock puppets converging on our position. They raced around corners, arms outstretched, fingers glinting silver.

I blurred and chopped my arms down into my attacker's death grip. The arms, as it turned out, were not actually wood but some resin designed to resemble it. The limbs came off at the wrist joints, vomiting sparks. Scrambling to my feet – one clawed hand still embedded in my thigh – I watched as the sock puppets converged into a single, slow-motion tide. Reaching for me...

...and blocking the way to medical.

I sidestepped their approach vector. Blurmod timing out, I took the only option afforded to me.

The hangar.

Behind me, a distorted warble of multiple Peznowski voices roared into normal time.

"*Traitor!*"

"*Traitor!*"

"*Traitor!*"

★　★　★

There was no way to tell what had triggered the station alarms. Klaxons rang as I bolted out across the access corridor, making for the nearest of dropship moorings. They were easy to pilot but useless in combat – built for speed and maneuverability, the technological equivalent of a skiff used to cross the Styx-like space between Phobos and the S-E.

If the station had revoked my admin rights then all would be for naught. Not that it mattered, because there wasn't enough time to begin the warm-up cycle for launch. Nonetheless, I touched my hand to the nearest biometric pad.

Nothing happened.

Two minutes until detonation.

I was going to die up here.

And maybe I deserved to.

To my stunned amazement, the door of the next dropship slid aside. I hurried inside.

A message from Gethin Bryce pinged my comlink: ★**I've got your ride prepped.**★

"Where are *you?*" I gasped.

★**Got something to do first.**★

"Are you *crazy?* Bryce, you don't have *time* to do anything!"

★**That's not true. I've got about two minutes.**★

"Bryce!"

★**You just ended the war, Harris. Congratulations. Now I'm sending you home.**★

Any further protest died as the link dropped and the ship detached from its mooring. The systems whirred to life. The hangar door moved aside like a shadowbox panel, revealing the caramel vista of Mars.

My vessel's thrusters fired, lurching me out from Stickney Crater. I waited, breathless, for the point-defense suite to blast me apart.

Yet they didn't. Bryce, and whatever illegal AI was hitching a ride in his sensorium, had rendered Phobos dead in the water.

My hand strayed to the shipboard com-array. I punched up a wide signal dispersal, all points, and spoke in a clear, crisp voice. The words poured out of me, driven along with a desire I barely understood.

"This message is for the Partisans," I broadcast. "You brutalized Mars. You captured and oppressed and tortured its people. You terrorized the populace with your shadowmen police! That ends today. I represent the Order of Stone. I am here to bring justice. I am here to show you that the injuries you inflicted upon Mars will not go unpunished. My name is Harris Alexander Pope, and I am the last thing you will ever see."

On the monitor, Stickney Base vanished in a flash of light. The shockwave chased my fleeing shuttle.

Peznowski was dead.

Monteiro, too. And Potts, Bishons, and the whole rotten crew.

And so was Umerah Javed.

Everyone left behind in the base would have taken their last breaths as the rupturing fusion core split the station like an apple. I lay back in my seat as the shockwave passed. My dashboard showed an automated route to the S-E.

And then my ship blossomed flame as it ripped into the Martian atmosphere.

PART TWO
SPY

This is Victoria Nightfire, reporting live from the foothills of Olympus with a breaking development. Something has happened on Phobos. Ground-based telescopes are tracking the aftermath of an explosion in Stickney Crater. As many of you know, a message was just broadcast from orbit...a message from someone claiming to be an operative with the Order of Stone.

Here on Mars, we have unconfirmed reports that Partisan units are surrendering. Not just on Olympus. Partisan units are apparently surrendering across the planet.

This is Victoria Nightfire. Stay tuned for updates as they come in....

—The War Word, *October 3rd, 348*

CHAPTER SEVEN

Homecoming

The morning was cold as I emerged from the S-E station into a Martian dawn the color of melted copper.

It had been a nine-hour descent from the orbital docking station to the surface. I'd been the sole passenger in a carriage designed for fifty. Before the war, the space elevator ran tourists and orbital workers up and down the gravity-well. When the Partisans commandeered it, they used the route to ferry prisoners, VIPs, and supplies to Phobos. It was how I'd gotten there over the years, whittling away the slow hours by watching newsfeeds.

This time, I steeped in solitude. Windows opaqued, walls dark. Three hours in, I rummaged through the service closet, pushing past boxes of MREs and medkits until I found a liquor crate. I selected a bottle of vodka as my traveling companion. By the sixth hour, I couldn't feel my feet.

Now, I stood outside the S-E station, bottle in hand, and breathed the chill morning air. The dust storm had passed through Hellas, moving its poltergeist-like rampage towards Tharsis and the Valles Marineris. To the south, I saw the shattered tramline connecting to the shuttleport. I scanned for whatever remained of Umerah's dropship, but it was nowhere in sight. Swallowed, apparently, by the storm.

There was movement to the west: a dust-devil on the horizon. I amped my vision to track its course and sighted a lone buggy approaching my position.

Instinctively, my hands strayed for my rifle and came up empty.

Right. I'd left the weapon on Phobos. Had shed everything but my armor. For the first time in years, I was defenseless. Homo Sapiens, warrior caste, declawed.

When the six-wheeled vehicle arrived, it pulled alongside me. The passenger door opened.

A trog was at the wheel.

"Good morning," he said.

I blinked. "Eric?"

The man who had killed me sixteen hours earlier held the steering wheel with one hand, watching me with violet eyes through his chain-looped visage. "Welcome back."

"Never thought I'd be seeing *you* again."

He shrugged. "Same here. I flat-out told Argos the plan was crazy. No one's ever successfully infiltrated the Partisans. But you did it." He hesitated, tongue pressing into one of his fangs. "Congratulations."

I said nothing. Couldn't think of anything *to* say.

"Order brass sent me to pick you up."

I climbed into the passenger seat. "Figures *you'd* be the kind of escort I'd get." I offered him the remainder of my vodka. He shook his head, pulled a dusty U-turn, and drove us back the way he'd come.

Towards the iconic shadow of Olympus Mons.

The cone volcano's wooded foothills – sequoias, redwoods, and evergreens – transformed the first several thousand meters into a verdant preserve. Even from a distance, I spotted activity: Anzu copters whirling, smoke curling from bomb craters, and troop transports threading the main roads. The war wasn't over yet.

"It's over," Eric said, reading my thoughts. "There will be mop-up operations for a while, but no one's getting commands from HQ anymore. You lopped the head off the Partisan monster."

"How very epic hero of me."

"You don't get all the credit. People love to claim that General Bishons was some big military genius...the next Alexander or Apollo. But in the end, he made the mistake of tyrants everywhere. His ego wouldn't let him share control. Had to run things himself. Holing up at Phobos was their Achilles' heel."

"So where are we going?" I slurred.

"Like I said, the brass wants you."

"For a parade, or an execution?"

Eric gave a sidelong look. "A debriefing is more like it. Are you really drunk?"

"Does it matter?"

We drove the rest of the way in silence.

★   ★   ★

Amazonis Seaport, in the shadow of Olympus.

I knew it well – the canal cities were nourished from here, with polar meltwater pumped out of the muddy basin to the cantons. My childhood home on Lighthouse Point lay only a few miles north, hugging the shore. David and I had spent countless afternoons there, watching a flurry of vessels coming and going, pretending they were various alien species that we – intrepid xenobiologist brothers – had come to document. Trawlers, freighters, water-taxis, ferries, private yachts, and sandships in a near-continuous traffic across the resurrected sea.

It wasn't a surprise, then, to see that the seaport was every bit the madhouse of activity I remembered, even under military occupation. The past nine hours had been eventful, apparently. Amazonis Seaport was now under Order control. I felt a wave of discomfort as I glimpsed their insignia on every buggy, dropship, and patrolling soldier we passed. Two dots flanking a large circle. Like a trifecta of blisters.

We drove through five hastily mounted security checkpoints. Each time, Eric flashed a badge and submitted to a quick facial scan, and we were on our way.

"Do you even need the badge?" I asked as we parked. "Can't be too many trogs working for the Order."

Eric scowled. "More than you might realize. We were the first group persecuted. We have more reason to hate the Partisans than most."

Together, we entered the seaport hotel. Immediately, I found myself in the midst of a goddam riot. An angry crowd had hijacked the place, and consisted of two opposing viewpoints. I caught only snippets of the shouted debate – a general demand for immediate elections in the wake of victory, and those who were advocating a delay – when the crowd noticed us.

The debate went silent. Heads turned, snarling mouths freezing in mid-argument.

I cleared my throat. "It's good to be back, thank you."

No one responded.

Every soldier imagines his or her own homecoming. We fancy our own funerals, too. My head remained a jumble of memories, a conflict of dual perspectives not so different from the lobby crowd itself, so I wasn't sure what kind of homecoming I'd ever imagined. Nonetheless, I was reasonably sure it wasn't this mausoleum of silence.

I was drunkenly plotting a retreat from the hotel when a voice split the quietude.

"Harris Alexander Pope!"

"Fuck," I muttered.

The crowd parted around the figure of Natalia Argos. She was dressed as last I'd seen her, armored and ready for battle. My commanding officer crossed the lobby with a politician's grace. Gave me a brisk salute and a broad PR smile.

"Congratulations on a successful mission, soldier!"

"The war isn't over," I murmured.

Natalia's grin slackened a millimeter.

"There are Partisan regen clinics at Agartha, Hawaiki Falls, Evermist, and Nova Basrayatha," I said. "If you don't hit them now, they'll flood soldiers back into the field."

Natalia nodded crisply. "How long do we have?"

"It's been nine hours. Replacement bodies are probably drying on the racks."

My commanding officer touched her ear, transmitting this intel. My gaze went to the lobby's news holos floating over the crowd. It was a parade of images and ticker-tape updates. In my inebriated state, I could barely read the wording there, but I gleaned enough to realize that Bishons' last command to bake the mountain had failed spectacularly; the

Order had anticipated the contingency, and the hijacked sandclaws had simply gone dark before the blast hit. Then they'd powered back on to continue slaughtering Partisan divisions. Celebrity newswoman Victoria Nightfire was relaying this in her intense, animated style.

I looked back to Natalia. "Where's my brother?"

"General Pope is safe."

"I said *where* is he?"

"Are you drunk?"

"Yeah. Where the fuck is my brother?"

I'm not sure I meant to project the words as loudly as I did, but they resonated in the lobby like a howitzer.

Natalia's smile seemed to burn on her face. "The general," she said, "is in a secure bunker."

"Then get me securely to him."

"Why don't we discuss this privately?" She gripped my arm, attempting to steer me away; my instinctive response to this manhandling was to aim my *jamadhar* palm into her face. For one drunken moment, I thought I'd activated the weapon. Wouldn't that be something for the history books? *This is Victoria Nightfire! Harris Alexander Pope, war hero, returns from Phobos to brain his commanding officer in full view of a hundred people....*

I imagined how the rest would play out. In the stunned seconds that would follow, I'd have to blur to the nearest chokepoint; bad odds, sure, as there were a hundred people here, and a fully armed garrison outside, and I didn't have my weapons. Nonetheless, I was already accessing the seaport blueprints, plotting my retreat....

Natalia seemed to read the storm in my eyes. She released my arm. Eric drew near; I felt the same tension as when they'd reactivated me at Bradbury. As if they were afraid I would revert, lycanthropy-style, to my shadowman self.

Natalia cleared her throat. "You've had a long day, soldier. Why don't you freshen up, and we can talk later?"

"I could do that," I said. "Or I could ask why an IPC praetorian came after Gethin Bryce."

My commanding officer froze, rock solid. "A *praetorian*? You ran into a praetorian?"

"Not sure what else it could have been."

"You recorded this?"

"Sure did. He tried killing Bryce. I barely got out of there alive."

Natalia and Eric exchanged a look; the trog appeared as surprised as her. Finally, aware of our audience, she whispered, "I'm looking forward to the debrief. The important thing is that you accomplished the mission regardless of asymmetrical interference. You got Bryce – and yourself – to Phobos."

Something in her tone and wording caught my attention. "Sure," I said. "But he died up there."

"You saw him die?"

"He was on Phobos when I blew the core."

I could tell my commander was fighting to control her emotions. "Did you *see* him die?"

I stared at her. "Didn't you hear me? He was up there when the base popped. Even if he ran at full blur to the hangar, no other ships departed Phobos. And there's no way anyone could have survived that explosion... not unless he leapt into space and landed on some invisible ship."

"Wouldn't that be something?"

"You know what, Natalia? I don't fucking care. Right now I'm going to see David, even if I have to steal a ship to do it."

I turned away. She interposed herself in my lane of retreat. "We can't have you leaving just yet."

I laughed. "Go fuck yourself."

She put her hand on my arm again. Astonished, I realized she really intended to stop me. Which meant I really was going to brain the bitch right there....

"Let him go!"

The voice boomed through the lobby, paralyzing Natalia and me like a pair of insects in amber. A woman shouldered through the crowd. An Earther, judging by that short, ropy body. She was a surprisingly tough-looking character – Martians tended to dismiss Earthers as privileged arcology types, ensconced in their ivory towers of decadence – but this woman exuded a near-electric sense of danger. Something cat-like about her movement. Aggression in the intensity of her stride.

She wore heavy armor of a style I'd never seen, too. Ablative, judging by the *segmentata* plates. Modular fittings of various origins. The kind of thing Victor Frankenstein might assemble, if his tastes ran to armor over necromancy.

As she neared, her ID bubble materialized on my HUD:

Celeste Segarra
Archon, Order of Stone

Her gaze fixed me in place. "Paladin Pope?"

"Um…archon?"

She addressed the crowd without looking at them. "Harris Alexander Pope just ended the Partisan War! Infiltrated Phobos and popped it like a pimple! He is to be honored for his service and bravery. Pope spent twenty years as an undercover spy and, when the time was right, he cut the enemy's heart out with his teeth!"

A slow trickle of applause leaked from the crowd, gained traction, and soon filled the lobby. Not exactly deafening, but it frightened me. The crowd was murky and half-visible, a nightmare arrangement of faceless silhouettes. A crowd of mouths and accusation. Not everyone was clapping. The realization pierced my inebriated fog.

I had killed people while undercover. Some of them were probably here now. Others were dead forever. Save clinics were hard to come by for guerrilla warriors. Mobile clinics were hard to build and maintain. And the biomaterials needed for printing weren't exactly available at Hellas Market.

Segarra watched me, a strange cocktail of expressions in her lean, hard features. Sympathy? Respect?

"Archon," I repeated awkwardly.

"What can I do for you, paladin?"

After swallowing hard, I said, "I want to see David Julius Pope."

"Flights are grounded except for emergency operations. And the general's location is classified." I began to protest, but she cut across the first syllables out of my mouth. "However, I will personally chart you a sandship to his location…as soon as I'm able."

I glanced to Eric and Natalia, then back to Segarra.

"Can I at least talk to him?"

Celeste Segarra smiled. It wasn't Natalia's clinical smirk, or Umerah's high-watt grin. Rather, it was a small, wounded expression that managed to convey a deep reservoir of feeling; a rare smile peeking from a palisade. "That," she said, "I can do. Follow me."

*   *   *

One of the presiding themes of the New Enlightenment was an aesthetic return to the classical age. For more than three centuries, the arcologies of Earth and aerostats of Venus and cantons of Mars had been molded in the stylings of famed origins – Ancient Greece, Rome, China, India, Egypt, Sumeria, and Babylonia. Terrestrial arcologies resembled Aztec step pyramids, Etruscan agoras, and Edo-period villages….

We had no arcologies on Mars, but the same sensibility had guided our colonial development. Amazonis Seaport therefore retained the Persian style I recalled from my youth – an entrancing combination of intricate arabesques and knotted florals framing proud griffins, bearded sphinxes, and guards in Achaemenid robes. All rendered in greenish soapstone and rich basalts, too. It was here that Dad would take my brother and me, after we met him at the end of his shift. He'd buy us ice cream at the hotel restaurant. Chocolate scoops for Dave. Vanilla soft-serve with crushed walnuts for me.

Now, I traveled that same corridor, passing by the restaurant on the way to the elevators. My footsteps echoed with the archon's in lonely, morose percussion.

We stepped onto the lift. Segarra slapped the button for the third floor.

I cleared my throat awkwardly. "Archon—"

"Call me Celeste."

"Nine hours ago, this place was in Partisan hands. They might have booby-trapped it." It was, I thought, what *I* would do, if forced to retreat before an enemy advance. Leave a secret housewarming present for the next tenants.

"We checked," Celeste assured me. "Didn't move in until we sent sniffers through each floor."

The doors opened and she led me out into a blue-and-gold carpeted corridor. Walking abreast of her, I said, "I'm not just talking about explosives. They could have waspbots, slotted to emerge at night and sting everyone to death. Tailored viruses. Golems hiding in a supply closet or ceiling duct."

"We were thorough."

"They had the place for twenty years."

Celeste halted before a door, palmed it open. "It's clear."

"Bradbury Shuttleport was clear, too. Right until a crack commando gave me the fight of my life." I hesitated at the room's threshold. "Honestly, it's not wise, all of you being in one place."

"We're not. Our generals are in the field or secure bunkers."

I looked at her. "But not you, huh?"

She studied me with an appraising, veteran's stare. "I learned to stop hiding a long time ago, paladin."

I considered the room. A queen-sized bed, workdesk, closet, kitchen area with food-printer and minibar, bathroom. "You said I can talk to my brother...."

Celeste went to the wall. As she reached for the holopanel, I noticed the scars on her arms. Like negative-value tiger stripes.

Defensive knife wounds. Someone had slashed the hell out of her long ago. Or maybe each scar had been earned from a different incident...except who the hell would have multiple encounters with people wielding knives? I noticed two old bullet wounds, too. And at one wrist, the unmistakable pattern of teeth marks...not human teeth, but some kind of animal. Where had she gotten that? Mars was free of dangerous fauna unless you went fooling around in a zoo.

She dialed a lengthy sequence of numbers. "This place used to host corporate bigwigs before the war," she explained, "so it's already wired for secure holoconferencing."

The room went dark.

For a moment, my soldier's instincts kicked in, sensing a trap. But the room pixelated into a real-time overlay of another location. A windowless room somewhere, with walls of hewn traprock. The sole piece of furniture was a mighty sandstone desk, a glowing map on its surface. A uniformed man leaned over this, hands flat on the edge.

I didn't recognize him. He was a hollow-faced stranger, sporting a nasty red scar below his left eye like an oversized teardrop. He looked famished and unwell and unwashed – the visage of a refugee scraping by on meltwater ice and lichens. Only his uniform was pristine, as if he'd freshly printed it that morning.

The man noticed me. His eyes widened.

"Harris?"

I blinked. "Excuse me. I'm looking for General Pope."

"That so?"

A cloth seemed to fall away from my eyes. I didn't know the man in front of me. But I realized that if I regressed him two decades, added fifteen pounds to his beanpole frame, and erased that scar from his cheek, this *could* be Dave.

And that uniform! Unlike the slick Partisan reds, the resistance had taken to printing uniforms and armor that resembled Martian traprock. It gave them all a blocky, chiseled appearance. Like Old Calendar knights outfitted by masons.

"David?" I whispered.

The general rounded his desk. My hotel room was engulfed by the hologram, aside from a dim chaperone-grid to prevent me from banging into things; Dave's image melted through the workdesk.

"Harris!" he cried, wrapping me in an embrace I couldn't feel.

I stood awkwardly. The archon watched, little more than a shadow in the holographic backsplash.

David resembled me, I suppose. Same oak-colored hair, hazel eyes, cleft chin. The soft face I remembered had been boiled away by hard living; his cheekbones resembled high Martian plateaus.

He released me, still grinning. "Stars, it's good to see you!"

A memory shuffled forward.

My brother and I as teenagers, climbing the spiral stairs of Penthisilea Lighthouse up the beach from our childhood home. Bracing ourselves against the protective railing, we gaze upon the wine-dark sea. "I'm really glad you're my brother," he says, apropos of nothing but this shared moment. The wind blows his messy hair around his face.

Dave gave me an up-and-down appraisal. "You look every bit the soldier, Harris. You look like...Dad, actually."

"Dad was never a soldier."

"He would have made a great one, though, don't you think?"

"Agreed."

"Remember hiking with him in the Valles?"

"Of course I do."

Silence fell between us. My gaze drifted past his shoulder to the hologram's environmental details. There were no windows, but that traprock couldn't be just anywhere. Wherever Dave was broadcasting from was either underground, or in a mesa's hollow.

"Where are you?" I asked.

He laughed. "You trying to zero my location for your old bosses?"

"No!"

Dave's laughter cut away. "I was joking. Sorry."

"Were you?" I walked through him and approached his desk. The chaperone-grid reminded me that I was about to collide with a wall; I hesitated an inch away, pointing to the glowing map. Its cartographical features were smeared. "I notice this isn't an unfiltered transmission," I said.

"It's not because of you," Dave insisted. "There are enemy holdouts that could be intercepting communications."

I nodded. Of course, that made sense. "You look good, Dave."

"Bullshit." His smile returned cautiously, twitched at the corner of his lips. "*You* look good. Like a beast!"

"Why did you leave me undercover for twenty years?"

My brother swallowed hard. He seemed to sense there was someone else in the room, or more likely, the transmission was telling him I wasn't alone. Dave and the archon exchanged a cryptic look.

"Do you think I wanted to?" he asked.

"That isn't an answer. I deserve an answer."

"You sure as hell do. I'm sending a transport for you in the morning – I'd do it today, but Mars is in total goddam chaos and air-traffic is not secure. Technically speaking, we've captured Olympus, but several enemy divisions either haven't gotten the message or they don't believe it." His expression turned as hard as granite. "We're hunting them now."

"Call for a general amnesty."

Dave laughed again, but this time there was no humor in it. It was a cold laugh, bitter and tempered with rage. "Not everyone deserves amnesty."

"Do I?"

He raised an eyebrow. "You remember this was all *your* idea, right? *You* suggested going undercover. *You* volunteered for it."

Another memory emerged, like a groggy bear trundling out of hibernation.

We're on a boat disguised to resemble a fishing trawler, bobbing listlessly on the sea. But below decks it's outfitted with a mobile regen clinic and top-line bioprinter. Mars is firmly under Partisan control; every canton has a military governor, each city has a local monitoring station. To keep people safe, they say. The secession from IPCnet is only a few years old and there's worry that blueworld agents are fomenting rebellion to the new regime.

The boat is dark. I'm lying on a gurney in the vessel's belly. Waiting for Order of Stone technicians to finish their explanation of what they're going to do to me. Neural reprogramming. A brainwash that will selectively obliterate the synaptic structures that make me sympathetic to the Order. It's fucking impossible, I think. Nothing can make me forget that my mother and father were 'disappeared' by the Partisans. That they were sent to an unknown detention center. That any record of them has been erased – two lives deleted.

But the technicians assure me that it is not merely possible, not merely probable, but an astonishingly simple procedure. Who we are is determined by our neural forest and which trees entangle, which neurons fire-and-wire together. Digital capture software has analyzed billions of human brains. Data-mining has revealed how easy it is to fundamentally change a human being's sympathies and allegiances. A shuffling of tiles into new configurations.

"The Partisans killed my parents," I say. "How the hell will your software spin that?"

The technicians huddle in the gloom, thinly drawn by the glow of equipment displays. Dave sits on the stairs leading to the upper deck. His eyes are large and sad.

"Forget it," he says. "My brother isn't going to have his brain destroyed for this. The Order will have to find another way."

"It's not permanent destruction," a technician insists. "We'll keep his original file backed up here."

"And if you lose the file?"

"We'll keep it safe."

"If you lose the war?"

"Nothing will matter then."

Dave hangs his head. In the murky luminosity, his resemblance to Dad is unnerving. "I don't want my brother to actually become *a Partisan."*

I clear my throat. "Someone has to make them pay for what they did."

"Harris, this is too much."

"No one's forcing me to do this. I'm volunteering."

"If something ever happens to the original file...."

"Don't let it," I plead. "And don't leave me with those fuckers long, okay? Let me get in there, learn what I need to, and pull me out."

He gazes at me a long time.

"I love you, bro."

The memory fell away like gossamer.

"You *do* remember, right?" David pressed. "The Order was desperate. In the past, a well-trained spy could study up on an enemy's culture and pull off a deception. During Earth's Old Calendar, one of the tests to ferret out German spies was to see if they could sing the American anthem, did you know that? Trial by shibboleth. But that was before

Digital Captures. Now, you can read a brain in a spreadsheet. A false identity would be instantly visible in the data. So—"

"So you rewrote my brain," I finished for him.

"You *do* remember!"

I paced around the room, a planet wheeling around a star named David. "I *remember* asking you not to leave me undercover for long."

"There were complications."

"What complications?"

"For one thing, we couldn't *find* you. When you went undercover, the war had yet to heat up. Partisan troops acted as local peacekeepers in their home cities. It was part of their strategy, feeling that provincial familiarity was an advantage. It also underscored the idea that they were helping to *protect* Mars. Literally defending the home front."

I considered this. "So you thought I'd be assigned to Lighthouse Point."

He nodded vigorously. "Or a canton nearby! And for a while that was true enough. My brother, decked out in reds, patrolling the old streets and piers where we'd grown up. We could have pulled you out then, but there was no point. You were a grunt. You hadn't learned anything valuable."

It had taken two years, he explained, before I was promoted. That promotion had come after I'd helped root out a burgeoning plot against the local Partisan office. I'd turned in old Mrs. King, who had once sold my brother and me pastries on the sandship pier. King had made the mistake of criticizing the Partisan regime in my presence. She'd compounded that mistake by inviting me to a resistance meeting. And so I went to the meeting – with a squad of troops – and led the arrest of the entire cell. I remembered the way Mrs. King's face changed from shock to cold hate when she saw *who* was arresting her. Remembered how she spat on me as she was taken away.

After that, I was promoted. Sent to Partisan Special Ops training. I'd shown an aptitude for combat and ruthlessness…the very traits that greased the wheels for any tyro looking to fast-track a career. Leaving me with some home-turf garrison was deemed a waste of my talents.

"And besides," Dave added, "the war was in full swing by then. The

Order was getting organized, cutting supply lines, printing weapons, assassinating officials. Even the state-controlled media could no longer insist it was the work of a few sympathizers. They needed soldiers in the field."

"But *twenty years*, Dave?"

"For six years, we had no idea where you were. Slowly, our operatives pieced together a scattered breadcrumb trail. The Partisans deployed you all over the goddam planet, bro. You survived some serious battles. The Siege of Noctis, for one. Thirty thousand people died there."

"I remember," I muttered.

"They gave you an Amber Star for your work there."

His voice had taken on a tight, restrained quality. What he *wasn't* saying, and what he didn't need to, was that any medal I'd earned was the result of murdering Order troops. And the Siege of Noctis had been nightmare-fuel...a forty-one-day horror in which Partisan and Order squads stalked each other through that fog-shrouded labyrinth. With turrets secured on the peaks to keep dropships away, what was supposed to be a quick operation devolved into something that might have hatched from a Roman emperor's imagination: a death trap battle royale.

"Eventually," Dave continued, "we heard rumors that you had been inducted into the shadowman program. We didn't know a lot about it back then. Just the name, really. But our troops were noticing a new threat on the battlefield – a breed of souped-up super-soldiers."

My legs were growing wobbly. I sat on the edge of my hotel bed. "Cut to the end, Dave. How did you find me?"

"As the tide began to turn, our intel became more reliable. The instant we learned you were operating in Hellas, we drew up plans for Operation Persephone. I'd love to claim sole credit, but it was really the brainchild of Gethin Bryce and Archon Segarra." He nodded to where Celeste leaned in the corner. "We let it slip that an offworld VIP – Bryce himself – was in the Order's custody. The Partisans took the bait."

So did the IPC, I thought grimly.

"So," my brother said. "I dusted off your old file. We shipped Bryce to Bradbury in the hopes that *you* would grab him. I personally ordered Argos's squad to intercept and reactivate you. The rest is history."

My inebriated state had evaporated into full sobriety. I glanced longingly to the minibar.

"What happened to our parents?" I asked. "After they were arrested?"

"You know goddam well what happened to them."

"I mean their Save files. They might still be backed up somewhere...."

Dave gave a stony look. "Once the IPC was kicked offworld, the Partisans took over the regen clinics. They didn't just execute their enemies. They *erased* them."

"But the IPC should have older copies! Mom and Dad emigrated from Earth, so there should be—"

"That's true. I've already confirmed that Luna has copies of our parents. From before their emigration here."

I staggered to my feet. "Then you can bring them back! Stars, David! We can be a family again!"

My brother was silent for a long while. "They're *old* files, Harris."

"Why does that—"

"From before they had us."

My protest died in my throat. Teresa Orsini and Edward Pope had relocated to Mars as part of the third-century diaspora from Earth; lots of blueworlders were leaving back then. It was common practice to back yourself up before taking an interplanetary voyage, in case of accidents.

Mars was the only life that Dave and I had ever known. But Mom and Dad had told us about their life on Earth. How they'd met in Rome, married in Athens, honeymooned in Xianyang. Sometimes they took us on holotours of those lofty, populous arcologies. When they decided to leave Earth, they got Saved before their flight.

In the intervening years, they had gotten Saved many other times. But with their arrest, local Saves would have been deleted.

I bowed my head. "Bring them back anyway."

"They won't remember us."

"I'd rather make new memories with them than never have them alive again. Wouldn't you?"

Dave exhaled. "It's better than oblivion."

His image stuttered. It must have been a general disturbance of the transmission, because he seemed to realize it too, and he hurried to me as if to offer another virtual embrace.

"...tomorrow...sending ship...okay?" He extended his arms, pixelating into a nebulous entity. "...love you...."

"Dave! I love you too...."

The image locked and froze. David Julius Pope, arms out, mouth in mid-speech. The hologram died.

I was back in the hotel room.

"What happened to the transmission?" I demanded of Celeste.

"This is Mars," she said coolly. "Even before the war, com-lines were twitchy. There could be enemy jamming actions. Chaff interference."

"Dust storms?"

"Maybe."

Instinctively, I tapped into the local weather stations for stormtrack updates. Satellites were watching three dust storms – the one I'd encountered in Hellas, one in Utopia, and a large gale blowing across Cimmeria. None of those regions were likely places for a secret Order of Stone bunker....

Celeste stepped away from the wall. "I need to get back."

"Post-war negotiations?"

"It's been a busy day, paladin."

"You can call me Harris."

"Okay, Harris. I congratulate you on a successful mission. Now, we are all sojourners in civilized life again."

I blinked, surprised by the reference and degree of bitterness in her voice. "That's from *Walden*."

The archon paced around the room, taking in everything with a disinterested glance. "There's a chapter in that old book where Thoreau watches two different colonies of ants. They're at war with each other. The fight of their lives, and for what? Dominance of a few fucking inches of dirt."

Not knowing what to say to that, I waited for her to continue. But

Celeste only shook her head, anger stamped on her face, as if she was contemplating tearing the room apart with her bare hands.

I said, "Aren't you glad that our side won the war?"

"We never should have had the fucking war!" Celeste snapped. She looked dangerous enough to make my blood run cold. I glanced once more to the grisly Braille patterning of her scars.

What the hell has this woman been through?

"But we *did* have a war," she said, quieter. "And you, Harris, are its big hero."

"The people in the lobby made me feel like a POW."

"Well, you did publicly tell your commander to go fuck herself."

"Yeah, I'm a regular Confucius. Still, they regarded me like a smear of dogshit."

"The hell with them. You want rationality? Sorry, but you joined the wrong species." She raised an eyebrow. "When's the last time you slept?"

I had to think about it. "Maybe thirty hours ago."

"Yeah, you look like it. I'm posting guards outside your door. No one will disturb you. And I'm giving you my private link." She made a small movement with her hand, and my sensorium flashed with an incoming email: Celeste Segarra's contact info. "If you need anything, don't call the desk. Call *me*, got it?"

I held her gaze. "I imagine you don't make this offer to every grunt."

"You're not every grunt. The war is over because of you."

"It's over because Natalia gave me a brace of antimatter rounds. How in the hell did she acquire something like that?"

Something happened in Celeste's eyes. Like different shades of black glass sliding over one another. "Is it important?"

"Well...yeah. No one outside the IPC is allowed to produce it. Its tactical uses are limited. So...where did it come from?"

"That's classified."

"Okay."

Silence again. The window rattled as an Anzu buzzed the hotel. My gaze crept to where my brother's hologram had been. "I still can't believe he became a general," I muttered.

"*I* can. He came to us when he was just eighteen. I was there when he approached us."

"*What?*"

Celeste's forehead creased. "I said—"

"My brother joined the Order when he was eighteen?" I didn't remember anything about that.

"The Order of Stone was only a few years old, meeting in secret places. There was this bar called the Oort Cloud in—"

"Ybarra Docks," I finished for her. "I remember. The night before my parents were arrested, Dave and I snuck off to Ybarra. Took a late tram. Grabbed drinks at the Oort Cloud. It was a stupid thing to do. Ybarra was dangerous. A trog ghetto."

I recalled that Dave and I had entered the smoky den, grabbed a corner table, and ordered beers. Must have been the start of an epic bender, as my memory of that night was as murky as the place itself. I remembered our waitress was a trog with killer legs, the tips of her mohawk painted bloody like a medieval mace. Remembered the open, frank interest in her violet eyes.

Beer after beer, Dave and I enjoyed the night. We'd played a few rounds of pool. More beer. I remembered Dave disappearing for a while to use the bathroom. And then….

"You sure you have the right night?" I asked Celeste. "The Oort Cloud? When Dave was eighteen?"

"I'm sure."

"That means I was with him the night he approached you guys."

The archon shrugged.

I struggled to retrieve more details. All I found were dim, ragged images, sodden with beer. At some point, the waitress's shift ended and she took me upstairs to the apartment flats. I'd spent the night buried between her thighs.

The next morning, I awake to a nasty hangover and post-sex bruises. Slipping out of bed, dressing quietly for fear of waking the waitress – her insatiable appetite had drained me into a husk. Sneaking downstairs. Realizing that my brother was gone. In a panic, I call his link. No response. Half-dressed, I summon an autocab to take me to Lighthouse Point, all the while trying to reach Dave.

From afar, I see the notice on my home's front door. Black letters on paper as red as arterial spray:

TRAITORS

The Partisans had ransacked our house. Emptied drawers and storage crates into the middle of the living room as if in preparation for a bonfire. I go wild, pinging Mom and Dad over and over.

But they're gone.

Celeste interrupted my grim reverie. "After your parents' arrest, Dave returned to Ybarra. He formally joined the Order. Started at the bottom of the chain, running messages by hand to resistance cells. Making and retrieving drops. Bluffing his way into warehouses and past checkpoints. Gathering intel. He had a gift for deception and guile. An intrinsic knack for strategy."

I said nothing. The person she was describing sounded nothing like the open-hearted innocent I'd grown up with.

Celeste seemed to gauge my state of mind. "War changes people," she said.

"I guess so."

"The war matured your brother, but it didn't break or embitter him. He carries this...this *optimism*. Darkness, anger, despair...they run off him. Your brother is a natural leader." She gave a shrug. "I'm old, Harris. I grew up in the Wastelands of Earth before you were born. I've seen battles you can't imagine. You live as long as me, life becomes an endless expansion of Serpinski triangles: the same kinds of people, the same mistakes, the same evils recycled under different branding...." She trailed off, her eyes going distant. "And just when you think you've seen it all, something surprises you. Your brother is unlike anyone I've ever known."

I sank back onto the bed, not knowing what to think or feel.

Celeste gave another of her wounded smiles. "Get some sleep if you can, Harris. The war is over."

She left, closing the door as she went.

I sat motionless, staring at the carpet. After a few minutes, I switched on the room's newsfeed.

Teary-eyed journalists. Order flags going up in canton after canton. Partisan troops emerging from tunnels, surrendering *en masse* at Olympus.

"It's over," I said, testing the words aloud.

I didn't know how long I sat there, but a bladder full of vodka finally impelled me to the bathroom. There, I stripped off my armor, skinned out of my clothes, and took a shower. Blood had dried black and sticky on my body. There was a curious satisfaction in watching it swirl around the drain, along with the grime, chalk-dust, and sweat that had caked my skin.

It's over.

Twenty years of fighting.

The war is over.

There was no sense of relief. No joy. My body seemed a hollowed-out shell. With a towel wrapped around my waist, I returned to the holo and stood, watching livestreams of civilians celebrating in the streets. I studied their happy faces.

The cameras panned to an interview with a grinning unit commander. Behind him, a Partisan dropship lay upended like a beached whale, derelict and forgotten.

I killed the holo and climbed into bed, curling under cool sheets. Out of habit, I made a mental review of my inventory. My multigun and other weapons were slag on Phobos, but I still had my *jamadhar* coiled in my left arm. My armor lay like a discarded tortoise shell in the bathroom.

I closed my eyes, heart pounding.

The Partisan War.

Is over.

CHAPTER EIGHT

Saving a Life

I tried to sleep, but continually woke in a blind panic, reaching for the rifle I didn't have. The bed felt too exposed, so I finally tore off the sheets and threw them into the tub with spare towels. I hunkered there and tried again. After maybe an hour, I awoke in such a frenzy – having no idea where I was – that I nearly put my hand through the glass shower stall. In the end, I climbed out of the bathtub and slumped, heart pounding, into a corner of the room and spent the remainder of the night distrusting the hotel's silence.

When the window brightened with dawn, I dressed in my dirty clothes and went to the hotel restaurant for breakfast.

It seemed no one else had slept, either. Many of the same people from the day before were out and about. My emergence drew plenty of stares, which I could handle well enough. What I *couldn't* handle was how the lobby doors kept banging open every time someone new entered the building. Five minutes of that and I took my breakfast tray back to bed, where I scarfed down the eggs, hash, and toast.

I was nursing the last sips of coffee when an email notification arrived.

TO: Harris Alexander Pope
FROM: David Julius Pope
DATE/TIME: October 4, 348
SUBJECT: Reunion
MESSAGE: Good morning bro. Can you be at Evermist by 1? Air-traffic is still grounded, but there's a 0915 sandship you can grab. We've got so much to catch up on. Peace (we can say it now). Love you.

I conjured a virtuboard and poised my fingers over its keys, uncertain of what to write in reply. In the end, I elected to send a wordless, thumbs-up confirmation. Straight and to the point. Then I ran a comb through my hair and fled my hotel room, leaving my Partisan armor behind.

The lobby wasn't as crowded as the night before; that singular mass of people had fractured into archipelagos of gossip. I pushed the doors wide and stepped into a bright morning.

Brandywine Cruises kept running during the war, as travel by canal was the lifeblood of Martian life, economy, and industry. And as a local company – as opposed to offworld corporate juggernauts like Prometheus Industries or Vector Nanonics – they were left strictly alone by the Partisans. Now, the company's vessels lined up at the pier as if for inspection. The arrival/departure board advertised an hourly schedule that could only be possible if Brandywine was deploying their entire fleet. Seemed the company figured business was about to boom; when I glanced at the crowd surging onto the boardwalk, bags over their shoulders, it was clear they were right.

I bought a ticket with a touch of my fingertips to the kiosk paypad, and went immediately to the selected ship, the *Body Electric*. A line of passengers was already forming there.

"All aboard!"

The line shuffled forward. My ticket grew damp in my hand. I viewed the sandship with a mixture of hope and anxiety. The vessel's fluted, serpentine design glittered in the low sunlight. Plumed sails blossomed from towering masts, tapering like the fins of a sea monster: an organic, flowing design like a living creature rendered in shapestone.

I didn't see Dad's old ship, the *Toynbee Convector*. Might have been decommissioned in the twenty years since he'd served aboard it....

"Hi, Harris," a voice said behind me.

I rotated in place to see a woman dressed in a tunic that was probably shapestone; it resembled the Martian rocks of the high deserts. Resembled the sandship.

"Natalia," I whispered.

A vein thumped in my neck.

Her eyes narrowed fractionally. "I'm sure you meant Commander Argos."

"I'm sure I didn't," I said, turning back as the line compressed another meter. "What I *meant* was, 'Fuck off.' The war is over. We won. My contract stipulates—"

"I know what it stipulates."

The actuators in my muscles clenched, potential violence crackling along strands of enhanced fibers. The sun was a small circle no bigger than a multigun muzzle, and the *Body Electric* sparkled as if coated by diamond dust.

"You have to get Saved," Natalia explained.

"I'm taking a cruise. My brother is meeting me at the first port of call."

"Terrific. You still need to get Saved. You were undercover with the Partisans for twenty years. Can't risk all that data vanishing from your head if you die."

"I don't expect to die aboard a cruise."

"Thirty minutes," Natalia pressed. "It only takes thirty minutes, and then you can take your cruise and see David and I'll never bother you again." She grabbed my elbow; I shook her off, and suddenly it was the lobby all over again, only this time the archon wasn't available to intercede. "Come on, Harris. Ship doesn't leave for *forty* minutes. Hurry up, dump your data, and you can retire."

I consulted my opticlock: 08:35 a.m. The ship departed at 09:15.

Most of the Save centers on Mars were at transportation hubs. Originally, the IPC tended the Great Library of human souls. As the tech was lent out to subcontractors over the years – the Luck Everlasting, Vector Nanonics, and of course, Prometheus Industries – the process of neural capture became widely understood. Enough so that, when the Partisans took power, they were able to build their own Save-and-regen clinics, creating a tyrannical local monopoly that could flatly erase enemies of the state.

"Harris?" Natalia said. "We're wasting time."

"At least I'm not wasting twenty years of your life," I countered, but felt myself relent. She had a point, even if I'd be damned to admit it to her. By my recollection, the last time I'd been Saved had been a week earlier in Hellas.

Natalia led the way to a dockside Save clinic that still bore the outlines of a Partisan flag. Once inside, though, I saw that the place had been fully commandeered by Order personnel.

There were rows of steel cubes. Naked people coming and going from them, their neurals freshly Saved to backup drives.

I disrobed in front of Natalia, my body a map of glossy scars. Knife wounds. Haze rounds. Two waspbot stings that had crystallized into circular deposits in my back, like knots that never left.

"If that ship leaves without me," I warned, stepping into the pewter-gray Save locker, "the Order of Stone better fly me to Evermist."

White light arced from the neurocapture nodes, erupting like a ghostly forest of bramble and limb and brush. A fabulous tangle of tracers, crawling in my head, forcing me to squint. Emerald-green holoprompts appeared like alien sigils on my optics, exciting certain pathways, capturing every synaptic contour, lighting up mental clusters. Just me and the hot light, washing over me like waterfalls. A scintillating, cleansing bath of the soul, more penetrating than the shower I'd taken the night before. White light invaded my mind in squiggles of energy, the prying feelers of the capture-jack copying every configuration.

I closed my eyes. The stuttering light wormed inside me, godlike and yet somehow base, a parasite, a tapeworm, an angelic hand, a magpie claw, a cosmic suction, a gravestone rubbing from hallowed epitaph to wax paper duplication.

The war is over, I thought, and then said the words aloud, softly, like a young wizard warily testing out an untried incantation.

Through the narrow door slit, Natalia said, "The war isn't over, Harris."

I looked at her. "Yes it is. I blew up the Partisan base. Top brass is slag, still cooking in the Phobos fusion reactor."

My former commanding officer nodded. "Sure. But some of the

Partisan top brass is unaccounted for."

"Oh well."

"Not very patriotic of you, to say that."

"I'm saying it anyway." I closed my eyes again.

*　　*　　*

The War.

The slogans of MarsAlone were circulating in force when I was a student at Edlund College. Offworlders were not wanted, people said. *Farewell Blue Hell! We embrace MarsAlone!* It was a fringe movement with fringe goals that most Martians shrugged off and, grudgingly, enjoyed how it made the IPC uncomfortable.

Technically speaking, Mars had been settled by the InterPlanetary Council in the year 99 of the New Enlightenment…an effort that finally justified the IPC's name. Luna had been colonized fifteen years earlier. From there, a tide of humanity had taken to Venus (living in aerostat colonies), and to the Belt (mostly burrowed down in Ceres), and to the mini-system of Jupiter (on the Ganymedan moons), and to Saturn (in orbital ring-stations). There were even habitats in Neptunian orbit – an uneven society of scientists and resource procurement specialists who didn't constitute enough of a presence to become a formal body in IPCnet.

Thing is, Martian history was more elaborate than the IPC liked to pretend. The *first* efforts to terraform the place had been started – not in the year 99 NE – but a thousand years earlier. In the Old Calendar. Before the collapse of Earth in the so-called Final War and the millennium of death and disease and bloodlust that followed.

Most of that era's records were lost. Digital information had been fried in the war, and so the bulk of what we knew came from hardcopy books and newspapers discovered in landfills. Pieced together from these disparate sources, it was largely accepted that the original Martian colony had been established at some point in the so-called twenty-first century. A small group of men and women from nations now forgotten had landed on Mars and set the first terraforming projects in motion. Men and woman bearing the title of *astronaut*. An international team of engineers and scientists meant to serve as vanguard for an all-out colonization wave, and who set up shop in lava tubes to carve out the Martian underdark. Orbital crews hung the initial aurora-belt satellites to bequeath a magnetosphere. The first cyanobacterial grids were established. The first mesa farms. The future must have looked bright.

And then Earth died.

Billions perished in the nuclear barbecue of the Final War. Millions followed in the hellish Warlord Century…a grisly curtain-call during which the fragments of nation-states fought over resources, ideologies, and power. New empires were forged in blood, only to collapse into dust. History's grimmest hits replayed as purges and inquisitions and conquests and genocides festered on the radioactive corpse of humanity's birthworld. Maggots fighting over the few scraps of digestible meat. Nuclear *seppuku* on a global scale. The Triassic impulse uncoiling and strangling the cerebellum's Eloi. Masks shorn away, all trappings of a civilized species gone as we showed what we *really* were…what we had *always* been: a bloodthirsty tribe of sadists who had come down from the trees only to rape and pillage and destroy ourselves. It all culminated in the march of Warlord Enyalios, who butchered one hundred million people in his attempts at unifying half the planet.

In the end, peace was brokered. The world was unified. A warlord named Apollo the Great brought Europe and Africa into one political body. Warlord Lady Wen Yin delivered Asia. Warlord Enyalios dragged the broken and bloodied and barbaric Americas to heel. From those three shards emerged the first global government – Earth Republic – with a new calendar to celebrate it.

And what of the colonists who had gone to Mars? When the nuclear guillotine fell, they found themselves cut off from the universe. No more supplies streaking down like friendly meteors to aid them. No more space agency command centers available via radio. Those first Martians – thirty-three of them in total – were forgotten as Earth committed self-lobotomy.

There were no rejuv treatments or Save centers in the twenty-first century. Back then, people were born only to begin dying and, when they died, they were really dead.

The Martian Thirty-Three died on Mars. Died in the act of bringing life to the planet. Died in the hope that one day, people might return.

A thousand years later, people did. Under the leadership of Earth Republic and a nascent IPC, Mars was settled *en masse*. A new aurora-belt was hung in orbit, new cyanobacterial grids established. The ice caps were liquefied, canals swelling fat. Mars awakened as a garden stretching green over the frost-bitten corpse of a billion-year winter.

And gradually, the bodies of the Thirty-Three were rediscovered.

First one, then another. I was eight years old when my parents took Dave and me to the Martian Museum of Colonial History. It was where I beheld my first dead man: a desiccated mummy behind glass, curled in a postmortem ball. I remembered staring wide-eyed at the ancient face atop that bulky, frost-split life-support suit. The bronze placard read:

William F. Szukalski
Number Fourteen of the Thirty-Three
Born in Philadelphia, United States, Earth
Discovered in 104 NE, lava tube, Hellas

It was the Thirty-Three that Martians looked to as our cultural and spiritual progenitors. The Thirty-Three who had helped change Mars, back before IPC hegemony. So strong was this conviction that it even affected a moment of the war. During a fierce battle at Elysium Mons, a bomb had blasted open a lava tube where the bodies of two more Old Calendar astronauts – Numbers Twenty-Nine and Thirty – were discovered. These turned out to be a man and a woman entwined in an immortal embrace. The newsfeeds went wild. Fighting was called off by both sides, our version of the Christmas Truce. Archaeologists shoved past Partisan commandos and Order paladins to carefully extricate the dead lovers, run tests, and build a shrine on the spot…a crystal house for the deceased.

Two corpses had temporarily stopped the war.

*   *   *

I checked my opticlock in the midst of the Save center's upload, which read 08:54 a.m. Twenty-one minutes until the sandship departed for Evermist. The arcing light continued probing my head, uploading my pattern to clinic storage. In a few hours, I'd be seeing my brother again.

Heart pounding, I glanced to the window slot. There was no sign of Natalia. Whether she had gone to the bathroom, or was getting coffee in the lobby, or had choked to death on a bagel, I didn't care.

I let myself wonder what a reunion with Dave would be like. Would we go strolling along the shores of a beach? Climb an old lighthouse? Grab beers at Ybarra like the fateful night before Mom and Dad vanished?

Words flashed on my HUD. An update from the clinic:

10 MINUTES TO UPLOAD COMPLETE

*   *   *

MarsAlone transformed into a political group calling itself the Partisans. In the election of 325, they captured Martian government in a landslide election. It was a shock to the establishment. It was a shock to my own family.

How did a fringe group gain enough support that they could win the planet? Analysts pointed to the fact that in 322, something strange and terrifying had occurred on Earth.

The so-called *Pax Apollonia* had encountered a mighty hiccup.

In 322, the IPC and Prometheus Industries had come within spitting distance of another war. Shots had been fired on both sides. People had died. The powers rushed to the brink of Armageddon and, at the last possible minute, ceased hostilities. Peace was brokered. A few months later, IPC and Prometheus Industries issued a joint statement claiming that they had been manipulated into conflict by artificial intelligences…a proclamation that led directly to the AI genocide.

Except Mars remained skeptical. Distrust of blueworld authority mounted. The Partisans' call for secession gained favor. In the election of 325, they captured the House of Laws, a majority of Oligarch positions, and local governorships.

And true to their promise, Mars seceded from IPCnet.

The pograms followed. Teachers at my school being 'transferred', replaced by instructors who wore the slick Partisan reds. Soldiers patrolling neighborhoods. The tip-line demanding action against 'blueworld sympathizers'.

The rest was history. A history the children of Teresa Orsini and Edward Pope had become intimately involved with.

A history now firmly in the past, like an island that fades from view as you push the throttle on your boat.

The war was over.

★   ★   ★

Nine mercifully quiet minutes passed. I opened my eyes again, glancing reflexively at the door-slot. Natalia was back and peering at me.

"Can I help you, Lieutenant-Commander Peeping Tom?" I demanded.

Natalia gave her patented scowl. "What does that even mean? Who's Tom?"

"Download a slang app. Your life will never be the same."

A notification appeared on my optics:

30 SECONDS TO UPLOAD COMPLETE

"You did good, Harris, in the war. You're one hell of a soldier."

"Who has earned one hell of a retirement."

22 SECONDS TO UPLOAD COMPLETE

My former commanding officer nodded. "Ever hear of a poet retiring? They don't, because it's what they are."

"I doubt you've read a poem in your life. Leave me in peace, okay? Before I get angry."

"The Partisans butchered thousands of Martians, Harris."

6 SECONDS TO UPLOAD COMPLETE

"The war is over," I said in my steel locker. "Do you hear me, Natalia? The war is

CHAPTER NINE

Son of the Damned

I found myself lying on a rubber gurney, surrounded by cement-gray walls, pale ceiling, and a portable console parked beside me. The warm air reeked of something like turpentine. Algae-lamps glowed in each corner of what appeared to be a ten-by-ten-foot jail cell. There was a single door, painted or printed white, with an inset mirror and black robe dangling on a wall hook.

My half-spoken comment to Natalia lay on my tongue; the sight of her eyes staring through the slot in the Save clinic door faded like a holo before the credits roll. My new environment had blinked into existence as if springing from unseen theatrical compartments.

I froze, soaking in the room's details.

I'm a POW, I thought. *Someone printed off my file from the seaport. I'm being held prisoner. But why?* This was followed by another consideration: *Who would have done this? The Order won the war... but there must be Partisan sleeper cells, loyalists to the regime who had... what? Stolen a copy of my Save? Printed me out in some bunker for... interrogation? Retribution?*

It was hardly my first time being killed and resurrected. Shadowman ops had been a cycle through regen centers, emerging naked with other back-from-the-dead soldiers to dress, receive our newest set of orders, and return to the field. There was always a quick mention of how we had died, too. Sniper-shot in Cydonia, three days ago. Dropship crash in Carter Concourse, two days ago. Brief, single line epitaphs. Lots of soldiers memorialized their death-summaries with tattoos. One of my squad operators – Petty Officer Cuddy – was a veritable illustrated man, including not one, not two, but *three* death-by-waspbot dates. Singularly disturbing karma, that guy.

Anxiety squirmed in my chest. I lifted my hand to the sensorium tab behind my left ear…

…and stopped short, noticing how long and spidery my fingers were.

Triggered by the movement, the bedside console flashed a message:

WELCOME BACK, PETER!

YOU HAVE JUST BEEN RESURRECTED IN THE LUCK EVERLASTING REGEN CLINIC IN HELLAS.

THERE IS NO CAUSE FOR CONCERN.

YOUR FATHER HAS BEEN NOTIFIED THAT YOU ARE AWAKE AND WILL MEET YOU IN THE LOBBY. PLEASE USE THE ROBE AND PROCEED TO CHECKOUT WHEN READY.

—YOUR FRIENDLY LUCK EVERLASTING STAFF

I staggered off the gurney and approached the mirror.

A stranger stared back at me.

As Harris Alexander Pope, my birthbody had been much like my father's. Muscular, tall, broad chest and shoulders. Sandy brown hair and hazel eyes. This new body was young – the face couldn't be more than nineteen standard – and scarecrow thin. Almost no muscle development. Brown-complexioned skin. It reeked of the bioreactor fluid in which they'd grown me.

I jabbed the sensorium tab behind my ear. A lavender menu pinwheeled over my vision. At the bottom corner, the date appeared that froze my blood:

DECEMBER 22, 358.

"Three-fifty-eight," I muttered, breathing hard.

I'd lost ten years.

Ten years!

The thought occurred that this was some hideous error, the result of a haywire print-job. Harris Alexander Pope had gotten Saved at Amazonis and then (hopefully) had caught the *Body Electric* and went to Evermist. What happened next? A reunion lunch with Dave? Beer at Ybarra for old time's sake? Whatever had transpired, my backed-up neurals should have remained safely stored as the years passed. This had to be a computer error. While the real me had gone on to a post-war life, this old copy must have been run off accidentally...and downloaded into the wrong body at that. A teenage kid had come back from the dead as a war veteran. All I had to do was explain the mistake. No need to worry; my other self must be ten years older. Maybe I'd gotten married.

Then my eyes flicked to the Message tab on the pinwheel hub. There were two unread messages. I clicked them open with a finger-tap on my virtuboard.

The first linked to a news article from two days earlier:

FATAL ACCIDENT AT BAYNE SEEDFARMS
Click for more

Ignoring that for now, an oily sense of dread uncoiling in my belly, I opened the second message.

It proved to be a video recording of a woman facing a camera or, more likely, facing her own reflection as she made a recording with her optics.

She had changed her hair over the lost decade. The only time I'd met her, she'd worn her hair short and layered; now it spilled blackly around her shoulders. She'd traded her *segmentata* armor for a tailored, basalt-hued uniform. The Order of Stone flag was printed above a breast pocket.

"Hello, Harris," Celeste Segarra said. "The last thing you remember is the Save clinic at Amazonis. You were scheduled to hop a sandship. You were supposed to meet the President – your brother – at Evermist. For whatever it's worth, we think you did arrive at your destination before the hammer fell." She swallowed hard, the room trembling around her. Was she recording this on a train? "Are you sitting down, Harris? Believe me, you want to be sitting down."

The last thing I wanted was to sit. But there was a darkness in Celeste's eyes that chilled me, a haunted and hellish distance such as I'd glimpsed in really ancient immortals, or in soldiers who had stared too long into the abyss. The thousand-yard stare. Unfocused, glazed, and...hollow.

I sat on the edge of the gurney and waited.

"You were right about the Partisans leaving us a housewarming gift," Celeste continued. "Right in concept, wrong in scale. Exactly twenty-four hours after Victory Day, the planetary defense grid fanned open and nuked the planet." The dead look in her eyes became darker still. "Mars was baked into a radioactive wasteland."

★   ★   ★

For several minutes, I only half-listened to the rest of her words. The horror of her report engulfed me, and I regarded my room's door with despair...fearing what I'd find when I drew it open.

Mars was dead.

A dead planet again, murdered by nuclear firing squad. The cantons reduced to smoking craters. The labor of centuries smashed open by a Parthian shot to end all Parthian shots.

And suddenly, I thought back to my conversation with Peznowski on Phobos.

"Our strategy doesn't rest on a volcano," he'd said. *"This is only a battle, compadre."*

"Wars are lost, battle by battle."

"They're won the same way, especially when you're playing the long game."

Phobos Base was destroyed, so there hadn't been anyone left alive with command codes to enact a nuclear protocol. General Bishons must have had a doomsday clock in place, forever ticking down. Maybe once a day, he sent a reset code from his private quarters, like a cultist making daily invocation to a dark god.

And when he died?

No further prayers.

The defense grid had rotated in orbit and unleashed its deadly payload on the planet. The sword of Damocles had fallen.

"We intercepted a third of the missiles in the upper atmosphere," Celeste explained, as I sat on the gurney wearing a stranger's body. "Ground-based lasers turned them into fireworks. But fourteen major cities were hit. Six million people died outright. Another million perished...in the aftermath...fallout...starvation. Things were...bad...."

Celeste seemed to freeze in place. My first thought was that the video had timed out, or that environmental interference was causing loss of signal. Then I realized the recording was fine; it was *Celeste* who was struggling to find the words.

Rumor was that really old immortals no longer felt anything; that their emotional capacities had stretched like old leather. Loose and flabby response parameters, like nerves burnt out through overstimulation. Was she old enough to be suffering from that?

Then I remembered what she had told me at the hotel: she had grown up on Earth. Not in luxurious arcologies, but in the battered and shattered wastelands beyond them. The blueworld ghettos separated from civilization in cruel apartheid. I remembered the nasty scars along her arms. She was a child of the ruins. Had gotten offworld. Had settled on Mars...

...*and now she was back in the ruins.*

Seven million dead.

My mind reeled. Buildings sheared open like cracked geodes. My beloved Mars baking beneath ten thousand fires.

And for *what*? A fucking *tantrum*? Had Lanier Bishons been so petty? If he couldn't have Mars, then no one would? There was no tactical, practical purpose I could think of.

Except for vicious spite.

Celeste Segarra wrangled her emotions. "You've been dead for ten years. In a way, that was a mercy, Harris. *I* have this strange habit of surviving every horror the universe throws at me. The seaport was hit. I was buried beneath tons of rubble. Took me two months to dig myself out. I ate whatever scraps I could dig out of vending machines." She pursed her lips. "But you want to hear about Mars. About its current state. In the past ten years, it's been rebuilt...though it's not the same world you remember. The new cities are 3D-printed – you should have seen the print-cranes operating day and night, like ancient oil-pumps. Literally rebuilt with rubble, ground everything up and spit it back out." Rage bloomed in her eyes. "We had offworld help, too. Look it up if you want to know more."

"What I want to know," I snarled to the recording, "is why you waited ten years to bring me back!"

Celeste tucked her hair behind her ears with a harsh, angry motion. "Harris? By now you've realized the body you're in is not your own. And before you ask: it *needed* to be you. There's no one in the universe better at undercover ops, or better at dealing with Caleb Peznowski."

Peznowski?

The name of the dead monster, thrown out so casually.

"He's alive," Celeste growled. "Regenned in a new body under a new identity, and emerged like some fucking cicada into the new Mars. Calls himself Mark Bayne. The old birth records were charred. Probably wasn't difficult to manufacture a new identity."

Mark Bayne? I glanced at the earlier email, linking to the news story of a Peter Bayne's death at some farm.

"Under this new identity, Peznowski somehow got hold of an entire seedbank of crops. Proved very helpful to the reconstruction. People were starving...and he was able to set himself up as the biggest food supplier on the planet. Got himself elected as governor of the canton, too...part of the first wave of elections since Detonation Day.

"No one suspected a thing until the Order started taking a closer look at everyone. Started scanning social media feeds and running patmatch analyses. One week ago, that searchlight fell on Mark Bayne and gave a sixty-one-percent match with Minister Peznowski's cadence, word choice, and style. He's back from the dead, Harris, and in charge of North Hellas."

I stood, naked and cold. Mere seconds of content remained to Celeste's message.

"We need you to kill Peznowski again."

As if I needed her to say it. I nodded wearily. Cold dread slithered… not a snake, but a hydra spreading into my limbs.

"Before you assassinate him, however, we need you to investigate. Is this his own private ego trip, or the edge of a rat-line? It requires a subtle approach. Surveillance, then assassination. I've embedded a dossier to help. Contact us on MyTribe once you're settled. Your handler is posing as Peter's girlfriend. And please understand, you don't have much time."

"Why?" I whispered.

Celeste sighed deeply. She appeared to shrivel like a clay figurine under hot lights, the illusion of youth spoiled by age-battered exhaustion. It was as if she could hear me across time and geography.

"The body that you're in," she said, "is Peznowski's son."

CHAPTER TEN

Reunion

I emerged from the recovery room into a drafty corridor that smelled of mint air-fresheners trying vainly to cover the turpentine odor of freshly printed bodies.

It was, apparently, a slow day at the clinic. Wearing only my black robe, I padded by a nurse station, where staffers were comforting a weeping, resurrected woman. No one noticed me, so I didn't stand around to be noticed; following my soldierly instinct, I searched for the washroom. In the field, new bodies are easy targets, as enemy waspbots will sniff out and zero them.

Four meters from the washroom door, however, a gray-haired doctor intercepted me. His name leapt to my nanonics: DR. HORACE WELLINGTON.

"Why didn't you call for assistance?" he demanded.

"I didn't need any." I stiffened at the nasal sound of my new voice.

Wellington was an alarmingly hairy fellow, what a Neanderthal would look like if snatched from the Paleolithic and forcibly dressed in a starchy violet lab coat. His face was a shrub of beard and bristly eyebrows. Beards weren't popular on Mars. Despite our self-reliant, mountain-man, *shinrin-yoku* ethos, we were also practical: beards interfered with dust-masks.

"You should have waited for assistance," Wellington chastised me. "If you fell while relearning coordination, your father—"

Would cut out your eyes? I thought. *The way he kept cutting the eyes out of Vanessa Jamison?*

"—would be displeased if anything happened to you."

"Well, I sure don't want him displeased."

The doctor seized my head, tilting it one way and another. He shone a light in my eyes, checking the pupils. I had the discomforting thought that he was scouring for an imposter beneath the skin.

"Your father is on his way," he informed me.

Good.

"Good," I said.

Wellington finally stepped aside so I could enter the washroom. I didn't need to use the toilet – this body's bladder and bowels were as empty as they'd ever be. But I rinsed off in the shower stalls, letting the bioreactor fluid and bits of jelly-like scaffolding wash down the drain. I lathered with soap, using my time to access Celeste's dossier on Peter J. Bayne, son of a Mark and Jessica Bayne of North Hellas.

Name: Peter J. Bayne
Born: November 13, 339
Place of birth: Ambersky, Mars

I blinked at the birthdate. If he'd been born in 339, that was nine years *before* Mars had been nuked. Which meant that Peznowski had been operating all along in multiple bodies – one on Phobos, and one on the redworld. He had apparently stayed under the radar, cloaked in civilian life, getting married to whoever this Jessica person was, and having a child.

Had other Partisans been leading these doppelgänger lives, too? What in the hell for?

In the shower, I washed my hair with the facility's shampoo and kept rifling through the dossier. The nukes had hit when he was nine, which was right around when the kid had started keeping an e-diary. After that, he'd gone underground with his family. Living in the tram tunnels – I instantly recognized the stations he referenced. Those platforms had become little Stygian villages since my death.

Ten more years stolen from me.

I shuddered, fighting panic and rage. Two decades spent undercover with the goddam Partisans! Coming up for air for a single day, and then losing another decade! The life of a time traveler couldn't possibly be more disorienting, and my anger bit deeper.

I squeezed my eyes shut. Focused on the water spraying over my body. Focused on the now. Umerah's voice arose from memory:

Now is what we own, Harris. It's all we ever really own.

Eyes closed, I studied Peter's e-diary. It described the lives of human moles. A cloistered existence that oscillated between his parents' basement storm shelter and sojourns to the tunnels for trading and bartering with other survivors. Peter's twelfth birthday was a special event, since it involved a brief return to the surface to meet offworld aid workers remotely neurocasting from orbit to distribute food and medical supplies. Pete had squinted at the caramel sky and saw Phobos for the first time since going to ground.

A year later, his May 3rd entry described a permanent return to the surface. He'd ascended the basement steps with Mom and Dad to view the dusty, vacant rooms of his childhood home. The caramel sky was now peppered with airship detoxifiers. The horizon was dominated by print-cranes rebuilding infrastructure.

July, 352. The Baynes relocate to a new homestead and convert the property into a greenhouse, growing ample high-nutrition crops to supplement – and soon supplant – the offworld supply drops. Their efforts feed thousands of Martians.

October, 355. The success of the farm propels the Bayne family into the public spotlight. Mark Bayne runs for, and is elected, governor of North Hellas. I'd never heard of North Hellas.

I was toweling off in the shower stall when I completed my overview. Peter's last entry was just three days before his death, and it was a single line:

December 15, 358: I've met someone.

My bare feet slapped porcelain tiles as I went to the washroom mirror and wiped it clean. I contemplated the brown teenager gazing back at me. I waved my hand; the boy returned the greeting. I made several faces, stretching my expression into ungodly grimaces.

Seven million dead on Mars.

Ten years lost.

I closed the e-diary and rummaged Peter's emails. Unsurprisingly, there hadn't been a lot of electronic communication during the nuclear years. Post-emergence, though, his inbox had ballooned with movie ticket receipts – Earth's cinematic imports finding an eager audience among Martians. At some point, public education returned, because I located class registration schedules: Peter was now a freshman at Thoth University. I'd never heard of Thoth University.

When I emerged from the washroom, Dr. Wellington was still there, waiting for me.

"How did I die?" I demanded.

"It was an accident," he said, handing me a plastic bag containing a change of clothing.

"What kind of accident?"

"You drowned."

I blinked. "I *drowned*?"

The doctor looked uncomfortable. "You were home from university for the holidays. You'd been drinking – your blood alcohol level was 0.248. You went into one of your parents' farmpods and must have fallen and hit your head. You drowned in a cistern."

I don't know what I was expecting – the news release hadn't been forthcoming with details. Harris Alexander Pope had been killed multiple times: stabbed, blown to bits, shot up and shot down. As often happens during war's freakish calculus, I'd emerged relatively unscathed from the forty-one-day horror of Noctis only to step on a sand-mine two days later while searching for an alley to piss in.

But *drowning*? That was a new one. It wasn't an especially common way to perish on Mars, either. The canals were always muddy; Martian dust thickens their surface into a syrupy, molasses-like medium. No one wants to swim in that shit. In fact, drownings were so uncommon that they're jokingly chalked up to the legendary sea monster Penthi.

So why did a nineteen-year-old kid home from college drink himself into such a stupor that he'd managed to drown? And in the security of his homestead?

"Get dressed," Wellington said impatiently. "Your father is waiting for you."

★   ★   ★

When I stepped into the waiting room, dressed in Peter's ghastly choice of neo-Victorian attire, three people were there. Two were young men, probably awaiting the resurrection of a parent; I wondered if it was the weeping woman I'd seen at the nurse's station.

The third man was Mark Bayne...new identity of Minister Caleb Gradivus Peznowski.

"Peter!"

Years back, I'd read an article in *NoWire* about why resurrectees make certain body choices. An unsurprising eighty-one percent of respondents regrew their birthbodies, minor alterations notwithstanding – smaller nose, bigger breasts, larger penis, thicker hair. The remaining nineteen percent fled to the opposite polarity, selecting entirely new mortal coils of calculated antithesis to what nature had dealt them. Blondes into brunettes, women into men, racial toggling....

Minister Peznowski had defied the stats. He was taller by inches, had traded his sandy-blond hair for mahogany curls. His Nordic genotype had been swapped out for something suggestive of Mexican or Xibalban heritage. Yet the face wasn't radically at odds with what he'd worn in his last life; he'd skirted eerily close to his birth features. Clever, this attempt at ducking the sniffers.

"Peter!" He embraced me warmly. His tangy cologne stuffed my nose. "Let me look at you. How does it feel? All checked out, no worries?"

"Sure, Dad."

He appraised me carefully, concentrating on my eyes. The worm in my stomach flipped around. There hadn't been time to study my new identity's speech patterns and word choices, so I was determined to be as monosyllabic as possible. I held his gaze.

Mark Bayne's eyes were the same as Minister Peznowski's.

There was no mistaking them. I had looked into those eyes too often to miss their hard blue power, charisma and cruelty, retinal patterns be damned.

"Come on," he said gladly, "Mom wasn't expecting you until Friday. You were fifteenth on the waiting list, but I pulled a few strings. Let's give her a surprise!"

I forced an expression of mirth. Endorphins flapped in my chest, my movements straining in odd directions. Peter's muscle memory would be a problem. So would his hormones.

Peznowski/Bayne signed the release at reception, and we departed together, father and son, into a public concourse. The walls glowed with advertisements. The first to catch my eye was a movie poster, depicting an unquestioningly Martian landscape behind a man and woman locked in a passionate kiss. Mushroom clouds sprouted on the horizon, the fireball licking the poster's edge. The movie's title glowed: *The Year of Passion and Death*. Starring people I'd never heard of.

The second advertisement was simpler. It showed a starry void, with white letters burning against blackness:

HELP US BUILD THE FUTURE
TEN THOUSAND WORLDS ARE WAITING FOR YOU

THOUSANDS OF JOBS – GUARANTEED

INQUIRE AT MARS/TENTHOUSANDWORLDS.IPC

I blinked, waiting for more of an explanation to appear. To my surprise, the words faded out, and the ad recycled.

The IPC had forbidden extrasolar colonization. A Congressionally approved Colonization Ban had been in place for centuries, confining the human race to Sol System. In the 200s, a batch of probes had been flung to the nearby celestial neighborhoods of Ra System, Dagda System, and Shakespeare System. Habitable worlds had been confirmed around those stars. But manned exploration? The IPC slammed the option. The

Colonization Ban was unbending...even in the face of rapid population growth straining Sol resources.

So what was this Ten Thousand Worlds they were advertising? Humanity was forbidden to visit even *one* extrasolar world, let alone ten thousand of them.

"You okay, Pete?" Dad asked.

"Yeah," I managed.

The concourse was a strange one. During the war, I'd gotten to know Hellas intimately; now, I considered an unfamiliar hall of aug shops, prefab offices, and stalls. Was Hellas Market still around? I suddenly wanted to be standing amid its colorful garden of herbs and fruits and vegetables.

Dad led the way up some escalators; I followed, taking note of the odd, institutionally white architecture. And then, as we crossed a skyway to the tram station, I caught a glimpse of the horizon and stopped short.

There were dinosaurs in the distance.

That was my immediate impression, forcing me to halt in place so quickly that Dad continued on, unbeknownst to me. I gazed through the curved glasstic skyway to a horizon dominated by printer-cranes that resembled a herd of theropods, long necks moving as if grazing. As it turned out, they were doing the opposite: each crane was spewing quick-set concrete from extruder nozzles, layering intricate structures in the Martian desert where no structures had ever been built.

The Hellas of my time had been constructed from local Martian stone; some cantons contained original architecture as begun by the pioneering Thirty-Three. New Mars – post-war and post-nuke Mars – was apparently a different story.

We were a 3D-printed ant-farm. Uniform, smooth, selected from a utilitarian catalog.

And the planet wasn't just being rebuilt. It was being expanded.

I managed to pry myself away from the sight and proceed to the escalators, where my father had finally noticed I wasn't with him. He stood at the crest, watching me.

"Something wrong?"

"Sorry," I said, joining him and proceeding to the trains. We took one bound for North Hellas and settled into our seats.

Dad squeezed my arm.

"With your birthday coming up, I was going to take us spelunking at Agatha Crossing. You still want to go? Your accident hasn't changed your mind, has it?"

I squinted at him. "My birthday? We've got eleven months before it's my birthday, Dad."

The Mark Bayne face grinned. "Right. Well you know me, always thinking ahead." He tousled my hair and sat back in his seat.

There was no air-conditioner on the ride home, but I couldn't stop shivering.

★ ★ ★

"Sweetie!"

Mom greeted me in the kitchen of the Bayne homestead, wearing a checkered apron and a wide, ruby-lipped smile. With a start I realized where I had seen this vision of motherliness: ironic reproductions of stay-at-home housewives from Old Calendar advertisements, long-since memed into banality.

"Let me look at you!" she cried. "How does it feel? All checked out, no worries?"

She possessed hard eyes, blue and cold and with a hint of cruelty. They were eyes I knew well. They were features I knew well.

Great fucking stars!

My blood transformed to winter slush. The nightmarish awareness that Peznowski's gaze was peering out from a second body was enough to sicken me, but that was just the ragged fringe of a deeper, almost cosmic blasphemy. According to Celeste's dossier, Peter Bayne was the natural offspring of his parents. Which meant that Peznowski, existing in two separate bodies, had naturally produced him. Grunting and ejaculating, the unholy union growing into a new child from the fruit of two loins of the same puppetmaster?

I almost attacked her right there.

Please, control. Please!

"Dear?" Mom's eyes widened in concern.

Please!

My smile cracked like a fissure in ice. "Sorry, Mom. I still feel like I'm in the clinic."

She hugged me. I noticed that Peznowski had given himself very large breasts. "Tacos tonight?"

My mind raced fluidly over reams of data. Was this another test? I nodded noncommittally. A reddish-brown dog padded toward me from an adjacent room, head low and tail wagging. Doberman. A hundred pounds, easily. It put its head into my hands. Wet tongue and cool nose.

"Looks like someone missed you!"

It's movie-fueled nonsense that pets can detect a stranger in their owner's body. Pure urban legend bullshit. The Doberman smelled the natural cologne of pheromones, body salts and skin oils. It couldn't telepathically sniff out an imposter any more than it could play chess.

Was it Peznowski also?

The freakish thought blasted through me. I stared into its liquid eyes for signs of my old enemy. Eyes like black pearls. Teeth up-thrust from cushions of pink gums. As if a caveman feeling out the primordial world, I thought: *Dog. This is dog, not man.* I scanned Peter's e-diary for the words 'dog' and 'puppy' and 'pet', and came across an entry from a year earlier.

Mars wasn't exactly crawling with pets anymore. Life underground had been difficult, and food was scarce. Many a pet had ended up on a spit to feed starving families.

So a year ago, Peter's dad had procured him a petbot. A robot designed to look like a dog, but which didn't have to eat. Which didn't have to be cleaned up after. Which could be muted if it barked too much, or have its vocal pattern reduced to warning growls if a stranger came around.

And that made sense. Peznowski probably had cameras on every square inch of his residence and – under the guise of getting a pet for his son – had added a robotic guardian, too. A Doberman-shaped Talos to patrol the Isle of Bayne.

The machine's name bobbed up from the dossier.

"Hey, Suzie! How are ya, girl?"

The tail wagged furiously. I scratched the faux fur behind its ears.

"Dinner is all set!"

During wartime, resurrections were followed by a swig of water and high-protein MRE to get nutrients into an empty bloodstream. In the Bayne homestead, dinner was tacos, Penthisilean ceviche, and Zulu-style sourdough flatbread. Mom and Dad joked and teased each other, interspersing their joviality with somber reflections on my accident. Two days ago, apparently, I'd come home from Thoth University and, late at night, polished off an entire bottle of rum by myself. I'd wandered into one of the farmpods, which surrounded the central Bayne residence in an interconnected grid of greenhouses. Sometime around midnight, my life-signs flatlined and Mom awoke to the security alert. She found me floating facedown in a cistern.

"You should never have had so much to drink," Dad admonished.

I bit into my taco. "I don't remember the accident."

"Of course you don't. But you'll make sure to never drink that much again, right?"

"Sure, Dad."

"So how is it, coming back from the dead?" Mom's question, her teeth a flash of white behind her wineglass. Dad watched me over the yellow rim of his taco.

I choked down the mush of tortilla shell and beef, thinking of recent movie receipts. "Waking up was like in the movie *Star Shiver*, when the main guy is defrosted."

Mom laughed. Dad nodded agreeably, scooping some ceviche onto a jagged edge of taco shell and shoveling it into his mouth. I glanced past his shoulder to the dome-like interior of the house, where Martian dusk shone through window-framing onto elaborate arbors of beets, tomatoes, watercress, and breadfruit.

What I didn't see were neighboring homes. When we had dismounted the train, a PDT had taken us into the valley of North Hellas. I'd glimpsed neat rows of residences in a snail-shell patterning like Parisian arrondissements; the Bayne manor acted as the central Arc de Triomphe.

What the hell had been here during the war? I reflected on maps of the region I'd seen. Never heard of a farming community here. Never saw one in sat-images, which I'd pored over regularly in the hopes of spying smuggler caravans bringing ordnance south into Hellas.

When dinner ended, Mom came over and kissed my cheek as she cleared away the plates. Dad caught Mom from behind and gave a playful tickle, to which she spun around and wrestled in his grasp. They moved like dancers, as delicately attuned as a well-oiled machination. Alternately, they looked at me and smiled.

I had no weapons or armor. No blurmods stitched into this body. No jamadhar coiled in my arm.

No killswitch.

Sweat dripped down my nose like a splash of hot rain.

CHAPTER ELEVEN

A Stroll in Stygia

Peter's bedroom was a shapestone burrow on the second floor of the Bayne manor. My impression was that private bedrooms hadn't changed much during my lost decade. The furniture fitted neatly into its ovoid curvature in the same treehouse style popular in my childhood. The window was wine-hued with Martian twilight.

There was a VR rig by the bedside, and I was anxious to fire it up and make contact with my handlers. Still, I used the moment to steep in local details. Movie posters on the wall, action frozen in standby. Closet, pilotchair, nightstand with touch-light, and a holographic pair of *katana* on the wall. Guess Dad doesn't let me have the real things. Couldn't make things too easy.

What confused me was the VR rig itself. It seemed little more than a router, with no visible holo-projector or static keyboard. Most people used virtuboards, sure, but there was always a physical backup, just as every autodrive vehicle maintained a switch to manual control if needed or desired. I was still puzzling over this when, as I stepped towards the pilotchair, the bedroom walls erupted in images that wrapped themselves around the furniture, floor, and ceiling.

I stared, agog. Images draped over the bedroom and transformed it into a floating pavilion. Clouds whipped past at high speed. Balloon-cities dotted the horizon.

The kid's room was rigged for wall-to-wall holoconferencing!

The last time I'd seen something like that was ten years earlier in the seaport hotel, talking to my brother. That had been fine for a facility catering to corporate needs. But for personal, in-home use? Interfacing with the redweb was typically done through the privacy of augmented overlays or VR rigs; even during the Siege of Noctis, my squad had brought a portable rig to databurst messages to command. VR rigs afforded privacy that even AR overlays couldn't; when you were strapped in, no one else could read your lips when you were talking, or deduce your virtuboard strokes when you were typing. And they also served as hardened transportable communication hubs with insulated matryoshka boards when intrusion-chaff screwed with databursts, or when the enemy broadcast sense-impact siege-chatter to disrupt comlinks.

By contrast, a bedroom with wall-to-wall holos was the very *opposite* of private; it left your communications wide open. Anyone could peep into the window and see what you were doing.

Was this the way a post-nuke generation had been brought up? Didn't Peter care about privacy?

Or was he not afforded it by the ex-spymaster extraordinaire?

Whatever the case, there was no way communications here were going to be secure. And yet I needed to contact my handler. Needed to get a read on the terrain.

What would a nineteen-year-old kid do, as soon as he came back from death?

With a sigh, I glanced to the bedroom door and noticed there was no lock – not that a lock would have provided anything more than atavistic comfort. My father could have cameras printed on every inch of surface in here.

You're behind enemy lines, Harris. The enemy is watching.

I settled into the cushioned pilotchair and extended my hands. A menu appeared, floating in the air between me and the cloudy vista:

**MYTRIBE   HOME   REDWEB   BLUEWEB
FAVORITES   ARCADIA
MORE**

Remembering what Celeste had told me in her recording, I selected the first option.

The holographic clouds yawned wide to reveal a starry firmament. One of the stars glinted brighter than the others, pulsated, and fell towards me. In a flashing impact, it turned into a woman.

"Hi, Pete!"

I stared. I hadn't expected to see a familiar face – it wasn't like the Order of Stone was going to send one of their operatives in here wearing a real-world countenance. Nonetheless, the woman who arrived was not what I'd expected. She wore a lacy corset, her blonde locks piled high like some monarch. Her skin was powdered to the sheen and pallor of calcite, excepting rosy cheeks. She seemed around Peter's age.

The woman gave me a hug I couldn't feel. There was a sensejack option in my head, but I wasn't up for cybersex with a total stranger, and in someone else's body, and in the house of my sworn enemy.

The woman folded her hands demurely in front of her. It was a casual move, but I read the Order sign language in the tap of her fingers.

Natalia Argos.

Just fucking great.

"It's so good to see you!" she crooned, meeting my gaze in meaningful linkage. "It was all over the news...I couldn't believe it! Glad to have you back, Pete." A hesitation. "Your parents must be happy to see you."

I looked deeply into her eyes.

"It's good to see you, too. My parents are certainly happy. Actually, Mom and Dad had the *exact same identical reaction*! It was surprising!"

My words found their mark. Natalia froze, clearly rocked by my implication. Swallowing hard, she stammered, "Are you...um...will you still be able...."

I cut in hastily. "I haven't told them about us yet. Today has been playing catch-up. They're mostly pissed that I drank too much and got myself killed. Figured it wasn't the best time to bring up my love life."

"But you'll...tell them tomorrow?"

I stared at her. "What's the rush?"

She hesitated, and there it was – the flash of annoyance I remembered from the shuttleport and hotel. Natalia was accustomed to soldiers who complied with her orders instantly.

"I think I'll bring it up tomorrow," I added. "I did have a few questions for you, though."

"What questions, Pete?"

"What if you're wrong?"

"Sorry?"

"If I *tell* Mom and Dad, do you think that will be enough? Are there other relatives of mine who should be told?"

She shook her head. "We would've...I mean...Mom and Dad should be enough." But she looked frazzled.

"You sure?"

She froze. Her face lost all composure. In a lab somewhere, a hasty conference was being held.

When she resumed, she was all smiles. "I'm sure. This isn't a casual fling for me, you know."

"I'm starting to get that impression from you." I pretended to scratch an itch on my chest, moving my fingers in subtle Order sign language:

Equipment? Weapons?

Natalia strayed to the rails, peering down at the clouds. I joined her, drinking in the faux view. Must be a recreation of a Venusian aerostat during their dayweek. If so, it was reason enough for me never to travel there; the super-rotation was making me dizzy, and being forced to live in a confined space – even in the larger cities like Ishtar – was not my cup of coffee.

"I want to see you," Natalia cooed in her stranger's voice. "You realize that since you're in a new body, you've never kissed anyone. Can you get away, even for a little bit?"

"What did you have in mind?"

"Breakfast at Ybarra Docks?"

This startled me. The Ybarra Docks I knew were a trog ghetto. An impenetrable thicket of bars, clubs, pheromod-traps, cage-matches, shell slaughterhouses, and for the *really* unlucky, a blackjack to the head... your unconscious body carted off to a chop shop. They had been friendly enough to the Order during the war, owing to the whole enemy-of-my-enemy bit. But thirty years earlier, when Dave and I snuck off for beers, we had taken a real risk. I couldn't imagine a skinny kid like Peter Bayne surviving a stroll there. And to get *breakfast*?

"The docks sound like a blast," I said finally. Again, I gave the hand signal for *equipment* and threw in a pair of specific requests.

Natalia smiled. "I'm really looking forward to seeing you."

"Oh, me too. Believe that."

CHAPTER TWELVE

Ybarra

The next morning was December 23rd standard, two days before Solstice. With Peter's university closed for intersession, I didn't have to worry about navigating his academic or social life. A few emails arrived from people I presumed were his friends; I let them sit, unopened, like little holiday presents. Let him handle that when the op was over and he got downloaded into his body again…although I was pretty certain that by then, answering emails would be the least of his concerns.

Mom and Dad had presumably spent the night decorating, because as I emerged from my bedroom I found the corridor outside my room green and forested with wreaths and holly. The stairwell was festooned with ivy, leading down to a 'living room' deserving of the moniker; as in my own childhood, Martian Solstice was still the celebration of garden and growth.

The annual Solstice Tree was up, too. In fact, someone was there, hanging ornaments on its branches.

"Good morning," I said.

The figure turned around.

It had no face.

I choked down my scream. The entity before me was dressed in a red-and-green apron, and it was wearing a cheery antlered cap. But it was a sock-puppet shell. Like the ones on Phobos. Modular limbs, plastic jaw. The thing stared at me with an eggshell-smooth visage.

"Good morning," it echoed back at me in my own voice, jaw flapping. And then, in a duet of Peznowski's male and female voices, it added, "Good morning! Good morning!"

I felt the hairs on my neck stand up.

On Phobos, the goddam things had been rudimentary bots. No intelligence, just a coldly relentless commitment to their orders. Peznowski had been capable of sightjacking with any of them. Steeling myself, I retreated several steps while the thing continued facing me, holiday hat askew on that wooden countenance. At five meters, I apparently exited its sensor range, because it rotated back to the tree and continued decorating with bells and garland.

For a moment, I was paralyzed by indecision and fear. Beyond the living room, the lower level was a gloomy, uninhabited space. I linked to the home-grid. Mom and Dad were not in the house, but were both up and about: Dad's ID blipped in Farmpod 16, and Mom was in Farmpod 5. Other signals dotted the grid, in other greenhouses. I wondered if these represented more nightmare puppets, or actual human workers from North Hellas.

Cautiously, letting the adrenaline thin out in my blood, I linked to the thing that was my mother.

Good morning, Mom.

The reply came at once: *Good morning, sweetie! Did you sleep well?*

Yeah, I lied. Sleep had been a fitful experience at best, as I kept waking up in a blind panic. *If it's okay, I was going to head out for a while. Some friends want to meet for breakfast.*

Friends?

Cursing, I reminded myself that Minister Peznowski had almost certainly wired the house for lie detection.

To be honest, I said, *it's just one person. A...girl.*

Silence on the other end of the link. The sock puppet creaked as it bent to a box of ornaments, fishing for things to hang.

From Farmpod 5, my mother said:

You didn't tell me you had met someone.

I can show you my fucking diary if you want, I thought. *Unless you've already read it, which of course you have.*

I'm just meeting her for breakfast. I promise I'll come right back.

Another stretch of silence. I focused on my breathing, trying not to think of my lack of weapons...or how vulnerable this untrained body was. Tried not to think of the faceless thing toiling at the tree, and how I'd watched others of its brethren torture victims into insanity....

Oh, sweetie! Mom purred at last. *Go see your friend! But be back for lunch, okay?*

I will, Mom.

That's my good boy! Love you, baby!

I severed the link and went out the front door into the maze of farmpods. Blurry shapes toiled behind glasstic walls. An imp of the perverse flitted in my thoughts, impelling me to press against the panels to better see what was going on inside. I defied the urge, not needing to witness what I'd already realized: that the Minister of Media Intelligence had peopled his estate with a labor force of mannequins. His experience with sock-puppet shells had found a civilian – even productive – use. Never tiring, never requiring food or sleep, they would follow their subroutines until their actuators wore out. Wind-up automatons which would plant, aerate, water, and harvest with the same cheerless efficiency as they had mutilated, tormented, skinned, and debased the prisoners on Paradise Row.

Like Vanessa Jamison...screeching for mercy that never came until I killed her and everyone else on Phobos.

Outside the house, a private road wound through the valley. I called a PDT, and waited anxiously for it to arrive.

*　　*　　*

Riding in the vehicle, I watched an unfamiliar Mars streak past the window. Bone-white construction projects on the rusted desert, like a blurry image of teeth and gums. Printer-cranes were everywhere, laying the foundations of future arcologies. The development seemed excessive, considering that seven million people had died. Surely not all those Save files had been recoverable.

Then I thought of the overpopulated masses on Earth, and in the Belt, and on Luna. A new wave of immigration must be gearing up. Our planet was being readied to receive them.

Ybarra was located by the canals. As I disembarked the PDT into cool, moist air, I was finally able to move past the anxiety of the last sixteen hours. *Here* was a type of settlement I recognized. The canals! Once the heart of Martian life – sprouting by readily available water sources as surely as Earth's civilizations had hatched by the blue veins of the Nile, Tigris, Euphrates, Yangtze, Indus, and other deltas. If Ybarra alone was continuing that tradition, I would not think poorly of her. I wondered what had become of Lighthouse Point. Wondered who was living in my parents' old house. Wondered if it had survived the nukes.

To be sure, Ybarra was a sprawling warren of alleys, storefronts, bridges, and enclosed concourses. Watercraft sliced past. navigating canals with pinpoint precision. High above, a procession of airships hung morosely against the clouds.

I shouldered through a crowd of dockworkers and passersby. There were trogs, of course, working in riverside garages. Red-dyed hair and studded countenances. They were sanding, soldering, painting, and riveting various watercraft...but they were working side-by-side with non-trog Martians and barrel-chested Earthers, too; a kind of motley, diversified gaggle I'd rarely seen outside of metropolitan hubs. Briefly, I wondered if Eric Mazzola had survived Detonation.

I accessed Natalia's link:

I'm here. Where are we meeting?

It was half a minute before she deigned to reply: *Okay, I've got eyes on you. Turn left and go to Trevor's Garage.*

Do they serve breakfast at Trevor's Garage? Because I'm actually hungry.

The link dropped. I traced her directions, passing machine shops, bars, purifying stations, marinas, and apartments of such peeling and dilapidated condition that I realized these were the original structures. Guess Ybarra hadn't been high on the nuke hit-list. Or else this was one of those saved by the Order's ground-based defenses.

Trevor's Garage turned out to be a five-story structure rising above the city like a medieval watchtower. I located an open loading door and walked in.

"What do you know," I said, looking around. "It's actually a garage."

Hovercraft and buggies littered the interior like some robotic butcher's shop. The air smelled of diesel and the sweet stink of hydrofuel.

Footsteps sounded on a metal staircase winding like a spinal column from upper levels. Natalia Argos descended, reached the bottom level, and beheld me across ten meters of oil-stained asphalt.

She hadn't changed much since I'd seen her a decade earlier. Same crystal blue eyes, angular cheeks, and morning-star hairstyle. The chief difference was she had traded her beetle-black armor for a granite-gray carapace.

Her eyes narrowed. "That really you, Harris?"

"You've got some nerve, asking me that." I made a show of looking around. "Is this place secure?"

"See the picosurvs?" She pointed to the greenish devices protruding slightly from the walls. "They could detect any airhound in existence. We're as secure as it gets. Now give me an update on the mission."

"You mean Peznowski Squared? They're alive for now."

She was as motionless as a tomb guardian. "What have you learned?"

"No, no. You don't get to bring me back from the dead and then fire twenty questions my way. I want to know if the Order won the war."

Natalia hissed out her patented sigh. "You didn't scan the redweb for info on the last few years?"

"I did."

"Then you know we won. We're in charge of the whole planet."

"Then send in a commando team to take out the Peznowskis."

"Can't."

"Why not?"

She folded her hands behind her and began a short pace, as if she were performing a cadet review. "For starters, there are political considerations."

I gaped, flabbergasted. "Political...*considerations*?"

"The Martian president is focused on moving us forward, beyond the war and Detonation. He doesn't want Partisans in the news again."

"The Martian president can kiss my ass. If criminals have escaped justice, people have the right to know. They'd *want* to know." I hesitated. "I warned you about the Save centers...."

"And we followed your advice. Seized every clinic on the planet and searched for files. Downloaded the bunch to disk. Brought them all to Order HQ."

"Surprised you had time. The hammer came down just twenty-four hours after Phobos popped."

"Procurement of enemy backups was given higher priority than mop-up operations. A resurrected Bishons or Potts was deemed a greater threat than a few rogue commanders."

I considered this, picturing Order operatives scooping up Partisan Saves into some demented shopping cart. The rapists and murderers of Mars, collected as a pile of trash like ancient DVDs. "What happened next?"

"The files were put under lock and key. We planned to subject Partisan brass to a military tribunal. Anything useful would be extracted, and then we'd give the whole collection an EMP bath. Scrub them from the universe."

"I'm guessing the nukes disturbed your barbecue plans. Is it possible the files survived Detonation? Maybe they were carted away by loyalists for secret revivals."

Natalia shook her head. "No. The stash was taken to HQ. No nuke found that place. It was too deep underground. That's the same bunker where your brother was operating."

"Is Dave alive? Is he okay?"

"Dave is alive."

"And the Save files?"

She gave what for her must have passed for a smile. "I wasn't there, Harris — I was buried alive at Amazonis. But as I understand it, your brother and other high-ranking officials went ahead with their tribunal. They consigned the Partisans to oblivion."

There was comfort in what she was describing. David Julius Pope, waiting out the radiation with other resistance fighters and commanders.

Rationing their supplies. Extending wary feelers like a fragile plant across the burnt remains of a forest fire, trying to ascertain the full extent of damage. I could sympathize. During the war, I'd often been cut off from my squad, forced to improvise, scavenge, hunker down, and wait. My thoughts returned to nights spent with Umerah. Dining on old MREs together, sipping water from canteens. Making love while we waited for orders....

Where was Umerah's Save?

She had been killed on Phobos. But surely there was a backup copy somewhere! I'd seen her march into Save clinics many times.

Then I realized: *Her backup would be registered as Partisan. Maybe she'd been killed by the Order's late-night barbecues....*

"What happened to rank-and-file Partisans?" I asked, heart pounding. "Soldiers, special ops. Were they destroyed?"

The impatience was brewing in Natalia's face again. "A conditional amnesty was declared for everyone below command level. Those who survived Detonation were forgiven. The grunts and officers were as shocked by the nukes as everyone else. Later, dead Partisans were resurrected as chain-gang workers, mandated by the courts to reconstruction for three-to-ten-year service terms as determined by a formal review of their crimes."

I let this roll around in my mind.

Then Umerah Javed might be alive again. She wouldn't remember Phobos. Wouldn't remember our last op at Hellas, where we'd nabbed Gethin Bryce.

Wouldn't remember the horrors of Paradise Row.

Standing in the garage, I linked to the redweb and ran a search for her in the public database.

NO RESULTS FOUND FOR "UMERAH JAVED"

My thoughts grasped vainly for other explanations. It had been ten years, I told myself. Many Save centers were destroyed in Detonation. Mars was a library that had been put to torch, and not every volume had survived. Maybe she had gotten married and changed her name? No, there would still be a record of that.

Was she Saved in another library? On another world?

I extended my search to all of IPCnet. Even at the speed of light, it would take hours for the request to return results. But I'd lost thirty fucking years...so what were a few hours?

"Hey." Natalia had the audacity to snap her fingers in my face. "Are you still with me? Minister Peznowski is alive and your orders are—"

"According to public records," I cut in, "Peznowski had been living a double life since before Phobos. Sorry...make that a *triple* life. He might not be the only one."

"We're investigating that possibility."

It made me tremble, thinking of my former comrades reconstructing themselves like some sentient cancer.

Why would the Partisans return? Or was this just Peznowski exercising his own ego trip?

I paced in a slow, methodical circle around Natalia. "Where is Celeste?"

Natalia scowled. "*Archon* Segarra is not available at the moment. *I'm* your handler, Harris."

"Handle this." I flipped her off. "I'm fucking done with the Order of Stone. You stole thirty goddam years of my life. Now you resurrect me in a kid's body and tell me to perform a double homicide."

"Technically, it's a *single* homicide."

"Technically, you're a fucking bitch. Let me talk to David."

"After the mission."

"After the mission I might blink and wake up a thousand years from now."

"I give you my word—"

"Your word counts for *nothing*."

A voice sprang to my audio:

*How about *my* word? Does that count for nothing?*

The sender link burned in the corner of my vision:

Celeste Segarra

Archon, Order of Stone

It counts, I whispered, some of the fight leeching out of me. I had no argument with the archon. She was the only one, since my reactivation, who had treated me as a person – the kind of humanistic empathy that is the domain of people who still remembered what it was like to *be* a person, beyond any trappings of social identity or cybernetic upgrade. Memories of her in my hotel room were still fresh; I could recall the precise scar patterning on her arms. *Are you listening to us right now?*

I'm sightjacking with Natalia, she explained. *I'd be there in person if I could, Harris, but I'm in a meeting with some VIPs.*

Say it again.

I could sense her surprise across the miles. *Say what?*

Give me your word that I get to see David when this op is done.

I, Celeste Segarra, swear by the River Styx that you will get to see your brother when your current op is complete. In fact, I'll do one better: I'll personally fly you to see him. How's that?

Natalia was frowning, and I realized she was only hearing my muttered side of the conversation. "Who are you talking to?"

"*Your* handler," I countered.

She visibly started at this. "Well...good. So, getting back to the mission...."

"Not so fast. It's been ten years. My official tour of duty is over. What are you offering me to continue this assignment?" My link to Celeste was still open, and so I added, "I'm asking both of you."

"Back pay for thirty years, for starters," Natalia said.

"That's a start."

"You're still ranked as a paladin, did you know that? The Order is prepared to bump you to First Sentinel, House of Guardians."

I laughed caustically. "Natalia, if you've been reduced to offering merit badges, I'll take my chances and go through puberty again, thanks."

"What *do* you want?" she demanded.

I considered this, aware of my dwindling time-frame to depart Ybarra and return home. I didn't want to explain to the world's most dreaded interrogator where I'd really been.

"I want the same thing I wanted ten years ago. I want to see my brother. Then, Natalia dear, I want *you* out of my life."

She smiled thinly. "Done and done. Now, get this mission rolling, soldier. Here, the equipment you asked for." She reached into her utility belt and handed me a small device. "We usually prefer airhounds for surveillance."

"Airhounds could trigger a homegrid alert." I considered the device in my hands. It resembled a meat thermometer, with a small main body at the end of a retractable needle, and a secondary piece that was little more than a short-range transmitter with admin and senseshare rights.

A neurojack.

Natalia's patented frown was back, like a Japanese Noh mask. "Not sure what you're going to do with that. It only works on bots."

"I asked for a weapon, too."

"You did, and my judgment is that a weapon could blow your cover. If the minister's home is as secure as you imply, it could pick up the silhouette of a pistol or knife...even concealed in your pocket. At least with the 'jack, you can conceal it in your shoe."

"So how do I execute the assets? Stab them to death with a kitchen fork?"

Natalia darkened. "While undercover, you once killed a pair of Order soldiers with a brick. I'm sure you'll improvise. Add two more to your epic body count."

I didn't have a patmatch sniffer in the body I was wearing, but I didn't need it to detect the bitterness in her voice.

Coldly, I said, "Or maybe I'll add *three* more, huh, Natalia?"

My commanding officer stiffened. She had to know I was bluffing – I was wearing the body of a nineteen-year-old stick figure. My combat training was intact in my head, but the accompanying body was mush. I could feel the fragility of Peter Bayne's bones. Even if I procured a blurmod, it would kill me on activation; the absence of distributed seedclusters, nerve-junction processors, and dermal arrays meant I'd fly apart into red goo. A hard-stop and Peter's organs would explode out of my chest like a piñata. And that was assuming I didn't burst into flames before that.

So Natalia could surely snap me in half if I attacked her. Nonetheless, there was genuine fear in her eyes, and I took private delight in it. Not all victories are big ones.

Now is what we own.

"One last thing," I said as I buried the neurojack in my pocket. "What if I get caught?"

Natalia watched me coolly. "Don't."

CHAPTER THIRTEEN

The Ghost of Christmas Past

Whatever mystique had grown up around shadowmen – that they were unstoppable combatants, deadly assassins, intrusion experts, master saboteurs – the truth was that the majority of my responsibilities had been intel gathering. A snippet of enemy conversation was often more valuable than a bullet. Hard-and-fast tactics were rare; my long-perished squad usually deployed to monitor a canton for many tedious hours, soaking up intel for the brains at command to examine. Beresha, Hammill, Conway, Shea, and (when he wasn't being stung to death by waspbots) Cuddy, lying low and watching, listening, piecing together the pattern of enemy patrols, resources, personnel, defensive strengths, and fallback positions. Often we'd focus on a single building or alley.

Upon my return to the Bayne manor, I fell back on that shadowman training. Figuring the place was on full surveillance, I slipped into the role of dutiful son. I decorated for the holidays. Peter's last Save had been a month ago; I used that excuse to wander room to room, unsure where the decorations were, pushing past the sock-puppet abomination, opening drawers, extracting ornaments while scanning for anything useful…any intel that might betray Peznowski's purpose.

There was a downstairs study. I took stock of an entire bookshelf of binders. Tax records. Census records. Agricultural reports. The kind of thing to expect from a governor.

I retreated upstairs, found some wrapped presents in Peter's closet, and in the act of bringing them downstairs made a detour to his parents' bedroom.

There was their unholy bed. The rest was teakwood furniture: dresser, workdesk, pilotchair, brace of nightstands, and armoire.

Was Peter the type to nose around for hidden presents? The very act of stepping into their bedroom was probably sending an alert. Thinking fast, I crossed the room and placed a single gift on their workdesk. Then I opened the top drawer.

Socks. Folded underwear. A leather billfold.

I flipped open this latter item. Inside, I found an interplanetary passport, and some paperwork from a place called Banshee Private Security. I hadn't noticed any security forces on premises, so I guessed that Peznowski wanted protection for when he traveled.

But what the hell did he need an interplanetary passport for?

I thumbed through documents. Apparently, Mark and Jessica Bayne had arranged for private military contractors to be assigned as bodyguards 'upon arrival'. What arrival, and who was arriving, and where and when this arrival would occur, was not specified.

Yet there were other items of interest: three Banshee ID badges, one for each member of the family.

Closing the billfold, I retreated for the stairs.

Lunch awaited me in the kitchen. A replovat tree curled out of the floorboards, bearing fruit, meat knots, and breadbulbs. Mom toiled at the counter, smiling as she wielded two knives over a stump of venison roast. The real thing, too, if the blood in the basin was any indication. Before the war, deer were common in the Martian wilderness, driven to the forests by sandstorms and atavistic instincts to hide from nonexistent predators.

"Hey there, lover-boy!" Mom cooed. "Lunch is on the table!"

"Hi, Mom." The smell brought me back to my childhood, when my real mother would prepare venison steaks following our monthly jaunt to Hellas.

"How was your date?"

"It wasn't really a date. Just met for coffee and a bagel." I regarded my plate of polenta, minced seaflower, toast, and a glass of cranberry juice. "Where's Dad?"

"He had to go to the office today."

"On Solstice Eve?"

"Only for a few hours. He'll be back any minute."

I gulped the juice and regarded the table knives. If I killed her now, the flatline notification would hit whatever regen center she was registered with; more ominously, a notification would reach Dad. I needed to kill them both together.

Wait until tonight. Slit one throat ear-to-ear, and while the body is bleeding out go after the other. Neat and quick.

The kitchen swayed as I was taking another sip of juice.

"Tell me about your date," Mom said, rinsing her knives in the sink.

"She's...um...."

"Yes?"

The kitchen looked fuzzy. My fingers slipped their hold on the glass. *Shit.*

It was the purest desperation that galvanized my action. I leapt at Mom, intending to break her neck.

She turned aside, viciously slamming my head against the counter. White lights burst in my vision. Blindly, I grasped for one of the knives. My arm moved sluggishly. She hopped backwards, retreating, as I stumbled after her.

The throat. I could go for her throat.

In the moment before all went dark, I glimpsed Peznowski's cruel eyes shining down from that imposter visage.

★   ★   ★

When I regained consciousness, my optic readout told me that sixteen minutes had passed. I couldn't move my arms or legs. My head felt like someone had put a drill behind my ear. I tried sitting up, but couldn't. I was bound to my parents' bed, limbs strapped to each post. The pillow was wet behind me.

Mom stood in the corner, holding bloody knives and beaming.

"Mom?" I asked quietly.

"Cut the charade," Dad said from the opposite corner. I twisted my neck and saw him hugging himself. He approached and flicked something at me. It landed like an earring on my chest.

My nanonic antenna. The bastard must have dug it out of my head while I was drugged.

"Who are you?" he demanded. "I already know you're not our son, so drop the act. We grafted a rotating verbal tic into his consciousness when he was young, triggered by code-phrase. He's not even aware of it. Subtle, comes across as mild OCD." When I didn't answer, Dad's nostrils flared. "I can use a magpie claw on you, you know? Tear chunks of your brain out. Not the best option, but I've had more experience than most. So why not save yourself the trouble and a good deal of pain? What's your name?"

"Carlos."

Dad didn't even look at Mom when he said, "Take out his eyes."

She approached the bedside, still wearing the checkered apron from the kitchen.

"What is it with you and eyes, Peznowski?" I shouted.

"Wait!"

Dad was almost too late. Mom's eagerness had put the blade points a micrometer from one eyeball. At that range, they looked impossibly tall, a horrific stainless steel V, her hungry grin behind them. Dad's frown appeared in my other eye.

"Do we know each other?" he asked.

"I know what you like to do to prisoners," I said.

"A name. I want a name."

One of the knife points touched the eyeball. I gasped and tried pulling away. The movement drew a scratch and my vision blurred with involuntary tears.

"Last chance."

"Thomas."

The same expression hatched on both my parents' faces. The slow burn of realization, eyes quivering as they accessed some patriatch filter. I wasn't sure what they were seeing; I was just throwing out random names. They were going to kill me, I knew that much. And it would

be a grisly death…but I wouldn't remember it when the Order brought me back. And Celeste had *promised* me that when the op was concluded she'd escort me to my brother, so I wasn't about to give anything useful to my interrogators….

Then I realized my mistake.

I'd spoken the name 'Thomas' once before in Peznowski's presence. Back on Phobos, making a cynical quip about….

"Doubting Thomas," Dad said slowly, enunciating each syllable. He gave a barking laugh. "That you, Harris? Really you?"

I said nothing. But my shock was probably visible in a hundred vectors of microexpression, pulse, and temperature. Sweat dappled my brow.

Dad paced slowly, considering this. Then he let out a great peal of barking laughter and did a fist pump in the air. "Oh! The universe loves me!"

Mom leapt upon me, knocking the wind from my lungs. Her laughter was shrill and hideous as she gouged out my eyes.

★   ★   ★

"Harris? Look at me."

Dad's voice, followed by wicked female laughter.

I turned in the direction of the voice, trying not to think of my mutilated face. My throat was ragged from screaming.

"You know," Dad's voice intoned, "I would never have figured it was *you* who screwed us over. But then you issued that broadband victory announcement. Harris Alexander Pope! Turncoat, mole, spy! Fucking war hero!"

"Guess time doesn't heal all wounds." The words scraped out of my raw throat. "I'll admit it was a special pleasure, making sure you all knew who'd fucked you."

"The Order pay you in thirty pieces of silver to betray us?"

"Yes. One piece for every year of misery you brought to the planet."

Mom asked, "Who sent you here?"

"The Ghost of Christmas Past."

There was a terrible silence. The pain in my eye sockets was nauseating. Hot fluid spilled down my cheeks.

You survived the Siege of Noctis, I reminded myself. *Forty-one days of horror. You can deal with this.*

"What was your mission?" I couldn't tell if it was Mom or Dad who asked it. Husky voice, a whisper. "Looks like you went through some drawers. What were you looking for?"

"Something convenient to kill you both – ahhh!"

Mom must have inserted a blade or even a finger into one of my savaged eye sockets, because the pain shot through me until it was all I could focus on. When she finally withdrew, I tasted new sweat on my lips.

"No one wonder Peter drowned himself," I managed.

"He didn't drown himself."

"Police report said—"

"I got him drunk," Dad snapped. "Walked him to the greenhouse, and drowned him with my own hands. Shoved his head underwater until he stopped screaming and kicking."

"What in the hell for?"

Mom's voice answered me. "To draw out the hunters, you little bastard. To find out who has been coming after us."

I hesitated. "What do you mean, who has been coming after you?"

"Who sent you?"

"The Ghost of Christmas Past, Present, and—"

It must have been a fist that smashed through my teeth. The attack stunned me into mute stupidity, the broken teeth in my mouth like peanut shells. I spat them out in a gob of bloody saliva.

"I'm going to torture you forever, you know." Mom's voice in my ear. "But not like this. Mark and I agree that Peter grew up too fast. We want a little baby again. How would you like being downloaded into a helpless creature, engineered to never age? Your mind trapped in that prison for all time, slowly turning to mush, while we feed you and wrap you up and change your diapers…year after year? Forever?"

A new scream started in my throat, shredding my resolve.

"Oh, sweetie! Don't cry! This is just the beginning!"

There was a time when the human body was considered the ultimate achievement of the gods, a temple of flesh housing a soul. That model was long-since dispelled. The human body was only muscle, bone, nerves, and organs. Bodies today were cranked out by rapid-processing clone banks. We understood them, could improve on them, and could cause as much pain as either nature designed or man could enhance.

"Who sent you here?" Mom purred.

"I'm really going to tell you."

"You really are, Harris. Of all the people in the universe, you should know that."

"You don't have your old resources anymore, *Mom*, and it will take more than a kitchen knife to move my lips."

In the darkness, the silence resumed.

"That's a really, really bad example," Mom said at last, and she sliced my lips away. They came off in thin rubbery flaps—

—*like the prisoners on Paradise Row. Ripped apart, faces hanging in red strips*—

—and she sawed the blade, stripping my mouth into a frightful skeletal freak, all stained teeth and gums. I had seen this handiwork before, and my memory filled in the blindness: thin yellow lines of fat underneath, pale nerves like little maggots....

All human faces were masks in the most literal way. Prisoners reduced to calaca skulls....

Mom wasn't done. She dropped the knife on my chest, grabbed what remained of my mouth, and savagely yanked. The flesh ripped from its roots. Wet tissue and skin hung in loose, ragged sheets against my neck. I felt my mind wanting to retreat from this moment; the impulse to burrow into merciful catatonia.

"Let me *guess* who sent you here," Mom grunted as she worked. "Segarra and Argos, right? Ah! There it is, honey! How do you like being their little tool? Their living Familiar?"

Something cold locked down over my mutilated mouth. Like a metal gag. There was an electric pinch. Vibration chattered along my jawbone.

I remembered this part from Phobos, too.

They were using a subvoc amp on me.

Like a black spider clamped over prisoners' mouths. Lit up blue when you tried to speak, and the voice permitted was a gross distortion, like a cyborg with a broken soundcard. I had witnessed Peznowski suture mouths shut, then fit the device into place. Take a tour of the cellblock and the prisoners sounded like tortured robots, wheezing and sobbing and whimpering in electronic ball-gags.

Dad was speaking again. "Let's get to it, Harris. You know the drill. I ask you questions, and you supply answers, and we keep going until I'm satisfied. You can't outthink me. And you can *never* kill me."

When I replied, my voice was inhuman. Like scratches on a waxen cylinder.

"I killed you once," I said through the device, pushing the words out through broken teeth and blood. "That was a warm-up for what's to come, *compadre*."

"Always liked your stubbornness, Harris. We'll see how well it holds up."

"Take a good look, Peznowski. I'm the Fury, stalking you for eternity. You'll never get away from me."

"Wrong, old buddy. I am everywhere. You just don't know it yet."

"Yeah?" I gritted. "Was it just you who returned to enjoy the strangest masturbation in the galaxy, or did your comrades follow?" I imagined how the gag was flashing in sizzling blue from each spoken word.

"Is he recording us?" Dad asked uncertainly.

Mom's knife poked at my face. "If he is, it's not like he can transmit anything."

"Good." A pause, interrupted by a soft chuckle. "You know, Harris, I never did get around to asking you how that pilot of yours was in bed. Was her cunt a velvet glove or—"

As far as I knew, it was only the three of us in the bedroom, so I was shocked when a new voice deftly inserted into our conversation.

"Who is he, Caleb?"

The bed creaked as Mom shifted her position. "Commander Harris Alexander Pope, shadowman. Decided to drop by."

"Kill him *now*," came the immediate reply. It was a masked voice, hailing from the wall opposite us and disguised by thick harmonics. Yet I could hear panic in those artificial tones. "Kill him and torch everything, yourselves included! I'll bring you back at the Face."

"I can get offworld without needing to—"

"Torch *everything*! Torch yourselves! That's an order, Caleb. I'll never warn you again."

The wallpanel switched off with an electric *thump!*

For a moment the bedroom was silent, as if everyone was holding their breath. My surrogate father spat. "Fuck him. Harris is coming with us. Chop his head and we'll meet with Vil. She can smuggle us offworld."

"Let me guess," I croaked. "Was that Bishons?"

Ignoring me, Dad said, "The hacksaw's in the dresser." I heard Mom fumbling for it, a holiday jingle of metal.

My face was slippery with blood. The amp was a vise around my mouth.

"Don't I get a last request?"

"You'll be begging for last requests until the heat-death of the universe. But sure, Harris! Give me your benediction!"

I tried sitting up in bed, as best as my restraints would allow. My eyelids stretched over sightless pits. In the corner of my vision was a sizzling fountain of color, the optic center of my brain firing scintillating bursts of orange and white.

I cleared my throat and spoke through the electronic voice.

"You are Minister Caleb Peznowski. A Partisan. You brutalized Mars. You captured and oppressed and tortured its people. You terrorized the populace with your shadowmen police. That ends today. I represent the Order of Stone. I am here to bring justice. I am here to show you that the injuries you inflicted upon Mars will not go unpunished. My name is Harris Alexander Pope, and I am the last thing you will ever see."

Mom's knives had done their cruel sculpting like a master surgeon. My nanonic antennae had been severed and extracted, leaving only a wet cavity in my skull. But I was a soldier. A soldier understands the need for contingency. A soldier knows how to improvise.

With my right thumb, I pressed the neurojack transmitter I had inserted beneath my fingernail. A short-range signal activated the neurojack...

...the one I had implanted in the *fourth* member of the family.

Suzie bounded through the bedroom doorway and attacked. The neurojack bypassed my severed antenna and provided me a front-row visual – sightjacked into Suzie's eyes – as she tore my parents into bloody scraps. Looking down the dog's snout at Dad's expression of terror. Mom made it to the door before Suzie clamped on her calf and dragged her back inside. Then she darted to Mom's face and chewed it off like a mask.

When it was over, I controlled Suzie to gnaw through my ropes; she was close enough that I could hear the whine of actuators in her jaws. Could smell Peznowski's blood on her steel teeth. Once free, I staggered to my feet, avoided my parents' corpses, and went to the kitchen to make a call.

PART THREE
ASSASSIN

By now you've seen the advertisements:

Help us build the future! Ten thousand worlds are waiting for you! Thousands of jobs – guaranteed!

You probably even know someone who went offworld for this mysterious multi-year contract. Maybe you bought them a beer the night before they shipped out and tried prying information out of them. "Where are you going? You really gonna zip off to space for nine years? What's the big secret?"

They didn't answer you, of course. Because even they didn't know.

As the months and years passed, maybe you got emails from them. "Miss you!" and, "Having a blast out here!" But no details were leaked. They all signed NDAs tighter than your favorite pornstar. All communications are filtered and edited.

So what the hell is going on? What are thousands of workers doing in space?

We here at NoWire have been sniffing around to see what we can uncover. Alas, we can't dispel the mystery yet, though we can provide a few morsels to chew over.

In the last nine years, four hundred thousand Earthers joined the IPC's mystery project. Thirty thousand Lunars went as well. A whopping one million Martians.

That's one hell of a workforce.

And we've got more for your cerebral mastications. The lion's share of enlisted workers have been the kind of folks you probably don't break bread with. Wastelanders from Earth. Trogs from Mars. Oh, there's lots of arky types too –

engineers of every feather and stripe. But most of this mass hiring has been, shall we say, colorful?

Obviously something big is going on in the deeps.

If that appetizer isn't enough to sate you, let us leave you with this: the first wave of multi-year contracts is set to expire in six weeks. That means those workers will be coming home...and their pesky little NDAs will expire when they do.

Six weeks, people! The IPC will pull back the covers, spread its legs, and reveal all....

—NoWire, *December 24, 358*

CHAPTER FOURTEEN

The President of Mars

"I said don't you dare kill that dog!"

My voice was shrill and electronic and terrible, and the physical trauma of the last hour had dumped so much adrenaline into my body that my legs felt as rubbery as young bamboo. From my parents' bedroom, I'd managed to stagger downstairs. Suzie was serving as my literal seeing-eye dog. Pain throbbing from my blinded sockets, I'd slumped at the kitchen table to await the Order of Stone cavalry.

Unfortunately, the Bayne homegrid security system must have been wired with an emergency response protocol, because I'd barely seated myself when the front door flew open and two local cops – accompanied by a pair of EMTs – stormed the place.

I'd flipped Suzie to her default passive mode; the petbot sat obediently by my feet. But the cops took one look at her gore-encrusted mouth and—

"Mikayla, get out of the way!" a police officer roared, drawing his pistol. "I need a clear shot!"

The cop's partner hopped aside; Suzie fled beneath the kitchen table as I hurriedly flipped her to HIDE mode. Sightjacked as I was, I watched the police officers and EMTs through a forest of chair and table legs.

"I said leave the dog be!" I cried.

"It's just a bot!" the female officer snapped. "It killed your parents, Peter! It mauled your face!"

"Back off!"

Through Suzie's eyes, I watched the burly male officer aim his pistol directly at the cowering bot. His fingers tightened around the trigger....

I kicked one of the kitchen chairs into him, bowling him over.

"My name is Harris Alexander Pope!" I shouted. "I'm an operative with the Order of Stone, and if you touch that dog I'll kill you. Leave her alone! *Now!*"

The burly cop clambered back to his feet, eyes flaring. "Mister Bayne, you need to stand down—"

I seized his pistol directly, twisting it against the joint. The cop's wrist cracked like dry wood. He crumpled to my feet as I wrenched the weapon free. His partner swooped at me with her stun-prod; I narrowly avoided the blow and spun around with a back-kick that connected hard with her chest. She was pitched into the EMTs.

The policewoman recovered nimbly, ready to spring back at me with the prod. Then she froze, seeing that I had snatched a dinner knife from the table and was holding it, arm back, ready to let it fly.

"I'll bury this in your throat," I warned, "if you don't stand down in six seconds."

The cop's eyes bulged in pure disbelief. She studied my ruined face, the knife, the electronic gag, and the poise of my arm. I saw her work out her fate.

Her partner staggered to his feet, nursing his crippled wrist. "Master Bayne, you've just assaulted two police officers...."

"I am *not* Peter Bayne. Are you listening to me?"

"Listen to him!" shouted a voice from the doorway.

From beneath the table, Suzie regarded a new set of intruders entering the manor.

Natalia Argos, followed by Celeste Segarra. Both wearing granite-like Order of Stone uniforms.

"About fucking time," I grunted.

Natalia put her hand on the counter and took stock of the scene. Something in the quiver of her eyes told me she was also accessing the homegrid's emergency response feed...perhaps even viewing the carnage and corpses upstairs.

She gave a quick, humorless laugh. "Well, well, Harris. Looks like you've really been working like a dog today."

I let the knife fly.

I assumed she'd have her blurmod set to auto-activate, giving her time to move away from the spinning blade. Maybe she hadn't bothered, figuring there was no need. Or maybe she was too absorbed in viewing the security feed. Whatever the case, the dinner knife landed with a meaty *thwak!* in her hand, pinning it to the counter.

She didn't scream. Rather, she stared, dumbfounded, at the sight of blood flowing around the impaling blade.

Natalia's mouth puckered. "You...you...."

"There are bandages in the cabinet above you," I said, and turned to Celeste. "The op is over. You offered to personally fly me to Dave, remember?"

"I remember," she breathed, blinking at Natalia's wounded hand. She seized the knife handle, pulled it free, and let it clatter in the sink.

"And I want your word that no one destroys the dog," I added.

Celeste held out her hands in confusion. "It's a fucking robot, Harris. Why do you care what happens to it?"

"Professional courtesy, from one tool to another. I made it kill the Baynes. Give me your word that no one destroys this thing for what *I* did."

She shrugged. "My word is given. Officers, we thank you for the excellent work you've done today. In case you didn't notice, this has become a planetary security investigation, classified by the Office of the President. Report immediately to our inquiry team outside."

"But—"

"It wasn't a request."

The policewoman glanced around in open, frank bewilderment. "But...Mark Bayne was just...er...he was killed by this...." Her obstinacy dried up as she realized who she was addressing. I didn't know if the recognition came from newscasts, or if her optics were finally registering the archon's ID bubble. Either way, she backed off with alacrity, escorting her wounded partner out the door. As they exited, a troop of technicians entered and, without a word, went directly to the stairs. I listened to their footsteps, tracking their progress to the horror show in my parents' bedroom.

For her part, Natalia Argos glared at me with incendiary wrath. An EMT wrapped her hand in a medpatch resembling a blue foam oven mitt.

Celeste raised an eyebrow. "You okay, lieutenant?"

Natalia swallowed hard. "Yes, ma'am."

"Good. Oversee the inquiry team and uplink to me."

"What about—"

"It wasn't a request."

Natalia gave a brisk salute with her oven-mitted hand. She went upstairs without giving me – or the archon – another look. Nonetheless, I could feel the hairs on my arm rise as she passed, as if I'd gotten close to a storm cloud. Celeste waited until the woman was out of sight.

Then she said, "She grows on you."

"Like a fungus?"

"Something like that."

Celeste touched the kitchen smartwall and conjured a display of the bedroom. She took in the view with a measured, clinical efficiency, as if she was preparing an inventory sheet.

The Peznowski corpses were a ghastly sight. Faceless, like chum from a butcher's slop pail. The technicians were dutifully setting the corpse heads onto the cutting board of a chilled neuro-extraction case. An instant later, the guillotine came down with a grisly *crack!* From there, they'd be flown to some Order lab for 'debriefing'. A methodical analysis of all synaptic pathways, combing for whatever data they possessed.

Far more merciful, all things considered, than interrogations on Phobos.

Celeste returned the smartwall to its paisley patterning. "Let's get you out of this body, Harris. I've already had a replacement grown for you. Going to wet-transfer you in. No upload, there isn't time."

"Before we even get to that goddam shell game," I interrupted, "you promised to take me to David."

She waved her hands impatiently. "It might interest you to know that the president wants to meet you."

"The president of what?"

"Of the Northern Brewery Guild, what do you think? The *Martian president* has heard of your success in executing a wanted war criminal. He's requested your presence."

"Tell the president to kiss my ass. I won't be diverted this time, Segarra. No Save clinics, no waiting rooms. Where the fuck is my brother?"

The archon folded her arms across her breasts. "Very well."

A second later, a comlink address appeared in my sensorium. It read:

David Julius Pope
President
Oligarchy of Mars

CHAPTER FIFTEEN

Mushrooms and Isotopes

When I was fourteen years old and a student at Carter Crossing High School, I took part in a field trip to the heart of Martian government: the House of Laws. It proved to be a *literal* field trip. The building was a round glasstic shell enclosing a field inset with acropolis-style seating. The dome was transparent, allowing anyone to see what was happening inside. It was how Martian government had been run before the war, eschewing the opaque arcologies of Earth Republic Congress for a grounded, out-in-the-open democracy. The House of Laws hadn't been a house at all.

I recalled how my classmates and I had sat in the grass and watched our politicians in action. Issues debated, laws proposed, and planetwide votes transmitted and counted in real-time. Afterwards, the president (at that time, it was President Josephina Ivywreath Tullo) escorted us to the nearby creek for a picnic. She proudly explained that Mars was the purest democracy since the Age of Pericles. A government of the people, for the people, *visible* to the people.

Forty years and several bodies later, I was back at the House of Laws.

And it was a bomb crater.

Martian government had taken a nuke full on the chin. Nothing remained of where my younger self had sat, cross-legged, the grass tickling my thighs. In place of that Emersonian vista, an unsightly 3D-printed monstrosity now sprawled directly above a crater. Like a gigantic white spider with its 'legs' acting as both access ramps to the central body and the support struts that kept it from falling into the abyss.

Celeste was as good as her word. She'd arrived at the Bayne manor by way of a sleek Griffin-model copter; from the house, she steered me into the dragonfly-like craft, where a technician strapped me into a gurney beside a freshly printed body. As the archon herself settled into the pilot's seat, the technician fitted a medical mask over my face and asked me to count backwards from ten. I'd made it to seven before waking up in the adjacent body, Peter's mutilated corpse being zipped up in a bag beside me.

Twelve minutes later, Celeste landed us in the House of Laws courtyard, flanked by a pair of massive algae trees.

I stepped carefully from the Griffin, testing out my new body. The joints were stiff.

Celeste twisted in her seat. "How do you feel?"

"Thirsty. Hungry. Dizzy."

"You need assistance?"

"I need to eat." I noticed she hadn't undone her harness. "Aren't you coming?"

"Have other meetings, Harris."

"With who?"

"That's classified." Her gaze softened. "But I'll tell you anyway: Prometheus Industries."

My jaw dropped. "You have a meeting with the biggest corporation in the universe? What in the hell for?"

"Sorry, I really can't say more. But I'll be just over there—" She pointed to a distant hilltop. "The meeting is in virtual. This bird of mine has been my mobile office for a while and I rather like it."

"You certainly seem to know people, Segarra. I'll give you that."

She gave a sidelong look. "You okay?"

I rubbed my new eyes – they itched like hell – and studied the giant spider-like building ahead of me. "It looks like this thing is going to spin me in a web and eat me."

Celeste laughed lightly. "There are glops crawling around Earth's Wastelands that can actually do that. In the ruins of New York, I once saw a guy pulled into an ancient manhole by some transgenic. The hole had shrunk over the centuries. Really wasn't big enough for him to fit through." Her smile fell. "The glop pulled him through anyway."

"How old were you?"

"Thirteen."

I shook my head. When I'd been thirteen, the most traumatic thing in my life had been losing my pet turtle. "Hard to believe Earth still hasn't cleaned up all those genetically engineered monsters from the Warlord days."

"Glops don't bother people in the arcologies."

"Not everyone is an arky."

"Yeah, well, those kinds of people don't matter to Earth's bean counters."

I blinked. "What's a bean counter?"

"Check your slang app, Harris." She removed her pilot's helmet, fluffed her hair. "Want to know something? All the shit I dealt with in the Wastes was *nothing* compared to what I've seen since leaving them."

I thought she might say more, but she only slapped my shoulder and gave a crooked grin. "Go see your brother. Tell him he still owes me a hundred tradenotes. I'll pick you up when you're done." With that, she jerked her thumb in the timeless hit-the-road gesture. I retreated several paces, and the vehicle ascended into the sky and landed on a distant hilltop. Sighing, feeling alone and cut off from all I knew, I shuffled towards the House of Laws.

I entered into one of the 'legs' and passed through a gauntlet of security booths, guards, and picosurv scanners. Every step of the way I was tracked by sensors measuring my retinal patterns, gait, biometrics, and breathing. I could feel the subtle weight of a new *jamadhar* coiled in my left arm; the heel of my palm sported the fissure from which the weapon would deploy. My joints felt wooden and stiff. I half-expected to flunk the battery of tests.

Yet I passed, unmolested, to the main building. Another guard – a trog – intercepted me and led me to a final set of doors, opened them, and bid me enter.

David Julius Pope waited inside, standing at a rounded second-century leather-topped desk. Whatever I'd been planning on saying to him was forgotten as I beheld him, in the flesh.

He looked mostly the same as when I'd seen him last. The wound I'd observed in his hologram had become a permanent, teardrop-shaped battle scar below his left eye. His forehead was more creased than I remembered; the weight of responsibility leaves its own marks.

But it was still David.

Or was this another hologram?

"Are you a hologram?" I asked.

He crossed the room and embraced me. Physical body, wrapping me in a kind of bear hug. He smelled of cologne and citrus.

"Welcome back, bro," he whispered.

"Am I welcome?"

Dave released me, looked into my eyes. "You're here, in the flesh. In *your* flesh." When I said nothing, he tried to conjure a smile; the expression hung delicately on his handsome face. "I had lunch prepared for us. You hungry?"

"Famished. I haven't eaten yet with this body." I considered his presidential desk. Sliced fruit, sushi handrolls, gyoza dumplings, and emerald-green seaweed salad had been arranged in colorful topography. A crystal decanter of whiskey was there, too.

I plucked a tuna roll and brought it to my lips. "Better eat carefully, right? If I choke to death, it might be another decade before you bring me back."

My barb found its mark. David looked at the floor.

"I get it," I pressed, embarrassed by the eruption of fluid from my salivary glands – a common, transitory side effect of newly printed bodies. I swallowed and said, "Mars was nuked. You've got the same scar from ten years ago, so obviously *you* survived Detonation. Survived the radiation that followed. Can't say I'm surprised, Dave. Last we spoke, you were hiding out in a bunker. We were supposed to meet at Evermist but the bombs fell before you got there. So you stayed put, safe and secure."

"Almost a year," he said softly.

I popped the sushi into my mouth, chewing slowly, letting the taste spread across my taste buds. "When you *did* emerge, that's when the real work began. Had to take stock of the damage. Remediate the soil.

Rebuild the sand levees. I've learned that millions of Martians died, but there were still plenty of refugees who needed care, work, and purpose. So you were busy for at least another year or two, right?"

Dave said nothing.

I strode to the window and pointed to the horizon, where printer-cranes bobbed and pivoted. "Those aren't local machines out there. After the nukes, other worlds sent aid. The IPC would have gone into full rescue mode, right? Their wayward son had stumbled through a school of hard knocks, but we were still welcome in the great solar family. A planetary reconstruction commenced. And since someone had to manage that influx of contractors, who better but the Order of Stone's victorious general?" My gaze strayed to the wall. A framed picture of my brother hung there; he wore a hazmat suit, standing amid rubble and sheared-open buildings. "You were already a war hero, Dave. I didn't have time to check, but I'm guessing your election as president was a fucking landslide. Doubt anyone bothered opposing you."

Dave hugged himself. "Keep going."

"Oh, I've already made my point. Resurrecting your brother wasn't as high a priority as everything else in your busy—"

He touched a button on his wrist, and the floor vanished.

For a moment, I thought he had actually retracted the floor and we were both about to plummet to our deaths. My stomach dropped. I nearly triggered my *jamadhar* to clamp onto the wall.

Then I realized I wasn't falling.

The floor was solid, but had switched to transparency.

David paced around, seeming to walk on air as he did. "Your tally left out a few details. Like *that*." He pointed to the bomb crater below us. "Take a gander, Harris. View the scars of Mars. Major cities were vaporized. Mars hadn't been part of IPCnet for twenty years, meaning there was no offworld storage for local Saves. When we cooked, all those stored personalities cooked with us. Permadeath."

He pointed to me. "*You* got lucky. The seaport clinic where you Saved wasn't fried by the nukes – but it collapsed and was buried by dust storms that swept, unchecked, over the following months. It wasn't until last month that excavation workers found the clinic, discovered intact files, sorted the data, and contacted me."

"And your first instinct," I said, "was to bring me back in the body of a teenager for an assassination?"

"My first instinct was to resurrect you, pin a medal on your chest, and throw a goddam parade in your honor. Cooler instincts prevailed. The people who did that—" he pointed again to the crater, "—are still alive. One of them doubled himself and rose to the head of provincial government. That's rather disconcerting, wouldn't you say?"

I chose a dumpling, scarfed it down. "I'd say that, legally, you've got a shitstorm brewing. You can't keep Peznowski a secret forever. Not even for long."

He poured two whiskeys, hand trembling. "I'm aware of that," he said.

"When news gets out that a secret Partisan survived and became governor...." I shook my head. I'd managed to catch up on some lost history during my ride to Ybarra. In the wake of Detonation, public trials were held in Cydonia. Partisan brass were declared Enemies to Humanity. Their Save files were torched. The legislation was even adopted by the IPC Senate – ever the stout humanists – who expanded the bill's reach to all worlds. The Partisans had no legal place to hide.

"Legally, you can't sit on this," I insisted. "The Baynes' purchase signals must already be in the queue at whatever clinic they're registered with. That will be public information. North Hellas will want to know where their governor is!"

Dave swirled his whiskey, ice cubes rattling. "Full disclosure can be delayed. This is an ongoing investigation, after all."

I lifted my own drink and clinked it against his. "You read my debrief? That third voice in the bedroom...."

"It was disguised, but we're running a patmatch. And we're scanning through Peznowski's neurals, but the bastard had a killswitch. Pureed most of his memories."

I sighed and took a sip of the whiskey.

"Still," Dave said, looking uncomfortable, "we did find something."

"Oh?"

"Something we need to act on fast."

His meaning couldn't have been clearer if he'd painted it on the sky with the Bat Signal. Weariness settled like winter-ice into my bones.

"I just got back, Dave," I managed. "Do you have any idea what I've been through today?"

"I didn't say *you* had to do it," he assured me. "There are plenty of other operators who can be sent."

"Another assassination?"

"Yes."

"And no due process again?"

"Fuck due process!" he snarled, eyes clouding with a sudden, incendiary rage. His scar flushed crimson. Then he saw my shocked expression and added quickly, "What I mean to say is, fuck due process *for the moment*. When it comes to the Partisans, I'm not interested in playing by the rules of civility or decorum. They were monsters, Harris. They sprouted from the worst traits of humanity. They tortured and killed our citizens, and when defeated, they didn't have the honor to go gently into that good night. Fuck the Partisans."

He had gone rigid, knuckles white where he held his glass. In the silence that followed, I could hear the buzz of the HVAC cycling air.

I touched my glass to his again. "Fuck the Partisans, indeed."

We drank to the toast. With a tight calm, Dave added, "There *will* be trials. I promise. Full disclosure, due process. For the moment, however, the investigation grants me certain extrajudicial powers for the sake of Planetary Security."

Neither of us said anything for a long while. I gazed into the crater – into the pit – and let the quiet gather.

Finally, Dave cleared his throat. "Let's pack a picnic, bro. Let's go for a walk."

*   *   *

The creek had survived, somehow.

The original waters must have vaporized when the nukes hit. But in the years that followed, rainwater had converged again through time-worn channels, resuming its liquid march. Back from the dead.

Like me.

We gathered the food, packing it away in a multi-tier cooler, and departed the House of Laws on foot. The creek was only a brisk, ten-minute stroll. David chose a place, laid out a blanket amid the red trees, and spread the picnic.

I scrutinized our lunch as it reappeared from the cooler. "No mushrooms? I'm disappointed."

David shook his head. "No mushrooms for a while, bro. Mushrooms soak up radioactive particles like a sponge. Unless you want me to order some replovat varieties. They do baby bells easily enough."

"I don't." In my experience, replovats were never able to get the texture of mushrooms right. Like chewing on vinyl.

He refilled our glasses. "The distillery in Lotus Gulf survived. Had this flown in special."

I nodded appreciatively. "It's good."

"Ice?"

"You know it."

I took a hearty sip, concentrating on the burn as it outlined my virgin esophagus. "I've been meaning to ask you. Back in the final hours of the war...."

"Yes?"

"Where did the Order come by antimatter?"

Dave's eyes bulged. "What? What do you mean, antimatter?"

"Natalia gave me two antimatter rounds for Operation Persephone. I used one to kill a praetorian. The other one I used on Phobos." His startled expression was raw and uncontrived. "Did you...not know that, somehow?"

My brother recovered from his panicked reaction. "Right, of course," he said. "Ten years ago. I keep forgetting there's a time differential between us. Your yesterday isn't the same as mine."

"Where did it come from?"

"Can you ask me something else, bro?"

"Why?"

"*Anything* else, I promise." His knuckles had gone white again.

I shrugged. "Fine. Ten years ago, you said our parents' files were available offworld."

He was visibly relieved for the subject change. "Sure, I remember!"

"So now that you're president of Mars, why don't you request those copies so we can be a...."

My words faltered as he dug into the picnic basket and produced two holocubes. They reflected the afternoon sun, luminosity catching on golden nanorods within the resin. They seemed magical things. Like the Golden Fleece or Cup of Christ or loot from Tir'na'nog. Dave held them, one upon each palm. He didn't need to say anything. I knew what I was looking at.

Teresa and Edward Pope.

Every memory they had up to their last Save. Everything they were, each dream, thought, and desire, captured and transferred to these physical storage cubes. A young couple about to take their first truly interplanetary voyage, captured in amber.

The twin reflections played along my brother's face. "Figured Mom and Dad would want to share this picnic with us," he said.

"Where did you get those from?" I whispered.

"Tanabata City, Luna."

"And they just *gave* these to you?"

"As next of kin I'm within my rights to request the transfer. The IPC practically delivered them on a silver platter. They could have sent them over as purchase signals, but they delivered the hardcopies along with a dragon's hoard of other Martian files. See, I requested all available copies of citizens who died under the Partisan regime. Unfortunately, the majority of deaths had no offworld storage. Still, the IPC was happy to oblige where they could."

My gaze strayed to where the soul-light crawled over the picnic blanket. "Let's get these to a regen clinic. Bring them back."

"They won't remember—"

"I know." I consulted my opticlock. "It takes about ten hours to grow replacement bodies. Hell, they can be back by midnight if there isn't a queue!"

David placed the holocubes on the blanket and looked patiently at me. "You're perhaps the leading authority on coming back from the dead, into circumstances that are unfamiliar and confusing. Is that really what you want Mom and Dad to go through? Remember, these are from Tanabata City. *Before* their immigration to Mars. We'll be resurrecting a young couple who was looking forward to life on the frontier, so when they step out of the regen clinic...."

"They get a post-apocalypse."

"And fully grown children."

"Wonder which will surprise them more?"

"So now isn't the best time to conjure them."

I scowled. "*When* is the best time?"

My brother's gaze swirled with secrets, hovering on the edge of a confession. "Not yet."

"Stars, Dave! Don't you think there's been enough secrets between us? Just tell me everything!"

"I will, and I'm *not* being coy. Tonight is Solstice Eve. I'm throwing a party right here." He indicated the stretch of lawn and courtyard. "Lots of VIPs and ambassadors. Very white toga. I want *you* here, to meet everyone. To meet *my* family. No more secrets between us, I promise...." He saw my expression. "Harris? What's wrong?"

The anguish – the shock – throbbed like a pulsar in my chest. "Did you say your *family*?"

He adopted a yoga-style posture and touched the picnic blanket, drawing up a photo-roll. I watched him make a selection, then spread it across the material.

A stunning raven-haired woman appeared. Her eyes were the color of sea-glass. After several seconds, the image dissolved and another formed. The same woman in a forested glen of tulips and daffodils.

My breath caught. "You rip this from a magazine?"

"That's Cassie Sedney, the famous chemist."

"Famous...*chemist*?"

"Watch a little longer and you'll see her become Cassie Pope."

I gaped. "This woman married *you*?"

"I got her really drunk before I asked."

"Naturally. How did you trick her into the ceremony?"

"Told her it was a sim. Pulled the same trick so she'd have kids with me, too."

A stabbing pain caught me in the chest. "Kids? You're a father?"

Sure enough, another photo pixelated onto the blanket. A marriage ceremony, in the cherry-blossom gardens of Hanmura Industries on Olympus. The guests were clad in Sylvan regalia, leafy greens and winter silvers and fiery scarlets and dusky purples. The wedding ceremony of my brother and this woman I'd never seen before. Another photo sprouted, showing them with their first baby. And then a second baby....

Dave's voice was proud. "A boy and a girl. They can't wait to meet you, Harris."

I took the decanter of whiskey, poured another glass, took a long swig that scalded my throat. "Sounds like the meeting could be awkward. Some political hack thought I'd make a good assassin. Not exactly the stuff uncles are made of."

"I...I told you that you've done enough. No more ops for you. I'm assigning other people to this investigation."

"What did technicians find in Peznowski's brain? Who else is out there, Dave?"

He closed the family photos. Began to scroll through others, rifling file icons. "During your flight over here, our analysts combed through the Bayne manor security footage. Ever hear of Tier Marsworks?" Before I could answer, he seemed to remember that I had been gone for ten years, and he blushed. "Sorry. It's the leader among dig-site recoveries. A Mars 10 company. They scout for buried loot. Dig up landfills and rubble. Then they exhume the stuff and sell to whoever's buying."

"Yesterday's garbage has a consumer base?" I asked skeptically.

Dave gave his characteristic sideways nod, an ironic gesture he had been doing since childhood. "You wouldn't believe it, bro. The Sylvan Age is big money. People who remember it, they want nostalgia they can touch. Museums lock horns over recovered stashes. It's a huge market."

He selected a photo, spread it for my viewing.

It showed a ribbon-cutting ceremony in front of a copper-hued structure. I could tell the setting was Olympus, even if the forest looked as brittle and red as the woods around the creek.

Lots of people milled about in the photo, wearing corporate smiles as a tall, blonde woman wielded oversized scissors to sever the ribbon. Behind her, the building consisted of two towers connected by skyways. The words TIER MARSWORKS were emblazoned on a lawn placard.

Dave pointed to the blonde. "Here's our person of interest. Vilhelmina Krohl, CEO of Tier Marsworks. Estimated net worth is seven hundred million tradenotes."

"Okay...."

"When Peznowski was...um...interrogating you...he made reference to someone he called 'Vil'. We put the patmatches to work and they pinged back with this: the CEO of Tier Marsworks. She doesn't give a lot of public speeches. Press releases sent in her name are almost certainly the work of a copywriter. Nonetheless, we dug deep. As it turns out, seventy-six percent of Krohl's word choice aligns with an allegedly dead Partisan general."

"Which one?"

"Eileen Monteiro."

Scoffing, I peered closer at the blonde in the picture. "Stars, Dave! She looks like some bar floozy. All legs and tits."

My brother gathered up a handful of dumplings and proceeded to eat them slowly, one after another, cheeks swelling. This was another childhood carryover. Dave adored food; the only explanation for his trim figure was that he kept his myostatin blockers cranked.

Eileen Monteiro. The human walking stick who had lost her sandclaw divisions to an Order hijack, then suffered the additional humiliation of watching Olympus Mons revert to the Stone Age. I recalled her avian face, eyes bulging in outrage. Her Pharaoh's crest of white hair.

Looking again to the hot blonde in the ribbon-cutting photo, I said, "Seventy-six-percent chance...meaning there's a twenty-four-percent chance you want me to murder an innocent person? Did you run a check on her Save?"

"Oddly enough," Dave murmured, "there's no record of Vilhelmina Krohl ever being Saved."

I shrugged. "Lots of Martians were twitchy about Saving. Remember that actor who died way back, Salvor Bear? He never got Saved, either."

"Which is why I'm sending someone to investigate first. She lives in residence at Tier's HQ. She—"

"You're sending me," I cut him off.

Dave shook his head. "The hell I am. You're coming home with me. We've got a party tonight."

He was reaching for a sushi roll when I stayed his hand.

"I'm going," I insisted.

"Harris, no! You just—"

"I'll go in, confirm her identity, and if she's the Partisan Crab Queen, I'm happy to kill her." I consulted my opticlock once more. "It's just after 1400. Send me the specs on this Tier place."

My brother seemed to change before my eyes. No longer the war vet and president of Mars, he looked young and scared and about to cry. "I...don't want you to do this."

I realized I was still gripping his hand. Gently, I released him, selected the sushi he'd been aiming for, and placed it on his palm. "The last time I saw Eileen Monteiro, she was as close to me as that oak." I pointed across the creek. "I never really got to bid her *adieu*."

Dave stared at the sushi I'd given him. He didn't look hungry anymore. He looked sick.

"I do have a question," I added. "You're keeping these assassinations off the books. Is that because of the IPC? They wouldn't take kindly to extrajudicial operations like this."

"We're not yet back in IPCnet," Dave said guardedly.

Something in his tone made me pay attention. I wasn't wearing Peter Bayne's body anymore; this new body, printed in my likeness, had an entire cyberwarfare suite at its disposal. With a flick of my fingertips, I could select a sniffer to measure my brother's words, vocal stress, and microexpressions.

That seemed rude, however. Instead, I said, "I figured rejoining IPCnet would have been a priority."

Dave leaned back on his elbows. "For starters, it's not my choice alone. We're putting it to a vote in March."

"No one asked for a vote until now?"

"We've been a little preoccupied, you know?"

I gave a meaningful look in the direction of the distant print-cranes. "You've already got IPC machinery here...."

He smiled slightly. "After Detonation, they flew us supplies. Humanitarian aid is part of their charter...keeping up New Enlightenment ideals. Lots of offworld companies tried courting us for reconstruction, but our economy was in shambles. So we approached the IPC. They offered to assist *pro bono*. Very gracious. Shrewd."

"And the Save files are part of that?"

"Of course. They're wining and dining us, bro."

"Before they fuck us?"

He picked a sesame seed from his teeth. "Obviously, the IPC wants Mars back in the fold."

"No doubt. Mars would help alleviate overpopulation from other worlds."

"It's more than that. They want our votes."

I raised an eyebrow. "What votes?"

"In the IPC Senate. The big vote coming up next year...you had to have heard about that."

"Dead ten years. Back two days...."

"Right, sorry. Overpopulation is fueling a new debate on the Colonization Ban. Lots of people want it lifted. The Frontierists made serious gains in the last two solar elections."

I laughed coldly. "That shit comes up every decade. No way it'll be overturned."

"The available worlds are being strained ecologically. There's momentum for a repeal."

I considered this. It was well known that there were habitable planets beyond Sol System. Hell, people had known that since the Old Calendar. In the earliest days of the New Enlightenment, scientific probes had been sent out in a one hundred light-year spread and beamed back images of Goldilocks worlds in nearby systems: worlds we had renamed as Osiris, Midsummer's Dream, Sagan....

"How do the votes look so far?" I asked.

"Dismal, of course. Two senators per planet, so do the math: Earth's senators will vote to keep the Ban. Venus will do the same: they've got an entire world to terraform, and want resources flowing to those efforts over some risky diaspora. Luna, of course, will follow Earth's direction."

"Luna isn't an independent colony," I reminded him.

He blinked. "They were granted independence eight years ago."

I shook my head, realizing how out of step I was with current events. My entire worldview needed recalibration. "Luna is independent now? Did they go all harsh mistress on Brother Blue?"

"Nope. They voted for independence, and the IPC ratified it."

"Really? Why the hell would...oh, got it." It clicked, and I gave a cynical laugh. "Luna's always been tied to Earth culturally and economically. So the IPC gets two more slam-dunk votes in the Senate."

Dave nodded. "Precisely. Earth doubled their voting bloc."

I ticked off the tally on my fingers. "That's six votes to keep the Ban. But some of the deepworlds opposed it."

"And some still do. So the Belt and Jovian and Saturnian Leagues will probably vote for its removal."

"So it's a deadlock. Six versus six."

"A deadlock upholds the law. But it's really goddam close, so you can appreciate why Mars – if we rejoined – could make a difference."

I frowned. "But even *if* we rejoined...how do they know we'd vote in tandem with the other brightworlds? Mars always did its own thing. Given our history, any Martian senators would probably vote against."

Dave studied me, and I didn't need a sniffer program to read his mindset: he was only now coming to terms with how little I understood of the modern world. "Stars, Harris. The IPC is making itself indispensable to our recovery. People I meet on the streets...they've changed their tune. It's no longer vogue to bash the IPC."

"Still, that's hardly a guarantee...."

"Mars has changed. We've all got PTSD – Planetary Traumatic Stress Disorder. The pogroms, war, Detonation...it remade our mindset. And there's a new generation which knows nothing of the old Martian autonomy. They've been raised in a connected universe."

I thought about Peter Bayne's online social activities. The offworld films and games and networks.

"There's something else, too," Dave added.

"Oh?"

"Something to sweeten the pot." Dave lowered his voice, even though we were clearly alone. "A bribe only the IPC could offer."

"What, an interplanetary fuck-a-thon?"

He sighed. I remembered that sigh from our childhood. He made it when faced with something he really didn't want to do but was resigned to doing it anyway. The sigh wasn't born from exasperation, or hopelessness, or annoyance; rather, it was a grudging admittance that he would *rather* be doing other things. I pictured a gigantic lever sticking up from the horizon like a space elevator, and my brother being told he had to push it to move the planet, Archimedes-style. And I knew how he would react: a shrug of his shoulders, that sigh, and then he'd move the goddam planet.

It was the same sigh he'd given on the yacht thirty years ago, when I chose to have my brains scrambled. When I chose to go undercover and become a Partisan.

"I can't say more just yet," he breathed. "But soon, bro. Sooner than you think."

"Whatever. Politics were never my thing."

"You don't have an opinion on the Colonization Ban?"

"I don't care." I touched the blanket, expanding the image of Tier Marsworks. "I'll need blueprints of this place. A full workup on Monteiro's security detail, schedule, and known history. And *this* body,"

I touched my chest, "will need upgrades if I'm going to infiltrate a high-security compound."

Dave beamed like a spotlight. It was his charismatic smile, and there was something else too, a lethal edge, like the glint off a knife blade. "That body," he said, "already has upgrades better than anything else on the planet. The archon and I decided its specs together."

"Yeah?"

"Blurmod, distributed healing system, three-hundred-sixty-degree sight wired to your optics, patmatch sniffer, full-zoom senses – even your fingertips can modulate for tactile analysis and print-capture. You also have a top-of-the-line Familiar implanted."

"What's its name?"

David blinked. "Xenophon, I think. I reviewed all the specs earlier today. Trust me, you're wearing the best Order of Stone tech, with the best of shadowman tech. You're the first hybrid soldier. Think you were dangerous before? Just wait."

I picked an edamame from a bowl, squeezed the beans into my mouth one by one. "I'm wearing the face I was born with. How effective could I be at undercover work when I'm...you know...famous? I announced myself to the universe. Won't people recognize me at Tier? Won't my name spring up as an ID bubble to whoever I meet?"

"More precisely," Dave said, "*any* ID we want will show up. The universe heard your message when you obliterated Phobos, sure. But *no one* knows your face. The Partisans scrubbed their shadowmen from databases. Made you more effective for the type of work you did."

"So no one will know me?"

"We can feed any identity we want. People believe what they're told. Always did."

My attention strayed to the holocubes. "How did Mom and Dad die?"

Dave watched me over the rim of his whiskey glass. "They died in prison. You and I went to a bar, and while we were there, they were arrested."

"*How* did they die?" My mouth was suddenly dry, picturing my parents subject to some years-long interrogation/punishment. They'd never been taken to Phobos, but there had been plenty of death camps on the redworld itself....

"I only learned this a few years ago. According to arrest records, Mom and Dad committed mutual suicide in prison. One of them – I'm guessing Mom – had smuggled in a poison. At some point during the night, she and Dad shared a neurotoxin cordial."

I exhaled a breath I hadn't realized I'd been holding. How pissed had that made the Partisans? Teresa and Edward, choosing the way of Greek philosophers and Shakespearean heroes, dying in a final embrace. It was just like Mom, with her sense of historical irony. If there had been cobras on Mars, she might have chosen to die by reptilian kiss. Denying the enemy's pleasure, like the Jews at Masada.

I didn't want to think of what happened next; how Partisan technicians had probably cracked open their dead skulls with a magpie claw, slicing and dicing for anything recoverable. But a dead brain isn't useful. The neurons begin breaking down almost immediately. Mom and Dad had taken their secrets – including the names of other 'conspirators' – to their graves.

It took me a minute to find my voice again. "I'm glad," I whispered, touching the holocubes. Picturing the frozen intelligences within them. Wondering what captured moment was there, what *in media res* moment characterized their thoughts at Tanabata.

When they come back, they won't know me or Dave.

Won't remember our journeys to Hellas Market together.

Won't remember getting ice cream at the seaport hotel.

Won't remember anything of this redworld life.

I regarded the dead forest, the spider-like House of Laws, the scar on David's face. *How much would I want to remember,* I mused, *if I was in their place?*

My brother cleared his throat. "You sure you want to do this?"

"Of course."

"You could say no."

I finished my whiskey. "I already said yes, Dave."

The wind died, and with it, all sound and motion. As if the world had frozen in place, my whiskey-tinged thoughts imagining that maybe *I* was the one frozen in a holocube.

"I want to do this," I repeated.

Dave raised his hands ever so slightly. Fingers tickling the air, sending a virtuboard message to someone.

In the caramel sky, like a hawk flying in for the kill, Celeste's Griffin was descending towards us.

CHAPTER SIXTEEN

The Castle on the Roof of the World

Tier Marsworks had operational centers across the planet, though their corporate headquarters were on Olympus. From the vantage point of Celeste's copter, I peered down at red forests interrupted by manicured rectangles of company estates: there was signage for AztecSky, Tornquist Corporation, and the stunning Japanese castle of Hanmura Enterprises. Together, they formed the planet's financial heart and, pledging neutrality during wartime, had kept the economy pumping. Consequently, they'd been spared destruction, nukes and all.

Even the fucking apocalypse won't mess with corporate power, I thought sourly.

"There," Celeste said, pointing. As we rounded the volcano, fading sunlight warmed a connected pair of towers – the same ones Dave had shown me in the ribbon-cutting photo. From a thousand feet, we viewed a serpentine road winding down from the towers, connecting to docks which linked to the larger canal system.

"I remember seeing those towers years back," I muttered. "But they didn't belong to any company named Tier."

"They once belonged to an Earth-based importer. The Partisans accused them of violating neutrality – supplying the resistance or something. Not sure if there was any truth to that. At any rate, they appropriated the place. Converted it to manufacture weapons."

I raised an eyebrow. "So our war criminal has set up shop in an old munitions factory? Not very subtle, is she?"

Celeste smirked; she was wearing her helmet again, and it made her seem like a happy kid at the controls. "You ain't seen nothing yet, Harris. Look at the docks down there."

The Griffin swept lower. The solitary road twisted and turned through a massive junkyard – mounds of scrap-metal and shattered masonry hemming in both sides. A few trucks ambled along the way, but what snagged my attention were the giant creatures crawling over the beach. They resembled crabs. Scuttling sideways, using their enormous claws to sift through debris.

"Sandclaws!" I cried, hardly believing my eyes. "Tier is using sandclaws for *cleanup*?"

Celeste's eyes turned cold. "Want to hear an inspiring story, Harris? Vilhelmina Krohl was supposedly a low-wage equipment operator during the war. After Detonation, she was forced underground with everyone else. Eventually, the rads dropped. She emerged like a new flower and – get this – stumbled upon some abandoned sandclaws. Your average person might have trundled past the derelict machines, but *our* girl had an idea! Why not—"

"Use them for remediation?"

"Bingo! There was a labor shortage, so Vilhelmina applied her 'heavy equipment skills' to commandeer the sandclaws. Put them to use. Built an empire out of cleaning the planet."

"With the very machines that helped destroy it?"

We tilted for landing. The sensation made me remember being with Umerah in her dropship, zeroing in on a plaza or alley or rooftop, the rappel cord in my hands.

To distract myself from anguished thoughts, I studied the forest below. They looked less like real conifers than sandstone: an illusion of geology, like faces in Cydonia, or the legend of indigenous lizards in the Martian desert. Out of curiosity, I conjured the redweb and searched for RED TREES OLYMPUS. The top result was from the Martian Forestry Service:

For three hundred years, genetically modified trees on Mars – especially in the Olympian foothills – offered a deciduous paradise to rival blueworld preserves. Sprouting in the rich cyanobacterial soil and taking advantage of the 0.376 gravity, forests proliferated and grew to staggering heights.

Detonation Day changed all that. In grim echo of Earth's Final War, radiation levels were absorbed by the forest like legendary sin-eaters, resulting in their Gorgon-like petrification. <u>Click here to read more.</u>

I closed the bubble and contemplated this bloody after-effect – another Partisan farewell gift. Centuries of biogeneering undone by one political regime's sadistic temper-tantrum.

Celeste reached backwards and punched my leg. "The forests will grow back."

I frowned. "You running a sniffer on me?"

"Don't flatter yourself. I learned to read people the old-fashioned way when I was a little girl."

Our copter alighted on a courtyard helipad. There, a young, ash-haired woman awaited us. She was smartly dressed in a fern-green suit. As I emerged from the copter, her ID bubble appeared:

Deborah Skyblush Drost
Executive Assistant, Media Relations
Tier Marsworks

Drost bowed, forming a forty-five degree angle so perfect it could have been drawn by a protractor. "Archon Segarra? We are deeply honored by your presence here. Welcome to Tier Marsworks."

Celeste removed her helmet and hopped out, nimbly landing on both feet as if ready for action. "Thanks for having us," she said, making a show of studying the grounds. Sensoramic manta rays glided languidly overhead, flapping their wings in lazy strokes. Picnic tables were threaded by a corporate garden and walking trails of flagstone and gravel. "The view is nice."

Drost smiled with clinical politeness. "The view will be better in a half hour, when the sun sets over the canal."

"I wasn't referring to the canal." Celeste nodded towards the mountains of trash hemming the road below. "*That's* what I'm interested in."

"Ah yes. Your office said you were looking to shoot some

promotional videos here. Interesting, since we don't think of ourselves as film-worthy."

"Depends on the film. I'm documenting the reconstruction of Mars. Did you have a chance to review my proposal?"

Drost conjured a hologram from her wristpad, bright squares of text floating in the air. The so-called 'proposal' had been drawn up by Order intelligence and emailed not more than an hour ago; I'd scanned through it on the flight over. As cover stories went, it was impressive: Celeste was supposedly commissioning a documentary on planetary cleanup. Whoever had written the copy had been clever, making shrewd contrasts between what Tier had achieved (in just a few years) while Earth – three hundred years in – was still riddled with Wastelands.

"I'm afraid Ms. Krohl has not had a chance to review it," Drost said, leading the way across the courtyard. "However, she is genuinely thrilled you would consider us."

Celeste strode alongside the secretary with a brisk, feral energy. "I appreciate you squeezing us in like this. Congress is going on holiday. Figured I'd at least get this rolling for next legislative quarter."

My gaze strayed to the main tower above us. Forty stories tall and crowned by the CEO's personal suite like a temple atop a ziggurat.

As we neared the entrance, another sight arrested me. A mighty statue gleamed in the courtyard, almost too bright to look at. It stood forty meters tall, depicting a faceless woman holding hands with an equally faceless child. Like a wife and son of the Colossus of Rhodes; they were even wearing classical togas. The difference was that unlike the famed Colossus, this one was composed entirely of greenish glass.

"War glass," I whispered.

Drost halted, raised an eyebrow. "Excuse me?"

I felt Celeste shoot me a warning stare.

Facing our host, I said, "This statue is built from war glass. As in, the glass created from sand fused by nuclear detonation." Drost looked surprised, and so I added, "I did some reading on the way over here. The statue was a gift from Tier's workforce, as an expression of gratitude to Ms. Krohl for providing them jobs after Detonation."

The woman's polished smile threatened to flush with genuine warmth. "Very good, Mister..." Her eyes flicked to my ID bubble. "...Porter. Tier Marsworks played a major role in remediating Mars, but we did more than that: we provided temporary housing to worker families. The cities were gone. We allowed them to live on premises. Do you understand? Ms. Krohl literally opened her home to them. Helped get supplies routed so they had food, clean water, and medicine. They were only too happy to gift her the statue. Isn't that a beautiful story?"

"It's a story."

We stepped through the main doors into an octagonal lobby of polished soapstone. Each wall displayed a bas-relief of the company's history. There were montages of canton ruins, bomb craters, bridges, and tramways like the bones of prehistoric beasts; buildings slashed wide to expose honeycombed interiors. In each scene, giant crab-shaped bots cleared away rubble, and I couldn't help a chuckle. *Here* was Eileen Monteiro's post-war legacy: the commander of legions reduced to a garbage picker.

My chuckle dissolved, though, as I reflected on the deeper implications. I'd grown up on sci-fi films, usually based on Old Calendar pulps whose copyrights had long expired. Such tales promised interplanetary colonies, rocket ships and robots. Here I was, living in a version of that imagined future, except the interplanetary colonies and rocket ships were props for battle, and the robots shoveled our radioactive trash. R is for Ruin, S is for Scrap.

"These machines you use," I jerked a thumb at the reliefs. "We need to see them up close."

Drost gave another precise bow. "Certainly. Would you follow me, please?" As she straightened, I caught her eyes. Zoomed in on the retinal pattern.

Hit RECORD.

My lips parted in a show of glee. "Can't wait," I said.

★　　★　　★

Descending by inclinator into a hollowed-out cavern, we arrived at what could easily have been an ancient necropolis. Halogen lamps dotted the gloom, illuminating a maze of debris that might have been the remnants of a dead civilization.

Then it hit me: that's *exactly* what we were looking at. The Mars of my childhood reduced to offal. The Sylvan Age in ghastly afterlife, its colonnaded buildings and Persian spires dissolved. Drost was our Virgil on this Stygian tour, leading us past toiling sandclaws. Light warped off metallic claws and shuffling legs. Servos droned. Human workers in bulky hazmat suits inspected the exhumations with patient, cheerless efficiency.

I even spotted the remains of a massive airship, perforated by anti-aircraft fire.

"The *Thassos*?" I gasped, seeing the stenciling along one swollen flank.

Drost looked impressed. "We found it in the Noctis. A massive troop transport. It was bringing Partisan reinforcements when it was shot down by the Order."

I remembered.

I'd *been* there. Had seen it happen.

Partisan brass had sent two divisions to capture the Noctis Labyrinthus, with three shadowmen squads to scout ahead, provide reconnaissance, and eliminate any small-scale resistance. The Order had been using the valley to run supplies. Brass figured it would be an easy offensive. A day, maybe two, to secure the place.

Right from the start, that 'easy op' degenerated into a grueling contest. The Order was entrenched in the valley, lining it with mines and turrets. They'd stationed sniper teams in the cliffs. They had cyberwarfare specialists operating in the caves. And the Noctis was home to an omnipresent fog that reduced visibility to a few meters.

It was a goddam nightmare.

Twelve days in, our forces are reduced by sixty percent. Out of the three shadowmen squads, one has been hunted down, no survivors. Chaff interference is screwing with com-lines. We're in bad shape. Desperate for reinforcements.

And at long last, reinforcements are arriving.

My squad has been holed up for two days, hunkered into CAMO tents. Sergeant Hammill is on lookout when he comlinks us excitedly. The Thassos is descending to the valley! An airship that could comfortably house ten thousand troops.

We emerge from concealment. Just to take a peek, amping our visions to see the vessel through the fog. Grinning idiotically, sending each other cartoonish graphics of champagne bottles popping as the ship blots out the stars.

And then hidden Order turrets – where no turrets should have been – strafe it. The airship is equipped with countermeasures, spiraling around like sparklers. But the assault penetrates, detonating chaff interference and saser pulses and every dirty trick the Order has up their rock-colored sleeves.

The Thassos comes screaming out of the night sky into the canyon. It explodes in a rolling fireball.

I turn to Umerah and see the horror in her eyes.

Someone tugged my sleeve. Brushing aside the memory, I saw that Drost had continued on ahead. Celeste pulled me, pressing us into a new lobe of the underdark.

We were entering an airy transport tunnel. The tunnel, Drost explained, led to the docks. Above, cut into the rock like Al Khazneh in Petra, a control tower looked out on the trash heaps. I zoomed in on the rectangular window there. Amped my view of the people inside.

CEO Vilhelmina Krohl was front and center. I recognized her from David's photos. The blonde was addressing a group of badge-wearing visitors – prospective clients, I presumed, seeking a low-cost and efficient cleanup somewhere on the planet.

Eileen Monteiro had never been an attractive woman. Unusually tall – even for a Martian – with stooped shoulders and a haggard quality. In her Krohl identity, Eileen had swapped every feature for something prettier. Her eyes were narrow and slender, Asiatic in inspiration. Her white hair was traded for platinum locks. Her height pushed an inch above female standard. The walking stick was now a comely butterfly.

And then a squirming, uncomfortable thought in my head.

How did I *know* this was Eileen Monteiro? Wasn't it possible the legend of Vilhelmina Krohl was real – an authentic rags-to-riches tale without any villainous parasite involved? Maybe Peznowski's mention of 'Vil' had been referencing someone else?

I buried the doubt for later analysis. My attention slid to the others in the control room. I recorded each face, just to be safe. They were a neat, well-kempt gaggle in professional togas and tunics. There was a bodyguard there, too, clad in a khaki-brown security uniform.

I focused on the bodyguard.

For a moment, I wondered if he might be a heavy-duty bot. His face was hidden by an AR visor, allowing for visual appraisals that standard optical augmentations couldn't pull off. Muscles built on muscles; he was squeezed into his armor. The armor wasn't any off-the-rack digs, either; multiple compartments along the sleeves and sturdy chest-plate spoke to a military-grade carapace. A multigun rifle was slung at his back; not exactly the kind of peacekeeper favored by corporations. At least, not ten years ago, it wasn't.

As if attuned to my thoughts again, Celeste whispered into my audio:

Guess the CEO doesn't fuck around with rent-a-cops. Check out the heavy behind her.

I'm already looking, I whispered.

The bodyguard didn't have a name-badge. The only display on his uniform was the Tier logo – a star above Olympus Mons – and the words SECURITY CHIEF on his breastplate. I connected to the local web and searched the company's public roster, but security personnel were usually unlisted, and this guy was no exception.

Avoid him altogether, I thought, *or kill him quick.*

Krohl edged to the glass, studying the strange vista of her domain. Her blue eyes were cold and flat.

Did she know about Peznowski's death? Dave said it was being kept from the newsfeeds, but the whole situation had been a mess, and messes were notoriously apt to leak. All it would take was one cop – maybe the fellow whose wrist I'd broken – telling his wife. Or an EMT chatting with buddies during lunch. *Hey guys, don't say anything, but I've got to tell you what I saw in North Hellas today! A bot went haywire and killed the governor and his wife! Then their blind teenage son beat the shit out of a pair of cops!*

Celeste waved to the CEO. "Is she coming down? Or are we going up to meet her?"

Drost touched her ear – the universal etiquette to show you're in a private conference. Krohl noticed us from her lofty perch. She gave a polite wave. Lips moving, issuing a subvocal command.

"Ms. Krohl apologizes," her secretary relayed, "but she cannot break from her meeting. She asked if 1830 would work for you."

"1830?" Celeste rubbed her chin, pretending to think this through. It was such an exaggerated act that I almost laughed; xenobiologists contemplating the evolution of life don't ponder as hard as the archon was feigning. "Hmmm. You know, I've got a 1930 in Falls Village, and that cuts it close. I realize this was a last-minute drop-in, so no worries. Mostly I wanted to see your establishment up close, to inform the planning stages for the documentary." Celeste straightened and gave a winning, oddly savage smile. "Please thank Ms. Krohl, and tell her I'm happy to meet with her any other day she finds convenient."

Drost touched her ear again. In the tower window, the CEO continued watching us.

"Ms. Krohl will contact your office tonight," Drost explained, "and will propose an alternate date. She offers to personally escort you through the facility. Is that acceptable?"

"Very."

I extended my hand like a spear thrust. "The archon appreciates your time."

The secretary shook my hand. In my optics, her fingerprint pattern appeared like alien sigils.

Celeste flicked my arm. "Are we good, Mister Porter?"

"We're good," I told her, and my eyes expressed the rest.

CHAPTER SEVENTEEN

Showdown

Two hours later, I slid off the side of a rented yacht into the canal and swam for the docks. Olympus was a shadow-colored pyramid, its cone summit framed against constellations. The canal was cold, gritty, and tasted like chilled blood.

It was just past 2000. Seen from the yacht, Tier Marsworks grew dark as lights winked off for the holiday; the beach, however, swarmed with sandclaws, and they glinted in the double-moonlight.

Keeping low, I breaststroked towards the marina. A pair of freighters lay moored, but their decks were empty. Likewise, no human workers were visible beyond the occasional PDT riding down the road. It was Solstice Eve, after all.

Nonetheless, I knew the grounds would be under tight surveillance. I slipped beneath the wooden docks, using the slimy posts to drag myself along. In that dank hollow, I activated my CAMO suit and crept ashore, invisible.

Tier Marsworks stood, castle-like, atop the slope. The single road was the most direct and ill-advised approach. Dangerously exposed. A CAMOed body still produces a shadow, and the most basic surveillance can detect footprints dimpling the ground from an unseen boot.

The beach provided an alternative. The massive delivery tunnel cut straight to the sifting floor where Celeste and I had been earlier. It had almost certainly been a lava tube – Olympus was riddled with them – expanded and reinforced per corporate need.

I moved swiftly along the beach, weaving around junk piles. A massive sandclaw reared up, servos humming, legs flinging sand as it strode past.

I watched it go. During the war, such walking tanks had been outfitted with a pair of fifty-caliber cannons, one at the center of each retractable claw. I very much doubted these repurposed monsters would be similarly armed, but it wasn't difficult to imagine.

<The sandclaws are not armed,> said a voice in my head.

I nearly leapt out of my skin. For an instant, I thought another CAMOed agent was on the beach with me.

Then I realized a frosted icon was aglow in my HUD. Faint, nearly as invisible as me amid the pale beach. Its pictograph showed a crouching gargoyle.

A Familiar.

David had mentioned this body was outfitted with a Familiar!

<Hello, Paladin Pope,> the voice continued in the painful silence that followed. <My apologies if I startled you. My name is Xenophon. I am the Familiar assigned to you for this and future operations.>

Catching my breath, I whispered, "Xenophon?"

<You may rename me if you wish.>

"I didn't activate you."

<My apologies for startling you. I was set to auto-activate upon your entry into the operational field. You may adjust this feature if you wish.>

"Meaning you've been listening and watching me since I came here with Celeste."

The Familiar didn't respond; I hadn't exactly posed a question, after all. Nonetheless, I fancied I could hear strained tabulations as it considered whether to respond at all, dissecting my words and tone. It wasn't the first Familiar I'd had. In combat, an AI-assist could be terribly useful. Hell, when I was a kid you could buy them off-the-rack for any number of applications ranging from 'homework buddy' to 'gaming partner' to 'social navigator'. Alas, the exclusively offworld manufacturers hadn't found Mars a profitable market; such toys were seen as indicative of blueworld decadence. From what I'd heard, the social landscape of Earth had been a veritable ecosystem of AI wingmen, advisors, mediators, and fact-checkers.

Of course, that had been *before* the IPC's genocidal purge of all advanced AI systems. Familiars weren't necessarily 'advanced' by the Turing cop definition, but they found themselves on the slab, too. The market went belly up. By the time of my Hellas mission, I hadn't used a Familiar since the Siege of Noctis.

Did I really need one now? Leaning against a junk pile, I considered deactivating the thing.

<You may deactivate me if you wish,> it said.

"You reading my thoughts?"

<I noticed you focusing on the sandclaws, and deduced you were looking for visible armaments. Consequently I saw fit to advise you that outfitting maintenance vehicles and associated machines would constitute an unlawful act. Likewise, your lengthy pause after your last statement led me to conclude you were considering deactivating me.>

"Maybe I should."

<You have that option, Paladin Pope.>

There was a sudden, noisy spill of metal, barrels, and other flotsam. A sandclaw clambered atop the next pile, framed against the starry sky like some mockery of a victory pose. As I watched, it pulled a twisted I-beam from the pile and carried it away, scattering trash as it went.

In my head, Xenophon said, <The sandclaws are not programmed for violent behavior. However, they are capable of alerting security if they detect an intruder.>

"You don't think one of those things could swat me with a chunk of rebar?"

<That would be a violation of federal and local laws. The InterPlanetary Council does not allow AIs to be armed with weapons.>

"Except that you – an AI – are armed with me."

That seemed to give Xenophon pause.

"From now on," I pressed, "you only activate when I call on you, understood? Your new default setting is to sleep unless I wake you."

<Yes, Paladin Pope.>

Sighing unhappily, I sprinted to the next junkpile, keeping to sandclaw footprints to minimize my own. From there, I had eyes on the delivery tunnel.

"I'm not used to working with an AI," I whispered.

<As I said, you are free to deactivate me if that is your preference. However, I am adept at tactical appraisals and support.>

"You've been deployed in the field before?"

<I do not have that information.>

I shook my head. Terrific. The man out of time working with an amnesiac Familiar. What a superhero team we were going to make.

<I appreciate that this is new to you. Perhaps a formal introduction would be in order? My name is Xenophon. It is a pleasure to meet you, Paladin Pope.>

"Whatever," I grumbled. "Just tell me you can hack into the security grid and advise on what's in the tunnel."

<Done.>

A visual of the tunnel overlaid my HUD, notated with textual sidebars. The tunnel ran for two thousand meters to the warehouse. Security cameras ringed the entrance in an Argus spread.

Studying the feed, I asked, "No defenses in the tunnel?"

<There are eight defenses in the tunnel.>

"Eight? What do you mean, eight?" Even as I asked the question, I counted the number of sandclaws roving back and forth along that stretch. "I thought you said they weren't armed!"

<The sandclaws are not armed. That would be a violation of federal and local laws. The InterPlanetary Council does not allow AIs to be armed with weapons.>

"Then how the hell can they be considered defenses?"

<They are capable of alerting security if they detect an intruder.>

"Fucking stars, okay." I pressed against the heap as another monster trundled in from the beach. It carried a sheared-away hab-wall as easily as I might heft a two-by-four. I ducked into its shadow and kept pace just behind it.

Into the tunnel.

It was several minutes before we reached the warehouse. My unwitting escort tossed its payload down the ramp with a thunderous crash. Then, it rotated in place and marched back towards the beach. I stepped aside and peered into the pit.

It was the view I'd had earlier in the day, though from the opposite end of the chamber. Yet that had been in full lighting, with plenty of human workers on premises. Third shift presented a different situation, as sandclaws – unsupervised by mammalian eyes – sifted garbage into material categories known only to their programming. They really did resemble crabs picking over a littered beach.

For a moment, I allowed myself to be unnerved. Here was a creepy vision of Mars if raped by another war; a dead planetary surface while forgotten monsters ambled in the underdark…recharging their batteries, toiling until their carapaces rusted, processors failing, lights blinking out. It gave me a chill. I wondered if the larger universe was like this: a cosmic curiosity shoppe long abandoned, alien relics tended by metallic homunculi dutifully fulfilling the wishes of long-dead masters.

Putting these grim fantasies aside, I threaded my way to the control tower. Without warning, headlights split the blackness. Cursing, I rolled into a squat and let a cart pass. Two employees rode inside, talking heatedly amongst themselves. I caught a few words of the conversation. Something about tickets to an upcoming game.

When they had driven off, I pressed onward. A gigantic lobster-thing scuttled by, so close I could see the greenish scratches in its copper shell. Behind it, the tower was ten meters away, ringed by bleaching lights. Purposefully bright. My camouflaged body would cast a shadow on the tarmac, so I altered my approach, prowling obliquely to the crudely hewn rock wall. It wasn't like I'd been planning on riding the elevator, anyway.

In the space outside the floodlights, I pressed my gloved hands to the rock and began climbing.

Then I pinged Xenophon.

<There is a ventilation shaft two hundred and sixteen meters above you,> the Familiar intoned.

I nodded, gloves and boots forming a gecko-like molecular bond with the rock. The immense lobster-thing was below me, a careless move of its claw knocking over a generator the size of a buggy.

<Krohl checked into her suite at 1946. No guests are listed, and her posted schedule is clear.>

"That's enough updates for now."

<Of course, Paladin Pope.>

"Look, just call me Harris, okay?"

<Of course, Harris.>

I paused mid-climb, giving in to the impulse to view the warehouse in all its otherworldly glory. Crabs and lobsters in nightmarish feeding frenzy. The patrolling cart returned, making the rounds, the two men laughing agreeably now. Guess they resolved their ticket debate.

I climbed, an invading spider in another's web.

★   ★   ★

After carefully removing the ventilation grate, I wormed my way to a juncture. Choosing the left path led to another grate and, beyond that, a women's lavatory. CAMO active and room dark, I activated my shieldfist's display at the lowest setting, spilling a sliver of light to examine myself in the bathroom mirror. Invisible, rock dust clinging to my legs, arms, and torso like some vague specter, I brushed myself clean before heading out the door.

The executive suite was another twenty-eight stories above me. I took the stairs, activating my thermal dampeners and knowing time was short before I cooked in my suit. I was drenched in sweat as I reached the fortieth floor, ducked into another bathroom, and vented heat.

<I detect no thermal surveillance,> Xenophon advised.

You might have said that earlier, I snapped.

By way of response, Xenophon ran a playback of my own voice: <"You only activate when I call on you, understood? Your new default setting is to sleep unless I wake you.">

Snotty little fuck, I thought. *Or was that simply the most convenient way of addressing my comment? The Order supplied me with antimatter ten years ago. Maybe they've given me a sentient Familiar, too.*

Making a mental note to ask Dave about this, I said, ***I hereby rescind the order.***

The fortieth floor was an expanse of pink marble walls and creamy carpet. Unoccupied workstations were arranged in a kind of hedge maze; they even resembled hedges, built out of faux topiary with fountain-stone desks. The only lights in this expanse were from a coffee machine, an industrial-sized 3D printer, and glowing EXIT signs.

I shifted my vision through the available spectrum. No cameras on the floor, no security beams or sensors beyond those related to fire detection. Ahead, a set of cedar doors were marked with the placard: GRAND HALL.

I crossed the carpet, changing my fingertips to the pattern I'd recorded that afternoon.

"Welcome, Ms. Drost," the system announced as I touched the biometric pad. The doors slid apart.

The Grand Hall was worthy of a terrestrial arcology. Black marble and pretentious, with sofa chairs and a floating sensoramic of planets wheeling overhead. There was a full bar and a star-shaped billiards table with more than fifteen numbered balls on the felt – a variant of the game I was unfamiliar with. Replicas of shaggy vegetation sprouted from the floor, festooned with odd vines and bulbous, tumor-like growths. A babbling stream ran along a narrow channel.

What the hell was all this?

"What the hell is all this?" I whispered.

<These are recreations of the fungal forests on the planet Osiris in Ra System,> Xenophon informed me. **<Recreated by probe transmission.>**

"Figures that Monteiro's tastes would skew to alien mold."

On the far side of the Grand Hall, a corridor met a final set of doors. Krohl's personal suite. The great CEO was in there, a queen in residence. The apparent emptiness of the corridor was suspicious.

"Xenophon...."

<There are pressure-plates and picobeams along that hallway.>

"Fuck me," I whispered.

If it was just pressure-plates, I could scramble along the walls or ceiling and avoid them. But picobeams? Even blurred *and* CAMOed *and* adhering to the walls, there was no way to cross undetected. Might as well waltz in at the head of a jazz funeral.

Which left the inelegant option of going in hard and fast, tripping the alarms, kicking down the doors, and pulping Krohl in her apartment. Assuming I *could* kick down the doors; they were probably reinforced with latticed nanosteel. In either case, the building would go into lockdown. I'd be subject to immediate arrest if the cops got here first, or killed-while-resisting if security beat them to it. Which, of course, they would.

Which meant that the next time I woke up, I wouldn't remember any of this. My last memory would be at the seaport, anxiously waiting to board the *Body Electric*.

None of those options appealed to me. So I elected to wait. Like a lion in the Savannah grasslands. Wait all night, until the murderous bitch emerged from her hiding hole. She'd have to pass this way, eventually. Then I could cut her throat. Insert an EMP into her brainpan. Beat a hasty retreat to my exfil. Unless....

"Are Krohl's biometrics linked to building security?" I asked.

<Yes.>

Meaning the *instant* she flatlined, the building would go into lockdown. Onsite personnel would sprint up here to investigate and try reviving her.

Okay, I thought. *Then I'll knock her out and drag her across the corporate level. Haul her over my shoulder and retreat to the warehouse, then the tunnel, then the beach, where I can execute her at the water line and bring her head back to David like Perseus after a hard day's work.*

I was still considering the logistics of this option when Xenophon announced, <Deborah Skyblush Drost is approaching the suite from a VIP elevator.>

★　　★　　★

There was just enough time to slip behind the bar as an elevator I didn't know about opened from a painting on the wall. I hunkered by racks of liquor bottles as heels clicked on the floor. Drost passed me unaware, looking hurried and burdened by ill tidings. Passed so closely I could view the silver earrings jingling at her tunic's neckline, the alligator pattern on her briefcase. Could smell her jasmine perfume.

Just before she crossed into the corridor, I flicked an airhound at her. It was almost too late. The device clamped onto her tunic fibers a split second before she reached the picobeams, tucking itself out of view beneath her hem.

Not slackening her pace, she attained Krohl's doors and palmed the biometric pad. Oddly enough, she left the briefcase in the corridor as she went in.

The airhound detached and flew to the ceiling, providing 360-degree coverage that blossomed into my eye. An elegant room designed in Nova Basrayatha style lay within. Winged gods and bas-reliefs of bearded warrior-kings. There was a central fireplace. One wall had been fitted with an immense aquarium, where tropical fish – imported from Caricom, by the look of them – darted beneath violet fluorescents.

Krohl lounged on a blue satin couch before a low table. The blonde wore silk nightwear, a fluted glass in one hand.

"Good evening, ma'am," Drost said, making one of her perfect bows.

Krohl regarded her. "What did you learn?"

"The archon's story checks out. According to our sources, she called a meeting this morning with her political advisors and a film director. Wants to create a series of holo-spots for interplanetary distribution. She's looking for locations."

"And Tier makes her short-list?" Krohl asked dubiously. "Hanmura is next door and looks like the Gardens of Babylon."

"That's exactly what she *doesn't* want. Hanmura Enterprises is a blueworld company. We aren't."

"Except the archon is a blueworlder."

"From the outlands of Earth, yes. That seems to be her angle, from what I gather. Earth hasn't lifted a finger in three hundred years to clean up its battle scars. Segarra grew up there…a street-rat. She escaped, settled on Mars, and saw it collapse…only *this* time, the IPC is doing what they never did for Earth. Probably burns her up." The secretary shrugged. "She wants to expose their hypocrisy. Can't say I blame her in the slightest."

Krohl swished the fluid in her glass, considering this.

"Actually," Drost added, "I think this could be very good for us."

"Why?"

"Pope's term is up next year. Segarra's term is up in a few days. I'm betting she's got her sights set on the presidency. By agreeing to her media project, we make an investment. Costs us nothing and might bear fruit for Tier."

"You didn't come up here to shill for her political career," Krohl observed.

"No. The Baynes died this morning."

The CEO stiffened.

Her secretary clasped her hands behind her back. "Apparently, Mark and Jessica were mauled to death by their robodog. Peter was attacked, too, but survived and was taken to the hospital."

"Which hospital?"

"I called around. None of them will confirm his admittance."

Krohl rose from the couch. She made a rapid pace through the room, hesitating by the aquarium. Striped fish gathered behind the glass, mouths puckering, tiny fins swishing like flight stabilizers. The CEO folded her arms across her ample bosom, glass in hand. Her head tilted in silent deliberation, chin thrust out.

I had seen that posture before.

On Phobos.

Standing at her command podium, watching the real-time display of her defeat at Olympus.

"There was nothing on the newsfeeds," Krohl said with an audible strain.

"Exactly. Which suggests that someone is burying the story."

Krohl touched the aquarium glass. Fish floated curiously towards her fingernail.

"The bot *could've* gone berserk," Drost suggested. "Radiation has been known to screw with their programming."

"Then why keep it off the feeds?"

"That's not so strange. With all the paranoia over AIs? Plenty of people would want to hush the story of a murderous robot."

"The way Sabrina Potts's murder on Luna was hushed?"

My breath caught.

Sabrina Potts!

General Sabrina Potts, who I'd last seen with an honest-to-stars eye-patch on Phobos. Sabrina Potts, who had been in charge of the death camps on Mars.

Fucking hell. With one utterance, any lingering doubt evaporated. David Julius Pope was *not* being paranoid. The trail I'd uncovered in Peznowski's house of horrors had led to another monster, and the Order was doing right by letting slip the hounds.

The Partisans had returned. At least two of them, conjured from hell. Three of them, if I was counting the mysterious voice who had spoken to Peznowski....

My mouth ran dry.

"Sabrina died in a buggy accident," Drost was saying.

Krohl hurled her glass across the room. "A *buggy accident*? A week later, Caleb dies from a malfunctioning bot? And now one of the fucking founders of the Order shows up on my doorstep?" The color drained from her face until she looked as pale as her platinum hair. She stared at the broken wineglass, the pieces sparkling by firelight. "They're coming for us."

Drost swallowed. "You don't know that."

"*They're coming for me!*"

The former general was breathing so hard it seemed she might hyperventilate. I rose from the bar, flicked my ammo wheel to standard rounds. Any notion of subterfuge fled my mind. I'd recorded her confession via airhound. In two seconds I could send that audio to David.

In the suite, the CEO said, "We're leaving. Now."

Drost hesitated. "Ma'am? It's Solstice Eve. My daughter is home waiting for—"

Krohl's eyes bulged. "She can go on waiting!"

"Where are we going?"

"Offworld."

"*Offworld?*"

Krohl glared at her. "The Order of Stone is coming for us, Debbie. You can't stay here. They know you work for me. They'll rip out your neurals. They'll ferret out everything you know about me. About the others."

The others.

Krohl sprinted to her closet and began to dress. Her secretary trailed after her, looking numb and shocked.

"If the Order is behind this," Drost warned, "they'll never let you on the S-E."

"We're not going on the S-E." The woman stripped, letting her nightgown crumple like a pool of mercury at her feet. Naked except for thin green panties, she dressed into a black tunic with red trousers, resembling a sci-fi interpretation of a ladybug. "We'll take private transport to the Face."

"The Face? But—"

"Get your things."

"Ma'am? I can't just leave my daughter!"

"*You'll do what I fucking tell you to!*" Krohl snapped, the terror in her voice splashing indigo colors across my patmatch sniffer. Then, seeing her secretary's bitter expression, she added a quick, desperate addendum: "I'll get her to the Face, Debbie. You have my word on that. But only *afterwards*."

"The Order will take her in for questioning!"

"And she legitimately doesn't know anything. Once things calm down, I'll send for her."

Drost didn't seem reassured, and scarcely moved as her boss handed her a travel bag. For her part, Krohl struck up a private conference, speaking subvocally. I cranked my audio, catching only a peppering of out-of-context words and lip-reading interpretations. I could examine the transcripts later, or just send it over to my brother's analysts.

<Harris,> Xenophon said, <an Anzu is on approach vector. Krohl is likely to leave by rooftop.>

"Thanks."

<There is evidence that Krohl's suite contains an emergency lift.>

"What evidence?"

<There is a redundant electrical grid in the suite, fitting the parameters of a mobile panic room.>

"Well, she's sure as hell panicking. One more piece of bad news and she might die of an aneurysm." I sighed, staring at the suite doors. I had to get in there before she was whisked away to whatever safehouse waited for her. And what the hell was the 'Face' she mentioned? Historically, it referenced Cydonia, where a trick of geology suggested a human countenance. Yet Krohl had said she was going offworld. Were there other Faces in the solar system? I knew there was a vulva formation on Pluto. A pair of eyes on Titan. A thumbs-up on Callisto. Only Mars, however, had a Face.

I shook my head. It didn't matter at the moment. I had an op to complete, another hydra head to lop off. I rose from the bar and headed for the corridor.

In the same instant, the suite doors opened.

My attention had shifted away from the airhound feed; I hadn't noticed Drost pivoting towards the doors, palming them open to retrieve her alligator briefcase. The woman was stooping to grab its scaly handle when she spotted me twenty meters away.

An intruder in the Grand Hall, caught red-handed. Her eyes grew wide. Lips parted, a cry of alarm welling in her throat.

Fuck.

With no better option, I blurred straight at her, shattering the picobeams. In response, the suite doors began sliding shut at a speed nearly to match my own, and they would undoubtably have succeeded in locking me out, but Drost was blocking their closure. For a morbid second I expected the doors to shut anyway, cleaving her in half like a tomato. But they stopped, klaxons erupting, lights dappling the walls.

Shoving the secretary aside, I raised my multigun and put Krohl in the targeting reticle.

For an instant, the CEO was as frozen as her corporate stooge, a well-dressed mannequin in mid-stride. When I pulled the trigger, she snapped into her own hyperacceleration. Body twisting, nearly tumbling over herself, she whirled away at five times normal speed.

I flicked the ammo wheel to **LASER**, and fired again.

CHAPTER EIGHTEEN

Security Concerns

A laser beam.

Impossible to dodge, stabbing out from my multigun batteries like a bright jousting lance. It burned into my target's thigh an inch below her femoral artery. The suite instantly reeked of charred meat. The world froze, the aquarium a still-life painting and the fireplace a Phoenix in its glorious epilogue.

Vilhelmina Krohl screeched and went down hard. Wound sizzling within a black-scorched rim of tunic, she was reaching for a private virtuboard when my next shot lasered her hand off at the wrist.

This time she didn't scream. Pale and sweating, her mouth stretched into a silent 'O', she gaped at the cauterized stump. I'd seen that look before; at Elysium Mons, Sergeant Beresha had been blown up by mortar fire, and as I dragged him to cover, he kept staring in astonishment at the rubbery loops of intestine in his hands. A portrait of pure disbelief. That was the expression Krohl wore as her stump hissed inches from her face. *Where is my hand?* some part of her mind was asking. *There's supposed to be a hand here....*

"Hi, Eileen," I said, squatting before her. "Been a while, huh?"

She blinked slowly, face slack. "You...you're—"

"*You,*" I cut her off, "are General Eileen Monteiro. A Partisan. You ordered the murder of thousands. You terrorized the populace with your shadowmen police."

She crawled backwards on her elbows. My blurmod gave its teapot whistle, timing out.

Following her, I continued. "I represent the Order of Stone. I am here to bring justice. I am here to show you that the injuries you inflicted upon Mars will *not* go unpunished. My name is Harris Alexander Pope—"

My mod snapped me back to real-time. Debbie cried out in the corridor.

"—and I am the last thing you will ever see."

I aimed into the CEO's face.

And then something struck me like a battering ram. I was pitched off my feet, impact data splashing the news that a fifty-caliber bullet had hit my shoulder. Rolling behind the sofa, I peeked at the doorway. Debbie Drost dashed for the VIP lift, but she wasn't my main concern.

Running from the other direction – nearly bowling her over as they came – was a squad of security guards in brown uniforms, weapons out. At the head of their column was none other than the visored security chief, his tricked-out multigun lining me up for another shot.

My panicked face appeared on his reflective visor. With the butt of his rifle tucked into his shoulder, he fired again.

★　　★　　★

It was a squad of six men who rushed me in three-by-three formation, the muscular heavy taking point. I didn't know where they'd come from; maybe the VIP lift, or a secret access panel in the walls. Whoever designed the place must have taken cues from a Japanese ninja house.

My blurmod gauge was climbing towards green. I rolled again, getting back to my feet and slapping down my protective visor. Opposite me, Krohl dragged herself towards a cubbyhole, wounded leg trailing.

There was just enough time to thumb **PHOSPHIRE** on my ammo wheel. I sprayed the entranceway as a half-dozen whirlwinds exploded into the suite.

Their arrival triggered what little juice was left in my blurmod. Two whirlwinds converged on me, coalescing into men as our speeds aligned. They fired wild and messy. One fellow wore spiked blond hair and a well-manicured goatee. The other had a squatter, ape-like build – had to be an offworlder. I rolled forward, into their approach. Flicked the wheel back to LASER, sliced off the offworlder's head in a lateral sweep. Mister Goatee cartwheeled sideways and dove for cover behind the sofa.

Several bullets caught me center-of-mass, knocking me about. I pivoted, opened my shield, and deflected the fusillade back to sender. Guards scattered, vases popping on shelves.

My blurmod stuttered, batteries draining.

One second.

Without warning, an opponent materialized in front of me. He was just a kid, though clever enough to have delayed his blur by several real-time seconds, putting me at a deadly disadvantage. My mod screamed, leeching emergency power from other systems to stretch the effect.

Acting out of instinct, I fired a grenade directly at the kid's feet.

One-second timer.

Even as it thumped into the floor, two more guards entered our timestream. Grim, angry fellows, committed to the moment, seeing me as the long-awaited bogeyman of their training: the hypothetical intruder made real.

With the last juice of my batteries, I shoved off after Krohl.

The grenade exploded.

The blast catapulted me sideways. There was a stunning oblivion, blinding and hot and colorless. For an instant I thought I'd been killed. Dead and reborn. The merciless glow of a regen clinic. Another ten years stolen from me....

Then my senses recovered. I lay prone, covered in glass and resinous debris. My multigun was several meters out of reach.

Krohl slumped in her security chief's arms like a crash-test dummy. Real professional, this guy: protecting his employer while his team dealt with the trespasser. He cradled her to his chest. They both disappeared in a blur.

Towards the dead-end cubby. A panel lifted for them, then slammed shut.

<Harris,> Xenophon said, <the target is heading to the roof. The Anzu is inbound, ETA sixty-seven seconds.>

"How do I get to the roof, fast?"

<The Grand Hall has a—>

A compartment in my shoulder popped open. A concealed turret blasted a man-shaped dust-devil as it bore down on me. The silhouette collapsed, clutching its throat. I found myself staring at Mister Goatee; he'd caught a round in the jugular.

There was barely time to register the sight before my turret fired again, blowing his brains onto the floor.

<My apologies,> Xenophon said. <There was no time to wait for your reaction.>

"You can hijack my systems?" I demanded.

<I am programmed with Survival Override. You may deactivate this feature if you wish.>

"How do I get to the roof?"

<The Grand Hall has a balcony. You can attain the building's exterior from there.>

I exited the suite to do exactly that, returning to the alien fungal forests and babbling brook. The balcony wasn't immediately apparent; Xenophon painted my optics with a yellow brick road rounding a brace of shaggy trees. Sure enough, there was a sliding door beyond them, leading to a balcony.

"Glass or glasstic?" I asked.

<The door is glasstic. You can tell the difference by the diminished filtering effect that—>

I carved a hasty oval into the door, draining the last of my LASER batteries. Then I ran full tilt, amped my legs, and kicked out the panel. I stepped through the breach into freezing air. Forty floors below, the grounds were coming alive with activity: emergency lights dappled the courtyard, corporate security vans converging at the tower's base.

The roof was one story above me, framed against the moons. The Anzu swept down like a pregnant gull.

Using my magfiber gloves, I scaled the wall. Hauling myself over the top, I glimpsed the security chief dashing towards the Anzu. He still had Krohl in his arms.

I thumbed my ammo wheel and fired for the aircraft's open door:
SPIDERBOMB

It was difficult to tell what happened next. The security chief seemed to teleport in front of my shot, his own shield knocking my projectile aside. Krohl was no longer in his arms; he must have tossed her clear of the explosive. Following that line of tactic, I spotted her ten meters to the south of the Anzu, sprawled on the roof and blinking in bewilderment. The spiderbomb careened off the ledge and burst harmlessly mid-air.

As impressive as my opponent's augmented reflexes were, he'd been a tad overzealous in pitching his employer to safety. She was now fully within my sights. I placed her in my targeting reticle, half-pressed the trigger to tag her silhouette for the next spiderbomb, and—

—was shot clear off the rooftop.

The impact took me square in the visor, not only blindsiding me, but blinding me in the process. I plummeted, stunned into imbecility. Cold wind rushed around my face. The bastard must have shot my visor clean off my head.

My fall was arrested by an involuntary firing of my *jamadhar*. I jerked, dangling by one arm. Helpless and blind, but no longer hurtling to my death.

Xenophon's voice entered my thoughts. **<Harris? You were shot by a laser.>**

"Is that what it was?"

<Yes.>

Of course, that made sense. The shot had been so instantaneous it hadn't even triggered my blurmod. My vision returned, optics both cybernetic and biologic recovering. Technically, visors were designed with reflective and ablative properties to deal with lasers; nonetheless, a concentrated burst of stimulated light has a way of fucking you up, regardless of what the manual claims.

<The dropship is leaving.>

"No shit." I could hear the change in pitch from the vehicle's turbines as it lifted into the night, and at an angle that didn't afford me a shot. Retracting myself up the *jamadhar*, I planted my magfiber gloves flat against the building.

<You have tagged your target,> Xenophon reminded me. <I would advise firing a spiderbomb straight into the air. It will find its mark.>

"Is the spiderbomb a self-guided missile?"

<It has that functionality.>

Before I could follow my Familiar's advice, the security chief's mirrored countenance appeared over the rooftop ledge. I snapped my shield open where I clung, braced for the next laser blast.

What I received, instead, was a stricken pause in the action. My opponent froze, visor reflecting me, clinging to the side of the building like an insect. He didn't fire. Didn't move.

Another security guard appeared beside him, unhelmeted and flush with combat high. This new enemy saw me and raised her weapon. My shoulder-turret fired across the rim of my shield; she was caught in the throat, tipped over like a clown, and plummeted forty stories in silence.

And still, the security chief didn't move.

"You!" he cried.

I stared through my shield. "You know me?"

He didn't reply right away. The single word he'd uttered ran through my patmatch like a pachinko ball. As the vocal print was measured by tilt and cadence and emotional qualities, my memory outpaced the analysis. I remembered sitting in a buggy ten years earlier. Remembered a gruff, wry voice....

"Eric?" I cried. "Eric Mazzola?"

He snapped open his visor.

I saw his violet eyes first – a natural mutation found in a percentage of the Martian populace. Eric had chopped his lion-mane hair, but the piercings, studs, tattoos, and chains were as I remembered them; a new tattoo on his neck, showing a daffodil, was the only obvious addition.

"It's you," I gasped. "How...how have you been?"

The trog glowered. "What the fuck are *you* doing here? Why attack my—"

"She's a Partisan."

Eric's frightful expression deepened. "Bullshit."

"There are no bulls on Mars."

"Which one?"

"Which one what?"

"Which *Partisan* do you think she is?" Spit flew from his teeth as he spoke the hated word.

"General Monteiro."

"The Partisans are dead," he insisted. "They fucking died, all of them! *You're* the one who killed them!"

"They're back."

Eric's wrath was a nightmare to behold, seething with conflict, doubt, and hatred as pure as anything I'd ever seen. Yet he lowered his rifle.

"You might want to step back," I advised, and fired my remaining spiderbomb into the sky. Against the swampy hue of Deimos, the projectile corkscrewed out of sight. I side-shuffled to the tower's corner, and gazed at the missile's trail.

The Anzu's explosion actually resembled a spider, a hellish arachnid-shaped cloud stretching fiery legs above the canal.

CHAPTER NINETEEN

The Labyrinth of Eternal Night

Tier Marsworks' campus was in full lockdown by the time the VIP elevator reached garage level. Eric didn't speak as we descended. He simply glared at me, neck tattoos flaring like gills. Forty floors passed in venomous silence.

It was a relief when we stepped out into a drafty, deserted garage. My dubious companion led me to a six-wheeled security van. He drove us outside…

…into chaos.

Krohl's aircraft had gone down over the docks. Even from a distance, the beach was a far cry from the 'beautiful canal view' that Drost had bragged about earlier that day. The wreckage was ablaze. Sandclaws encircled it, interrupted in their usual duties but not authorized to disturb an emergency scene; the result was that they seemed like parishioners encircling a fiery idol. A swarm of fire-suppression drones, first-responders, and security forces descended on the site. Com–chatter percolated with the news: Tier's CEO had been killed in the crash, along with the pilot and three security personnel.

The garbage-picker had joined the trash.

Eric drove us past one security checkpoint after another, his badge and biometrics acting as protective talisman. We made our way to the public road.

"We've got to find Debbie Drost," I said, settling back in the passenger seat. "She has a good fifteen-minute head start on us. Can you call her?"

Eric scowled, knuckles white on the steering wheel. "And say *what*?"

"You're head of security. There *was* an attack on the company. Tell her she's needed for debriefing."

With undisguised reluctance, the trog touched his ear. Further south along the road, the local sandship docks appeared like a carnival. Streetlamps illuminated a rippling crowd. Every employee this side of Olympus was heading home for the holiday.

"Her infolink is down," Eric said at last.

I nodded. "Not surprising. She's running dark."

"Can you blame her? She just saw you trash the place and murder her coworkers." There was real anger in his voice, showing as orange tint in my sniffer program.

"I killed her coworkers in self-defense," I countered. "They'll come back, Eric."

"You murdered the CEO, too."

"Yeah. *She's* not coming back."

Eric's glower deepened. With his tribal scarification, smoldering tattoos, chains, studs, and earrings, he seemed some dieselpunk interpretation of an Old Calendar pirate, all exposed rivets, seams, and bolts. Helmet discarded, the red-dyed lion mane shorn away to a mohawk splitting two shaven sides.

"Debbie Drost isn't a Partisan," he grumbled.

"She's involved in this."

"I don't believe that!"

"This isn't about belief. I recorded her convo with the boss."

Eric shook his head, chains jingling. "You show up after ten years, barging into *my* workplace, shooting up the place...."

"You spoke to Natalia Argos on that rooftop, didn't you? She confirmed everything."

"I spoke to someone who *sounded* like Argos, sure. I'm not part of the Order anymore." He swallowed. "I'm in the private sector now, dammit! I've known Debbie for *nine years*, and I'm telling you she's no Partisan. She'd never work for them."

"Plenty of people worked for them," I scoffed. "That's why we had a goddam war."

"You don't get it," he insisted, flashing a thicket of fangs. "They're the most hated people in history. No Martian would go along with that."

"I spent twenty years among people who went along with everything they—"

"*That* was the war! I'm talking about what they did *afterwards*." He jerked the wheel and we pulled into the dockyard commuter lot. Parking the vehicle, Eric gave me a boiling look. "Debbie is a friend. She was part of a refugee group I hunkered down with after the nukes. We became close." His eyes narrowed. "You and I are *hardly* friends. We're barely compatriots! *Our* bonding was when I put a hole in your chest!"

"You still know how to follow orders, right?"

"I'm not a soldier anymore!"

I shook my head. "We're always—"

An explosion lit up the sky and I cried out. Fireworks, bursting over the canal like dropships taking fire.

For a moment I was back in the trenches. I tasted adrenaline. The sonic booms impelled me to reach for the van's door.

<They are only fireworks, Harris,> said Xenophon.

"Shut up," I whispered. Seeing Eric's murderous expression, I quickly added, "Sorry, wasn't talking to you. I've got a nosy partner in my skull."

"You're hearing voices?"

"It's a Familiar."

He said nothing.

Peering through the window, I counted three sandships taking on passengers. The east–west length of Canal Penthisilea crawled with other vessels. Private yachts. Fishing trawlers. Holiday ferries. They were too distant for Drost to have gotten aboard in fifteen minutes.

"She'll leave by one of the sandships," I guessed.

"Debbie takes the tram home each day," countered the trog.

"She's running dark. You don't go home when you're running dark."

"She's not going to abandon her kid!"

I mentally sifted the mission dossier. Krohl was its main focus, of course, but there were links to known associates, security detail, and administrative retinue. Drost belonged to that latter category. Her public address was listed as Padilla Flats, ninety miles from here. I emailed Dave with the relevant page number, and instantly received a ping of acknowledgement. The time was 2056. My brother's holiday party had been going on for an hour. I pictured him making the rounds, glad-handing the attendees, the timeless platitudes of, "So good to see you!" and, "How is the family?" and, "Are you enjoying yourself?" abruptly punctuated by my email. More platitudes, while Dave secretly read the message and orchestrated a response. He'd dispatch personnel to Drost's home. Put surveillance on her friends, family, and anyone else within five degrees of her social network.

"She won't go home," I repeated. "And she'll avoid the tram. Every passenger is biometrically logged on entry and exit."

Eric followed my gaze to the marina. "Same is true of the sandships."

"Except you can't jump off a hundred-mile-per-hour tram. It isn't difficult to ditch a ship."

"You sure about that?"

"Yes. My father worked the sandships. They scan you at boarding, and scan you at departure. But mid-transit? You're free. A fugitive can drop over the side. Swim to shore."

Eric shook his head. "Not a chance."

"This isn't Earth," I said. "There aren't sharks or glops in these waters. She could jump overboard and make for the nearest safehouse."

"Debbie isn't a Partisan! She's not a soldier! She doesn't have that kind of training."

"Due respect, we don't know *what* she is, or what kind of training she's had."

Eric was quivering with fury as he exited the van. That concerned me. Ten years ago, he'd been a glacially cool customer. Having fought me, killed me, and revived me, he'd treated the entire matter with professional calm. Later, after the destruction of Phobos, he'd maintained that demeanor. I would have hated to play poker with the guy.

Now, he was barely holding it together. My sniffer lit like a Solstice Tree from his emotional indicators: fast breathing, flaring nostrils, clenched fists. It wouldn't take much to push the needle into flat-out violence.

Which meant I needed to mind my words.

Stepping from the van, I plucked the last three airhounds from my utility clip. Eric watched as I flung them into the sky.

Reluctantly, I pinged Xenophon.

<Hello, Harris.>

"Yeah, hi. Please link to the airhounds and scan for Drost."

That would be a challenge. The secretary was average female height and build: six-foot-two and lean. Coupled with the volume of passengers and the fact that most would be in dust-masks and goggles, target discrimination was going to be a bitch.

Eric walked abreast of me as we made for the pier. "What's the op concerning Debbie?"

"The op?"

"You were sent to kill Krohl. You did that. What happens when we find Debbie?"

I stared at him in disbelief. "First of all, there's no 'we' at this point. Thank you for standing down on the roof. Thanks for the drive here, too. But this is *my* mission. You're a soldier, you know what that means."

"I'm not a soldier anymore." His face was a jungle cat glowering through steel instead of vines. "And I'm coming with you."

"You're not authorized to—"

"I'm entrusted with the protection of Tier employees. Debbie's an employee."

"My orders—"

"Fuck off with your orders."

I felt my protest wither at this defiance; in fact, I almost laughed, a genuine laugh that made me wonder how long it'd been since I'd done that. Sighing, dialed into the shoal-like eddies of the crowd, I said, "Fine. My op was to kill Krohl, but its parameters have changed. Deborah Skyblush Drost has become a person of interest. I'm going to apprehend her."

<Harris,> Xenophon interrupted, **<I have three possible silhouettes matching the target.>**

"Let's see them," I snapped, and then to Eric, said, "Sightjack with my link. I've got three probables you should see."

Mazzola's presence whumped into my head as he accepted the neural invite. Sightjacking with even a single airhound can be disorienting for the uninitiated; trying to parse a trifecta of views overlaying your HUD can make a veteran woozy.

The crowd was coalescing into three lines, one per sandship. Mercifully, the marina was well-lit, and the airhounds held position – mosquito-like – above the streetlamps. People squeezed up the gangplank, passing one by one through the manned security booth for embarkation.

Too many faces. The human brain can only process so much.

Men and women and little children. Families returning, I presumed, from picnicking along the canal, or else from a bring-your-kids-to-work day. The children were bundles of energy, oohing and ahhing at the vessels. The adults, by contrast, were a painfully reserved bunch. They exhibited an economy of movement that betrayed real trauma.

These were the nuclear war survivors, I figured. People who had experienced the horror of traditional war with a radioactive chaser. They knew the food shortages, radiation poisoning, life underground. Some might have died, which meant they'd returned to a disfigured, transfigured Mars. That was a trauma all its own. Both groups were trying to resume the business of living…and from the sheer number of children I saw, it seemed that 'business' had included a super-bloom siring.

As I zoomed in on the crowd, I could see it in their eyes: the scars only war can bestow. The memory of suffering. The realization that nothing is permanent or assured. That a world which could die once could die again. Perhaps, I mused, the neurotic fear that they might be dreaming and, any second now, would wake up in their survival bunkers.

I could certainly relate to that.

Linked with the airhounds, Xenophon outlined the probables in green highlight. Three women. All similar height and build. All masked. Two sported ash-blonde hair of similar cut and length to Debbie's; the third wore a wolfsbane-purple *hijab* with black webbing.

I nudged Eric. "Any ideas?"

He squinted at the images. "Each is going to a different ship. Think they're decoys?"

"I don't see how. When would she have had time to call them?" Saying it aloud, though, made me wonder. It was *probably* just coincidence – there were several hundred people on the pier, after all.

"We're not going to kill her," Eric said.

"I already told you we're not."

One of the women lowered her mask to sip from a flask. It wasn't Debbie; the airhound watching her moved off, shifting its coverage.

Two probables.

"The one without the *hijab*," Eric said. "That's her."

I amped the view-field. "How do you know?"

"I've known her for nine years, remember? I recognize her dust-mask."

"Okay, let's get in line."

From the pier's mounted speakers, a voice rang out. "All aboard!"

★   ★   ★

Our sandship was the *Dandelion Wine*, and stepping into its shadow made me feel like a kid again. Waiting for Dad to disembark. His immaculate uniform. His high-watt smile as he appeared atop the gangplank and walked us home, or to the hotel for ice cream. The musketeers – Dad as Mars, his sons as little moons in tow. The uniform made him a retro pulp hero, Flash Gordon perhaps, or a fabled rocket man on home leave.

An icy breeze brushed the memory away. I shuffled forward, shivering.

"It's awfully cold for December," I noted.

Eric stood behind me. "Technically, the planet is still in nuclear winter. Average temperatures dropped six degrees after Detonation."

As we edged to the security kiosk, the sandship design was looking more and more unusual to what I remembered. Still serpentine, but oddly stylized. Like a Viking longboat painted by a cubist. And larger, too. It's exterior glittered with reflected starlight for six hundred meters. Plumed sails blossomed from masts. The overall effect was of paradoxical realities: the organic, flowing design of a finned maritime creature rendered as Cycladic art. I stepped aboard and the hull rippled with shapestone feathers.

I counted seven decks to the *Dandelion Wine*. The Lido was topped by a restaurant and observation tower.

"If she's going overboard," I said, "it'll be when no one's looking. She'll wander aft and slip over the edge."

Eric made a scoffing sound. Our target strayed to the port-side rails, gazing solemnly across the canal. I broke the link, leaving the airhounds in default follow-mode.

The ship pulled away from the harbor. The deck was crammed with foldout chairs; I found a pair of empty seats and turned to Eric. "You look good, by the way."

"*You* look freshly printed," he countered. "They just ran you off the line today, didn't they?"

"With *this* body, yeah. But I've been back a little longer than that."

"How much longer?"

"Since yesterday."

He raised an eyebrow. "When was your last Save?"

"Amazonis."

"I didn't ask where, I asked *when*."

I mentally searched for the Save receipt. "It was 9:05 a.m., October 4, 348."

Eric mulled over this date, absently running his tongue along the tips of his fangs. "So you didn't live through Detonation. Didn't see those years firsthand."

I settled into my chair. "No, I didn't see that."

"*I* did."

"How did you survive?"

"After dropping you off at the hotel, I went home to Ybarra." He gazed onto the canal, the black foothills, the stars and aurora-belt overhead. "Guess a trog ghetto wasn't high on the kill-list."

"I don't know whether to offer congratulations or condolences."

"What I *want*," he snarled, "is for you to understand that no one who saw what followed would work with…" He glanced around, voice dropping nearly to subvocal. "…the Partisans. Ain't no way Debbie is one of them."

"There are lots of ways, actually."

"She's been my friend for nine years."

"That code for fuck buddies?" When his eyes kindled in offense, I added, "Eric, I'm not judging. She's attractive, and I'm sure you were a good protector. Hell, I'd be surprised if something *hadn't* developed between you two."

He withdrew into silence. After half a minute, he said, "My point is that she's not a Partisan."

"My job is to arrest her—"

The vessel gave a sudden lurch.

My initial thought was that we had taken a torpedo. Or maybe a sandclaw had pursued us and was clambering up the side, causing the vessel to list.

To my astonishment, I realized that the *Dandelion Wine* was lifting off the canal. Climbing into the sky!

I raced to the starboard rails to see water streaming off the hull in a gentle, hissing curtain.

"What in the fuck?" I gasped.

Eric came to stand beside me. "It's been ten years, Harris. Still think Debbie will drop overboard?"

★   ★   ★

There were ships running Penthisilea and ships running to the sea and now, apparently, ships that flew above the desert. The *Dandelion Wine* ran a route that had never existed in my time: from Olympus Mons to the canyon belt.

And included on that route was a stop at the Noctis Labyrinthus.

My mind balked as the captain announced our string of destinations over loudspeaker. Noctis? That twisting maze formed by natural valleys, craters, and mesas, where my squad had watched the downing of the *Thassos*. Where I'd survived forty-one days of horror....

Thirty thousand people died in the Siege of Noctis. Air support had been ineffective. Sandclaws, ideal for navigating difficult terrain, were easily picked off by aggressive mine placement at the chokepoint. Complicating matters was the fact that Noctis hosted a permanent ice fog; a microclimate steeping the canyon in a relentless, obscuring miasma. It had therefore fallen to soldiers – ordinary human soldiers – to try securing the place. What transpired was our variant of the Battle of Gettysburg, of Stalingrad, of Enyalios's massacre of militias at the Rio Grande....

I felt a cold sweat at the thought of seeing it again, even at altitude.

Little kids scrambled to the rails, pointing to the lights of a city coming into view. A city I didn't recognize, on a stretch of desert that had never been inhabited before.

"Now arriving at Annwyn," the captain's voice announced.

My airhounds orbited the *Dandelion Wine*. Debbie Drost had retreated to the Lido bar. Absently, I watched her nursing a martini in quiet, grave concentration.

Eric went looking for a bathroom and when he returned said, "She's having a drink in the bar."

"I know."

He raised an eyebrow. "You okay?"

"Taking in the new sights," I said, nodding towards the unknown city's pier.

"The IPC built new cities out here, away from the blast zones. The deserts are home to at least a dozen communities, hot-off-the-press."

"But in the *desert*? They planning on expanding the canals? How do people get water?"

"They extended the water-lines. Maybe they'll extend the canals, too, who knows?" The ship drew to a halt. Several families migrated to the gangplank, while my attention was captured by Annwyn's pale spires, medinas, and covered skyways…this city that seemed to have sprung from the pages of *One Thousand and One Nights*. Gigantic sand levees were under construction, like ramparts over the desert.

The IPC wasn't just repairing Mars.

They were remaking it.

And yet Dave had told me that Mars wasn't back in IPCnet. All this reconstruction must therefore be an incentive, softening the beachhead of public mistrust.

How generous…and shrewd.

When the last Annwyn passengers were gone, our vessel floated off again. The captain's voice returned.

"Next stop, Noctis Labyrinthus."

My pulse thudded in my wrists. Fucking Noctis. How the hell could a port be there? There must be thirty thousand corpses hidden below its fog-line!

"You ever deploy out here?" Eric asked.

"Not out here," I rasped. "But at our next stop, yes."

"Me, too. I wonder if we shot at each other." He stared hard at me. "Though probably not. I tend to kill what I aim at."

"You're thinking of putting another hole in my chest, aren't you?"

His breath curled in lacy plumes. "Thinking about it, yeah."

"I'm *not* going to kill Debbie. I'll arrest and interrogate her."

"She has a kid."

I sneered, "I do love how people trot out their reproductive success as a hole card. If she's a war criminal, spreading her legs doesn't erase that history. Hell, Peznowski *fucked himself* to reproduce."

Eric darkened. "Minister Peznowski is alive?"

"Was alive."

"You interrogated him too?"

"That's one way to put it."

"What I'm saying," Eric added, eyes glossing over with that traumatic sheen I'd noticed in the crowd, "is that there *has* to be due process. Something you didn't give Krohl back there. And I presume you didn't afford Peznowski, either."

I regarded him with amazement. "That sick son of a bitch got exactly what he deserved. And I was following orders."

"Gee, where have I heard *that* before?"

"Are we going to have a problem?" I snapped.

To my surprise, Eric looked amused. "Do you know why I joined the Order of Stone? Most trogs wanted nothing to do with either side. We kept to ourselves, as our ancestors had kept to themselves when the planet was being settled...descendants of Earth's unwanted. The rejected, unwashed masses who grew up in the shadow of arcologies. We came here as cheap labor. *We* built the first Martian cities! The stone was barely set when Earthers moved in and kicked us out." He smirked, eyes like black flame. "There was even talk of sending us back to Earth, did you know that? But see...we had gotten offworld, and *no one* was going to send us back. People called us barbarians...so we *became* barbarians. Beholden to no one but each other."

"That is your reputation."

"When the Partisans took over, it meant nothing to us. Meet the new boss, same as the old, right? But they turned out to be worse. Consolidated strength by targeting 'blueworld sympathizers' and 'radicals' and 'enemies of the state'. Lots of trogs laughed, seeing the civilized world eating itself. Most had treated us like shit anyway."

I said nothing. There hadn't been many trogs in Lighthouse Point, though I occasionally glimpsed them at Hellas Market. I remembered my mother quickly steering me away. *They're dangerous, Harris. You stay away from those people.*

Eric continued in what was the longest conversation we'd ever shared. "But me, I could see around the corner. People arrested without trial. People deleted from the books. There was *no question* in my mind that sooner or later, the Partisans would come for us. So I did what few trogs cared to: I joined the Order of Stone. At first it was to protect my people. In the end, it was to protect *all* people. You said earlier that soldiers don't ever retire, but my loyalty wasn't to a flag; it was to a Mars where people can be free from persecution. So I'm telling you now, Harris, if the Order starts pulling that same shit...."

"My brother won't let that happen," I insisted.

Silence fell between us. In the distance, black peaks and claw-like geology began to appear. We drifted, like a parade float bearing down on a phalanx of spears.

An alert flashed from my airhounds. Drost was pushing her empty glass across the bar and returning to the deck. I watched her cross my actual field of vision. She looked afraid.

An expression that matched the terror in my own galloping heart.

CHAPTER TWENTY

Crawlnest

Our vessel glided into the Noctis.

The cliff walls surrounding us were festooned by fire balloons. They exuded pale luminosities on frightful precipices, fang-like stalagmites, and grotesque silicate goblins; essentially mobile lanterns, they were able to affix or detach as needed. The place seemed as cartoonishly exaggerated as I remembered. My eyes strayed to the peaks for signs of enemy turrets.

The turrets were long gone, of course. I didn't even see ceremonial replicas, such as I'd observed while holotouring Earth's Caricom. The *Dandelion Wine*'s passengers admired the bulging knobs and melting white-streaked cliffs. I didn't budge from my position in the crowd, but I did punch up the airhound view; seen from above, our vessel resembled a longboat drifting on vaporous seas.

The fire balloons thickened at the next boarding platform, which had been built into a jutting mountain ledge. To my astonishment, the ledge was familiar....

"Roc's Egg," I whispered.

Eric frowned. "Say again?"

"Never mind."

Years earlier, I'd seen that ledge through a rare break in the fog. *The Siege of Noctis has been roiling for fifteen days. My squad is scrambling in the mist, seeking concealed enemy positions, evading traps while setting our own. We're all tired, doped up on sleep-deps. Strained to the breaking point. Wandering the canyon like lost spirits denied any view of heaven and suddenly....*

Umerah and I are taking point, when a gust of wind tears a rift in the oppressive ceiling. Like an invisible zipper. We gasp at the view of stars.

"Harris, look!" Umerah whispers excitedly. "It like an old picture I saw as a kid! *The Second Voyage of Sinbad!*"

Warily glancing around, I mutter, "We're exposed out here. We shouldn't stay."

Ignoring this, she continues, "Sinbad the sailor was marooned on an island. He saw a strange white dome on a cliff top. He went to investigate, and discovered it was the egg of the greatest bird in the world, the powerful roc. Look up there, Harris! See that pale boulder? It looks like a roc's egg!"

"If only our biggest concern was a goddam bird."

"Harris—"

"Umerah, this is dangerous...."

"For five seconds, can you just look?"

"Five seconds of letting our guard down is all it takes to—"

"Now is what we own, Harris. Please, own this moment with me."

And despite every trained instinct, I gaze at a boulder that – in our sleep-deprived and panicky states – really does resemble some mythical egg. I suddenly want to be on an adventure with Sinbad. Finding treasure and monsters and wonder.

When the fog closes in, I nearly weep.

Years later, the pale boulder was still there, though now it had company. A village had been constructed with igloo-like homes carved out of local rock, bristling with weather instrumentation and radio antennae.

"Now arriving at Noctis Labyrinthus," came the captain's gratingly cheerful announcement.

"Who the hell would live up here?" I asked. "And why?"

"A scientific community," Eric explained. "Mostly geologists and climatologists. Aero-farmers, too, taking advantage of the fog desert. The town is called Starpoint."

I liked Roc's Egg better.

The ship pulled along the pier. A handful of passengers disembarked; I glanced to Debbie to see if she was trying to steal ashore, but she remained at the rails, absently viewing the vaguely Neolithic architecture of these clifftop dwellers.

I nudged Eric. "It's time."

We made an oblique approach to our target. The *Dandelion Wine* moved on.

★　　★　　★

"Scouting more locations, Mister Porter?"

Drost asked the question without turning, her rigid grip on the rails so firm it seemed she was welded there.

I took position beside her, near enough to catch a whiff of her sandalwood perfume. "If I was, this would be the place. A billion-year-old labyrinth. Can't beat that."

"And you're the Minotaur." She was breathing shallow. Eric sidled to her right flank, and she brightened at him. "Eric? Stars, it's good to see you!"

"Hi, Debbie," he said stiffly.

The secretary seemed to read his face. Finding no help there triggered new desperation. "Eric, I don't know what this maniac told you, but he attacked Vilhelmina!"

Eric nodded. "I was there."

"Then you saw—"

"The recording," he cut her off. "I saw the recording of your conversation with her."

Drost nodded vigorously. "Yeah? Know what you *didn't* see? How that fucking bitch forced me into servitude. How she kept me as her message-runner to the others!"

"What others?" I demanded.

"Are you here to murder me?"

"I'm here to ask questions."

"Is that what you were doing at Tier? Asking questions?"

"Back at Tier," I growled, "I was eradicating a parasite."

"I'm not one of them!"

"No, you just work for them. I want to know how that started. How you became involved. And where these *others* are. I also want to know what your exit strategy is."

"What guarantees do I—"

"None."

She looked forlornly to Eric. To my eyes, there was nothing unusual in the gesture, yet my sniffer painted an indigo pattern from how their bodies mirrored each other, their postures, the dilation in Eric's eyes, the tilt of Debbie's head. In clinical terms, it read: MUTUAL ATTRACTION, ROMANTIC INVOLVEMENT 89% LIKELY. It wasn't surprising. These two in a gloomy bunker. Eric returning from scavenging runs. Intimate conversations in the dark. Secret sojourns to a supply closet. Clothes unzipping, tunics hiked up. In war, everything is cranked to heights that civilian life can never equal.

We were passing another fire balloon; it illuminated one side of Drost's face. "I worked as her secretary, Mister Porter."

"Know what the word 'secretary' means? 'Keeper of secrets'."

"I'll spill them, in exchange for my life and the life of my daughter."

"Krohl doesn't have a neuro-block on you?" I asked skeptically.

Debbie laughed bitterly. "No, Eileen motivated my silence another way. Look at me." She faced me, arms spread. "This is the *only* me. My boss never permitted me to update my Save. It's all very legal, too. I 'voluntarily' signed an NDA, to abstain from clinics during my employment contract. That kind of blackmail ensures cooperation."

Eric frowned. "You'd still come back if you died...."

"With no memories of the last few years! No memories of my daughter! Her first steps. First words. First laughter."

I stiffened. She seemed to notice, and adjusted her stance towards me, eyes scanning my face. Was she running her own sniffer on me? Seeking emotional chinks in my armor?

"Krohl is dead," I told her. "Permadeath, sister to insensible rock. It's been an hour, so her purchase signal has gone out. But that's as far as it'll get. Vilhelmina Krohl will cease to exist. She'll be excised like a faulty gene snipped from DNA."

Debbie swallowed hard. "I'm glad to hear it. She blackmailed me and my daughter into—"

"Stop talking about your daughter. I want to know if she had other backups."

"She didn't."

"So certain, are you?"

A waiter came by, offering champagne. Drost looked at me. "*In vino veritas.*"

I shrugged. She snatched a glass with a trembling hand. I glanced to the Noctis cliff tops. On a whim, I tapped the redweb and downskinned an informative overlay to my HUD: the cliffs filled with infobubbles like fire balloons of their own. The Siege of Noctis became an augmented reality diorama, showing a *very* truncated chronology like a demented Event Calendar. The waxing and waning of Partisan and Order control of the place. The names of downed ships. Estimated body counts.

Drost drained her champagne glass by half. "A year after Detonation," she said, "I was living in the ruins with a group of radiation-scarred survivors. Living with Eric." She touched his wrist meaningfully. He returned her stare with such longing that I couldn't help but wonder if I'd felt that way about anyone.

Umerah Javed? Did I love her? And if so, was it the other *Harris Alexander Pope who loved her…the false me, the cover identity?*

Drost downed another gulp. "As the rads fell, the IPC began dropping emergency crates. We made brief trips to recover them."

I glanced skyward. Phobos was there, a water stain between stars. "Who went on these trips?"

"Eric and I usually went together. We were the healthiest of the group. And it was good to get out of the bunker…if only for a time."

Eric seemed as rigid as Italian marble, staring to the dreamy vista. Her words were having an effect on him.

The secretary finished her champagne. "One day, I was making a supply run alone. Out in the wastes, I intercepted a radio broadcast. It claimed to be from another group of survivors. I made a detour to investigate."

Eric spun to her in wonder. "You never told me that! Where was I?"

She stroked his wrist. "The IPC had opened detox stations. You—"

"Had gone to check them out," the trog said, brow furrowing. "Wanted to make sure it wasn't a trap."

"So with you gone, I went out by myself to recover a drop."

"That was dangerous! I *told* you I was coming back!"

"Sweetie, we were running low on medpacks. We needed replenishment. And besides, you and I had made so many trips together, I knew the area without needing an MPS overlay." She chanced a wounded smile. "Do you know I still take my daughter out there, to show her where—"

"Stop talking about your daughter!" I hissed. "You mentioned a radio signal! What did you find?"

She leaned over the rails and let her empty glass drop away like a pin into cotton. "I found Eileen Monteiro."

"You mean Vilhelmina Krohl," Eric corrected her. "Eileen was killed on Phobos. Her replacement body was Vilhelmina."

"Yes, but she told me who she really was."

"Why the hell would she do that?"

"Because she recognized me the moment I stepped into her bunker."

Her tone was pregnant with dark implication. It all came together for me. Like reverse-footage of a plate shattering on a floor.

"*You were a sympathizer!*" I cried, aghast.

Drost retreated a step. My hand snapped over her wrist, staying her. Eric pivoted towards us, and for a moment I wondered if we were about to reenact our life-and-death waltz at Tier.

But no...what Eric did was touch Debbie's face and lift it so he could stare into her eyes. "Tell me it isn't true," he whispered.

Tears cut trails down her cheeks. "I was a sympathizer," she whispered.

My sniffer program detected such a whiff of potential violence from Eric that I was no longer worried what he'd do to me – it was Debbie who was in trouble. Outrage seethed in his eyes, stiffened his muscles into an attack posture held in check by a fast-unraveling thread of limbic connection: memories of hard-won survival, coming through disaster together, shaking off radioactive dust and creating a life of normalcy....

"I was a fool!" she insisted, clutching his hand. "I was a young idiot!

My family were early supporters. They bought every lie those bastards peddled. Growing up in that household, I did the same!"

Her outburst was attracting attention. Fellow passengers glanced disapprovingly at us.

"Lower your voice," I said.

She turned to me. "I was a sympathizer, okay? I will carry that shame with me until the sun burns out! I'll carry it whenever I see my little girl, and think of all the families that—"

"I told you to stop talking about your daughter!" I jerked her away from the rails. "Seven million people died because of your *sympathies!* Flaunting your offspring won't get you out of this."

Eric interposed himself. "She's cooperating...."

<Social vectors are turning hostile,> warned Xenophon.

I wrangled my fury, bottling it until my eyes shivered in their sockets. "We're going below decks. We're going to have a nice, private conversation where no one can disturb us."

Debbie bowed her head. "If you think that would be best."

*　　*　　*

In the time it took to descend the aft stairwell to the passenger cabins, Xenophon had hacked the *Dandelion Wine*'s manifest, located a vacant room, and overridden the lock.

I shoved Debbie inside. There was a queen-sized bed within, a narrow bathroom, and a portside window. When my father worked the line – when sandships were limited to traveling by water – cabins had been available for holiday rent; ships would deviate from utilitarian routes for a more listless, romantic meander. Now, with ships capable of traveling wherever they wanted, I guessed that renting cabins was more common than ever. Through the window, the fog-line resembled an actual ocean scrolling past.

Eric was last through the door, and he slammed it behind him. "A lot of people went along with the Partisans," he said. "They didn't know what they were doing."

"Sure," I said, watching Debbie where she stood across from us. "But I'll wager Debbie was more than a civilian cheerleader. If General Monteiro *recognized* her, she must have been an enlisted woman."

The secretary swallowed. "I was her communications officer."

I tried seeing past her basalt-hued corporate digs. Tried imagining her in Partisan reds.

Eric paced like a caged beast. "Deb, you played the fool during the war. But why help her *after* Detonation? You aided her concealment! You could have blown her cover at any time!"

"You don't understand," she said.

"I'm *trying* to understand! In that bunker...you and I...we both *saw* what they did to our planet!"

"What *they* did to our planet? You really believe that?"

Eric's jaw hung agape. "What are you talking about? We both suffered through the aftermath. We saw their attack on Mars!"

"I saw what they did *for* Mars!" There was a swift change in her demeanor. Her anguish dropped like a discarded party mask. "They fought to keep us free! To drive out the vermin who were ruining the planet!"

"They *nuked* Mars!"

"*I don't believe that!*" she snapped, eyes full of hate. "Those bombs *had* to have been fired from someone else! How do you know the Order didn't do it? Or the IPC? The Partisans were the best thing to happen to us, but the two of you...*you're* the ones who destroyed Mars! *You*—" she screamed at me, eyes flashing, fingers quaking as if accessing an overlay. "You were one of us, Harris Alexander Pope, and you ended the dream of a free Mars! You *fucking traitor*!"

<Harris!> Xenophon cried. <Aspect change, activating—>

Several things happened at once. Eric cut in front of me, shoving his old lover into the cabin wall. His teeth bared, eyes tearful, he was grasping her by the shoulders when—

—a cloud of white erupted from her mouth.

The eruption triggered my blurmod. Debbie Drost froze in place, mouth stretched so wide I could see her tonsils. A chalky cloud ballooned from her throat and spread into the room. It had already hit Eric in the face and was splitting around him.

Moving five times normal speed, I grabbed him by the back of his armor and yanked him away, trying not to breathe.

<Crawlnest detected!> cried Xenophon. <**Recommend immediate EMP!**>

A memory bobbed in my personal fog. *There's a brochure in my Advanced Countermeasures class, back in shadowman training. Page 17, glossy sidebar, showing a nasty little weapon. The voice of my instructor, a grim masochist named Fernfaith Calaelen, saying, "Hopefully you never run into this one, tyros. Nanite crawlnests. Once in the body, they use bioelectricity for a brief but painful career. They spread with the blood, taking up preconfigured places in the arms, legs, neck, brain. You could say they're fast-acting. But if you get hit with one, trust me, you'll wish they acted faster."*

The goddam thing had been developed during Earth's Warlord Century. Nanotechnology's answer to the African *siafu*. Got into your lungs and stomach. Unfurled mandibles and began chewing. Victims died shrieking, venting blood like the Red Death.

I drew my multigun. Selected EMP and fired point-blank at Drost as the crawlnest emptied from her mouth.

The EMP exploded. Electricity flared, tiny machines popping like firecrackers. I pushed off towards the cabin door, dragging Eric as I went.

And snapped back to normal time.

Debbie continued vomiting the crawlnest like a fire extinguisher. The room was caked in foamy residue. In the hallway, Eric struggled in my grip.

"Just saved your life!" I cried.

"What the hell happened?"

"Later!" I pushed him towards the stairs. "Get topside now!"

We scrambled for the stairwell. Eric stumbled, coughing. His face was a smear of powder.

"I breathed in some of that shit," he panted. "What was it?"

"Crawlnest."

"Oh *fuck*!"

I shoved him up the stairs. "I fried the initial blast."

He clutched his chest. "I think I can feel them working on me."

"Psychosomatic. They usually take a good minute to start."

"It's *been* a minute!"

"It's been thirty seconds." Nonetheless, I touched my ear and activated one of the few audio links I knew. "Segarra! I need emergency medevac!"

Celeste's voice was in my ear. "What happened? Did you get the target?"

"We were hit by a crawlnest."

I heard her sharp intake of breath. "Are you...."

"I'm fine, I think. But I ran into an old compatriot. Eric Mazzola, remember him? He was part of Natalia's squad. He took the crawlnest head-on."

We had attained the main deck. Eric was breeching for fresh air like a whale when he collapsed to his knees.

"Send a medevac!" I cried. "We're on a sandship called the *Dandelion Wine*. Position is midway through the Noctis."

There was a hesitation in my audio. "Did you get the target?"

"Not yet."

"What do you mean, not yet?"

"Fuck you, Segarra! Eric needs help *now*!"

"Harris, you—"

"*Send it!*"

Her voice fell. "You're right, of course."

I dropped the link. Eric spasmed like a fish, clutching his chest and stifling a shriek. His violet eyes were wet. "I can feel them inside me! Oh, fuck! Fuck!"

Shit, he really did inhale the crawlnest.

"Help is on the way!"

The look on his face moved me. I saw his hopes wash away as he realized he was going to die; even now, the nanoscale robots were swimming upstream towards his heart in a perverse antithesis to sperm cells bearing down on an egg. A detachment would go for the brain, too, and shred it like spaghetti in a blender. It had happened to Private Hammill, after he'd triggered a crawlnest in Cydonia.

He licked the paste of dead machines. "Take my head!"

"What?" I cried.

"I'm Saved. I'll come back."

"When was your last Save?"

He vomited messily, bile and blood hanging in syrupy tendrils from his chin.

"Eric! When was your—"

"Last month!"

I shook my head. *If I killed him, he'd come back with no memory of any of this. No memory of Drost's betrayal. No memory of what had transpired at Tier.*

"Segarra is sending a medevac," I said. "Deaden your nerves!"

"I've deadened everything I can!"

There was another cry from the crowd, this time coming from the ship's bow. I could see nothing where I crouched beside Eric, but my airhounds were still in their holding pattern. I linked with them and got a top-down view of the deck.

Debbie Drost had emerged from the bow stairwell. She was certainly a sight – splattered with pale dust like talcum powder. She was bleeding, too; blood caked in clownish lines from the corners of her mouth; the force of the crawlnest expulsion must have ruptured tissue.

She whirled, wild-eyed and panicking. The crowd screamed as the terrifying apparition dashed towards them and leapt over the deck rails with a piercing scream.

My airhounds plummeted after her into the mist. Telemetry pinged back: we were twenty meters above the canyon floor.

Drost had just committed suicide!

Or was she still alive down there? Twenty meters was a hell of a leap, but a properly augmented jump-rat could survive it.

Eric clutched at me. "Harris! Please, just…."

I turned back to him. "Sorry about this."

I deployed my shieldfist, shaped it into a spear-like configuration by manipulating the track-ball in my palm, and slammed it into his chest. Twice. One for each lung. Cracking through his EMP-resistant dermal layers.

Then I aimed into the holes I'd made and fired one EMP charge each. The detonations went off like sonar buoys, and Eric's head lolled.

"Freeze!" a voice shouted. I rotated to see a security officer standing behind me, pistol drawn.

In my right eye, the airhound feeds were a tri-paneled view of gray mist. Zipping above the canyon floor, fruitlessly searching for Drost's broken body.

Where the hell had she gone?

To Eric, I said, "I think I toasted the crawlnest."

"Suppose this makes us even," he murmured, barely conscious from pain and blood loss.

The security officer barked, "Get on your knees!"

I activated my blurmod.

The officer, to his credit, must have been primed for this move, because he fired the very microsecond I disappeared. The bullet whispered by my head as I dashed for the sandship rails. I cast one final look at Eric…

…and then I jumped.

Down into the fog.

Plummeting, as if fast-roping from Umerah's dropship.

Into the Noctis.

★　　★　　★

I landed hard – my legs' shock absorbers squealing from impact. Cartilage crunched; my nerve clamps thumped like over-cranked guitar strings. For a moment, I half-expected to see my old squad-mates landing around me, rappel cords in hand.

Like we'd done at Hellas. Hitting the tarmac. Sprinting into the shuttleport in a coordinated advance. Walking right into a goddam trap….

The canyon floor was strewn with boulders, exposed Martian geology carved by merciless erosion. The water vapor had added its own stylistic touches, producing icy, abstract shapes reminiscent of ferns, quills, and mammoth tusks. Down here was an unending protean art, the Martian day and night as rival artists toiling in ice and heat. An eternal contest of form and formlessness, like Penelope forever weaving and unweaving her tapestry.

I craned my neck to see the sandship moving on. My airhounds, denied anything in the way of helpful visuals, wheeled about in concentric, prescribed search patterns. Their feeds were gray smudges in the corner of my eye.

Now is what we own, Harris.

In the canyon's quiet, I cranked my audio to listen for footsteps. Sound carried poorly in the flat Martian air.

Fog.

Silence.

A gentle smell of sandalwood perfume.

I switched my view to thermal.

<Harris,> Xenophon said, <it is likely the target is lying in wait for you.>

How flattering. Maybe she just bugged out.

<Unlikely.>

Why?

<Because she knows you will never stop tracking her.>

I frowned at this unexpected editorial. *Why the hell would I never stop tracking her?* My subvocal speech skirted close to full audio, and I stiffened, realizing that if Drost was indeed waiting to ambush me, the slightest sound could betray my position..

My Familiar, however, had been asked a question. Its reply came straight away: <I do not have that information.>

The click of a skittering pebble caught my attention. I selected **PHOSPHIRE** and fired in that direction. Glowing fluid lit the fog, spattering the ground with incandescent puddles.

My blind hope was that I'd paint Drost wherever she was crouched. No such luck, though the spatter provided a new source of illumination, and my airhounds quickly zeroed in on a faint set of footprints.

A woman's footprints.

<Confirmed match with target,> Xenophon said, something like

excitement infusing its voice. <She is heading southwest. It appears she has been injured by her jump and is limping.>

★　　★　　★

In the seconds before leaping off the *Dandelion Wine*, I'd felt a kind of primal horror swarming my resolve. I'd already been a time traveler of sorts – jumping ten years in a subjective instant – and I imagined that by hurtling into the Noctis, I might somehow travel again through time. Not forward, but backward...

...to the Siege of Noctis.

Yet that hadn't happened. The Siege of Noctis could no longer harm me. It was in the past, and there was an entire generation who knew nothing about it or the war that had sired it. To my surprise, I found myself grinning.

Now is what we own.

The frosty breeze on my face, the fog scattering before me...*this* was my present reality. There were no platoons here. No turrets, tanks, or troops to trouble me. Memories unfurled, but they seemed like wind at my back. I had faced a forty-one-day siege and had survived it.

I would survive it now.

I dashed through puddles of phosphire, careful not to get spatters on my boots. Xenophon auto-outlined my quarry's footprints: she was making a beeline southwest, running at a decent clip despite an injured foot.

Then the footprints evaporated.

"She jumped," I guessed. "Changed direction and jumped."

Such a kangaroo hop wasn't possible on Earth. In the lower Martian gravity, enhanced muscles could propel a person beyond the immediate vicinity, despite her injury.

She knows I'm following her. Might have her own airhound in play.

Without warning, my blurmod ignited. I snapped open my shieldfist as a dozen rounds flattened against the barrier. Then I deflected them back.

A woman screamed.

My airhounds changed direction at once, converging on the sound.

I approached, shield out. The mist separated and I saw Debbie Drost on her knees, clutching her stomach. Her corporate tunic was no substitute for armor. Two rounds had caught her in the gut; dark blood spilled over her fingers. With her other hand, she gripped a pistol.

"Drop the gun," I commanded.

The weapon landed softly at her feet.

"I-I surrender," she stammered.

"Yeah? The way you surrendered on the ship?" Keeping my shield between us in case she had any more tricks down her throat, I said, "Your old boyfriend took that blast in the face, you know."

"It wasn't meant for him."

"Crawlnests aren't exactly a precision weapon."

"We can't all be you."

I eyed the canyon. "Where were you going, Deb? Gonna hobble out to the Face by yourself? Hate to break it to you, but you were heading in the wrong direction."

I saw the flicker of resistance in her eyes. Telltale signs of a patmatch program, readying a menu of anti-interrogation tactics, so I grinned at her. "I'm not surprised the Partisans had a contingency plan. That all traces to General Bishons. He liked plans atop plans, all hidden passageways, escape routes, and booby traps. People say he was the most brilliant strategist since Apollo the Great."

Drost's lips compressed into a thin line.

"He even had a failsafe contingency," I said. "Blew up the whole planet."

"The Partisans *didn't* nuke Mars!" she snarled. "They would never do that! They cared for this planet unlike any administration before. Unlike your fucking brother, who sells out our...*ah! AH!*"

Her scream could have shattered glass as I reached under my shield and slipped two fingers into her stomach.

"*Mercy!*" she cried.

"Mercy?" I echoed, withdrawing my dripping hand. "Badmouth my brother again and I'll show you the extent of my mercy."

Debbie had turned as pale as the residue on her lips.

"And by the way, your bosses *did* the nuke the planet."

"Propaganda!"

"I was *on* Phobos. I *heard* them talking about a fallback plan."

She gave a sick, blistering laugh. "A fallback plan? Of course there was a fallback plan! But it wasn't to fry Mars! The IPC must have hacked the defense grid!"

I shook my head. "The Partisans never took kindly to criticism. The Martian populace was rejecting them as word of their atrocities got out. So they—"

"The Martian populace loved us!"

"—decided to punish everyone."

"I don't believe that!"

"And that's *your* problem," I growled. "Your reliance on *belief*. Every example of mindless patriotism grows from a wellspring of *belief*. You weren't a political administration…you were a *cult*."

She settled into silence, face going as expressionless as the stones of Cydonia. I wondered if she was flooding her body with painkillers.

Or else shutting down. Activating a killswitch.

I pulled a tool from my belt. "See this, Deb? This is a magpie claw. It goes in through your eye, pushes into your brain. Scoops out memories. It's messy work. Nowhere near as good as a Save file. But it's effective enough. See, I'm guessing you have the means of terminating yourself here, trying to prevent me from taking your head intact. The magpie is designed to grab what it can, even from a brain that's self-destructing."

She made no expression.

"But your daughter, I'm sure *she* doesn't have a killswitch."

At last, a genuine emotion other than hate manifested on her face. "My daughter…?"

"If I don't get what I need from you, the Order will get it from her."

"She doesn't know anything!"

"But you do," I prompted. "Tell me who else came back. The day you left your bunker and 'discovered' a radio signal…you didn't just encounter Eileen. There were others."

"Monteiro was the only one in that bunker!"

"But you met the others. You knew about Peznowski."

"He came back in two bodies, yes. Told me he could get more work done that way."

I'm sure that was the reason, I thought sickly. "Who else?"

"Peznowski was the only one I personally met. But Monteiro mentioned that Sabrina Potts was resurrected on Luna."

"Why Luna?"

"I don't know."

"Tell me about the Face."

She hesitated, but when I reached for her stomach again she sputtered wildly, "It's our rendezvous point! We're all supposed to regroup there!"

"That's crap. The Cydonian Face is an open park. Not exactly the choice locale for a secret moot." I frowned. "Unless it's *not* the Cydonian Face, right? Eileen said the two of you were going offworld. So where offworld is this 'Face'?"

"I don't know!"

"Liar!"

"I swear! I'm not a general! Eileen was going to get us offworld, posing as workers."

"What workers?"

"For the Ten Thousand Worlds project! Hundreds of thousands of people from all over the system have been working on it."

I thought back to the advertisements I'd seen. "What is the Ten Thousand Worlds project?"

Debbie shook her head, shifting her body in a vain attempt at alleviating the pain from her gut-shot. "No idea, honest. Some gigantic construction project in space. Could be around the Sun. Or on Pluto. It doesn't matter, does it? So many people going into space…we figured we'd use the project as cover." She groaned when she saw the dark puddle of blood that had formed around her; by the glow of my shieldfist, our reflections stared back at us.

"If you had to guess where this Face is…." I prompted.

"Then I *guess* it's in the Jovian League. That would make sense, don't you agree?"

I looked back to the canyon. It did make sense. If I was part of the most wanted criminals in history, I'd want my regrouping point to be well outside brightworld influence.

That left the deeps.

The Jovian League was a shadowy rival to the brightworlds. Nearly a mini-solar system in its own right, with Jupiter acting as the local 'sun' around which the Galilean moons served as individual worlds. And the Belt, with its resources and opportunities, were within easy reach of Jovspace. Unexplored dots on a map. Lots of places to hide.

Technically, the Jovian League was part of IPCnet. Actual circumstances were complicated. The IPC was headquartered on Athens, and their focus – economically, politically, strategically – radiated from there. The deepworlds were remote, wild, less regulated. Local IPC offices held nominal control, sure, and IPC battleships patrolled the region like ominous sharks. Yet it was scattered territory. Harder to control, harder to monitor. You could charter a ship, locate a rock, claim it for your own, and strip-mine your way into fortune before state officials caught wind. The Belt was a viper's nest of piracy, privateering, and espionage. And the largest corporation in history – the planet-spanning Prometheus Industries – operated out there. Lots of corporations, legal and downright shady, jockeyed for power. Stealing, murdering, plotting in the void.

The perfect place for a safehouse, except....

"If you fucks are heading to the deeps," I said, "there has to be someone aiding you. A local partner of some kind. But who would risk that?"

Drost stared listlessly at her own reflection in blood, saying nothing.

I considered the possibilities. What offworld faction would dare assist the Partisans? No one gave a shit about Mars when we were at war with ourselves. The Partisans, isolationist freaks that they were, didn't give a shit about anyone else, either. All the fighting and dying had, in grand total, been a provincial spat. If someone was offering a helping hand, what did they have to gain?

I looked back to Drost. "Anything else?"

"No."

"We'll see, won't we?" I slapped my hand against her forehead and pinned her to the ground, while I maneuvered my other hand into place.

She went wild in terror. "Wait! Please!"

I realized my free hand was still gripping the magpie. "Oh, this? Relax, Deb, I'm not going to use the magpie on you. This was in case you had a killswitch…which I've figured by now you don't have. Besides, magpies aren't very effective. They grab a highlight reel of recent memories. Most of it would be useless. So really, I was just bluffing." I leaned close, met her pleading gaze. "But I do have something important to say. You listen, okay?"

She sobbed.

"You are Deborah Drost, a Partisan. You brutalized Mars. You captured and oppressed and tortured its people. You terrorized the populace with your shadowmen police. That ends today." I brought my hand closer, the shieldfist gauntlet mere inches from her neck. "I represent the Order of Stone. I am here to bring justice. I am here to show you that the injuries you inflicted upon Mars will not go unpunished. My name is Harris Alexander Pope, and I am the last thing you will ever see."

The decapitation was clean.

CHAPTER TWENTY-ONE

Solstice

There was a temptation to stay, submerged in the fog like some relic tossed into the sea. Which, all things considered, was about right.

For several minutes, I sat cross-legged on the canyon floor. Watching the sandships glide overhead, as if I were a marine biologist studying a pod of whales. Mars didn't have whales; our imported sea-life were fish and mollusks and crustaceans existing mostly in underground pools and household aquariums.

Sitting there, alone in purgatorial gray, I dialed back my combat suite and steeped in merciful solitude....

Harris? Are you receiving?

I sighed as Celeste's link appeared on my HUD. "Go," I replied.

What's your position?

"I meant 'go'. As in go away, Segarra."

A shape blotted the fog, less a whale than a manta making a slow, pelagic circle.

Harris, I've got an EVAC in your general area. Signal your location, okay? A hesitation. ***Mazzola's been air-lifted to Bickford Memorial. He's in critical condition, but they've got the best trauma ward on the planet.***

With a reluctance as heavy as iron slag I sent up my MPS location. Immediately, the manta-shape dipped below the fog-line and painted the canyon with floodlights. Dredging myself to my feet, gripping the cryobag that held Debbie Drost's head, I approached the hovering craft.

"Bickford?" I asked, climbing aboard. The EVAC was empty, lacking even a human pilot. "I was born at Bickford. Surprised it survived the nukes."

Celeste's signal transferred to the ship's audio system, sounding tinny through the wall speaker. "Well, it's in the heart of a mesa. The first colonists knew how to build things to last." I heard her take a breath. "Hey? Sorry about my attitude earlier."

I shrugged, realized she couldn't see the motion, and said, "No worries. The mission comes first, right?"

"We'll do everything we can to save Mazzola."

"Okay."

The EVAC soared out of the canyon. I leaned against the cool window, affording myself one final view of Noctis. Crooked black shapes, foggy channels, and sandships now as small as guppies. I strapped myself into a harness and said, "Take me to Bickford Memorial."

The speaker crackled. "Your presence is requested at the House of Laws."

"I decline the request."

"It's Solstice Eve, Harris. David wants you at the party. Lots of food, drink, VIPs. I'm there now, actually."

I glanced at the blood-spattered cryobag. "I'm not bearing the kind of gift that goes under a tree."

"Leave it on the copter."

"Not really in the mood to celebrate, Segarra."

"Come on, I'll buy you a drink."

"I'm covered in dirt, blood, and phosphire. I'd need a change of clothes."

"I'll buy you that, too."

I let out a weary, musical sigh. Should have stayed in the canyon, where I could continue imagining a life as a marine biologist. Instead, here I was talking to invisible goddesses and being whisked off on magic chariots.

"Okay, Segarra," I relented, stretching my wounded leg. My knee was warm where the medpatch nanites busied themselves weaving new cartilage and muscle. "A drink and a change of clothes, unless you

want me showing up to David's looking like a butcher. Do you need my measurements?"

"I've seen your DNA and neural patterns. I've got your measurements." An onboard 3D printer began to hum. "How about something in black?"

★　　★　　★

The annual House of Laws Solstice Party, glimpsed on descent, seemed a bizarrely alien destination. The grounds where my brother and I had enjoyed our picnic lay buried beneath a surf of guests; redworld elites and glitterati. Fire balloons festooned the event. The pair of algae trees were ablaze with their bioluminescent colonies like constellations of ruby and emerald light.

Dave awaited me on the helipad. Dressed in a formal purple toga, he watched me disembark.

"Mister President," I said.

He embraced me. The EVAC shot into the Martian dusk like a meteor in reverse. I briefly thought of its grim package: Drost's head on ice, being summoned to the technicians of heaven.

Not how she'd been planning on spending the holidays, I was sure.

"Welcome back, bro." Dave released me, steered me towards the gala. I limped alongside him. "That's a lot of people," I said.

"It's Solstice Eve."

"Still...."

The holiday crowd was largely garbed in bygone Sylvan styles I recalled from childhood, a veritable garden of ferns, hollies, daylilies, and bluebells. The bulk of attendees were representatives from the three houses – House of Guardians, House of Scholars, and House of Laws. I even glimpsed Natalia Argos, wearing a wasp-waisted vermillion tunic and – I observed with some amusement – elbow-length gloves hiding the wound I'd gifted her that morning. She noticed me, and promptly pretended she hadn't.

Yet there were offworlders in the mix, too, as sharply delineated from the natives as *katakana* script in a sea of *kanji*. Short-and-squat Earthers in pastel-hued togas. Graceful, wisp-like spacers. IPC military personnel in smoky blues trimmed with gold. An Earth senator in full Athenian raiment. In a way, it reminded me of the crowd from the sandship...a masquerade not of dust-masks (the House of Laws sat below the storm levees) but of professional smiles and floral wardrobes. For my part, I wore the black monastic livery that had unraveled from my EVAC's printer; there'd been just enough time to strip off my armor and dress into my new threads, the fabric still warm.

My brother linked his arm with mine. "Everyone's here. The beating heart of civilization."

"You're not kidding," I said, and to my amazement I recognized IPC Secretary of State Donna McCallister. The third most powerful human in the universe (right behind the IPC president and vice president), she sported a silver sequin toga; encircled by her administrative retinue, she called to mind the centerpiece of a metallic orrery with clockwork planets in orbit. To my surprise, her gaze found me. She nodded in greeting and – wonderingly – I nodded back.

"Stars, Dave!" I said as we continued on. "Isn't this a little much?"

He shrugged. "Plenty of sympathy for us right now."

"Still...."

"I sent invitations across the system, from Venus to the frontier." He lowered his voice to a whisper. "Made the invitations public, to pressure attendance. No one wanted to refuse lest it be seen—"

"As *insensitivity?*"

"Yep."

I shook my head. "Why do you care so much? Is Mars trying to host the Olympics?"

"Maybe. Come on, I want you to meet people."

The crowd split around our trajectory. A sea of strangers. I'd powered down my sensorium in the canyon, but now – out of sheer curiosity – I activated it and ID tags peppered the attendees like dialogue bubbles in ancient comic strips. A senator from the Venusian Republic. Industrialists from Luna. Corporate reps from TowerTech, AztecSky, Hanmura Enterprises...

…and Prometheus Industries.

Even without the ID bubbles, Promethean employees were impossible to miss in their green-and-silver tunics. There seemed an unusually high number of them, too. Like aphids in a garden. The Partisans had expelled all offworld corporations from Mars, so I assumed the Promethean presence meant they were back.

Before I could press David about this, he pointed ahead. "My family," he said. "I want you to meet them."

I balked. "Can I shower first?"

"You look fine."

"I'm more worried about how I smell."

"You smell fine, too."

It was like we were kids again – David leading the way along the beach to look for 'fossils' of Martian cryptids, like the fabled canal monster Penthi or the stone-like lizard Thoat. Twenty-five minutes earlier I'd been decapitating a woman. Going from that to a goddam party was more than a little disorienting.

So I let myself fall into my brother's wake, a derelict ship tugged into tango with a passing comet.

And then, quite by accident, I bumped into a miniature version of him.

A young boy, no older than eight-standard. Same chestnut curls as my brother's, cut in the Mediterranean style. High cheekbones, squarish face, cleft chin. His tunic displayed scarlet geometries on sable.

The boy's eyes were bright as he regarded me. "Hello!"

"Um…hi," I gasped.

"Where's your name?"

"My name?"

"Your ID," the boy pressed. "You don't have it on."

My eyes strayed to the bubble above him, where his name floated: RUDYARD SARGON POPE

"I'm Harris," I said. "And unless I'm mistaken, I'm your uncle."

David tousled the child's hair and grinned. "You're not mistaken."

"Uncle Harris," Rudyard said, trying out the words. A woman with short, pixie-style bangs approached. Her sun-blushed complexion formed an attractive contrast with the turquoise *nova gaelic* gown she wore; low-cut though not indecent, it flowed water-like as she moved. Her eyes were flecks of sea-glass. She held a young girl in both arms, identified as LUTHIEN DIDO POPE. Her own name was—

"Cassie," she introduced herself. "It's so good to finally meet you, Harris!"

"Um, thanks. The pleasure is mine."

While little Luthien stared curiously from her arm, Cassie Pope managed to herd Dave and me together and regard us with cheerful appraisal. "Stars, you both could be in holos! Seriously! The Pope brothers conquer Mars!"

Dave slung his arm around me. The crowd was taking notice of us, tuning in to the nameless visitor standing with the Martian president. It made me uncomfortable, and I glanced to the House of Laws, plotting a stealthy escape to some deserted room.

A little hand tugged my sleeve. I glanced down, seeing my nephew.

"Are you really my uncle?" asked Rudyard.

"I really am."

"Did you get me a present?"

"I did," I lied. "Did you get *me* one?"

The boy nodded fiercely. "Uh-huh!"

"Well then. I look forward to the gift-exchange tomorrow."

"What do you like? For presents?"

"Monsters."

"Monsters?"

"Yeah. Anything with monsters."

The boy's face set in tight concentration. He was pretending to be deep in thought, as if I'd said the most fascinating thing in the universe, but the telltale quiver to his eyes told me he was likely combing some online 3D printer catalog for appropriate purchase.

Cassie's sea-glass eyes sparkled. "I've wanted to meet you for so long, Harris."

"Wish I could say the same. Didn't know you existed until today." I felt a thrum of unaccountable anxiety. "Then again, I've been away...dead."

Her brow furrowed. "We have a lot to catch up on. You're going to stay with us now. I had a room made up just for you."

"That's very kind. When did Dave tell you I was coming back?"

"Saturday. He told me your Save file had been discovered in the rubble. He was almost in tears." Something of her earlier smile returned. "I must have listened to your broadcast fifty times on Victory Day. Kept playing it, over and over. Never thought I'd actually meet the man behind it."

"Or that you'd marry his brother," I managed, fighting sudden panic.

Xenophon broke in. **<Harris, your heart rate is accelerating. Shall I administer a sedative?>**

Cassie squeezed my arm. "We have so much to catch up on. The war hero! Elder of the Pope clan!"

"Point of interest," I rasped, "Dave is now older than me by seven years. Weird world, huh?"

<Harris, you are having a panic attack. May I suggest you retreat from the party?>

Ignoring this, I regarded my brother's wife and – for a hideous moment – imagined Peznowski's eyes staring back at me. Not just from her, but from my niece and nephew. From Dave, too. And from the crowd, revealing itself as a living masquerade under which Peznowski lurked, the Demon with a Thousand Faces.

Sickness bubbled in my throat.

I was outnumbered. Engulfed in a sea of unknown people. Even the few people I knew...how certain could I be?

I'd left my weapons on the EVAC!

My armor, too! I'd been tricked into wearing this monastic garment that could barely stop a splinter! I never should have come here. Should have stayed in the fog.

In the past.

Before I was aware of any conscious decision, I broke away from Dave and his family. Unable to breathe. Beset on all sides.

Heart attack.

I was going to drop dead of a heart attack. My fingers were pins-

and-needles. It made me think of the Phobos sock puppets. Razor fingertips. If the crowd attacked they'd eviscerate me in seconds. I'd vanish as if in an industrial blender.

I bumped into someone.

"Harris?"

"Celeste?"

The archon held my arm firmly, two inches above the elbow. "Can you do me a favor?"

"What?" I croaked.

"Count to ten."

I blinked.

"It'll help with the panic," she explained. "The others here may not realize what you're going through, but I saw it across the patio." She drew close. "It happens to me, you know? Too many stimuli, too many vectors. Count to ten, and I swear I'll beat the shit out of anyone who bothers you in the meantime. Please?"

A nasty, metallic taste flooded my mouth. My throat seemed to have irised shut.

Robbed of my voice, I nodded and counted, silently.

When I finished, I was sweating. Yet the counting had anchored me, with Celeste as my focal point.

I zeroed in on the details of her clothing. Gone was the granite-hued uniform she'd worn at the Bayne homestead; instead, she had come to the biggest party on the planet wearing Terran-style cargo pants and a white button-down shirt that hugged her figure well, despite looking like a warehouse supervisor's uniform.

"Why are you dressed like that?" I whispered.

She raised an eyebrow. "Excuse me?"

"I mean...sorry, but...."

"Not formal enough for you, Harris?"

I shrugged. "To be honest, I don't care."

"Good." A waiter approached with a tray of champagne. I grabbed one of the glasses.

Celeste frowned. "What the hell are you doing? I said I'd buy you a drink."

"What do you think this is?"

"Donkey piss, that's what I think."

"What's a donkey?"

She pulled the glass from my hand and flicked its contents onto the patio, nearly splashing one of the guests. "No vineyards survived the nukes. They all had to be planted fresh, which means the champagne is barely fermented soda pop. Come on, let's get you the real stuff."

★   ★   ★

"Just shut up and walk with me," Celeste said, pulling a flask from her leg pocket as we ranged beyond the courtyard, into the less-populated expanse of lawn. "There are things I want to tell you, so just listen, okay? I think it's horseshit how you've been treated. I know I'm partly responsible, but Dave is too, and this is my way of apologizing. So shut up, okay?"

I hadn't said anything since accompanying her away from the crowd. Glancing back, I spotted my brother searching for me.

Celeste knocked back a swig of her flask, handed it to me. I took a sip and gagged.

"Stars and storms!" The drink was like sipping from the putrid seepage of a rotten fruit. I gagged as the pulpy sludge crawled down my esophagus and hit my stomach. "What the hell is this?"

She took it back. "A taste of home."

"Not my home!"

"*My* home. Back on Earth. We homebrewed whatever fruit we could get – the sweeter the better. Add a little bread for yeast, and *voila*! Libations fit for Hades and Persephone!" She grinned, pointed to Deimos and Phobos. "Double-moonshine."

I shook my head. The drink was already shooting into my head like a neurotoxin. "So where are we headed, Segarra? Another assassination mission?"

Celeste looked as if I'd slapped her. "Okay, I deserve that," she managed. "But you need to appreciate *why* Dave threw you into one op after another. It wasn't really his choice."

"He's president of fucking Mars, Segarra."

"He's not a fucking warlord, Harris."

Again, my gaze strayed to the courtyard. Dave was no longer in sight, lost in a colorful sea of people. They looked like an *avante garde* theatrical play: the House of Laws as enormous backdrop, the courtyard as the stage, the algae trees an eccentric lighting experiment, the actors in costume. A few couples had wandered off, and I caught glimpses of them in pockets of woodland privacy, clothes shorn away.

I turned back to the archon. "My missions were sanctioned by the president. How did he not have a choice?"

Celeste took another swig of her Wasteland hooch, imbibing like it was some full-bodied red from the south of France. "There was political resistance to your return."

"What resistance?"

"You were a Partisan."

"I was *playing* the *role* of a Partisan!"

"Sure. But you played it well. Too well, by some estimates. Went full Mister Hyde."

I snatched the flask back from her. "So I've got a scarlet letter over my head for all time?"

She shook her head. "What you've been doing, hunting those bastards down…we needed it done, and you really were the best person for the job. Shit, Harris, you mopped the floor with everyone you faced in the past forty hours, including Tier Marsworks security. *Obviously* you were the best person for the job. But this was also proof that you weren't a Partisan anymore. Sending you after your old masters exonerated you in skeptical eyes."

"I ended the goddam war!"

"Sure…and a few hours later, Mars was nuked into oblivion."

"So? They think *I* had something to do with that?"

She shrugged. "Some do, some don't."

"What do *you* think?"

Celeste met my gaze with a painfully frank honesty. "I think you're a war hero. Full stop."

"Good. Because I'll tell you what, archon: *I'm done now*. Even the slaves of Rome could buy their way out of servitude, and I've more than paid my tab. From this day forth, you subcontract your goons from another pool."

Celeste had an interesting way of listening. She carried her head in a sidelong fashion, ear toward me, as if measuring each word. Resuming her pace, suddenly arm-in-arm with me, she charted a roughly elliptical route around the grounds; the Solstice trees interlaced in parallax as we went.

"What *are* your plans, now that you're retiring?" she asked, as we passed beneath a flowering trellis. Absently, she touched the creeping ivy, brought a pliable vine across her face, and peeked at me between its leaves.

Mirroring this, I pulled a vine across my own face, a heathen in Dionysian dark, hidden by bramble for a peek at Artemis bathing. "Apparently I've been given quarters at the House of Laws."

"Oh?"

Through the trellis, I glimpsed the building. Figures I'd come back from the dead to live inside a giant spider. From a distance, the courtyard gala seemed like bits of incandescent gas swirling around a nebula's young heart.

"It's not going to be your brother's house for long," Celeste said, following my gaze. "David's term is up next year."

"Any predictions on who the next president will be?"

"You won't like who's polling to run."

"Oh?"

"Natalia Argos."

I downed another throat-scalding gulp from the flask. "Well then. She won't get my vote."

Celeste laughed. It was an unexpectedly delightful sound. "Mine either. Argos was a good soldier during the war, but I think she's a lousy human being." She gave me another sidelong look. "What do you want for Solstice, Harris? If you could have anything, what would it be?"

I took a breath and the answer poured out of me. "I want to delete my memories of the last twenty years. I want the last thing I remember to be the yacht – the time and place where I decided to get my brains scrambled. I want everything after that – my time as shadowman, reactivation, *everything* – gone. I want to wake up fresh." I regarded her. "You and I will be strangers again. Not that we really knew each other anyway."

Celeste nodded thoughtfully. "That can be arranged. All this—" she waved her arm around, indicating the grounds, "—can disappear for you."

We walked onward. "What about *you*, Segarra?" I asked. "You're a fucking cipher if I've ever met one."

She wove in and out of a neat line of Italian cypress trees. "What does it matter, Harris? You won't remember."

"Rumor is you were at the center of all that weird shit on Earth."

"Afraid you'll have to be more specific."

"The Incident of 322," I clarified. "Some kind of first-contact situation, right? People insist that AIs were behind it, but there are plenty of alternate theories."

She halted, taking back her flask. "That's a long story. Not one I want to share."

"You were involved in it, though," I pressed. "Your name was all over the newsfeeds. You and that guy I brought to Phobos."

"Gethin Bryce." She said the name softly. "Yeah, he and I had ourselves a merry adventure on Earth."

"I'm sorry."

She raised an eyebrow. "Why? We came out of it okay."

I gaped at her. "He fucking died on Phobos, Segarra."

She beamed. "Think so?"

"I *know* so! He was up there when the reactor exploded. Everyone died."

"He escaped."

"The hell he did!"

Celeste rounded another cypress and said, "Gethin Bryce is a conniving, shrewd, and strategic genius, and often a major pain in the ass. But the guy is a survivor. You've no idea the enemies he's gone up against. Frankly, you can't imagine it. He *volunteered* to be bait for you, Harris. The Order of Stone needed an excuse to get you to Phobos, and Gethin needed a way to get offworld."

"But—"

"I had a ship." She was breathing heavily, her words spooling out in rapid confession. "Back on Earth, I flew a vessel called the *Mantid*. It was an example of supreme artificial intelligence. One of several that existed back then. Created by AIs and leased to a group I belonged to."

This stunned me. "I knew there used to be an AI city on Earth," I said. "Didn't realize they'd partnered with anyone. What...what group was this?"

She watched me with hooded eyes. "Let's call them would-be revolutionaries. People from the Wastes who'd had enough of the apartheid. Those who were denied everything arkies took for granted: the longevity treatments, basic medicines, and opportunities of the elite." She grinned icily. "See, the IPC is all about preservation of humanity. Really fucking noble...except the unspoken sidebar is 'preservation of the status quo'. Maybe they started off with good intentions three centuries ago. Earth was a wreck back then: radiation, viruses, transgenic predators, antimatter bombs, waspbots keyed to gang turf." Her movements took on an aggressive energy – no longer a wistful wander through the garden, but a steely patrol. Her words, too, were suddenly lapsing into a subtle accent I'd never heard before.

"The arcologies," she snapped, "were protected enclaves. In time, they united into a global government."

"So?"

"So they did what all governments do: they based their power on fear. *That's* why the Colonization Ban exists."

"I thought the Ban was to protect us from malevolent aliens."

Celeste nodded. "Except we don't know if aliens exist. The IPC consolidated power by stoking fear. That's how they justified the AI purge."

I met her gaze. "The ship you mentioned…the *Mantid*. It survived the purge, didn't it?"

Celeste's eyes became distant, focusing on a point of lost history. "Yes," she said. "It's the last of its species, in a way. Hiding out from the IPC."

"And that's how Gethin Bryce fled Earth? Back when I was a kid, he was the most wanted fugitive in the universe. He smuggled himself to Mars. You *both* fled to Mars—"

"By way of an AI ship capable of advanced camouflage and evasive strategies."

A dark thought crept through my mind. "Why Mars?"

She gave an incredulous look. "Where else would we go?"

"Mars was part of IPCnet at the time," I pressed. Connections were coming fast, outpacing my conscious thoughts. "You and Bryce fled to Mars…and then Mars conveniently seceded."

"You want to know if Gethin and I triggered the secession. If we were behind the Partisan movement."

"You're goddam right I do!"

"Yes."

For a moment, I wasn't sure I had heard her correctly. My head swam with drink. My galloping thoughts took a turn for the surreal, made potent by the spectral moonlight.

What did she mean, 'Yes'?

"What do you mean, 'Yes'?"

Celeste sighed in a resignation suggestive that she had been anticipating this moment. "Gethin and I orchestrated the secession of Mars," she said, lifting her eyes to meet the fury in my own. "We were behind the Partisans."

CHAPTER TWENTY-TWO

Habitats

Holotours were a classroom staple, as teachers supplemented syllabi with VR walkabouts through literary, historical, or contemporary landscapes. I recalled a history class I'd taken in high school during which the teacher led us on a holotour of Tuscany, Italy. There was nothing on Mars resembling that pastoral tranquility. I remember finding the neat, side-by-side rows of cypress trees particularly fascinating. Those trees, our teacher explained, marked ancient Roman roads; the empire had planted them to provide shade for armies on the march. The roads were long gone, swallowed up by weeds and earth, though the cypress trees continued to mark the way. I remembered absorbing this knowledge in awe, juxtaposing the serene horizon with the violence implicit in the vegetation.

That same abrasive contrast possessed my drunken thoughts as I regarded the archon, cypress trees around us like green spearpoints. In the distance, the gala was like a distant music box.

"Tell me," I growled, "why I shouldn't kill you right now."

Celeste held out her arms, legs spaced apart. It wasn't a fighting stance. Quite the opposite; an open display of vulnerability tinged with a plea to listen. To listen! My mind raced to find reasons why I should ever listen to her again.

"Bishons," she said, breathing shallow, "Potts, Monteiro, Peznowski, Kleve – the whole rotten gaggle – we had *nothing* to do with them! Mars had been stewing for rebellion for years. Gethin and I merely stoked that fire. Took a culture of loose communities and gave them a political voice. We dialed up the heat…and watched the water turn to steam."

"You fomented a *war* to hide from the cops?" I cried.

"That's a distortion of the truth. We fomented war as a desperate, last-ditch effort at derailing something terrible."

I squared off to her. "*Something terrible* is what happened on Mars, due to *your* actions!"

"I agree." Celeste was sweating, standing poised between rich shadows and interlacing moonlights, a compositional chiaroscuro image. "And yet it was better than what the IPC was planning."

"What were they planning?"

"Do you know *why* Gethin is a fugitive? He was a special investigator with the IPC. He discovered something he wasn't supposed to: a hideous plan gestating from their elite. My guess is that it had been gestating a long while, but the events of 322 – the close brush with war – convinced them to move it from drawing-board to implementation. There was no other way, Harris! Someone had to throw a wrench in their plans. Mars was the only viable option."

"What plans are you talking about?"

"I can't tell you that."

"Fuck you, Segarra." I spun away, not knowing where I was going except that it needed to be away from her.

She seized my arm; I seized her back and pitched her between two cypress trees. We fell together, the branches clawing at us. I collapsed atop her, and she fisted her hand in my tunic, holding me firm as I gripped her throat.

"We didn't want the Partisans in charge!" she insisted. "That *wasn't* the plan! Revolutions can be necessary, Harris, but they rarely go according to plan."

"The understatement of the fucking century!"

"You don't understand! The Order of Stone was supposed to channel MarsAlone sentiments into a rational, sovereign government."

My face was inches from hers; I could smell the sour odor of her alcohol-tinged breath. "So what the hell happened?"

Celeste gave a bitter, empty laugh. Like the clanging of a bell in a dusty attic.

"What happened," she said, "was that we underestimated the ugly truth of the human race. What did I tell you ten years ago in that hotel?"

The memory was only a few days old for me. "You said, 'You want rationality and consistency? Sorry, but you joined the wrong species.'"

"Our plan – Gethin and me and a few others – was hijacked by extremists. A cabal of xenophobic assholes built a cathedral of hate and sadism upon the foundation *we* established. The Order of Stone was swept aside in favor of the Partisans' more extreme interpretation. The election of 325 saw Mars seceding, sure, but with *maniacs* leading the charge. The pogroms, secret police, death camps? None of that was part of our plan."

I slackened my fingers from her throat. "If you invite pyromaniacs to a party, don't be surprised when they burn your house down."

She hadn't released my tunic. One of her legs locked behind me, holding me in place. "We didn't invite them."

"The hell you didn't. You courted the same constituency, Segarra, but lost the branding war. 'We will secede peacefully and make a rational government' isn't as catchy as 'Burn down the fucking sky.'"

The hollow, thousand-yard stare had returned to her gaze. "We found that out the hard way."

I shook my head, my wrath swallowed by disgust. "Sounds like even harder lessons are in store for you. From what I've seen, Mars is poised to rejoin IPCnet; there's a vote early next year. Whatever nefarious plan the IPC was hatching will surely come to pass. Talk about a Pyrrhic victory."

My words dispelled some of the darkness in her eyes. "It's not over yet," she said.

"The Partisan War *is* over."

"I'm not talking about the Partisan War. Gethin is alive. For the last ten years he's been orchestrating—"

"Another fucking war?" I snapped.

"Something more impactful than war."

"Maybe I *should* kill you, Segarra. Seems the universe would be a safer place without you." I tried pulling away from her, but she wrapped another leg around my waist. She was feeling the drink – I suppose we both were. Her flush cheeks weren't the only indication, either; the friction of her body against mine had taken on a deliberate rhythm. I realized I was sporting an erection so stiff it throbbed, and by the glimmer in Celeste's eyes, she was well aware of it.

I glanced around the shadow-drenched gardens. We were alone. The only illumination came from the sky; the moons, stars, and greenish blush of auroras. There was another light there, too. The pale presence of Jupiter among the constellations....

"The Jovian League," I said. "If Bryce really escaped, the best place for him to go would be the deepworlds. Your *Mantid* couldn't rescue him from Mars, because even a CAMOed ship makes an entry-bloom, and the planetary defense network would have shot it down. That's why he needed to get to Phobos."

"Yes."

"And from Phobos, the *Mantid* slipped in and grabbed him."

"Slipped in," she echoed, her free hand sliding between us, "and grabbed him." She cupped my erection and I gave an involuntary groan. Her other hand pulled me towards her lips.

Our first kiss was soft and ethereal. Like kissing in a dream. Our lips lingered over the heat of our mouths. She undid the buckle on her pants with one hand; I gripped the belt loops and tugged them over her hips; in the same instant, she slid my tunic off my body. The night air was cool on my back.

Celeste kicked off her pants, skinned out of her top. The sight of her nude body made my breath catch. Organic architecture like a sleek Gothic cathedral, rib and groin vaults, the masonry of her blueworld muscles, the rapid tolling of her pulse within her chest cavity. As her hand stroked me, I buried my face in her neck, exploring her with my lips...the clear lines of her collarbones, the twin slopes of her breasts. She gave a delighted cry when I took one nipple in my mouth, my tongue drawing wet circles as I suckled, my free hand mirroring the movements on her other breast.

She rolled me over. Her hair was a wondrous mess as she straddled my hips, her hand continuing to grip my cock by the base. Framed by starlight, she became a silhouette, so I shifted my optical spectrum and there she was in thermal view; breasts upturned, swollen nipples as large as cherries.

Positioned atop me, she took in my first couple inches. Held herself there, eyes closed in rapt concentration, teasing herself with the tip of my member. I grunted softly, transfixed by this woman, the Martian night behind her, the aurora-tinged sky like Thessalonian wings from her shoulders.

We pressed to each other, discovering a steady, mutual pace that kept us both on the edge, a looping indulgence of desire and denial. We were a single machine keyed to one impulse, seeming to shapeshift as we changed positions, forestalling the inevitable as best we could. My hands ran along her spine. The shadow woman and the shadowman. I flipped her around, pinning her to the gravel path between trees. She clasped herself around me, raising her hips in an escalating crescendo. Her climax took over her entire body, head back, grunting, swearing, nails like flesh-hooks in my back.

When I finally came, it seemed I was unraveling inside her.

★   ★   ★

She lay in the crook of my arm, head against my chest. The night had grown colder, and in absence of sheets I drew my tunic around us. Our afterglow was steeped in the timeless, wordless epoch that is the epilogue of pure and perfect sexual chemistry.

At last, she said, "Your brother is about to send out a search party. He's been pinging me as to your whereabouts."

"Tell him you're debriefing me."

"Ha freakin' ha." Celeste peered into my face. She looked younger than she had moments ago. Innocent was never a word I'd breathe in the same sentence as her name, but I thought there was a vulnerability peeking out from her armor. How much of that toughened exterior, I wondered, came from emotional scabs that had calcified over her life? How much was forcible projection? Or was it like shifting gears for her – reading the terrain and adjusting accordingly?

Not that my own experience was to be dismissed so lightly. From shadowman to paladin to teenager to combatant to party guest of dubious honor, it made for a Moebius strip: one consciousness remade and reactivated, then Saved and destroyed, then reborn and wet-transferred.

"How do you think the *Mantid* rescued Bryce?" I asked suddenly.

Celeste blew strands of hair out of her face. "And here I thought we'd moved past that discussion."

"Is that what you were trying to do by fucking me?"

"No. I just wanted to fuck you."

"So how did the *Mantid*—"

"My guess is that she probably shadowed your Lofstrom pod…from orbit to docking. An AI ship can run cold. Invisible to optics and thermals. She would have trailed you in. Bryce could have gotten aboard before the explosion. The hangar doors were open as you left, remember?"

I rolled over and propped my head up with one hand. "Trailed my pod," I repeated. "Without detection? No CAMO in the world is that good."

"The *Mantid* was created by the most advanced AIs in history. Trust me, it's that good."

"Not good enough to save its species."

She pursed her lips. "Perhaps not. But then again, we really don't know, do we? The IPC *claims* to have destroyed them all…but they barely understood what they were dealing with. Maybe some AIs survived. Like dragons, deep in the jungles or seas or caves. Taking up residence on uninhabited islands. Waiting with a patience humanity will never possess or comprehend."

I stroked her face. "The *Mantid* took Bryce to the deepworlds, didn't it?"

She said nothing. My fingers gently scraped the top of her chest and she gasped pleasantly.

"What did he discover more than thirty years ago?" I pressed. "What made him go AWOL?"

"It's not up to me to break that secret, Harris."

"Is it the Ten Thousand Worlds project? I've been seeing the teasers all over the web, but no one seems to know what it is."

"That's not the reason he went AWOL. But I can tell you what that project is."

"What is it?"

"Habitats."

I frowned. "Habitats? You mean space stations?"

She rolled towards me, mirroring my posture. "I mean colossal artificial habitats capable of housing millions, even billions or trillions, of people. The biggest space stations ever constructed. Self-contained O'Neill cylinders, rotating to create perfect gravity."

"'Perfect gravity' is an awfully subjective phrase."

"Well, the IPC is building a fuck-ton of these things. I'm guessing some will be dialed to Terran G's, others to Martian or Lunar."

I tried picturing what she was describing. "So that's how they're going to address the overpopulation issue? They have no intention of overturning the Ban, so they're creating worlds right here?"

"Yep." Celeste sat up and fished for her clothes.

I watched her dress. "Why not just let people spread into the universe?"

"Because they would lose control of us."

"Come on! It can't be that simple."

She looked back at me with open amusement. "Oh no? Faster-than-light travel is impossible. If humanity shatters and scatters, the IPC becomes irrelevant. They've maintained absolute stewardship for three hundred years. Spreading beyond that sphere of control terrifies the shit out of them. It goes beyond the worry that the galaxy might contain nasty aliens. If we spread into the universe, we'll change. Genetically, culturally…we'll fracture into a thousand separate subspecies. The word 'human' will lose all practical meaning."

I shook my head. "That word has lost all meaning anyway."

She slid into her pants. Watching her sent blood rushing back to my loins. I wanted to be inside her again.

Celeste stood, topless, and fumbled with her shirt. She pointed to a star that, according to my knowledge of the firmament, shouldn't have been there. "You can see the vanguard of that plan already. A massive O'Neill cylinder built several years ago. It's called the *Coachlight*."

I beheld the distant light. "A single O'Neill cylinder is one thing. But ten thousand of them? Come on, Segarra! That would take decades!"

"One decade, and millions of workers, to be precise. At least to create the first batch. I don't know if 'ten thousand' is hyperbole or the end-goal." She noticed my renewed erection, and grinned. "I'd love to stay," she purred, in a tone that suggested she really meant it. "But I have things to do."

"You could do me again."

She leaned into my lap, took the head of my cock into her mouth, and gave a quick suction of the glans. Then she peered up at me. "You really going to erase your memories?"

"Yes."

She sighed, stuck out her hand. "Guess this is goodbye then. It's been nice working with you, war hero."

I shook her hand. "We might run into each other again, who knows? Mars is a small planet."

"We won't see each other again," she said decisively. "I'm leaving Mars at the end of the week."

"You are? Where are you...oh." The answer was obvious. "You're going to the deepworlds. Gonna see your fugitive buddy and cook up another war."

"Not another war."

"Right...something 'more impactful' than war, whatever the hell that means." I hesitated. "You *could* come back someday."

She folded her arms and considered me. "'I left the woods for as good a reason as I went there. Perhaps it seemed to me that I had several more lives to live, and could not spare any more time for that one.'"

"*Walden* again," I said, stricken by her imminent departure. "Do you always make decisions based on fifteen-hundred-year-old American diaries?"

"Good advice is good advice, irrespective of age."

"A cipher," I grumbled. "You're a fucking cipher, Segarra."

Despite my air of calm, her words caused me a thrum of panic as my world's tenuous stability was sliding into new configurations. It was ridiculous, of course; I barely knew her, and our history was as rapid-fire as everything else. Nonetheless her impending disappearance burned like a hot coal in my heart.

"When are you shipping out?

"End of the week."

"The *week*?"

Celeste's forehead creased. "There a problem?"

"Of course not," I said quickly. "You ever been to the deeps?"

"There's a first time for everything. How much worse can it be than anywhere else?" She stared at me awhile. "You could...."

"Could what?"

She hovered on the cusp of confession or revelation. Then she smirked, mouth twisting sideways. "Never mind. Goodbye, Harris Alexander Pope."

I watched her saunter off. She didn't return to the party, but melted into darkness.

"Hey, Xenophon," I mumbled. "You there?"

<Yes, Harris.>

"Were you listening to all that?"

<You suggested that my eavesdropping aroused your discomfort.>

"Were you listening to all that?"

<Yes.>

"What do you think she was going to say there, at the end?"

<I assign an eighty-one-percent likelihood that she was going to say: "You could come with me.">

"Say it in her voice."

<That would be a violation of likeness rights.>

I closed my eyes. The warmth of Celeste's body, her smell, the immediate memory of our time together, hung around me like a pleasant energy. "Say it anyway."

<"You could come with me.">

Of course, that was a silly idea. Why would I leave Mars? The bad guys were dead and I was back with my brother. It was time to settle down. To feel Mars beneath my feet. I sure as hell wasn't going to relocate because of a woman I barely knew.

Stretching languidly, tucking my faltering erection to the side, I considered the idea anyway. The only logical reason to accompany Celeste to the deeps would be to follow up on what Debbie Drost had told me: that the Partisans were reconvening offworld. As intel went, it was barely more than gossip. Besides, I knew enough of the Belt and Jovian Leagues to understand they were a jungle forest of hiding places.

Still…I might be able to pick up a trail.

A message from Dave suddenly pinged my sensorium.

Hey bro? Where are you? That was kind of rude, bugging out the way you did.

Sorry, I said.

Come on back. The party's wrapping up.

I dressed into my tunic, and hesitated. My brother had made me wait thirty years. He could wait a few minutes longer for me.

With a wave of my hand, I connected to the redweb and found the link for Bickford Memorial Hospital. The operator put me through to Eric Mazzola's room.

His gravelly voice muttered, "What the hell do *you* want?"

"Happy Solstice, Mazzola!"

"Fuck."

"Don't know if you're up for that right now. But I wanted to see how you were doing." The link in my optics flicked to a hospital feed; an overlay of Eric in his recovery bed, hooked up to an IV. He looked ghastly – a bloodless, scarred Grendel banded by leech-like medpatches feeding nanites into his injuries. The doctors had removed his facial piercings and chains; I wondered if the nanite treatments were going to heal the holes. His mohawk fell flat to one side.

Eric tried sitting up in bed, but grunted in pain and stayed where he was. "This is how I'm doing, you bastard."

"Glad the medevac got to you in time."

"Me too."

"Did the cops ask you to make a statement?"

"I said I didn't want to press charges."

"Considering that I pressed charges *into* you…I wouldn't blame you."

"Well, you did save my life."

"Your life was already Saved. I just didn't want you to come back without the fun memories we've made. And if you'd died on the sandship, it would be ten whole hours before you returned."

He shook his head. "Trogs don't get priority resurrections. Ten *days*, is more likely."

"Better than ten years."

He grimaced. "For what it's worth, I'm sorry for what you've been through."

I shrugged, genuinely unconcerned with all that. Amazing what a good fuck can do for your mood. "I'm not going to dwell on the past, Eric. Time flows in one direction. You can't step twice in the same river…you know, all that stuff."

Eric's violet eyes narrowed. "You sound oddly refreshed. Something I should know about?"

"It's been the strangest day of my life."

"And that's saying something."

I walked towards his bed. He couldn't see me; there were no cameras or airhound feeds to transmit my image. "What's your prognosis?"

He glanced dubiously to the datapad on his nightstand. "They've scrubbed the crawlnest from my lungs, and pumped nanites to repair the bronchial tissue. I'll be tip-top in a couple days. Not how I wanted to spend the holiday, but we don't always get what we want."

"Now is what we own," I agreed. "And you've still got a job at Tier."

"Not for long."

"Oh?"

"I'm giving my notice. Can't work for them anymore."

"It's still a legit company. With Monteiro gone…."

But he shook his head vigorously. "I worked within spitting distance of that murderous bitch. And Debbie...." He trailed off. "I'll never set foot in there again."

"So what are your plans?"

"What are *your* plans?" he asked with interest. "I can hear it in your voice. Something happened, didn't it? You're all charged up."

"Am I?" In the distance, I watched my brother and House of Laws security draw an ever-expanding search pattern that reminded me of a supernova. "I've got some things to consider. Listen, I'm going to let you go. Have to get back to the party."

Eric stared. "Party? You practically de-lung me, shoot up my workplace, and then go to a *party*?"

"Believe it or not, I was following orders."

"That's a shitty excuse." He hesitated. "There are more Partisans, aren't there?"

"Yeah."

"You know where they are?"

"I know where to start." My eyes lifted to the sky and the diamond glint, like a far-off lighthouse, of the *Coachlight*.

PART FOUR
AGENT

How much longer will you allow Earth to rule your lives?

Why should a distant blue speck exert control over you, your children, and your future? Earth is NOT the center of the solar system...but WE are!

Out here, we have freedom!

Out here, we have community!

Out here, we are the future!

—Pamphlet from the 'Jovian Liberation Front'

CHAPTER TWENTY-THREE

Deepworld Greetings

I awoke to find myself hanging upside down like a bat, a harness banding my chest. My legs dangled over an unlit space. It might have been a cave – there were innumerable cave systems on Mars, and many of these were still unexplored despite an influx of eager spelunkers from around the solar system. The air was cold. From somewhere in the blackness, a snake hissed warningly.

I had no idea where I was.

Peter's bedroom in the Bayne homestead? My CAMO tent in the field? Or had I fallen asleep aboard Umerah's dropship and was dreaming that I was Sinbad in the valley of serpents? Maybe one of those reptiles was slinking towards me, jaws unhinged to swallow me.

Each hypothesis fell away. I fingered the harness, feeling strangely lightheaded. My blood seemed to be pooling in my head.

Someone coughed in the dark. Creaks and confused murmurs percolated the cave – or wherever this was – and rose above the relentless hissing.

Had I died again?

I must have died again…and other dead people were awakening around me.

★ ★ ★

As the year 358 had drawn to a close, I'd been living in the House of Laws' residential leg, in a guestroom just two doors down from my brother and his family. The days had settled into a kind of gray routine: every morning we took breakfast together in the residence's tearoom, after which Dave would be whisked off to various meetings until, around 1300, he'd summon me to his presidential office for lunch. The Pope brothers would eat together on the floor, sitting cross-legged on the Order of Stone seal while slurping pho, sushi, pasta, cutlets, and rice, or whatever else struck our fancy.

Throughout, Dave refused to talk about current events; considering they were his constant focus as president, I couldn't blame him. Rather, he wanted to review the past with me – the *good* past, the past of our childhoods. Beaches, lighthouses, games in the family den, recess yards, ice cream, and vacations. A lost age in which the Pope family was the center of our universe and everything else an abstract concept with little bearing on our lives.

After lunch, Dave would courteously eject me from his office as his duties resumed. I wouldn't see him again until dinner. We'd eat, and play tabletop games or watch holos. Dave, Cassie, Rudyard, little Luthien... and me.

All things considered, the days weren't bad.

Nights were a different tale.

My guestroom was cozy enough. I had my own bathroom, a soft mattress, plenty of books, a pilotchair (which I never used), and a single window (which I never opened). Safe and secure accommodations.

Yet every night I awoke in a frantic, sweating panic. Reaching for my rifle. Not finding it. Lying silent, trying to remember where I was. Straining for signs of danger. Terrified that I had made another involuntary hop through time.

By the fifth night, I'd taken to leaving the bathroom light on and the door slightly ajar. The resulting vertical glow became a visual anchor for me, a grounding element to help me recall where and when and who I was.

★   ★   ★

I searched in vain for that vertical light. Instead, a host of luminous dots were kindling like wary constellations. Wrist-lights! Blooming all around me, they revealed that I wasn't in a cave. People were stirring awake, strapped into seats lining the concave space of an interplanetary shuttle's main cabin and....

The shuttle!

I conjured my opticlock – 6:14 a.m. January 24, 359 – and it all came rushing back.

After eight days as my brother's guest, I'd booked passage aboard VG Flight 9956, Mars to Ganymede. He hadn't taken my decision well. I'd just gotten back, he maintained. Why was I leaving? I mustn't be thinking clearly! Why was I so eager to flee...and to go offworld at that?

Cassie especially was determined to get to the bottom of my decision, and she went from questioning me to bartering with me, as if the matter was a high-level negotiation. She probed ("Why don't you just talk to us?"), offered bribes ("We can get you a bigger room!"), and tried cramming activities into my schedule ("You need to keep busy, Harris!"). The night before my departure, she apparently lost patience and snapped, "Fine – why don't you just *tell* us what you want?" As if I hadn't told her already.

What I wanted, I explained for the thirtieth time, was to go offworld.

She stared at me with pure disbelief. Even the next morning, when the PDT arrived to take me to the shuttleport, Cassie seemed to be expecting some last-minute confession or demand.

Officially, David pulled strings for me. The Order assigned me a new undercover identity – Bellerophon Rybka from Haiwiki Falls. In this capacity, I was going to the deeps as one-half of Celeste Segarra's personal security detail, with Eric Mazzola constituting the other half. We met in the departure terminal that morning. Rode the S-E to the docking station. Checked our luggage.

And launched for the deeps.

Now, I looked at the shuttle passengers hanging in their seats. I listened to the hissing sound which could only be....

"Oxygen," I said aloud. "We're losing oxygen."

"It's worse than that," someone grunted beside me.

By the dappling glow of wrist-lights, I saw Eric in my neighboring seat. The trog had already undone his harness and was perching, like a ninja preparing to drop down from rafters.

"Eric! What the hell happened?"

"They shot us out of the sky."

"*They?*" I asked. "Who are *they?*"

"Don't know." He scratched his face, jingling the chain looping from his right nostril to the corresponding ear. "But whoever they are, they're demanding our surrender."

★　　★　　★

It had been a three-week voyage from redspace to the Jovian League. Three weeks so uneventful that the days had bled into one another. Most of my fellow passengers spent it in virtual, plugged into creche wetports when they weren't hitting the gym. Some stayed plugged in there too, while they pedaled or jogged with clouded eyes and drooling mouths.

For my part, I settled into a strict routine. Awakening at 0500 each morning, I'd run the ship's rotating torus for an hour. This was followed by two hours at the gym, surrounded by semi-conscious dreamers. Next was a sonic shower before taking breakfast at 0830 sharp, after which I'd devote a few hours to personal studies – learning what I could about the political, cultural, corporate, economic, and environmental ingredients that gave the deepworlds their distinctive flavor; there were travel advisories aplenty, and I read them, external links and all. At 1400, I'd meet Eric and Celeste for lunch. By 1600, I'd plug into virtual and work my way through an array of VR target-practice scenarios – open battlefields and close-quarters combat, tweaking the gravity value to deepworld standard. That would end by 1800, when I'd go on another run of the torus.

For his part, Eric joined me for my evening run and virtual training sessions. We ran scenarios that escalated in challenge and mixed up the variables. Sometimes we were outnumbered by ten, twenty, or thirty NPC opponents. We fought on the rings of Saturn, on recreations of Earth's Wastelands, on Venus, on Luna. Sometimes we'd win...and sometimes we'd lose until we figured out how to win. Three weeks into the voyage we had scaled our practice to fifty opponents with gravitational conditions that toggled every five minutes.

And Eric was a good soldier. Excellent tactical instincts. Cool under fire.

He never asked me about Debbie Drost. Never inquired into her final moments in the Noctis. Considering what was trending on the newsfeeds, I suppose he didn't need to.

Back on Mars, the cover story used to explain the Baynes' executions was coming apart at the seams. The citizens of North Hellas were demanding to know where their duly elected leader was; robo-dog incident aside, the governor and his wife should have been resurrected within a day or two. Three weeks later, they were still MIA. The Martian Justice Bureau issued a public statement: the deaths had been declared a matter of Planetary Security and classified as part of an ongoing investigation. It would buy a little more time...but only a little.

As for Peter Bayne, the claim was that his injuries had rendered him comatose. A coma was a good excuse – it could reasonably delay a purchase signal, as doctors worked to determine if an injured brain could be saved, or if it made more sense to euthanize the patient and resurrect him fresh. Nonetheless, when journalists filed to obtain hospital records, the MJB claimed he'd been moved to a 'secure and classified' location as part of the investigation.

This same bureaucratic evasion was applied, with considerably less success, in the matter of Tier Marsworks' CEO Vilhelmina Krohl. Her death was the top news item on Solstice Day, and had already been reported as a homicide. Martian media went into an uproar. Stalling techniques were stretched to the breaking point. A drip-feed of leaked intel painted a lurid picture: an armed intruder had attacked Krohl in her suite on Solstice Eve. Corporate security had been engaged, and there were several deaths. Krohl's personal secretary, one Deborah Skyblush Drost, had been murdered the same night. Both resurrections were being delayed. Another 'planetary security investigation'.

The media was connecting the dots. Reporters learned that on the same night of Krohl's death, there had been a disturbance on a sandship called the *Dandelion Wine*. Witnesses spilled what they'd seen. The Lido deck bartender confessed he'd served a woman matching Drost's description. Tier's HR department reported that their own chief of security had been involved in the incident but had since left the company.

And then last week, Drost's ten-year-old daughter (who had been taken in by relatives) made a social media video where she asked, in teary-eyed sincerity, where her mommy was.

Stars and storms, I thought. *What a shitstorm is brewing!* Dave did have a hole card to play: the Baynes and Krohl and Drost had *actually been* Partisans. He'd be able to explain – within the outer reaches of truth's gravity well – that it had been necessary to keep things hushed in order to trace the rat-line.

But the excuses, procedural countermeasures, and legal acrobatics were hurtling towards a finale. The only chess move left was for my brother to hold a press conference and spill the entire, macabre odyssey.

And when that happened, Mars was going to experience a different kind of Detonation, with its own special fallout.

As for my other shuttle companion, Celeste was an amiable if cryptic presence. Archons didn't typically leave Mars, but then Celeste was no longer archon: her term had expired with 358. She was a civilian again, even if her presence among the passengers created a continual stir, with more than a few asking for her autograph.

Despite my attempts, she wouldn't reveal *why* she was heading to the deeps.

"I know we're going to the *Coachlight*," I said one night before climbing into our separate sleeping creches.

She nodded. "That's good enough for now."

"No, it's not."

"My op is classified above top secret, Harris."

"I'm your security detail," I protested.

"Information will be provided onsite, *as needed*."

"That's crap, Segarra."

"Those are our orders."

"Story of my fucking life." I don't know what bothered me more, that I was being kept out of the loop, or that not once during the three weeks of our voyage had she said anything about what had happened on Solstice Eve. Nor did she invite me into her creche...or make any attempt at joining me in mine.

In the end, I supposed it didn't matter. To my surprise, it felt good to be away from Mars. I wasn't sure if it was the change of locale, the jitters of my first interplanetary flight, or the simple fact that I'd made a decision for myself...no longer a pawn in someone else's strategy, but charting my own course.

Did Eric say we had been shot down? Who the hell had shot us, and why?

⋆   ⋆   ⋆

"Who the hell shot us?" I demanded. "And why?"

Emergency lights snapped on, drenching the main cabin in red. My fellow passengers hung from their recessed cubbyholes like larval wasps in a hive. They groggily unfolded themselves. Lots of frightened, glass-eyed stares. Slow to react, slow to understand that we were in danger. That the torus was no longer rotating. That we were losing oxygen.

Stars almighty, sometimes civilians are like a separate species that I'll never understand.

"You need to see this." Eric tugged at me.

"We crash-landed on Ganymede," I guessed, unstrapping myself and drifting down after him in the low gravity.

"Yeah."

"Where's Celeste?"

He pointed along the cabin's curve that was presently the 'floor'. Celeste was there, strapped into her seat, and clad in a form-fitting eel-skin suit, unconscious.

I ambled over to her, avoiding a passenger who dropped like an errant icicle from the ceiling. Oxygen masks floated out of the floor like sea anemones; I fitted one securely over Celeste's nose and mouth, checked her for injuries, and looked back at Eric.

"You were saying?" I prompted. "Someone shot us down?"

The trog jabbed a finger towards the crew module. During the voyage, the door there had transmitted a holo displaying our flight in quaint maritime imagery: the Jovian moons as islands, our vessel as trireme, and the local void a mass of squiggles showing Jupiter's radiation belts, flight paths, and moon-to-moon trade routes.

Now, the door displayed a different view: Ganymede's scabby, cratered surface of silicate rock, with Jupiter as a swollen orange presence beyond it. Icy oases glittered amid crocodilian ridges and striations. During the voyage, I'd learned that these features were forever in flux during a Jovian year; hot geysers altered the topography, meaning that old maps were useless. Go tooling around in your buggy and you might plunge into a ravine that wasn't there last spring. Cartographers must work their asses off here.

There was something else on the display, too. I noticed a small vessel, holding position above the moon. It was visible as an irregular speck against Jupiter's umber vista.

"Is that what attacked us?" I asked.

Eric nodded. "I think so. They fired while we were on descent. Took out the engines with one shot. They've been signaling, promising to shoot again if we don't surrender."

I glanced around the cabin. "So let's surrender."

"Didn't want to make a unilateral decision."

I pushed off towards the crew module, landed, and hopped inside. The captain and two crew members were dead in their seats.

From the dashboard, a distorted voice was speaking. "Respond or we will fire again. We require your surrender."

I pressed the audio. "This is VG Flight 9956, a *civilian* transport. Do not fire! We're receiving you, but the captain and crew are dead."

A hesitation. "Give us control of your systems."

Eric frowned. "Why the hell would they want that?"

"Cargo or passenger manifest, maybe," I guessed. "Maybe these guys are pirates."

"Give us control of your systems!" the voice repeated.

"How do I do that?" I replied. It wasn't an act; I wasn't a pilot, and the only vehicles I had personally controlled during the war were the occasional buggy and – during an ambush in Carter Crossing – an aerobike I'd hijacked to escape to a rooftop. In both cases, vehicle controls had been a snap; by contrast, the shuttle's dashboard was a convoluted landscape of buttons, switches, panels, and screens.

A cry of alarm went up from the main cabin. Eric and I glanced back to see several passengers crowding the starboard porthole, pointing and gibbering.

Eric started towards them. "What the hell are they seeing there?"

He had taken two steps when Celeste dropped out of her seat and saw us.

"We've got problems," she called.

"No shit," I countered.

"Punch up the starboard monitors."

I held out my hands helplessly. "How?"

She was in the cabin in three strides, moving with unexpected grace in the low-G; what spacers referred to as *long-gom*, an assured and skillful way of moving. The bright luminosity warped over her eel-skin suit. Celeste studied the dashboard, fingers gliding over two rows of black buttons. She switched on an exterior camera view, and I was suddenly looking at the Ganymedan surface.

Four people were out there. They wore glistening voidsuits as they converged on our downed vessel. All of them bore heavy laser-cutters in their hands.

"Holy shit," Eric stammered. "They're going to breach us!"

"Probably why they wanted ship control," I said. "To override the airlocks remotely and get in."

Celeste punched up a diagnostic chart and recited the details there. "We're lying on our port side, six miles from Ambrose Base." Her fingers moved again, opening an audio link. "Ambrose Base, are you receiving?"

The response came at once: "We are."

"Any plans to conduct a fucking rescue?"

"We've contacted the IPCS *Sargon*! ETA is one hour."

"An *hour*? What about base responders? Don't you have your own defenses?"

"Two of our Furies were disabled by the same bogey that attacked you! We have no active resources to reach you."

Eric gave a caustic laugh. "Substitute 'courage' for 'resources'."

A scream went up from the main cabin.

"They're cutting their way in," I said, watching the monitor.

Celeste activated the intercom. "All passengers head immediately to the starboard escape pods! I repeat, all passengers to the starboard escape pods!" The passengers didn't stand around pondering this directive; they stumbled over each other to oblige.

Celeste linked back to the enemy ship. "What do you want with us?" she demanded.

"We want one of your passengers."

"Which passenger?"

"Gethin Bryce."

She stiffened. "There is no one aboard by that name."

"We'll find that out for ourselves," came the response.

The audio went dead.

I gripped her arm. "Gethin Bryce?! Why the hell do they think he's aboard? I mean, he *isn't* aboard, right?" Most of the passengers had stayed in their creches during the voyage, but over three weeks I figured I'd seen them all. It was unlikely that someone could have kept hidden…but certainly not impossible.

"He isn't aboard," Celeste assured me, and added thoughtfully, "but *they* think he is. That's interesting."

I gaped at her. "*Interesting?*"

"Our immediate priority is getting out of here."

"Yeah, right." I studied the screens. "The engines were taken out and we're lying on our side like a beached whale. If we launch the pods, they'll just pop-fly into the dust. Then *these* fellows will catch up with us." I jerked a thumb at the voidsuited figures cutting into our ship.

Celeste considered that. "What if we give the pop-fly a boost?"

"Sorry?"

"Four escape pods," she said. "Two are aimed at the sky, two are directly against the moon...."

"Yeah, but...." It clicked in my head. "Stars, Segarra, that might work!"

Her hands flew over the dashboard again, setting a sixty-second countdown for the landlocked pods. The three of us bolted, corralling a few stray passengers as we went. At the starboard pods, we climbed in past anxious men and women and sealed the door behind us.

The countdown launch displayed on the wall.

Five.

Four.

Three.

Two.

One.

★   ★   ★

It was the Lofstrom from Hellas all over again.

The synchronized launch of the groundward pods blasted the ship off Ganymede like a mass driver. My fellow passengers lurched in their seats. Our shuttle was one hundred meters off the lunar surface in six seconds. Metal squealed and groaned like a living thing.

On Mars such a launch would have been a bunny hop. Here, we ascended dreamily, frictionless, into the black sky. I had a glimpse of the moon below – the four people in voidsuits had been knocked into the dust by our unexpected flight. We reached the zenith of ascent, and gravity reasserted itself.

"Now!" Celeste ordered, transmitting her command to our neighboring pod and slapping the LAUNCH control. Both escape pods jettisoned from the doomed shuttle like lateral torpedoes in the direction of Ambrose Base. Behind us, the shuttle fell back to Ganymede.

The force of launch made the passengers scream. I settled into my seat beside Celeste, watching her with admiration.

"You've done this before?" I asked.

She smirked. "Told you I used to be quite the pilot back on Earth. Before you were born, *senor*."

Landing was a terrible affair. The pods auto-deployed parachutes as we came down; nonetheless, we landed sidelong and rolled, a circus ride for the damned. The passengers screamed again. We tumbled, splintering rock and ice, and finally slid to a halt.

My friends were upside down. Eric squinted through the nearest window and snapped, "Looks like someone from Ambrose grew a set!" The tiny shape of a buggybus was threading Ganymedan craters, on its way to pick us up.

I shook my head.

Welcome to the deeps.

CHAPTER TWENTY-FOUR

Fugitive

The Jovian League offered the nearest thing to pulp-era depictions of the future that had ever been. My mother introduced me to those garish, Old Calendar magazines, full of muscular heroes and scantily dressed heroines who caromed among the planets in a matter of hours. The Jovian League fulfilled that promise: with Jupiter as the local 'sun', the Galilean moons of Io, Calisto, Enceladus, and Ganymede were easy-to-reach worlds. Subsequently, they had developed a vibrant, interconnected economy. Proximity to the Belt meant they also benefited from the water and precious metals trade. To top it off, they acted as commercial hub to the colonies around Saturn, Uranus, and Neptune.

They were the gateway to the frontier. A mercantile power threatening brightworld hegemony.

Maybe that explained the look of Ambrose Base.

As the passengers of Flight 9956 shambled through customs, I marveled at the local décor. It drew inspiration from nautical motifs. Sensoramic coral, barnacles, and kelp entwined pillars and struts. Arrival and departure boards were done up in maritime imagery. The lighting was blue and green. Combined with the low gravity, the illusion of being underwater was impressive; I suppose if you have to live in an underground bunker on a low-G moon, you don't want to be reminded that you're in an underground bunker on a low-G moon.

We were a rattled bunch. One by one, we passed through customs. My passport was scanned and I saw my new identity on the security panel:

Bellerophon Rybka
Executive Protection Officer
Haiwiki Falls, Mars

A uniformed fellow intercepted us before we could disperse into the station. A trim, ascetic-looking guy, he was so neat and manicured he appeared vaguely plastic. "I'm Security Chief Turro," he said, making a showy, inauthentic bow. "On behalf of Ganymede, I apologize for what you've been through. If you'll follow me, our medical staff is at your disposal."

Turro was accompanied by seven security officers, all dressed in the loam-green uniforms of the Jovian League.

"Quite the welcome committee," Eric whispered beside me.

"Not feeling very welcome," I whispered back. I didn't like the look of the officers, the assault carbines in their hands, or the intensity of their stares.

They're running patmatch scans on us, I realized.

That was surprising. We'd already had our identities confirmed at customs, so why this secondary check? Did they not believe the results?

"Please follow me," Turro repeated.

Celeste broke in. "Hang on. Who attacked our shuttle?"

"It was an unregistered vessel. No transponder. Now, if you'll come this way—"

"I'm more interested in answers than bandages."

The security chief regarded her with undisguised annoyance. "Madam Segarra, is it? Welcome to Ganymede. I'm afraid I can't comment on the situation yet. Rest assured we are investigating. Now, if—"

"But you must have some ideas," she pressed.

"It's happened before," he said.

"Has it?"

"Unfortunately, yes. There are criminals out here who prey on local traffic. Mostly they're after cargo."

"Space pirates?" Celeste laughed. "You're telling me we were attacked by space pirates?"

Turro frowned. "It *is* a problem here."

"We weren't a cargo ship. What, were they looking to steal our underwear? They attacked us in *your* airspace, chief. Seems an awfully big risk to nab someone's carry-on."

"Kindly follow me," he snapped, in a tone that was significantly less than kind.

★　★　★

Despite what we'd been through, I was uninjured. My unconsciousness following the crash had resulted from an initial loss of cabin pressure, not concussion. Celeste, Eric, and myself sailed through the medical scan without issue. In the space of a few minutes, we were released.

The maritime theme persisted beyond customs. In fact, as we entered a main agora, my impression was that the place was unspeakably ugly. Imagine several dozen galleons colliding in a maelstrom, their cargo washing up as so much flotsam. Merchant stalls of every kind crammed the available floor-space. And wall-space. And the ceiling. My jaw dropped at this verticality; customers moved along nylon rigging like nimble crabs. The effect was incredibly disorienting. Hellas Market, it was not.

"We've got three hours to go before our connecting flight," Celeste said, looking around. "Let's see the town."

"I think the town will just be more of this," I said.

"Where's your sense of adventure?"

"You mean today hasn't already been an adventure?"

"Come on. I could use a drink and a fuck."

I bristled, stunned by her frankness. Must be an Earther thing.

"I can buy us all a drink," I said awkwardly. "But...um...."

A sleek cab pulled up, skimming the edge of the agora. Celeste hailed it and one of the doors opened, allowing us to enter.

As the door shut behind us, two facts entered my sphere of awareness. The first was that the vehicle had no driver. This wasn't surprising: autodrive cars were the dominant mode of ground transportation on Mars,

Earth, and Luna. Consequently, there was no delineation between front and back seating; the seats faced each other in a rounded arrangement.

The second fact was that we were not alone in the cab. Seated across from us, reclining like some mafia don, was Gethin Bryce.

★ ★ ★

The bastard looked pretty much the same as ten years earlier. Black hair trimmed an extra inch, perhaps. He wore a sea-foam tunic matching the aesthetics of Ambrose Base. Otherwise he was as fit as I remembered. As if he'd been spending most of his exile in an artificial environment spun up to terrestrial gravity.

That was surprising. Spend ten years in space, and it changes you. Not even nanite treatments can entirely counter muscle atrophy and bone loss. Chief Turro and his gaggle had been skinny, stringy specimens of humanity; hell, it even aligned them with the nautical theme, making them seem like marooned sailors. In the cab's dim lighting, Gethin Bryce looked formidable by comparison.

I crossed my arms and glared. "You know what, Bryce? I've had just about enough of you."

He regarded me in surprise. "Nice to see you, too, soldier." His attention skated to Eric before settling on the third of our company. "*Buenos dias,* Celeste."

She grinned, and the expression ignited the air. "Hi, Gethin. Figures you'd flee Mars to land in a fucking aquarium."

Something seemed to happen between them. It went beyond body language. They were suddenly in their own universe consisting of just two people. Without needing to utter a word, information and familiarity seemed to crackle along invisible circuits. It had the effect of making me feel like an outsider: Bryce and Segarra were a rocheworld sharing the same atmosphere while Eric and I were transitory comets flashing past.

Gethin shrugged. "Speaking of aquariums, sorry for the splash you took getting here."

Celeste mirrored his shrug. "Wasn't really a surprise."

Our cab pulled away from the agora and was passing into an underground tunnel system. In that blackness, I cut in. *"Wasn't a surprise? Celeste, are you saying you* expected *us to get shot down?"*

"A little."

"A *little*?"

Pale lights lit on the floor. Eric frowned, glancing from Celeste to Gethin and back again, and said, "How could you possibly expect that we were going to be attacked?"

"I made a call to Gethin aboard the shuttle."

I cried, "You *what*?"

Her gaze unlatched from Bryce and found me. "I didn't use the shuttle com, Harris. I used my own nanonics. In my own sleeping creche. It was a private call, voice-only."

Eric absently scratched his chin. "Voice-only? So you spoke aloud in your creche?"

"I wasn't very loud, to tell the truth. Neither was Gethin."

"Gethin's voice doesn't matter if he was speaking in your head," I said irritably, and then I noticed something in her expression. "What?"

"I routed his voice through an external speaker," she said. "Again, not very loud...barely more than a whisper. But to anyone eavesdropping, it would seem like I had company in my creche."

My mind raced. "You think the shuttle was bugged?"

"Yep." Beyond the cab windows, a seething cluster of traffic moved around us, taking various exit ramps from the tunnel.

I frowned. "Do you think...could someone have put an airhound on you?"

"Possibly, but unlikely. It would be easier if they installed a hidden microphone in my creche."

"Just yours?"

"Maybe yours, too. Who knows?"

"And during our flight," I continued, "you made a phone call to the most wanted man in the universe and pretended he was stowing away with you?"

"Yep."

"Stars, Segarra! Why the hell would you *do* that?"

She hugged herself. "Call it a privacy test. If anyone was listening, I wanted them to believe that Gethin was with me, if you can imagine."

I'd rather not, I thought sourly.

Eric broke in, "You're implying that the IPC bugged the shuttle. But whoever attacked us wasn't the IPC."

Bryce had been silently watching the exchange; now he leaned forward and steepled his fingers. In the murky light, it was easy to imagine we were back in the Hellas underworld, hiding from his would-be assassin. "No, they wouldn't bloody their hands in such an obvious way," he said. "I'm guessing my former masters did a little subcontracting."

Eric said, "Why bother? It's no secret they want to arrest you."

"They don't want to arrest me. They want to *erase* me. A public capture brings the press, lawyers, and lots of questions. So I'm guessing the IPC did what all powerful groups do when stymied by the law: they outsourced the dirty work."

"Seems like a lot of trouble, just to catch you."

"I'm quite the catch."

"While you're being so witty," I snapped, entertaining the fantasy of punching him in the teeth, "maybe you should be concerned that they have you cornered now."

Eric protested, "Do they? How? Security didn't find him. Neither did that medical scan they foisted on us. Why would they think he's here?"

"Because their chat would have no time-lag." I looked at Celeste, saw her nod, and continued. "That would tell the IPC that their Most Wanted is local."

Gethin said, "Doesn't mean I'm on Ganymede."

"Except you *are* on Ganymede!" Our cab emerged from the tunnel and joined a roundabout of other vehicles. I glimpsed a cobalt-blue police cruiser in the mix, several cars deep.

Security might have an APB on us, I thought. *From the concourse, they'd have seen which cab we got into.*

We navigated the roundabout and flowed into another tunnel. I glimpsed a signpost announcing: HALI, 6 MILES.

Fighting a sudden bout of claustrophobia, I said, "So this is where you've been hiding, huh? Jumped from one moon to another?"

Gethin flashed an ivory smile. "I don't have a permanent address. As you might imagine, I move around a lot."

"How?"

"I'm afraid that's above your pay grade."

"Yeah? You mean you haven't been chauffeured around by an AI ship that the IPC would like to destroy as much as you?"

Gethin froze in place. He was a cool customer – one of the most controlled people I'd ever met. But my words rocked him, and it gave me a small thrill of pleasure. You take the victories you can get, however small.

"I see someone's been talking," he said finally, eyes flicking to Celeste.

She shrugged. "He's got as many secrets as we do. How *is* my ship, by the way?"

"Keeping out of sight, as it does so well. Concerned for you, as it always is."

A look of anxiety passed over Celeste's face. It was as if she was getting news about a lost parent or child. Once again, I was aware of how much an outsider I was; a minor blip in a larger epic involving people and forces I could barely fathom.

"Hang on," I interrupted. "You've been zipping around the solar system in an invisible, sentient ship. The same ship – the *Mantid*, if I recall correctly – that was able to infiltrate Phobos and rescue you."

He nodded.

"Invisible or not, it would still be detectable in space."

"Think 'camouflaged' instead of 'invisible'," Gethin explained. "The *Mantid* can use real-time optic distortion, but it can also make itself look like an errant asteroid, of which there are plenty. It can pose as a mining ship. It can imitate transponder codes, jam signals, send false chatter. When it's not traveling, it hunkers down into a network of craters. The *Mantid* is a lot smarter than any of us, and it has technology the IPC doesn't know about."

"It's also the last of its species," added Celeste. "It *wants* to survive."

Police lights dappled the windows. I bolted upright, seeing two cruisers cutting off the road ahead. The traffic instantly bottlenecked and halted.

"Sh-shit," I stammered. "Better turn us around."

"We've got a cop on our tail, too," Gethin said softly.

"So let's try to lose them!"

"This isn't the Plains of Cydonia. We can't outrace authorities here."

Anxiety twisted a dagger in my chest. Meeting his green stare, I said, "Why the hell does the IPC want you? What the hell's going on, Bryce?"

He settled back like a Turkish sultan reluctantly forced to hold court. "It's complicated," he said.

"Fucking try," I countered.

"I discovered something they were planning. Something I need *your* help to stop."

From outside the car, a voice rang out: *"This is the Ganymede Transit Authority. Cab 182 is ordered to pull over!"*

I glanced to Eric. He had stiffened, hand instinctively straying for his weapon and then remembering that our weapons had been transferred with our luggage to a connecting shuttle.

"Pull over your vehicle!" the voice repeated.

Our car slowed and drew onto the curb, its autodrive protocols hijacked. Two cruisers boxed us in, lights flashing.

Desperately, I looked to Bryce. "I didn't sign up to fight the IPC. I'm here to hunt Partisans."

Gethin raised an eyebrow. "Partisans? They're dead, Harris. You should know that – *you* killed them."

"I've got actionable intel that they came to the deeps."

He closed his eyes. "If they came out here, it would have to be by databeam. Meaning they would need someone to resurrect them."

"Agreed."

"Any idea which Partisans you're looking for?"

"The top brass," I said, heart pounding as I watched two cops emerging from their cars, weapons drawn. "And that would include Lanier Bishons."

"Bishons would be exceedingly problematic to conceal." Gethin's eyes were still closed. I felt sick, realizing his capture was mere seconds away. What that meant for us was probably akin to aiding and abetting a wanted fugitive. This was bad.

Gethin said, "It would be a terrible risk for anyone to help the Partisans. That's good news, as it limits the possible suspects. Few groups would have the resources to pull this off, or the incentive to."

"What incentive could *anyone* have?"

"To enlist Lanier Bishons. To benefit from his military genius."

"He still lost," Eric growled.

"But he was a genius," Gethin insisted, opening his eyes at last. "Your brother, Celeste, and I went toe-to-toe with his strategies. Bishons' Waterloo was his retreat to Phobos. It was a dead-end castling move. You were able to deliver the knockout blow because of that error."

A third cruiser pulled up, and three additional cops in full body armor hopped out. One of them boomed, "Come out slowly with your hands up!"

Speaking hurriedly, Gethin said, "I don't know anything about the Partisans being back, but I'd recommend you continue on to the *Coachlight*. Celeste has business there anyway. Go see an associate of mine at a place called the Electric Lagoon in Drop Town."

Celeste had gone rigid. "Are you going to be okay?"

Gethin sighed, seeming to deflate as he did. "Being hunted by the IPC is something I've gotten used to. I know their strategies. It's the local element I'm more concerned with. I have a dangerous enemy out here, Celeste. A crime lord who hasn't taken kindly to my activities."

I watched the cops approach. "Stars, Bryce. You're more dangerous than a goddam radiation belt."

"I didn't come out here to make friends. I came here because your brother asked me to, and his plans coincide with mine."

A cop tried the door, found it locked, and drew a baton. "This is your last warning!" the cop said. "Unlock the door and come out with your hands up!"

Gethin touched Celeste's hand. "Good luck, *senora*."

"To you also, *senor.*"

I was looking at their hands – I couldn't help it – when I realized that something was wrong. Gethin's hand had passed through hers, as if he was a ghost.

To my open-mouthed amazement, the figure I'd assumed was Gethin Bryce dissolved into holographic pixels.

Somewhere within transmission range, the real Gethin Bryce had just severed a broadcast. Son of a bitch....

Celeste opened the car door and smiled sweetly at the baton-wielding cop. "Good morning, officer. I'm Celeste Segarra, former archon of Mars. Is there a problem?"

CHAPTER TWENTY-FIVE

The Night Witch of the Electric Lagoon

"Welcome to the *Coachlight!*" the young woman announced at debarkation, local time 1532. "You have arrived at Gateway District. Please let us know if there's anything we can do to make your stay a memorable one!"

"It's already been memorable, sister," Celeste said, marching through the biometric kiosk. Eric and I followed, and the receptionist's professional smile faltered as she took stock of us. We certainly stood out from other arrivals; about half of VG Flight 9956's passengers had taken the connecting flight, and *they'd* used their time on Ganymede to freshen up. By contrast, Celeste's eel-skin uniform was spattered with sodium bicarbonate, and Eric and I wore full armor. We seemed the embodiment of a joke: an Earther, a trog, and a soldier walk into a space station....

"Now *that* is a sight," I exclaimed, craning my neck to regard the sky.

There was no sky.

Just a dizzying sprawl of buildings, roads, and green parks in every concave direction. *Coachlight* was an O'Neill cylinder, revved up for spin gravity and with all its structures on the walls, which I needed to think of as the floor. The resulting centrifugal effects were welcome after Ganymede. And the gravity was set close to redworld standard. It almost felt like Mars.

On the other hand, it sure as hell didn't look like Mars. The wraparound horizon was incredibly disorienting – what a metropolis would be if designed by M.C. Escher. Stare at the inhabited 'sky' too long, and you worried about falling into it.

"I reserved us three rooms at Chilon Tower," Celeste explained, pointing to a bristle of artificial stalactites almost directly above. One stood out in spectacular fashion, like a ruby-gold fang. "Our baggage will be there within the hour."

I followed her outstretched finger. "So much for keeping a low profile."

"Actually, it's the ideal place for our purposes. Chilon is privacy compliant. No cameras, no surveillance allowed. They even offer privacy masks."

"How very Halloween."

"It's a good place to conduct business."

"*You're* here to conduct business, whatever that business is. Me, I'm on a hunting expedition."

Celeste considered me with a skeptical look. "So you've told me. You realize if you make a mess, you're on your own, right?"

I flashed a broad smile. "As far as I'm concerned, Segarra, that's a welcome change of pace."

She didn't appear pleased with that answer. "We've got 2030 dinner reservations. The Floating Islands restaurant. It's mandatory, so I trust you two won't be late. Gotta run now."

As she sprinted for the tram station, I said, "Hey! You're not going to clean up first?"

She gave an exaggerated pivot in mid-stride. "You saying I don't look fresh as a daisy? I sponged down this morning."

"Your meeting. You're going there alone?"

"Yep."

"What kind of meeting is it?"

"The secret kind."

"*Where* is it?"

Celeste raised an eyebrow. "At the local Promethean office." She scanned the sky like an astronomer looking for a constellation, and pointed to a greenish building that jutted sidelong, like a defensive pike angled against a cavalry charge.

"Maybe you should have bodyguards," I said, not liking the look of the structure.

"Thought you and Mazzola had a date?"

Eric shrugged. "He's right. We're your security detail, we should be going with you."

"I don't need security where I'm going. My meeting is at a top-floor executive suite of the biggest corporation in the universe."

"I had a top-floor executive suite meeting," I reminded her. "Remember how that went?"

She smiled. Stars above, she looked adorable when she smiled.

"And I once jumped out of an airship without a parachute," she said. "I'm not going in blind. I have high-level contacts at Prometheus Industries; you could even say I have friends there. Still, I promise to maintain situational awareness. If I need to bug out, I will."

She turned and headed for the TRAINS signage.

"The rooftop!" I shouted after her.

Jogging, Celeste glanced back. "Sorry?"

"If you run into trouble, get to the rooftop! Spin-gravity effects are lower when you're that far from the station walls. You could jump like Superman up there."

She shook her head, but I could see she was laughing. "I'll keep that in mind. You just watch after yourself, *senor*."

Then she dissolved into the crowd.

*   *   *

The *Coachlight* transportation system was a model of efficiency and cleanliness. Each train was a *shinkansen*, so white and polished they hurt my eyes. Eric and I caught a 1548 to Drop Town station. It was an eight-minute ride. I used the time to study the color-coded wall map of *Coachlight*'s various districts. Drop Town was purple.

Despite the open seats, Eric elected to stand during the ride. He gripped a hanging strap, watching the curved landscape through the windows. "You think they're right?" he asked.

"About what?"

"Was the IPC behind the attack on our shuttle?"

I absently touched the glass, watching my body heat form white halos around each fingertip. "It's a tad convenient that we get shot down not long after Segarra made her call. And those cops went after us on Ganymede."

"Doesn't mean they were looking for—" He stopped himself from speaking the name aloud.

"The IPC wants him," I insisted, and in a low voice added, "Ten years ago they sent a goddam praetorian to kill him on Mars."

Eric's eyes glimmered with interest. "So it's true, then? You actually scrapped with a praetorian?"

I swallowed, remembering. It was still fresh for me, a matter of weeks. The blocky silhouette in CAMO. The head-to-toe shielding, like an interred Chinese emperor come to life. Our cat-and-mouse chase before I vaporized the fucker.

"I'd love to hear the details," Eric pressed.

"Maybe later."

"Selfish prick."

"What did *you* do during the war?" I asked. "Aside from killing me, I mean. Were you always with Argos's squad?"

My compatriot switched hands holding the hanging strap. "That was the first and last mission I ever had with her. I was serving with the 188 Special Tactics in Elysium. Was their top sniper. One evening we got the call that I was needed for a mission in Hellas. They briefed me on the way."

"And the others on her squad?"

He shrugged. "They mentioned a similar experience: all hand-picked for Operation Persephone. We didn't get a chance to know each other."

"Why?"

"Because you killed them, remember?"

Silence fell between us. My gaze returned to the curved landscape. Green and yellow blurs that were crop fields. Grey blurs for residential blocs. Blue for bodies of water – harvested from asteroid ice.

"Actually," Eric said conversationally, "I was in demand all over

Mars. My sniping skills were first rate. Not bad for a trog who started as a ghoul."

I perked up. "Really? I'd love to hear about that."

"Maybe later," he said, and grinned.

Ghouls were special operators who also went by the slang of vultures, cleaners, firemen, and maintenance. Most units had a detachment of ghouls who'd stay behind after major engagements to ensure that any dead soldier from their side was 'torched'. It served an important tactical need: you don't leave your dead on the battlefield, where enemy recovery specialists could get at the bodies. You harvest what you can – their spare clips, rations, and dog tags – and you burn everything else. Ghouls even purged skulls, using blender-magpies. Like Egyptian priests de-braining the dead.

But ghouls served a secondary purpose, too. Like their mythological namesake, they went searching for the enemy's dead. Ripped out neurals and sensoriums.

So it was no wonder that Argos had chosen Eric to take me down. A ghoul with sniper skills. I owed my life to how clean he killed me. My reactivation wouldn't have worked if someone had blown my head off during the fight.

The *shinkansen*'s conductor announced, "Next stop, Drop Town."

*   *   *

Drop Town was the oldest part of the *Coachlight*. The IPC's largest habitat had been built, Frankenstein-like, from old stations and stripped-out asteroids; Drop Town had originally been the largest refueling station in Beltspace outside of Ceres. A watering hole for a cosmic Serengeti, it hosted the miners, pirates, engineers, and laborers who toiled in the void. When the *Coachlight* was being constructed, Drop Town had become part of it. Like a chunk of DNA cut-and-pasted into another species.

As Eric and I emerged from the train, we found ourselves in what seemed to be an artificial mangrove forest. Drop Town, as it turned out, was a suffocating ghetto threaded by madly congested buildings, neon storefronts, and holography. Even the 'sky' was hidden by extensive crossways and advertisements.

"What are *you* smiling about?" I asked my companion, seeing his chain-link grin.

"Just thinking," he mused. "I spent most of my life underground. Ybarra's underdark. The dust shelters. The bunker after Detonation. Now here we are in space, and it's a cave, too."

"Everything old is new again." I accessed the local web and downloaded an area map, then summoned my personal genie, Xenophon.

<Good afternoon, Harris.>

"Hi. Please show me the way to an establishment called the Electric Lagoon."

<The Electric Lagoon is four blocks northwest. Follow the yellow brick road.> In my optics, a yellow line painted a footpath, with a navpoint counter showing how many meters to go.

We strolled past gaudy storefronts. They reminded me of holotours I'd taken of Earth arcologies. Millions of people resided in the ziggurats of Babylon, the Shimizu Pyramid, Scotland's World Tree, Egypt's Avenue of Sphinxes, and the Zulu Cloud Forest. The *Coachlight* seemed designed on that model, pressing its population into residential stacks that made optimal use of available space.

Even so, based on the pastoral blurs I'd glimpsed from the train, the *Coachlight* was producing far more food than it needed. I could appreciate the value of storing away food – Mars's dust storms made that a necessity. And of course, surplus made for good trade. Nonetheless, it seemed like overkill.

Then I remembered what Celeste had told me on Solstice Eve.

There were other habitats being constructed, hush-hush. *Coachlight* was not a single marvel of human ingenuity, but the vanguard of an imminent wave. Other O'Neill cylinders were on the way…the IPC's solution to overpopulation. Someday they would be self-sufficient, but for now their work crews required food and water.

The yellow arrow in my vision banked left at a T-intersection. On the corner, a signpost advertised the Electric Lagoon. It was a citadel-like structure, reminiscent of a lighthouse. I went to the doors and read the lettering there:

ELECTRIC LAGOON
HOURS BY APPOINTMENT ONLY
NO TRESPASSING

"Well, that's helpful," Eric quipped. "A company that doesn't say what they do."

"They're listed as a 'specialized manufacturer' in the *Coachlight* directory."

He rolled his eyes. "Yeah, that's so much clearer. Like people who told me they were 'contractors' during the war."

I rubbed my chin. "Twenty tradenotes says they build custom spacecraft."

"Big spender, you."

"My investments didn't grow as much as I'd hoped while I was dead."

We shook on our bet. I drew open the doors and stepped into a hive of bee-people.

They must have been local specialists. Men and women as bald as chess pawns and wearing golden goggles. They worked in curious segregation-by-trade; engineers and computer technicians and others, hunched over workbenches, monitors, and an art gallery's worth of holodisplays.

No one looked up at us. We stood, awkward and uncertain.

"Excuse me," I began. "Can one of you help us? We're looking for a friend."

"Friend?" a woman said on the stairs above us. "Not sure you have friends here, Harris Alexander Pope."

She wore a gray silk business suit with a white shirt beneath, top button undone to show her slender brown throat. She might have been a young heiress of the fashion model industry. She exuded easy confidence, the elegance of a lioness. Her black curls were longer by inches, dangling around her face.

"Umerah?" I breathed in astonishment.

She folded her arms across her chest. "Together again, huh?"

CHAPTER TWENTY-SIX

Revolutions

One of her gold-eyed associates detached from his workstation and led us up a zigzagging staircase to a loft office, then scurried away like a bee on a pollen-collecting expedition. Umerah Javed seated herself in a chair of true Nebraskan leather. She crossed her legs, folded her hands in her lap, and looked at my compatriot.

"Eric Mazzola," she said, nodding. "Recruited by the Order in 331. Seven hundred and eighty-five confirmed kills. Twice awarded the Jade Heart. Recipient of the Guardian Medal. Last wartime mission was a shadow-op known only as Operation Persephone. After the war, you were hired by Tier Marsworks as chief of security." She raised an eyebrow. "Is Tier looking to expand offworld? If so, they should consider rebranding."

"I'm no longer employed there," he said.

"Oh?" Her hands moved gracefully, paging through private virtuscreens. "And what business are you in now, Mister Mazzola?"

"Personal security detail."

"That does seem a good fit for a man of your skillset. I was going to order some lunch. Any preferences?" Her eyes flicked to me. "From either of you?"

I couldn't seem to bring my thoughts together. Seeing Umerah – alive – sent a thrill of shock through me. She hadn't been listed in any planetary database! I'd sent the query around the solar system!

My lips twitched. "You...."

Her forehead creased. "Something to eat, Harris? Sushi perhaps? I remember you enjoyed sushi."

How was it possible? As pilot for a shadowman squad, her Save would have been stored in a priority clinic like mine. Maybe that clinic had been obliterated during Detonation. Maybe it was still buried beneath rubble. The Order had regenerated all but the most heinous Partisans, mandating some of them to hard labor as atonement for their crimes while others – the run-of-the-mill soldiers and officers – were officially forgiven. My search for *any* record of Umerah had come up with nothing. No file anywhere. Hell, she hadn't even showed up in birth or enlistment records! She was like a legendary book known only through obscure reference in ancient sources. An Alexandrian volume reduced to ash.

Yet here she was. And she recognized me!

"Umerah," I pronounced the syllables, feeling their musicality on my lips.

She seemed to be sizing me up with a gaze both calculating and impish; *kitsune* eyes. "Harris," she countered.

"You're alive."

"I'll order you some sushi. There are fifty-six varieties of seafood raised local. If you can look past the fact that our rice is replovatted, the sushi isn't bad." She touched her ear, placing an order.

"How are you alive?"

"A strange question to ask in our modern age, no?"

"The laser-branding on your neck." I pointed. "I remember that scar from ten years ago. Meaning you're still in the same body. You didn't die on Phobos. You've got the same war wound!"

She touched the old scar. "This isn't a war wound."

"You never told me where you got it."

"And I never will."

I glanced to Eric, wishing he was somewhere else. "Umerah, I—"

"You didn't mean to kill me," she finished for me. "The Order of Stone sent you on a mission, and everything else was collateral damage. You had your orders. I don't blame you for blowing Phobos to hell."

I looked sidelong at her, hearing the surreptitious tone. "But you blame me for something else?"

Eric shifted uncomfortably. "I could take a walk...."

"Do that," I snapped.

"Stay put," she countered, and the trog fell back in his seat as if yanked back by magnetism.

My old lover took a breath that told me she'd been preparing for this. And of course she had; everyone in the universe knew that I'd destroyed Phobos. Harris Alexander Pope was a folk hero by now, like Johnny Appleseed or Jolene Fort. Folk heroes don't have definitive conclusions...their lives are always an ellipsis trailing off into rumor and myth. Harris Alexander Pope, slayer of the Partisans, had vanished with Detonation...but that didn't mean I was dead. Maybe Umerah had run searches on me...and found no files.

What a pair we made: two people who didn't officially exist.

"I know you've been back for about eight weeks," she said. "And I know that most of that time was aboard a shuttle. As for me, I've had ten very active, very busy years."

"You look like you've done well for yourself," I admitted. "I'm happy you survived Phobos...I just...I don't understand...."

The eyebrow arched again. "How I escaped?"

"Yeah."

"Gethin Bryce."

My breath caught. "He rescued you?"

"I was trying to reach you when the base alarms sounded," she said. "I told you we needed to talk. I wanted to try reconciling the horrors I'd seen on Paradise Row with the man I—" The merest of hesitations. "—thought I knew."

"I was trying to reach you—"

"There's even the possibility," she said, "that I was going to kill you."

I swallowed hard.

Her eyes took on a cold sheen, like frost on a window. "I was looking for you," she continued, "when suddenly I get a message from Gethin. I didn't know how he located my link. He told me he was departing Phobos, and that if I wanted to live I had thirty seconds to get to the hangar." She shrugged. "I wanted to live."

"There wasn't time to rescue you," I insisted, remembering my fight with Peznowski's nightmare puppets. "How was there time for *you* to reach the hangar?"

"Every security door opened for me. I had green lights straight to where he was waiting."

I remembered how easily Bryce had overridden the doors in Hellas. "He had an AI in his head. It must have hacked the entire base, overrode their security protocols. Opened doors, deactivated turrets." I had to remind myself to breathe. "And from the hangar…?"

"We got out of Dodge on his invisible hot-rod," she said. "I've been working for him ever since."

"Working for him," I echoed, waiting for her to elaborate. Her face was an inscrutable mask, a *Mona Lisa* painted Persian.

The loft settled into uneasy silence, disturbed only by the white noise of her bee-people below. Behind her head, a spate of monitors displayed enigmatic sigils; she would have the decryption key hardwired to her sensorium. Briefly, I wondered what it was all about. Was she translating an alien language? Manufacturing illegal AI ships like the *Mantid*?

I should have stayed on Mars, I thought suddenly. *Should have accepted a tedious life in the House of Laws. This cloak-and-dagger work is not for me anymore.*

Umerah interlaced her fingers beneath her chin. "Let's to business, shall we? Gethin mentioned that you're seeking a group of people who may or may not exist. He said you have no hard leads. That the meager intel you possess came from a low-level secretary, and can be summarized thusly: a cabal of war criminals are allegedly meeting somewhere off Mars. Is that about right?"

"Deborah Drost wasn't a low-level secretary," I said, finding my voice. "And she believed those war criminals were being regenerated in the deeps."

"Belief is a shitty thing to base your life on."

"I'm not basing my life on it. The Partisans *did* return."

She nodded. "Two of them, as I understand it. Caleb Peznowski and Eileen Monteiro."

"Four, by my count. Krohl – er, Monteiro – said that Sabrina Potts had been operating on Luna."

"*Had* been operating?"

"She was assassinated."

"By you?"

"Not by me, I've never been to Luna. She died a couple weeks before I was resurrected."

Umerah looked thoughtful. Her pink tongue moved cat-like across her lips. "Who's the fourth?"

"Lanier Bishons."

"You know this for a fact, or you're speculating?"

"Here's what I heard in Peznowski's bedroom." I conjured the audio file and played it from my wrist-gauntlet. Two voices, one masked through distortion, the other coming from Peznowski's female version:

"Who is he, Caleb?"

"Commander Harris Alexander Pope, shadowman. Decided to drop by."

"Kill him now. Kill him and torch everything, yourselves included! I'll bring you back at the Face."

"I can get offworld without needing to—"

"Torch everything! Torch yourselves! That's an order, Caleb. I'll never warn you again."

As the recording ended, my former compatriot had lost her professional, measured calm. She looked unsettled. Old memories, old demons, stirred in her eyes.

"That's not proof," she managed.

"Who else could order Peznowski around like that? Who else would orchestrate their reincarnation?"

"Still…."

"Someone is helping them," I insisted. "You think they'd bother, if Bishons wasn't part of the deal?"

Eric cut in. "The question is *who* would dare."

Umerah stood and paced around the office, the screens winking around her stride. "I know exactly who would dare," she said. "He's the biggest criminal out here. Goes by the name of Quinn."

"Quinn," I repeated. "Who is he?"

"A very bad man, Harris. Know what the biggest commodity is out here? It's not food – we grow plenty. It's entertainment. Behind legitimate venues is a forbidden underskin. Gambling dens, snuff arenas, slavery." She expelled that last word as if it was dipped in acid. "Quinn came out here decades ago. He was a weapons smuggler from Earth. A Wastelander, if rumors are true. Quinn invaded the ecosystem, clawing and killing his way to the top. Impressive, actually. He has his hand in every illegal trade."

I considered the terrain she was describing. "You know that our shuttle to Ganymede was attacked, right?"

"It's all over the news."

"Bryce suggested the IPC was behind it, but that they subcontracted the dirty work. Could that have been—"

"Quinn? Certainly. No one would play skeet with an IPC shuttle unless he sanctioned it. He might have taken the job *pro bono*."

"Why?"

She leaned against the wall in a pose that reminded me of Hellas, waiting for the S-E tram. Umerah was famously calm and methodical; it warmed me to realize that she'd preserved that temperament. The deeps hadn't broken her; if anything, they seemed to have polished her talents. "Gethin and I came out here ten years ago. We had to stay low, under the IPC's radar. That meant dealing with unsavory types. We started up this company to aid our objectives."

"Eric and I were wondering exactly what the Electric Lagoon does."

Umerah beamed. "Just what it says on the tin. Specialty manufacturing."

"That could mean anything."

"And it often does. Within a year, our activities came to Quinn's attention. He attempted to muscle us out. We fought back, and the last several years have been…shall we say…a series of *arguments* between our operations." She laughed. "Quinn is a dangerous customer, but Gethin is slicker than snot. They've been waging an invisible war. At this point, it isn't even about money. Quinn wants Gethin dead. If the IPC asked him for assistance to that end, he would have jumped to it."

"And this Quinn," I said, bristling at the familiar way she was referring to Bryce. "You think *he'd* be willing to aid the Partisans?"

"If there's pay in it, yes." Lunch arrived on a silver tray, and Umerah indicated we should help ourselves.

I didn't feel hungry – I felt sick – but training overrode my nausea. When you're in the field, you stock up on calories when you can. Brandishing chopsticks, I selected a rainbow-hued sushi roll. "What kind of paycheck is there in helping the Partisans?"

Umerah studied me with brooding intensity. "The Order of Stone would pay well for Bishons' head on a plate. Maybe Quinn smells an easy sale: bring the Partisans back so he can fuck them over."

"You don't believe that," I said.

"I don't believe they're out here," she countered. "I think a few came back and you killed them and that's that. I think you've lost your mind."

"*Deyyange haal kawila,*" I said, repeating an old Martian sentiment. The expression was Sri Lankan, explaining insanity by claiming the afflicted had eaten divine rice.

The words snuck past Umerah's professional armor. She gave a light, cautious chuckle. "Okay, let's say you're not fraying from too many resurrections. We'll float the hypothesis: Quinn is helping the Partisans. Knowing the bastard as I do, he wouldn't run them off a printer just to cash them in for a one-time transaction. He's playing a long game. That's what he does."

"What long game?"

She stepped towards the food, leaned down, selected a tuna roll with her fingers. "Revolution," she said, and popped the morsel into her mouth.

★   ★   ★

Interplanetary travel is notorious for killing appetites. Most shuttles are diminutive enough that you can feel the spin-gravity, which messes with inner ear balance and spatial awareness. Motion sickness is reported by nearly half of all travelers. Compounding matters is the common practice of taking nanite infusions and bio-conditioning to prepare for your destination's gravity; it works well enough on that account, though tends to screw with your electrolytes. And to be frank, shuttle food sucks. You arrive at your destination as a nauseous, dizzy, constipated wreck.

I'd been spared those curses. The trade-off was that I'd been shot down by space pirates, had been detained by Ganymedan cops...

...and was now facing the woman I had written off for dead. The woman I'd abandoned only weeks ago, whatever the calendar said.

Raw panic churned my already sickened gut. Umerah Javed returned to the wall, arms folded as she watched Eric help himself to the platter. That pose! Whenever I gave mission briefings to my old squad, it was always the same arrangement: the guys crowded around Cuddy and Beresha, with Hammill and Conway on opposite wings. Shea tended to sit off by himself. And Umerah, our trusty flying ace, lingered in the corner, watching and listening in pensive attentiveness. Sometimes she'd be in the shadows beyond a campfire or lamp, and all I'd see of her was the reflective glint in her eyes.

"Revolution," I echoed, fighting to keep the one sushi roll I'd eaten down my throat. "*What* revolution?"

Umerah studied me. "The deepworlds are chomping at the bit for independence."

"That's not revolution," Eric countered. "That's our fractured human drama playing its usual tune."

She shrugged. "There's new kindling in the mix. First up is the Martian vote next week. Will they rejoin IPCnet?"

"Polling suggests they will," he said.

"And then a much bigger vote is slated for next month."

I forced down another piece of sushi, barely chewing it; it felt like a wad of cardboard in my throat. "The Colonization Ban," I said. "Regardless of the Martian vote, the IPC Senate will cast ballots on whether the Ban is lifted."

Eric frowned. "How does that vote herald revolution? Suppose the Ban is overturned. Any extrasolar ships would still be under IPC control.

Any alien worlds would be settled by IPC committee. They're the only ones with ships capable of making the voyage anyway—"

"The Ban will stay in place," Umerah said.

"You don't know that. Polling shows a dead heat."

"The vote is theater. The script has been written, along with the outcome. The vote preserves the illusion of choice."

"Conspiracy theory bullshit," I snapped. "They can't control how individual senators vote."

"You're still you, Harris," she said, a smile edging into her voice. "Gethin told me to expect you, but I wasn't sure what that meant. Now I understand. Across a thousand deaths through flesh and stone, you're still...you."

"Um, thanks?"

The smile faded. "The deepworlds want to break with the IPC."

"Bullshit."

"There are no bulls out here."

"Any war with the IPC would be a slaughter," I insisted. "They've got battleships. Millions of troops. Supply lines. Advanced weaponry. Fucking antimatter...."

Back on Mars, the Order of Stone had gifted me two capsules of antimatter. No one told me where they had come from, or what purpose the illegal production served.

"You're producing antimatter out here," I guessed. "Is that the 'specialty manufacturing' you and Gethin are up to?"

Umerah's lips compressed in a cryptic line. "That would be illegal, Harris."

I reclined on the sofa, connecting the dots. "Ten years ago, I used antimatter to destroy Phobos. The Order didn't have the facilities to create it on Mars. There used to be some in the terrestrial Wastes, but that was a long time ago. So the Order must have gotten it elsewhere." I watched her for reaction. "They got it from the deeps. But you and Bryce weren't set up here a decade ago. So where did it come from?"

"Ten years ago," she said, "the Order made contact with deepworld revolutionaries. Bryce himself facilitated the arrangement. He was valuable to them; a former IPC investigator who knew their resources and strategies. And these revolutionaries were valuable to him: they could produce small quantities of antimatter for a potential war...a war which has yet to happen. Bryce had them smuggle the stuff to Mars. *You* used it to end the war."

"Fuck," I breathed, stunned by the revelation. Once again, I realized my life had merely skimmed the edges of larger machinations. "So after Mars, he came out here to join up with those same revolutionaries, and *that* led to a power struggle with Quinn." An unpleasant thought occurred, and I glowered at her. "A would-be revolution might benefit from enlisting the Partisans."

Eric's neck tattoos flushed. "What the hell for?"

"They're the *only* political body to achieve independence."

"They didn't achieve that through military victory!" he cried.

"Does it matter?"

"*Yes, it matters!*"

"I'm saying they engineered a secession that—"

Eric could barely sit still. Blood rushed to his face, so that his mohawk seemed a jagged lid on a kettle about to explode. "They engineered *nothing*! The Partisans were elected on a tide of xenophobia! They enjoyed power until they got their asses kicked." He pointed to me. "Until *you* vaporized them!"

Umerah's eyes grew wide, gauging how best to handle a pissed-off trog. "I dislike giving the Partisans credit for anything, Mazzola. But I'm also a realist. Their initial victory may have been political, true. But in its wake, Bishons conducted a top-to-bottom reorganization of the Martian military. He took a notoriously scattered group of cantons and scaled them up for worldwide dominance. That's no mean feat. Anyone interested in revolution could benefit from his talent."

I rose from the sofa. "So Quinn might know where the Partisans are. Is that the best lead you can offer?"

"It's all I have," she insisted. "I think you're out here on a fool's errand. No one in my network is talking about Partisans. I'll make inquiries – maybe someone's heard something – but I wouldn't bet the farm on it." She sighed. "Check your slang app."

"I'm familiar with the expression." An urge to embrace her flooded me; I fought it back, glanced at my boots, and said, "What about this 'Face' they referenced? That's where they're supposed to be regrouping. Any ideas?"

She pursed her lips, thinking it over. "The only 'Face' I know of is on Mars. Sorry, Harris."

Eric ate a last piece of sushi and then stood, bowed, and followed me towards the stairs. I placed a hand on the rail, hesitating. I looked back to her, but she had already turned to the monitors, typing furiously in some encrypted correspondence. I waited for her to finish, and slowly realized there was no end in sight.

So this was what had happened to my former lover. She had escaped one war, and was preparing for another. This time, she wasn't flying people around, but had become a kind of field commander. I was happy for her.

I missed her.

After clearing my throat awkwardly, I said to her back, "It's good to see you, Umerah."

Without turning, she said, "Both of you take care."

CHAPTER TWENTY-SEVEN

Coachlight Hospitality

We departed Umerah's compound to find the slots of daylight through Drop Town's overpasses dialed back to the blush of tempered steel. It was the onset of evening, 1802. The artificial sun had moved along its track. At the same time, the district was awakening with a surplus of pedestrians and end-of-shifters, like foraging ants on the prowl. Eric and I shuffled past Zulu eat-houses, ramen shops, conveyor-belt dim sum, bakeries, taverns, and autotroph feednodes with adherents plugged in like electric cars recharging their batteries.

I messaged Celeste as we struck north towards the trains, advising her that we were en route to Chilon and would meet her at the bar. Eric veered down a crowded alley.

"Where are *you* going?" I asked him.

"Need a Brockhouse coffee," he grumbled, indicating the indigo pyramid of the interplanetary chain a hundred paces off.

"There was coffee at the Electric Lagoon."

"It wasn't Brockhouse. Want anything?"

The little food I'd forced down felt like slag in my stomach. I sighted the coffeehouse and dialed up their menu on my HUD. Scanning it for something fortifying and liquid, I said, "I'll take a bowl of chicken pho."

Eric strode off, effortlessly cutting through the crowd. I hung back and thought of Umerah. It wasn't just the meal that was sitting uneasily with me. It seemed that something was clamping down on a part of my soul, a tourniquet staving off normal, limbic reactions.

Normal reactions, I thought bitterly. *What's the baseline for normalcy anymore?*

I didn't know what to feel. Maybe that's what happened to the oldest immortals. Emotional parameters stretched like putty. The usual stimuli and responses eroded by time until there was nothing left but an empty canyon. A Noctis Labyrinthus. And if it wasn't just the years but the mileage, then perhaps I was skirting that hollow territory. A discarded shell...considered human only because of its shape.

Someone bumped hard against me in the crowd. I almost didn't turn, but the bump was so unmitigated that it seemed to demand a response. It didn't occur to me that this was precisely what I should *not* do, that someone wanted me to engage.

I found myself face-to-face with a squat, bearded, Slavic-looking fellow, barrel-chested and with arms befitting a gorilla.

He jabbed a stun-prod to my belly.

"That's right," he said, licking his lips. "Don't try anything, ruster. We're going to take a short walk, over there." He indicated with his head a poorly lit Xibalban restaurant. I smelled plantains frying from its doorway.

"You're going to shoot me in this crowd?" I asked evenly.

His eyes were hard. "People 'round here mind their business."

I considered this. *Coachlight* was IPC-controlled, but we were in a bottlenecked rabble. Cops would need an aerobike just to get here, and by then....

"Who are you?" I tried.

He jammed the prod deeper. "Gonna have us a private talk. Now move!"

I moved. Without even activating my blurmod, I smashed the dome of my forehead into his nose. The cartilage popped, blood gushing into his beard. He moaned, drew his hands protectively to his face, while I snatched the prod. People saw the altercation, but the flow of bodies was too steady to permit a reaction beyond fleeting, open-mouthed gapes.

I aimed the prod into his chest and triggered it. He dropped like a cut marionette.

<Detecting hostile vectors,> piped Xenophon. <Three bogeys south.>

I spotted them. A trio of men shouldered their way against the north–south flow of traffic, bearing down on my position. Unfriendly faces in the human river.

Turning north, I pushed towards the Brockhouse. One of my pursuers possessed an Earther's density. Nearly as wide as he was tall, he shoved people out of his way as if they were dolls.

I would never make the coffeeshop before that flesh-tank was upon me. Darting into a software shop, I rushed past occupied wet-ports. The clerk cried out as I kicked open the rear door. There was a flight of stairs zigzagging to the roof, and I reached the crest in seconds.

From there it was an easy leap to the next rooftop. I hopped the gap as the flesh-tank hoisted himself up ahead of me. Must have been a staircase there. Or else he had a magfiber grip and had scaled the building like a singularly fat beetle.

More importantly, he had successfully anticipated my retreat tactics. That suggested either luck, or he had eyes on me. An airhound, or someone in a crow's nest.

"Not bad," I said.

He grinned wanly. My dealings with Earthers had been limited. In childhood, they'd been a common sight at Hellas Market until Partisans depleted the immigrant population. During the war, I ran into a few holdouts who'd stayed to harass Partisan lines. In the end, their presence amounted to some diversity on the battlefield, as their lesser stature made them like dwarves in a racially varied fantasy saga. The only Earthers who had ever impressed me were Celeste and Gethin.

My rooftop opponent was unique even by those standards. He appeared unusually thick, as if his body wasn't flesh as much as flesh-hued concrete. Visually, he seemed to weigh in at perhaps two hundred and eighty pounds, yet I sensed he was heavier than that. Dense like a neutron star.

Which suggested he was built from more than bone and muscle. Jacked to the eyes with tech.

An arky.

"Which one?" I asked.

He frowned. "Which one what?"

"You're from the arcologies, right? Never met an arky. Would love to hear about—"

He threw himself forward, trying to incapacitate me with a flurry of chops. I whirled low and swept his legs. He fell with a crash.

I activated my blurmod.

He followed.

The ambient noise from the crowd morphed into a slurring, deep-voiced chorus. I sprinted to the next rooftop, and the next, while the Earther bounded after me, his muscles giving him a powerful boost to close the distance. I faked a direction change, spun about, and ran headlong into his charge. He ducked my first blow and slammed into me, delivering the first surprise: an electric stun effect that knocked me off my feet. The attack triggered our blurmods' safety features, dropping us out of hyperacceleration. The noise of the crowd returned like a lion's roar.

<He delivered four thousand volts with that attack,> warned Xenophon. <I hypothesize his body contains stacked electroplaques in his limbs to generate voltage.>

I rose unsteadily, the hair on my arms standing up. "That was different," I admitted.

The arky smiled, having barely broken a sweat. "I'm from the Apollonian Ring, by the way," he said proudly. "I've been fighting longer than you've been alive, ruster."

"'Ruster' is no longer accurate. Mars hasn't been covered in iron oxide for a long time."

"Right, just radiation and bones now, huh?"

"See," I growled, "that was just rude."

Something landed on my neck. I swatted it off, heard it skitter to the rooftop. At the same time, the arky leapt at me again, going for a grappling move.

Instead of recoiling, I stepped into his attack, blocking both his hands with an inside-out slap, and then punched for his throat. He saw the blow coming, but didn't realize it was a feint. Blurring again – and too close for him to react – my other fist caught him on the side of the head and caved in his face. There was a coconut crack; one eye hanging grotesquely from its socket. Then I shoved him into the crowd below.

Staying in blur-time, I spun around for whatever had alighted on my neck. Xenophon auto-outlined it for my convenience.

A waspbot. Rising from the roof and circling me, seeking exposed skin.

I swatted it again, this time catching the thing with a palm strike. The impact destroyed it, wings and thorax flying apart.

Dropping back to normal speed, I messaged Eric.

Hey! Where are you?

The response came at once: ***Stars, Harris! Be a little patient, okay? I just got to the counter!***

I'm under—

My blur kicked in. Red arrows indicated an attack from the southwest.

Twisting, riding the elastic sensation, I took half a barrage of needle-fire on my armored flank. Two rooftops over, three additional men were rushing towards me. One held a needle-gun, the rounds whispering from the muzzle.

I deployed my shieldfist.

Then, without any warning, I dropped out of blur.

The mod hadn't timed out; something had disrupted it. In horror, I realized my hands were peppered with waspbots. Blue-black and ugly, jabbing their pincers.

My muscles spasmed. The wasps swarmed, biting and stinging.

The only course of action that made sense was to hurl myself off the building. I lurched drunkenly for the ledge. The fall might break my neck but I wasn't concerned about that. Broken necks could be healed.

Two men scrambled up behind me. One smiling, one glowering, like living theater masks.

"Don't make this difficult," said the glowering man. He sported two patches of whiskers above his lip, and held a stun-prod in one hand. I mentally tagged him as Mister Rat.

My face was going numb. I stumbled for the ledge. My strength leeched and I tipped like a listing vessel. In a last-ditch effort, I tried to fall off the roof, but it was a couple steps away. I dropped to the men's feet.

The smiling man said, "Look what we caught!"

My shoulder turret popped up and his head exploded in a pink cloud. Mister Rat vanished as I fired at him, too. He reappeared by my side and pressed his stun-prod to my forehead.

"You're in the deeps now, little fish," he whispered.

There was an explosion of white light...

...followed by blackness as pure as the heat-death of the universe.

★   ★   ★

I awoke to hushed voices and the sensation of being dragged.

My feet trailed on fibrous carpet. My head lolled, drool streaming from my mouth. Little clusters of pain riddled my body like nodes in a network. It was a familiar sensation – I'd been stung by waspbots before. Enemies could feed the little bastards a variety of poisons; in my case, someone obviously wanted me alive, so they'd loaded a flavor of liquid paralysis. There were grimmer options, however. I'd once seen Lieutenant Cuddy dissolve like a time-lapse candle as he was swarmed in a room he'd failed to properly check.

Medical crosses flickered in my HUD, superimposed over my body diagram. The damage report told me what I could already feel: I'd sustained fourteen stings. I'd also taken a round from the needlegun, in the wrist just below my gauntlet. Hadn't even felt that one.

My hands were cuffed behind me as I was dragged. How many hostiles were there? I listened, tallying them by sound and pattern. Two men had me by the arms. One person strode ahead, and a heavy fellow trailed as rearguard.

I chanced opening my eyes. We were in a lengthy, lightless corridor; the only illumination came from doorway edges we passed.

Keeping myself limp, I tried reaching Eric. A NO SIGNAL alert replied to the attempt.

<They are jamming communications,> Xenophon whispered.

Whispering in subvoc, I said, *Do you know where we are?*

<You were unconscious and I could not see through your eyes.

Based on the footsteps, I estimate you have gone one hundred and fifty meters from where you were captured.>

Not very helpful, I mused. From what I'd seen of Drop Town, one hundred and fifty meters covered a hell of a lot of establishments. Still, it was better than no intel at all.

Anything else?

<I have no further information.>

Why are you whispering? It's not like they can hear you in my head.

<Sorry, Harris. I am keyed to adjust my intonations in sympathetic reaction to your circumstances. You may deactivate this feature if you wish.>

As I was hauled past the next door, I used its feeble light to view my abductors. The fellow marching point wore full armor of an unfamiliar style. My right arm was being supported by Mister Rat, and my left by someone I hadn't met. Couldn't see the person behind me, but the thudding impact of his boots suggested he was a formidable heavy. Music thumped in trance-like, bass-driven beats nearby. Were we in a nightclub? Above – or below – a bar?

"He's got a Martian accent," Mister Rat was saying. "We should brain him and space the bastard."

"Once we finish the interrogation," answered a calm, measured voice from my six.

Fuck. I knew that voice.

The arky. Alive, awake, and assigned to rearguard. Guess electrical attacks were just one trick in his bag; he must have top-line healing augs, too.

One of the many doors ahead flew open, spilling buttery light. A naked woman with a diamond collar around her neck crawled out, scrambling on all fours. She saw us and gave a stifled cry. There was something familiar about her; I was pretty sure I'd seen her in films. Realizing we weren't a rescue squad, she padded off in the other direction as fast as she could manage. I briefly wondered why she wasn't running, given the anguished desperation in her face. Then I caught sight of her legs.

She didn't have legs. At least, not human legs.

The familiar 'L' of kneeling human limbs had been swapped out for truncated, jointless stubs, like a pig's hind quarters. She'd been surgically altered to be a quadruped.

A portly figure lumbered from the room she'd fled. He was half-dressed, shirt unbuttoned to show a hairy belly. He saw his escaping captive. He extended his hand, fingers splayed.

The effect was astounding. The woman yelped and scrambled back to him. There had been no hesitation. She didn't *want* to return, yet she was doing it, and I suspected I knew why. In the war, we sometimes used a field ADS system to disperse crowds. It sprayed dissidents with a 150-kilowatt radio frequency. Caused all the water molecules in the target's body to boil. When it hits, you flee or get cooked alive. Or in her case, you comply with your master's commands.

He gripped her by the collar and steered her back into the room. The door slammed shut behind them.

<That was Angelica Shivanand,> Xenophon noted.

More likely a clone of her, I guessed. Shivanand was Hollywood royalty. There was no way she could be here, captured by thugs, reduced to that crippled and pathetic thing I'd seen. I knew there was a thriving black market for celebrity DNA. A discarded napkin, flushed toilet paper, sweat on a doorknob…that was all it took. A subset of criminals known as gene-lickers would trail celebrities. Once they obtained a DNA sample, they sold it to illegal clinics. Facsimiles were grown for sex slavery or snuff arenas. To counter this, celebrities employed professional cleaners to accompany them, scrubbing down things they touched. A moment's carelessness, however, and it was all for naught. The celebrity would continue on…unaware that a secret version of them would soon be consigned to short- or long-term hell.

My captors drew open a door. I was lugged into a twenty-by-twenty-foot room and forced to sit in a wooden chair. Mister Rat set my multigun in the corner and regarded it with open amusement. There was a single window across from me. A single light in the ceiling.

The arky was last to enter. He guarded the door, arms folded like a bouncer. With no small satisfaction, I noticed that half his face was deformed into a hideous swelling of tissue and fractured bones. Those healing nanites had their work cut out for them.

"He isn't alone," the arky grunted. "He was traveling with a fucking trog."

Mister Rat blinked. "You got eyes on?"

"No."

"Why the hell not?"

"I had my hands full taking this guy down."

Sneering, Mister Rat said, "From what *I* saw, your hands were full with your own brains. He wiped the floor with you."

My mom often noted that some people resemble animals, and we used to giggle at bears and lizards, apes and hawks we'd notice in public. Biodiversity's greatest hits peeking out from primate masks. Mister Rat looked even more rodent-like up close; the epitome of a flatfilm gangster stooge by way of *The Island of Doctor Moreau*.

I regarded my third captor. Clad head-to-foot in modular, blue-black voidarmor – the room's lighting gave me a better view of it. There were compartments on his arms, shoulders, thighs, stomach. I guessed most were for extra ammo clips or medpatches. One large compartment over his ribs was about the right shape to host a grenade, and there was a manual release knob there; in combat you want manual overrides so you're not screwed when an EMP fries the circuits you require to access a pocket. The turret seams at his shoulders were almost too fine to be noticed, but there's inevitably some wear and I made a note of it. His face was concealed by a black visor.

His most interesting feature, though, was the green insignia on his left shoulder patch. It depicted a ghastly woman, eyes crazed, hair billowing in a nimbus, and mouth stretched into a howl. Cut off from the local web as I was, it wasn't difficult to figure that I was looking at the Jolly Roger of Banshee Private Security…

…the group Peznowski had secured travel papers from.

The final figure in the room was a brown-skinned man wearing a gunmetal-blue tunic. His stature betrayed Earth origins, though he differed from the arky by every metric. He possessed a scarecrow frame. His beard was so neat it appeared sketched on by black marker. In a way, he exuded the famished quality of a refugee.

Yet he reeked of danger. The others were clearly deferring to him.

He studied me quietly for a time. His was the cold gaze of an accountant. Tabulating the situation, balancing the books. "Bellerophon Rybka, is it?"

"Every syllable."

"I've never heard of you."

I shrugged in my restraints, hands cuffed behind me. "Don't be too hard on yourself. There's sixty billion people in the universe."

His eyes quivered, reading some augmented display. "Well, Mister Rybka. My name is Quinn."

Ah! I regarded my host with new appreciation. The crime lord himself! It wasn't so surprising, really, given that Drop Town was a logical place for his base of operations.

"What brings you to the *Coachlight*, Mister Rybka?"

"*Schaefer's Nine Worlds of Sol*," I said. "I'm working my way through all the planets."

"Most tourists don't carry armaments like yours."

"Most tourists don't *have* armaments like mine."

From the door, the arky spoke through swollen lips. "Quinn, this guy is wired with military tech. And he's got a ruster accent."

I craned my neck to look at him. "Sounds like I gave *you* an accent, too."

The arky's face turned the hue of near-strangulation. He started forward. Quinn stopped him with a slight motion of his hand.

"You too, Quinn," I said, winking. "You've got an interesting accent yourself. In fact, I've only heard it one other time. Hudson Valley, New York, right?"

The man cracked a smile. It was a cruel expression, and I didn't need any patmatch to read what lay behind it. His smile told me that he'd seen bravado of every shade. Tough guys and gals, full of defiance until he broke them one by one.

"Very good," Quinn said, chuckling. "And I'll bet I can guess *where* you've heard it. See, I may not know you…and I don't know your trog buddy…but the VIP in your company, well, she and I go *way* back." His eyes shone with near-sexual luster. "Celeste Segarra has come to the deeps!"

Mister Rat made a face. "Who the hell is Celeste Segarra?"

"An old *associate*." Quinn enunciated the word deliberately, though spit flew from his teeth. "A Wasteland bitch who became the wannabe warlord of Mars."

I cleared my throat. "The former archon's schedule is full today, but she might be able to squeeze you in tomorrow. How's tomorrow sound?"

"There's no tomorrow for you," Quinn said. "You're going to die here. How fast or slow is up to you. See, I've got questions. I want to know what Segarra is doing here. I want to know why you went to see Umerah Javed—"

"She's fucking gorgeous," I interrupted. "Who wouldn't want to see her?"

Mister Rat stomped around in an impatient little dance. "Stars, Quinn! Let me take a crack at this guy!"

But my host remained cool. "Hang on, Harlan. I want to be fair, you know? Our Martian visitor doesn't fully appreciate his circumstances. We're really good about keeping people hidden, Bellerophon. I can keep you here forever if need be. It's not the kind of eternity you'd enjoy."

"You've got big shoes to fill, Quinn. I've been taken to hell before, and by the very best."

That seemed to give him pause. "When's the last time you Saved? Answer truthfully: I'll know instantly if you lie. You came from Mars, right? So you probably got Saved before your flight." He cocked his head. "Yes?"

I nodded.

"Then all you have to lose is a matter of weeks. Answer my questions and I'll kill you clean, that's a Quinn guarantee." His lips formed another smile. This time there was genuine warmth in it. "Truth be told, I've had a soft spot for Mars. It was my first offworld contract, once upon a time. Used to smuggle weapons there."

I stiffened. When the Partisans took power, they had heavy-duty ordinance they shouldn't have been able to acquire. Under IPC restrictions, large volumes of weaponry could never be legally shipped there. Especially to a faction which wasn't discreet about wanting to secede. Of course, a 3D printer could churn out thousands of cheap firearms – that was how the Order of Stone built their initial defiance. Yet the Partisans had gotten hold of complex, arky-tech weapons you couldn't just run off a printer, and the best theory was that Bishons – xenophobe as he was – had dealt with offworld smugglers.

Smugglers like Quinn.

"So let's start with your real name," the crime lord said. "Bellerophon Rybka is a fake if I've ever heard one."

"It's Russo-Greek."

"Your real name, please."

"The Ghost of Christmas Past."

"Why is Celeste here?"

"No idea."

Mister Rat tagged me with the stun-prod and I was blasted into a world of agony. Every nerve ending blazed. I jerked, screamed, fought in my chair.

My assailant hit me again, and again. Finally, he withdrew the prod.

"If you refuse to cooperate," Quinn continued, "we'll magpie your brain. Has to be done while you're alive, you know. Capture the activity in action. Not as good as a Save but we've had practice. Gotten good at keeping people alive while we dip and scoop."

The pain didn't subside immediately. Little aftershocks of sensation crackled through my body. Absently, I pulled at my cuffs, testing their strength.

Quinn whistled musically. "Really, man? You think we're stupid? Whoever the hell you are, it's obvious you're somebody's attack dog. We didn't scrimp on caging you. I don't fuck around with security, never did."

"Was worth a try." I sighed. "What do you want to know?"

"Why did you visit Umerah Javed in—"

"Get rid of the bot first."

"Excuse me?"

I regarded the armored merc beside him. "I don't deal with bots."

"Bots?" Quinn spoke with a degree of surprise. It was like he'd never heard the word, and I briefly wondered how deepworlders referred to robots. Mechs? Gearboxes?

"You've got a bot here," I grunted. "I say nothing until it leaves."

Quinn looked amused. "We don't use *robots* as bodyguards. Now, what business did you have with Umerah?"

"My business is none of yours, you Wasteland prick."

He heaved a sigh that conveyed a shallow reservoir of patience. Nonetheless, he kept his voice neutral as he repeated, "Segarra must have sent you to the Electric Lagoon. Why? What interest does the former archon have with a smuggler like Umerah Javed?"

"Smuggler? I thought she was a manufacturer."

"Answer the question."

"Fuck off." I glared at Mister Rat. "Go ahead and light me up again! I won't say a thing in front of the bot!"

Quinn jerked a thumb at the mercenary. "This is a human being, you fucking moron. We don't use robots here."

"It's a *machine*!" I snapped. "The whole Belt is full of machines! You want to chat? Tell the gearbox to fuck off." Before he could respond, I added, "Mars dealt with its share of robots. Sandclaws, waspbots, and everything a factory could crank out. We weren't exactly rolling in robotics experts, so I'm guessing they were purchased offworld. I know the deeps must be crawling with them."

"That's not the lay of the land here."

I found this to be a quaint metaphor, considering we were having our conversation in a rotating tin can on the edges of Jupiter's radiation belt.

The walls vibrated with a nearby sound system. Again, I wondered if we were adjacent to or above a dance club. Or were customers cranking the volume to cover their perverse pleasures?

Quinn rubbed his chin thoughtfully. I tried imagining what dealings Celeste would ever have had with this guy.

"Celeste," he hissed, as if reading my thoughts, "is a crafty little cunt. If she's out here, sending her lackeys to Drop Town, then she's up to something. What business does she have with Umerah?"

"I doubt she even knows who Umerah is. It was *my* idea to go see – whoa!"

The arky had apparently lost patience; he rounded my chair, gripped the front of my armor, and smashed the dome of his forehead into my nose. It hurt far worse than I'd expected; my nose was crunched flat. Blood squirted down my throat.

I was still reeling from the attack when he kicked my chair backwards. As my head struck the floor, he raised one boot above my face. Crazily, I thought back to Peznowski's bedroom...my broken teeth in my mouth.

"Stop!" Quinn commanded. "Sit him up!"

The arky, misshapen face quaking with wrath, grabbed my chair and righted it. There was something petulant in the action; I imagined him as a spoiled brat in his arcology.

"I can crack this ruster," he slurred.

Heart pounding with relief, I tried to think of stalling tactics. I didn't want to die. Didn't want to forget what I'd been through. Sure, I'd been Saved before the flight, but I didn't want to start over. Didn't want to wake up and think Umerah was dead.

I licked blood from my lips, spat, and said, "Quinn, I'm prepared to cooperate. Already told you that."

Quinn raised an eyebrow. "Then why aren't you—"

"*Get rid of the fucking bot!*"

He sighed with exasperation and bowed his head.

The Banshee merc finally moved, though. He crossed the distance to me in two menacing strides.

He swung his faceplate up.

A human man glowered beneath it. "This satisfy you, asshole? Now start answering the man's questions or—"

That was as far as he got.

With his faceplate helpfully out of the way, I pivoted my body, adjusted my hands, and shot the *jamadhar* directly into his face.

CHAPTER TWENTY-EIGHT

Scuffle

The *jamadhar* sprang out at twenty-three meters per second, a speed fully capable of triggering a blurmod. Unfortunately for the Banshee, the point-blank shot negated his reaction time. The weapon's galvanized tip speared his brainpan and sensorium, and he was dead on his feet.

Nearly in the same movement, I retracted the weapon – which is to say that my body and chair were jerked towards his still-standing corpse. Hands cuffed, I grasped the grenade pocket override, pressed the activation sequence, and used his body as fulcrum to shove towards the window.

The arky was on me an instant later, hooking his hands into my neck. Quinn and Mister Rat hopped sidelong to avoid the dead merc; they were both staring at the body when the grenade exploded.

The arky was pitched sideways by the blast. Mister Rat was crumpled in a corner, while Quinn was down but alive. The detonation had shattered the window. I lurched towards it, pausing only to grab my multigun – an ungainly action with my hands cuffed behind me. Quinn was trying to get to his feet, wobbling drunkenly; I kicked him in the windpipe and he dropped like felled timber.

Then I jumped through the window.

I landed on the neighboring roof. The NO SIGNAL warning cleared as I removed myself from local jammers. I was sifting for Eric's link when the arky hopped into the window frame, his hands shapeshifting into razor claws that – so help me – called to mind the iconic *nosferatu* of ancient cinema. He leapt at me, swinging both claws in a flashy, crisscrossing attack.

I hopped out of range of his claws – they whistled an inch from my face. Fumbling with the multigun, I selected LASER and twirled in place, firing.

The beam caught him across the face; he screeched, blinded. Then I kicked him off the roof; he fell, distended claws and charred countenance, into the alley. With a careful angling of my next shot, I severed my handcuffs.

I mulled over escape options.

I'd had enough of rooftop chases. I wanted to be street level as quickly as possible. That meant magfibering down a wall, or....

My eyes locked onto an unexpected sight. Someone had built a greenhouse up here. There was an open hatch visible within.

As points of egress went, that would do just fine.

Acting fast, I dashed towards the greenhouse, tucked my body in, and threw myself sideways through the panels.

Cheap glass crumbled around me. Inside, stacked trays of mushrooms were being grown on earthy substrate. I went down the hatch, discovering a stairway leading down into the building.

On the bottom floor, I emerged into an arena.

A soldier learns to react fast to new situations; you don't stop and gawk like a stricken deer. Nonetheless, I needed a couple seconds to understand what the hell I was seeing.

I was in an oblong chamber crammed with patrons. They wore full VR rigs. From what I could glean, they seemed divided into four teams and were battling each other with nonexistent weapons...swords and pikes, by the look of all the jabbing and swinging. Esoteric glyphs burned on every forehead. Overhead, floating against the ceiling, a gigantic aerostat *thing* moved about, like a silverfish or millipede, dangling feelers into the crowd; whoever was touched gave a convulsive jolt.

I shouldered through the arena, warily avoiding whatever the hell was above me.

<Harris!> Xenophon cried. <An armed individual is entering the club!>

Sure enough, a Banshee raced into the room and scanned the

crowd with a heavy rifle. I ducked behind a tangle of legs; one of the faux combatants – a kid no older than Peter Bayne – tripped and fell over me.

"What the hell, man?" he cursed, lifting his goggles to glare at me.

"Sorry," I muttered.

"This is the siege of Darkwater! Who the fuck are you?"

"Lower your voice, please."

He looked ready to argue. Then he took stock of my bloodied face, my armor and rifle. He soaked up these details with a wide-eyed stare and whispered, "We in trouble?"

"Just keep your head down and—"

My blurmod snapped into action. I twisted aside and took a shoulder-full of needles. They whined and pinged against my armor as I dropped and rolled twice. From the floor, I spotted the merc – a woman, the butt of her rifle tucked in the crook of one shoulder.

My rifle was still set to LASER. I fired through a breach in the crowd and torched a hole through her throat.

Getting back to my feet, I regarded the kid. "Good luck with Darkwater," I said, and sprang for the door.

Outside was a city square, hemmed in by narrow roads and buildings. I had no idea where the hell I was, and didn't have time to consult the map. Besides, my face and shoulder throbbed; my med-system was pinching off veins and clamping nerves, but unpleasant sensations slivered through.

Xenophon, plot me an escape route!

The response came at once: <There is subway access three blocks west of the square.>

I considered that direction. Lots of windows in the surrounding buildings. Lots of people milling about.

I was in enemy territory – the fiefdom of a deepworld thug. The square was dangerously exposed.

Interrupting my hesitancy, Xenophon spoke in a grievous tone: <Harris, street-cams show two snake-cars converging on our position.>

Before I could inquire what the devil a snake-car was, the first one came coiling out of an alley and blocked my westernmost route.

I formed quick impressions of it. Silver in color, it moved like neither a car nor a snake, but with a kind of gyroscopic fluidity. The vehicle stretched into a crescent-moon barricade, convex side opposing me. On the protected side, doors fanned open, and eight people in civilian clothing emerged, weapons hot.

I opened up on them with desperate, suppressive fire. The vehicle erupted under the fusillade. Hostiles leapt aside. Pedestrians screamed and scattered.

A second snake-car rolled up behind me, cutting off a southern retreat. The new arrival unloaded five Banshees in full armor. One by one, they dissolved into CAMO.

Acting out of instinct, I sprayed a wide arc of phosphire at them, emptying my entire cartridge, going for broke. The invisible figures were splattered, reappearing as patchy, luminous half-torsos.

Dangerously outnumbered and outflanked, I fell back to the club entrance. Something sailed over my head and landed at the doorway. Figuring it was a grenade, I leapt to the side, taking cover behind a falafel stall whose owner was already gone, his fleeing shape halfway down the street.

Instead of a grenade blast, the device erupted into a fixed nanoshield, sealing itself over the door.

I'm fucked.

The calculus of my situation unfolded in my mind. Thirteen hostiles in two flanking groups, each behind cover. Could I magfiber up the side of the club? Sure, but I'd be an easy target for everyone with a gun. Could I strike out north or east? Sure, though several enemies were blurring around me…zipping about like dust-devils, taking position.

I'm going to die.

A sudden crossfire opened up on my position and the falafel stand disintegrated into chaff. Aiming at a half-invisible figure, I returned fire; he sidestepped the shot in the graceful move of an experienced combatant.

My mouth went dry. A laser sliced an inch past my ear. In desperation,

I fired my *jamadhar* into what remained of the food cart, clamped onto it, and hurled it in the direction of the beam. The CAMOed sniper was closer than he should have been; phosphire had painted half his face and one arm, and the food-cart slammed into him with a sickening crunch.

My own blur ended as the batteries died. It was what my attackers had been waiting for. Two shapes flickered towards me. All I could do was deploy my shieldfist and spray-and-pray over its rim.

Then there was a sudden burst of light around us.

An EMP blast.

I hadn't even seen where the cannister came from.

The blast tore my attackers from their accelerated states. They sprawled almost directly to my feet; I decapitated them both with my shield, cleanly slamming it through their necks.

Eric's voice arrived over comlink: ***Can't even get a coffee without you fucking things up.***

I almost wept. A laser shot out of the east alley, cutting down two half-visible ghosts.

There are at least nine of these guys left, I messaged my compatriot.

Why are you still here? Bug the hell out!

I've been trying to!

The mercs collapsed into an impressive *testudo* formation to deal with the new tactical situation. No longer in CAMO, they condensed into a tight squad protected by green shields in front and on top. Moving as one, they marched on Eric.

For his part, Eric stood his ground. He fired over the rim of his shield, letting loose a fantastic wave of flame and plasma. The dual assault crossed the distance to the Banshees and lit them up. Their shields deflected the brunt, but heat made it through the barricade. They began to lose formation. I added my own firepower into the widening seams. It was like pulling apart taffy; as individuals broke off, Eric and I coordinated our crossfire and killed two more.

The civilians from the first snake-car looked stricken – bullies who were realizing they'd miscalculated. They presented an almost comic display of panic as we burned people alive in front of them. It wouldn't take much to shatter whatever morale they were clinging to. I decided to push them towards that outcome.

With Eric's fiery siege repelling the mercs, I lobbed an electric caltrop into the civilian midst. It landed, rolled...

...and exploded, arcing electricity onto everything in a ten-meter radius. Quinn's thugs were killed instantly, jittering like flies sprayed by insecticide.

Banshees are still up, came Eric's voice. *I'm depleting ammo fast.*

I glanced to my levels. *Me too.*

The remaining Banshees tightened their formation. They were backing slowly from us, across the square.

Can't let them gain the alley! Eric warned. *If they reach it...*

...they'll hunt us down at their leisure, I finished for him.

A laser scorched the doorway above my head. The heat singed me; in the foul-smelling mist, the laser was visible as a pink spear. This was followed by another of Xenophon's advisories:

<Two more snake-cars en route, arriving in eight seconds.>

Mazzola, I comlinked, *disengage and—*

Spotlights stabbed into the courtyard. In the vapors of battle, the lights seemed as solid as alabaster columns.

"Discard your weapons!" a voice bellowed from the sky. "All persons in Sector 38 stand down! This is the CCPD! You are ordered to cease hostilities and stand down at once!"

I glanced skyward. Gold-bedecked figures were gliding towards us on winged aerobikes, a flight of angels descending on the damned.

CHAPTER TWENTY-NINE

Nipping at the Heels of Gods

We were stripped of our weapons and taken, not to the Drop Town precinct, but to the InterPlanetary Council's office in Gateway District. The CCPD paddy wagon didn't bother with a ground-based route; rather, it lifted straight into the sky. Of all the modes of transport I'd taken – including the Ganymedan shuttle – this ranked dead last in my preferences. Spin-gravity was lost as we transitioned. Weightlessness had me fighting nausea for several unpleasant minutes.

The vehicle landed atop a hexagonal skyscraper. The IPC's logo spun in blue-and-gold holography.

Rooftop landings were rare on brightworlds. Here it seemed the way of things. From the helipad, we were taken to a processing station. MPs fitted us both with disruption collars that forcibly shut down our sensoriums. Next, a physician walked us through a cursory health scan. With no small amusement, I watched his bewildered expression as he viewed the results: my subdermal plating and EMP-dampeners, reinforced skeleton, virtuboard fingertips, *jamadhar* coiled in my left arm, and distributed seedclusters for blurmod and tissue regeneration. Poor guy was more perplexed by Eric's scan. Guess we were outliers from whatever he was used to seeing. No fucking surprise there.

Following this, we were separated. Eric was escorted into a detention cell, while my destination lay further down the hall. Three MPs showed me into an ovoid room of marble flooring, oak-paneled walls, and a gold-leaf ceiling. In place of windows were massive paintings, done in nineteenth-century realist style, oil on canvas. My first impression was that they depicted exploits from mythology. Then I gave a closer examination.

History, not folklore, was the gallery's focus.

The history of the human race.

Not the brutal prelude of the Paleolithic, nor the storied epic of ancient city-states, burgeoning empires, or age of sail. It didn't bother with the Industrial Revolution. It skipped over the failed superpowers of the so-called twenty-first century. Hopped past the Final War and the centuries of genocide, disease, and barbarism that followed.

Rather, the gallery featured the greatest hits of the New Enlightenment. In one frame, three individuals – Apollo the Great, Lady Wen Ying, and Enyalios the Mad – ringed an Athenian plinth that, like the *omphalos* of old, was to become the cornerstone of the world's rebirth. In the next painting I saw the construction of Babylon arcology over the ruins of New York. Another painting depicted the establishment of Tanabata City on Luna – the first permanent offworld settlement – with its glasstic dome catching sunlight like a mythical city on the hill. Yet another showed the founding of Mars (not from the Thirty-Three, I noted dourly).

My eyes slid from one majestic panel to another. The construction of the Apollonian Ring (which gilded the Mediterranean Sea). The laying of the Transatlantic Railway. The hollowing of Ceres. The hanging of Venusian aerostats like balloons in a cloudy sky….

Then I realized I wasn't alone in the room.

An IPC praetorian stood across from me.

I must have taken him for a fixture of the gallery – a suit of armor. It was tribute to my wearied state that I had missed his unmistakable silhouette. I started, adrenaline surging.

Holy shit! The praetorian from Mars!

The fight-or-flight instinct struck me like a bullet train and I broke into a sweat. Bradbury Shuttleport! The desperate chase ranging from terminals to loading zone, pitting me against the most implacable foe I'd encountered in twenty years of combat. My actuators tensed for a fight. The panic was so visceral that I found myself hyperaware of every detail: the seams in the praetorian's armor, the banding around its legs and arms and chest from which body-length shielding could spring, the eggshell-smooth visor regarding me coldly....

"He's not the same one," a woman said behind me.

I turned to see a stately figure cross the room. She wore white senatorial robes, and sported a shock of silver hair. Her ID bubble displayed on my HUD:

Donna McCallister
Secretary of State, InterPlanetary Council
Athens, Greece
Earth

McCallister was more than two hundred years old, and it seemed to show in her solemn visage. It was chic to go government gray; she was dutifully observing the style. Her face was all elongated slopes that, oddly enough, made me think of Drop Town's rooftops. Her eyes were flat and inexpressive.

"You were wondering if this was the same opponent you fought on Mars," she said, indicating the praetorian. "He isn't."

"Awful casual about treaty violations, aren't you?" I asked.

The secretary of state raised an eyebrow. "And who would you tell, exactly? There was no evidence left behind – thanks to your jaw-dropping *coup de grace*. You're outfitted with a disruption collar, so you can't record anything. We have a chance for something truly rare, you and I."

"And that is?"

"Pure, unbridled honesty."

I said nothing. McCallister studied me so long that I suppose another man might have begun to sweat, but I was exhausted past giving a shit. My nose throbbed. I could taste sticky, dried blood on my lips. The wrist which had caught a round from the needlegun ached where nanites toiled.

I wanted to sleep. More than that...I wanted to crawl into a foxhole and hibernate.

And still the secretary of state analyzed me. That was fine. I'd slept on my feet before.

"Harris Alexander Pope," she said at last.

"Every syllable."

"This is a treat. I should get your autograph while you're here."

"Should I just sign the arrest warrant?"

McCallister rounded a massive desk. The seat across from her looked awfully comfortable.

"You've certainly had a most eventful day," intoned my host. "Thirteen dead in Sector 38. Discharge of weapons in a protected zone. Destruction of property. Disturbing the peace."

"Disturbing what peace?" I asked.

McCallister grinned without humor. "You look nothing like what our computers calculated, you know. After Phobos, we were interested in learning about the legendary war hero. There were no photos available; your dossier had been scrubbed from Martian databases. I understand the Partisans did that for their shadowmen, tapeworming identities out of school and hospital records, social media posts, and planetary archives. But the Order of Stone had no records of you either."

"I was an ugly kid."

"With nothing else to go on, we ran hypotheticals. What might the brother of David Julius Pope look like?" Her smile broadened like a fissure in ice. "A thousand variations, and none of them came close."

She glanced meaningfully to the items on her desk. There, my weapons had been arranged as if at a criminal bazaar: my multigun with the ammo wheel safely ejected; my shieldfist gauntlet; my armored cuirass with shoulder turret attached; combat knife with rotating microblades; and toolbelt of countermeasures, airhounds, caltrops, and waspbots. Eric's belongings were there, too, and formed a more barbaric row behind mine.

McCallister laced her hands and made an excruciatingly slow examination. "So these are the toys that made a mess of Drop Town."

"Check the tape. It was self-defense."

"Looks like you packed for a war."

"It's a dangerous universe out there, Madam Secretary."

McCallister's eyes were creeping me out. They were utterly devoid of feeling, like the cold receptors of a machine. Even her smile had done nothing to inject emotion. With the white robes and gray hair, she seemed a dusty golem.

Those eyes lingered on the weapons as she said, "Did you know that the Japanese *katana* only came about because of the Mongolian invasion of the thirteenth century? The Japanese learned the hard way that their old swords were ineffective against boiled leather armor." She inspected my shieldfist gauntlet. "And that led, indirectly, to this."

I approached the desk. "I didn't receive a script. Do you want me to model these for you? Or am I supposed to quake in fear?"

"Actually, your profile says you're a hard man to impress. You played a fiction for twenty years. Save clinics might as well charge you double."

"As opposed to a single politician who must qualify for a group rate?"

Her smile returned, cold as asteroid ice. "Ten years ago, your victory broadcast became the most downloaded clip in history. A brilliant propaganda move, truly. Informing Mars that the Order of Stone had beheaded their gorgon…and at the hands of an undercover operative, no less! Suddenly the Partisans, who had never been infiltrated, wondered who *else* might betray them. It turned their own culture of secrecy against them. They ate each other."

"Fascists need someone to destroy," I said. "Even if it's their own."

"Is that what you've been doing? Destroying the leftover Peznowskis and Monteiros?"

I fought to control my surprise.

How the hell did she know that? McCallister was showing off, of course, playing the omniscient hand so customary of the IPC. Nonetheless, it staggered me. David had kept things locked down. If Mars didn't know, how could offworlders have any idea what really had happened?

Keeping my expression as flat as her reptilian gaze, I said, "Not sure what you mean, Madam Secretary."

She tilted her head in a vaguely bird-like movement. "Really? Perhaps with all your Drop Town antics, you didn't tune into the 'feeds today?"

In fact, she was right; I hadn't checked the newsfeeds since arriving on the *Coachlight*. During my connecting flight, I'd perused the local web to see what authorities were saying about the shuttle attack; otherwise, I'd been out of touch.

McCallister didn't wait for me to bluster through an evasion. She tapped the desk, opening a news holo:

PARTISANS ON MARS!
Click for more

POPE CONFIRMS THAT GOVERNOR, CEO, WERE WAR CRIMINALS
Click for more

PARTISAN AGENTS UNCOVERED, INVESTIGATION EXPANDS SEARCH
Click for more

"It's the top story in *every* feed," McCallister said thickly, watching further headlines spread across the holographic space. "President Pope held a press conference. With the time delay, it just hit the deeps…and *everyone's* talking about it."

She hadn't opened individual articles, just the headlines. The top nine out of ten news stories were related to the unfolding drama. David, as it turned out, had come clean. He told everyone about Caleb Peznowski and Eileen Monteiro. Subsequently, Tier Marsworks was doing backflips to distance themselves from their CEO, announcing an immediate 're-assessment of personnel files'. The deputy governor of North Hellas was calling for a referendum vote on Mark Bayne's successor. Witnesses on the *Dandelion Wine* were coming forward. The Martian Bureau of Justice announced that they were deepening their investigation into any known associates of the dead criminals.…

I almost didn't read the tenth item on the list, but its wording snagged my attention:

TEN THOUSAND WORLDS PROJECT UNVEILED!
IPC ANNOUNCES FIVE NEW HABITATS FOR IMMEDIATE COLONIZATION!
Click for more

I burst out laughing.

McCallister's eyes narrowed. "What do you find amusing?"

"You've been teasing this big mystery for months! And on the day you reveal it, Mars steals your thunder! Ha!"

My laughter was entirely out of proportion to the moment, but I couldn't help it. How long had it been since I'd really laughed? The fucking irony was devastating: the IPC had been building anticipation for their secret project, keeping the fires stoked with a drip-feed of little hints and a daily countdown...

...and on the big day, their announcement gets knocked from the spotlight by battered, broken Mars!

My laughter resonated in the luxurious chamber. I tried to speak a few times, each attempt dissolving into more guffaws. McCallister didn't interrupt me. She seemed to have petrified in place, stony expression and barely a hint that she was breathing.

I finally managed to expel some words. "My brother didn't do this on purpose, Madam Secretary! He *had* to go public! Media was breathing down his neck! He had already delayed as long as he could!" I wiped tears from my eyes. "It's just bad timing for you!"

"Bad timing?" she echoed in a brittle voice. "You expect me to believe this was coincidence?"

"Come on! Is *this* what you're upset about?" I pointed to the final headline. "You made your reveal! These habitats aren't going away! Although if you don't mind me saying so, five is a far cry from ten thousand, you know? I'd have a serious talk with your marketing department if I were you."

McCallister closed the holos as if crushing gnats in her hands. "Your brother is up to something."

"Excuse me?"

"No, don't deny it. He timed your arrival with his press conference."

My mirth faded as I reflected on this. The timing *did* seem rather suspicious. "So what if he did? There's strategic sense in putting a hunter in place when you shake the trees." I shrugged. "Not everything is about you, Madam Secretary. If criminals are here, it helps to have a guy on the ground."

Her face tightened fractionally. "Criminals...like Gethin Bryce?"

"Who's he?"

"He *was* on Ganymede."

"Was he? Didn't notice...you know, with me being shot down and all."

The lizard gaze returned. "The former archon has had direct communication with him."

"You have proof of that?" I demanded. "Because that's a serious accusation."

"You know perfectly well that I have proof. Unbridled honesty, remember? Segarra and Bryce go way back. I'm not surprised they're hatching some devious plot." She gave another bird-like tilt of her head. "What interests me is that they've involved your brother in it. The three have their own little conspiracy, how cute."

My attention glided to the painting behind her. Another advent panel of New Enlightenment history, this one depicting a fleet of IPC battleships against the Sun's molten backdrop. As with the others, it had been painted with an eye for realism – the battleships were nearly photorealistic, with antimatter batteries like little igloos dotting their flanks. Yet something about it smacked of classic propaganda posters: the might of the great fleet, wreathed in holy fire. Join the IPC! Rule the solar system!

My gaze returned to McCallister. "Not to change the subject, but does the *Coachlight* host many celebrities? Movie stars like Angelica Shivanand?"

McCallister blinked. "Are you autograph hunting?"

"I ran into her illegal clone in Drop Town. She's being held as a sex slave. If you send the cops now, they might even grab the monster who runs the place." I stared meaningfully at her. "Goes by the name of Quinn. Check your recent call-list, I believe you two are acquainted."

At last, there was a flicker of emotion in her face. Her jaw muscles tensed, a vein thumping in her throat. I'd gotten through her arctic shielding, and it made me smile as I added, "Unbridled honesty, remember?"

"How's this for honesty?" she snapped. "I don't care about you or your brother. I want Gethin Bryce. I want you to tell me where he is."

"Do you really think you scare me, McCallister? You think I can be bought or intimidated? You have any fucking idea what I've been through?"

Another tilt of her head. "You feel no loyalty to the man."

"You're right, I don't."

"Aiding and abetting a fugitive is a federal offense."

I held out my hands. "I'm not aiding *or* abetting him. You want honesty? I have *no idea* where he is." My broken nose throbbed. I wanted a drink. I wanted to collapse into bed. Nonetheless, I couldn't help but ask, "What is it with this guy, anyway? Why do you want him so badly? Didn't he used to work for you?"

The secretary of state let her hand glide absently over my weaponry. "Yes, he did. I knew him personally. Bryce is a natural contrarian. A throwback who fights against the system, whatever that system is. I won't claim the IPC has achieved utopia, but we have presided over a three-hundred-year peace…that's a record never achieved before in history. Older cultures profited from war. We profit – the entire species profits – from stability. That's always been our goal."

Her cheeks flushed with genuine color. She was warming to her own speech, and while I harbored no illusions that she had given it many times, there was an electric quality in her bearing that told me she believed every word.

And for all I knew, she might have legitimate reasons for wanting Bryce captured. He had sabotaged a lab and killed people. More to my concern, he was indirectly responsible for what had happened to my homeworld.

"The goal of Gethin Bryce," McCallister continued, "is chaos. He is discord and conflict. An outlier in the equation. There are advantages to that, I'll admit. His skills served us well for a time. But make no mistake: he's the snake in Eden."

"You didn't send a praetorian after him because—" My words cut off as the doors flew open behind me.

I had never seen Celeste Segarra angry – really, truly angry. But now the archon strode into the august chamber on a hateful tide of energy that practically gave off sparks. The praetorian advanced a step towards her; she gave it a withering look.

"Back off, you armored prick!"

The secretary of state exuded another lizard smile. "Ms. Segarra? I see you retain your way with words, as always."

Celeste halted beside me, her eyes boring into the woman. "Hey, Donna. News travels fast. I had to see for myself that an Order of Stone operative was being held without charges."

"We were merely having a conversation."

"And that conversation is over." She turned to me. "Grab your equipment, Harris."

The flush to McCallister's cheeks deepened. Her smile turned wicked. "It's been a while, hasn't it? You're better dressed than last we met...forty years ago, right?" She moved her hand, and another holo materialized over the desk.

I blinked at it. It seemed to be a still from a recording. There were two people in frame. The environment was unusual – it appeared to be the interior of an unknown vessel.

Gethin Bryce was centered in the feed. Hair a little longer and tousled, eyes green in the reflected light of an unseen monitor. Bryce's mouth was opened in the midst of speaking. His hands were splayed to stress whatever point he was making. It was clear he had made a call to someone – to Donna McCallister, I presumed, and we were seeing her side of the recorded conversation.

There was a second person in the image, though. It looked like she had just taken a shower, because she was topless and beaded with water...

or sweat. The pattern of her scars was unmistakable. The still-frame had caught her just as she finished crossing in front of Bryce...unaware or unconcerned with his conference.

Celeste regarded the holo and laughed. "Wow, Donna! How long have you been hanging on to this? Go ahead, plaster my tits over the solar system for all I care."

The two women beheld each other, fire and ice, while I gathered all the weapons from the table. Once the last ammo wheel was tucked in my arms, Celeste shepherded me out the door. Eric was already waiting for us in the hallway, and together the three of us exited the building in silence.

CHAPTER THIRTY

Man Dissolved in Fog

Her grip was akin to an industrial vise clamped on my forearm as she steered me to the elevator, then across the building lobby, then into the street, and then during the four-block hike to the nearest train station. Celeste was keyed up, galvanized by hostile energy. I didn't dare break that charged silence – and neither did Eric. It wasn't until we were aboard the *shinkansen* that she finally relented and shoved me into a seat.

As the train pulled away, I gave an awkward clearing of my throat. "So...how's *Coachlight* been treating *you*?"

Celeste didn't smile. She stood, clenching the hanging strap and staring absently at the floor.

"How did your meeting go?" I pressed.

"Better than yours." She scowled at me. "Remember the last thing I said to you?"

"Sure."

"I said if you got in trouble, you were on your own."

I scratched an itch on my swollen nose. My healing augs had set a repair crew of nanites on the broken cartilage, and the flesh was hot to the touch. "That's not actually the last thing you said, Celeste."

She twisted the hanging strap. "For fuck's sake, we weren't separated for long! How did you get arrested by the IPC?"

I was too weary for an argument. A pithy comment bubbled in my throat but died there.

Celeste's glower flicked to my companion. "Mazzola?"

Eric shrugged. "Don't blame me. I was getting coffee."

"What happened *after* you got your coffee?"

The trog started to reply, but I cut across his response with an acidity that surprised me. "You know your good buddy, Gethin? He sent us to meet an associate in Drop Town…a woman named Umerah Javed." I studied her face for reaction but there was none. This was her first time in the deeps, I reminded myself. She was as much a fish out of water as me.

"So," I went on, "within a half-hour of that meeting, I was assaulted, captured, tortured, and came within a nanometer of returning to Mars by way of purchase signal. Does that answer your fucking question?"

My outburst attracted stares from our fellow passengers. Celeste glared them down. In a swift pirouette, she went from standing to sitting in the empty seat across from me.

I braced for an escalation, but she only said, "Are you all right?"

"Never better."

"Who captured you?"

"Same person who shot us down, I think. Some crime boss who took an interest in me, and a *very* big interest in you."

Celeste blinked. "*Me?* I haven't been here long enough to—"

"His name is Quinn."

It wasn't so much shock that passed over her face, but a physical reversion, as if she was aging backwards. The notoriously rough, jaded exterior dissolved like time-lapse footage in reverse. She fidgeted with her hands. Her mouth hung slightly agape.

"Quinn…." she whispered.

"He's a big deal out here." I softened my voice, moved by her reaction. "How the hell do you know this guy?"

A tea-kettle whistle broke the silence, and we both jumped. It took us a moment to realize it wasn't a blurred attacker, but just the next stop notification.

Celeste's heartbeat was visible in her neck. "It's a long story."

"Is there anyone you *don't* know, Segarra? Criminals, fugitives, and Donna fucking McCallister?"

She stood, lost balance as the train slowed, and plopped back into her seat. "Come on," she said, voice flat. "This is our stop."

*   *   *

My favorite movie as a kid was Colin Specter's 219 version of *Journey to the Center of the Earth*. It offered more fidelity to Verne's ancient novel than any previous attempt, a few minor deviations notwithstanding. My favorite scene was the sea serpent battle, of course, followed closely by the harrowing escape from a twelve-foot Gigantopithecus and his herd of attack-mastodons. The most visually striking sequence, however, was when Professor Lidenbrock, Axel, and Hans stumble upon a gemstone wonderland. The movie's set-designer depicted this as a gaudy funhouse of mineralogical hues.

Seen up close, Chilon Tower resembled a prop from that scene. It was a reflective, ruby-hued skyscraper covered in a leprous matting of gold thread. Guests entered and exited via spinning doors, and PDTs lined up to accept or disgorge their fares.

From the train, we trekked several minutes without speaking. As we approached the hotel, Celeste said, "I don't know her, not really."

"Know who?"

"The secretary of state. We'd never met before today."

I halted at the spinning doors and looked at her. "Could have fooled me."

She swallowed hard; Eric picked up her cue and passed through the doors into the lobby. "McCallister was a lieutenant before her political career," she explained. "Gethin worked for her. Back in 322, he called her while we were aboard the *Mantid*."

"You weren't dressed for the occasion, apparently."

She shook her head. "You know why she played that clip, right? It wasn't for *my* benefit."

I frowned. "You're saying it was for mine? Why?"

"She was trying to get under your skin."

"Why would *that* get under my skin?"

"Did it?"

"Hey, you can fuck whoever you want. It's none of my business." Something occurred to me, and I said, "McCallister was at the Solstice Party. She probably saw you and me wander off together."

Celeste nodded. "The IPC prides itself on knowing everything. They like to show off. And they like to manipulate people."

I shrugged, wrestling with feelings I didn't want to identify. Part of me felt like laughing at the hormonal cocktail flooding my body; I was acting like an adolescent. Hell, I'd *been* an adolescent only a few weeks earlier, and while those hormones were not present in this body, it was possible I was experiencing an autonomic echo. The term 'muscle memory' was a misnomer; learn to ride a bike in one body, and you'll bring the knowledge over to another. Neural configurations are what matters.

It was 1954, just over a half hour to our dinner reservations. I was desperate for a shower and a drink – the two desires burned like a pair of navpoints. Yet as we passed through the spinning doors to enter the hotel, I froze.

A crowd of guests was gaping at the lobby newsfeed.

The holo showed celebrity anchor Victoria Nightfire, looming like a goddess. She'd changed her hair from her days with *The War Word*; the lusty, shoulder-length chestnut locks were now braided like a wreath of oak leaves around her head. She was speaking in her compelling, energetic style:

"—can confirm that each planet will be receiving a habitat from the Ten Thousand Worlds project." The holo cut to an O'Neill cylinder. For a moment I thought it was the *Coachlight*, until text appeared beneath:

KRONOS
  Scheduled for orbit around Saturn

The holo fractured into multiple panels, each highlighting a different cylinder and different text. I scanned them in open-mouthed wonder:

APHRODITE
  Scheduled for orbit around Venus

ARES
  Scheduled for orbit around Mars

GAIA

Scheduled for orbit around Earth

SELENE

Scheduled for orbit around Luna

ZEUS

Scheduled for orbit around Jupiter

POSEIDON

Scheduled for orbit around Neptune

DEMETER

Scheduled for orbit around Ceres

Nightfire spoke over the images. "Each habitat will provide living space for an initial population of two million souls. According to the Bureau of Stellar Engineering, however, they can comfortably maintain a hundred million people each! You heard that right, folks! Applications went online this morning. One billion unique uploads have already been received. I spoke to applicants from each world...."

Celeste went to the reception desk, where she formally checked us in.

"We're all on Level Fifty," she said, handing me my keycard.

I absently took it and jerked a thumb at the holo. "You seeing this?"

"I told *you* about it, remember?"

Eric's tongue ran along his fangs. "Eight new habitats," he said. "Room for eight hundred million residents...."

The holo was showing interviews with civilian representatives of each world. They formed a diverse spectrum of viewpoints. A cheerful arky from Paris. A skeptical miner from Luna. A guardedly optimistic medical assistant from Mars. A wonderstruck teleoperation specialist from Venus. In the corner of each interview, the relevant habitat hung in miniature.

"It'll start with eight," Celeste muttered, "like individual franchisees, each cylinder responsible for its own populace."

Eric chuckled, the sound originating far back in his throat in a way that reminded me of Mongolian throat singing. "When I was a kid in Ybarra, it was a special treat to get ice cream after dinner," he said. "Now, we're all getting a free moon!"

The optimism in his voice sounded genuine. I shook my head but didn't have the energy to argue.

*　　*　　*

One glass.

Two ice cubes.

Two hundred milliliters of rye whiskey from the minibar.

In my hotel room, I sipped my drink and felt the notches of anxiety slowly loosen. It wasn't merely the medicating effects of the alcohol, but the sense of normalcy that came with it; ice cubes clinking in the thick-bottomed glass, and my room offering privacy, security, and *time*. I was able to steep in nothing but my own thoughts. Not even that, because I wanted to escape from thinking as much as from pain and fear and danger. The room was as quiet as a suspended animation cube. Might as well be a portrait: *Man with Drink*.

When was the last time *anything* had felt normal? Nursing my whiskey, I contemplated the question. Time aboard the Ganymedan shuttle might be normal for a spacer, but not for me; my best efforts at establishing routine had never dispelled the unpleasantness of being in a spinning can.

Had it been my brief life at the House of Laws? Certainly the ingredients for normalcy had been there: a loving family, warm meals, gifts and wrapping paper. But I'd never felt truly comfortable there, either. Besides, Cassie and Rudyard and Luthien hadn't been *my* family. They'd treated me wonderfully, doting on me with authentic love; Rudyard especially had taken an instant liking to me, dragging me into his private world of puzzles and toys and Arcadium games. I'd been gracious, but the truth was that I'd learned – as many soldiers do – to don a smiling mask. The ugly truth was better left unspoken: they would never understand me.

I barely understood myself.

I finished the whiskey in a long, masochistic gulp. Then I ran the shower hot enough to steam the bathroom. I shed my clothes and equipment, leaving them in an ugly little pile. On the bathroom door, a bone-white privacy mask dangled, wrapped in plastic, for when I headed down to dinner.

The shower felt good. As water ran over my body, I let the mist envelop me completely. I was another painting: *Man Dissolved in Fog.*

At 2016, I toweled off and composed a message to David. The *Coachlight* was presently six hundred million kilometers from Mars, so there would be a time delay. That fit my state of mind well enough. An email rather than real-time conversation. I kept it short: a truncated overview of my misadventures, a few queries on how people were reacting to the Partisan scandal, and my best wishes to Cassie and the kids. I sent the message, reflecting that by the time I received his reply, I'd be too drunk to understand it.

I sifted through my luggage for something to wear. The bags had emerged from the Ganymede incident without a scratch. I selected the Solstice gift Cassie had given me: a burgundy tunic with a black sash. Clad in my new outfit, I considered myself in the mirror.

A stranger gazed back.

It was my face and body, no denying that. Subtle differences, though, triggered a roiling discomfort. My broken nose had healed up nicely, though there was still puffiness around my eyes.

My birth-body had been killed years ago while serving the Partisans – I'd resurrected several times since. Dressing as Peter Bayne hadn't been my first foray into switching identities, either.

The stranger in the glass watched me. Memories swirled. Each recollection was like a specimen in a preservation jar; murky except where light catches on angles and swollen contours. They felt like someone else's memories. In a way, they were.

What had I been before my Partisan days?

A memory floated up.

I'm twelve years old. Mom is helping me fit a sash over my forest-green tunic for my coming-of-age ceremony. She wears a proud, sad smile as she sets the final piece — my wreath of oak leaves — upon my head. It itches and tickles.

"Look how handsome you are!" *she says, steering me to a body-length mirror.* "Today you become a man!"

I glance around my bedroom, noting the toys on the carpet, the games stacked on my desk, the adventure books so numerous they seem a garish-colored fungus creeping over the shelving. Something about the scene makes me giggle. Mom holds me, and says, "Becoming a man doesn't mean you have to grow up in here." *She touches my chest.* "I love you, Harris."

Then another memory. This one is fuzzier.

Dave and me sneaking off to Ybarra District. We're drinking at our corner table. There's an argument between us. Dave storms off. The waitress brings me another beer. I go upstairs with her and spend the night between her legs.

The next thing I recall is the morning after. Slipping out of bed. Getting dressed. Pinging Dave and receiving no answer. Heading home, and seeing the scarlet TRAITORS sign on my parents' front door.

What had David and I fought about?

A knock sounded. I crossed the room, scooping up my multigun and holding it parallel to the doorjamb. A close-range shot could kill a blurred enemy instantly.

Drawing the door open, I found Eric standing there. He'd slicked back his mohawk into a kind of samurai's topknot. His piercings looked polished. His robust frame was clad in a sky-blue tunic with navy slacks.

It took me a moment to gather my thoughts. "You look...um... different."

Eric's eyes narrowed. "That what passes as a compliment from you?"

"Never saw you in blue before. It—" *Emphasizes your ghoulish pallor so you look like a corpse walking.* "—is really different."

"Bright colors are popular in the deeps. I'm trying to fit in."

"Why bother? It's not like we're staying." I fitted my shieldfist gauntlet over my left hand, snatched my keycard, and stumbled into the hall.

My compatriot gave an inscrutable look. "We're in space, Harris. You and I are half a billion kilometers from the only planet we've known.

I think that warrants dressing up, don't you?" His voice swelled with something akin to pride. "I'm a trog-kid from Ybarra. Never thought I'd get offworld."

I tried to think of something glib to say, but feared it might come out cynical. "Well," I slurred, "you did it, Mazzola. I'm happy for you."

He frowned. "Are you drunk?"

"Yeah."

"We've been back less than an hour!"

"Gather ye rosebuds while ye may."

CHAPTER THIRTY-ONE

The Floating Islands

Hang out in a Martian ski lodge long enough, and you'll inevitably hear someone talk about Yama Uba.

The reclusive ghost is said to inhabit the most unforgiving altitudes atop the redworld's Five Peaks. She's never seen in daylight or fair weather. Never haunts the foothills. Yet press onward, where biosuits are needed to survive and the horizon bends like a frown, and you are encroaching on *her* territory. At such dizzying heights, you encounter few people. There's an existential loneliness, the chill of the Wellsian time traveler witnessing the end of the world. Exhaustion sets in. Your legs burn, your biosuit chafes until you're bleeding. You settle down, scraping glacial ice to replenish your canteen. Then you pitch your tent and rest.

At some point in the night, Yama Uba pays you a visit.

She appears, so the legend goes, as a hauntingly beautiful Japanese woman in a kimono. Cold black eyes and blue lips. She lies across your body, whispering, "Rest now and forever, as I keep you warm." Her lamia breath tickles your ear like frost on a window.

And then you die.

The folk tale probably arose from the unsettling body count stemming from attempts at scaling Olympus Mons. The slightest tear to your biosuit, or a malfunction in your rebreather, and you're hit with high altitude pulmonary edema and a deadly euphoria. People have died with smiles on their lips.

Some imbecile had seen fit to decorate Chilon Tower's restaurant with Yama Uba motifs. The sinister ghost wasn't alone, either. A ghastly parade of haunts, poltergeists, ghouls, and revenants adorned the place, for reasons I could hardly fathom. Nothing says "Bon appetit!" like being ringed by the undead.

Eric and I arrived wearing our privacy masks. A cheerful maître d' guided us to a private tatami room. Inside, three unmasked guests awaited us.

My eyes registered Celeste before anyone else. She was as elegant and formal as I'd ever seen her, wearing a violet-and-black Sylvan Age tunic that hugged her curves and legs. She was in mid-conversation as we entered; her eyes skated over us, and then she went back to talking with the second person in the room, Gethin fucking Bryce.

The green-eyed Earther held a tumbler in one hand, sipping an amber-colored fluid that might have been brandy or cognac. I scanned for holographic trickery and found only a dense, physical presence.

"You look real," I said, removing my mask.

Bryce gave my hand a firm shake. "It's good to see you again, Pope. Mister Mazzola, it's a pleasure."

Then I noticed the third and final guest in the room.

"Umerah Javed." I breathed the name. She was in the same gray business suit she'd been wearing earlier. "Together again, huh?"

Never apart for long. I waited to hear the words from her, and felt a pang of anguish when she only nodded and said, "I heard what happened in Drop Town. For what it's worth, I'm sorry."

We took our seats around a low table, which put me to Gethin's left.

"No more smoke and mirrors, huh?" I snapped at him.

He shrugged. "Our situation requires my real presence."

"Despite the real risk?"

"I could throw an old Mencius quote at you, about disliking certain things more than death. But the fact is we're at a pivotal moment. Our Phobos moment, if I can make the reference."

"You and I had very different experiences on Phobos."

Eric sat across from me, the five of us positioned like points of a star. He helped himself to an appetizer of gyoza dumplings. The way he bit into the glutinous, translucent shell to extract the shrimp inside made me think of wolves sucking marrow from bones.

Gethin poured a bottle of chilled *sake* for everyone. To me, he said, "I understand you tangled with Quinn personally."

"Technically he tangled with me." I downed the *sake* immediately, communal toasts be damned. Grudgingly, I had to admit it was the best *junmai* I'd ever had; we preferred hot *sake* back home, but this serving was like the kiss of glacial meltwater. My gaze strayed to the tatami walls, where a painting depicted a lonely, floating outpost. It looked like Titan. There was an ochre sea beneath morose clouds. A winged figure floated above the water. Some mothman dreamt up by people on the frontier.

Gethin sipped his drink. "I've never met the guy, myself. I'm sorry *you* had to. As dangerous as he is, Quinn is hardly our chief concern."

Umerah cut in. "Did Harris tell you what he saw? Quinn is growing celebrity meat dolls. That's a concern of *mine*."

"I'm sure that's true," Gethin said. "Quinn probably has a lab of bioreactors growing most of Hollywood. Once the meat doll is ready, the customer rents a special room and does...."

"Whatever they want," Umerah finished coldly. Her eyes had a brutal, venomous gloss. I'd once seen her dick-punch Sergeant Hammill when, during an intel-gathering operation in Blacksand, he'd pointed out an attractive corpse – legs spread – and suggested he 'needed a few minutes alone with her'.

Gethin lowered his drink. "Quinn isn't our problem."

"He's *a* problem," Umerah insisted. "And I'm terrific at multitasking."

Celeste made a caustic sound. "Javed, right? We're not going to jeopardize our plan because of a small-time criminal. I've had dealings with Quinn since before you were born. His time will come."

Umerah grinned coldly. "Is that right, old lady? Maybe if you'd finished Quinn off before I was born, he wouldn't be troubling us now."

Their eyes flickered like swordplay. No false smiles of polite society here, but open suspicion and an unspoken threat.

Gethin cleared his throat. "Glad we're hitting it off so marvelously. If you're both done, let's get down to business."

I drummed the table. "What business, exactly?"

He steepled his fingers. He was playing it cool – that seemed his default modus operandi. But I detected a strained bearing in his demeanor, his eyes darting anxiously to the *shoji* door.

The fox has come out of hiding, I thought. *And he knows the hounds are legion.*

"We'll keep introductions brief," he said, and indicated Umerah. "Ms. Javed and I have been working together for ten years. She's a former pilot. A damned good one, too. As far as the universe is concerned, she died on Phobos and her service record was destroyed in the war. That's been an effective combo. She's conducted espionage, infiltration, and secret missions that made this moment possible."

I considered my ex-lover, trying to imagine this shadowy season of her life-after-presumed-death. And suddenly I remembered our first meeting.

In a Partisan hangar, I approach a dropship for my next deployment. A woman sits astride one of its wings, wrench in hand, tinkering with the rotor. Dressed in her loam flight-suit, she resembles some Old Calendar pinup combining patriotic we-can-do-it sentiments with stunning sex appeal.

"Hey up there," I call to her. "This your bird?"

She wipes her forehead and levels an appraising stare. "It is. I presume you're the shadowman I'll be working with."

"Harris Pope."

"Umerah Javed."

"It's good to meet you."

"We'll see about that, won't we?"

Gethin moved on with his introductions. "Eric Mazzola's service record speaks for itself. As I understand, he played a key role in ending the war. I'm glad to have you aboard."

Eric gave an appreciative bow.

"Harris," Gethin said, eyes finding me. "Not sure you need an introduction. The war hero who shouted his victory like Odysseus on Cyclops Island. We only collaborated once...a memorable little episode. Thing is, he didn't realize we were collaborating at the time. I aim to remedy that with full disclosure."

I folded my hands and watched him.

He turned to Celeste, and there it was again – a magnetic quality flowing between them. "The former archon and I met on Earth. In New York, as it happened. We shared a kind of Grand Tour through Athens, Turkey, Japan, and China. We've tangled with terrorists, gods, and monsters. Survived an airship crash and a mountain collapse. They don't come much tougher than her. I trust her with my life."

Celeste rolled her eyes. "You're sweet and all, Gethin, but get to the fucking point, okay?"

He laughed, and I couldn't help observe the dilation to his eyes, the blush in her cheeks. An ecosystem of primal reactions. Not as overt as a Kabuki shrimp mating dance, but honestly, not that fucking far off either.

"Very well, then. You're all here because we're at war. It's a war without bullets and without bombs. The stakes are nothing less than the fate of our species."

"What are you talking about?" I demanded.

"I'm talking about a plan to turn the human race into prisoners."

"You're talking about the Colonization Ban. Keeping us corralled in one solar system."

"That merely set the stage for what they're planning," Gethin said. "When the Ban was put in place three hundred years ago, the reasoning behind it was that humanity couldn't risk coming to the attention of hostile aliens."

I sighed. "Maybe the IPC has a point. If there are malevolent empires out there, maybe we should keep our heads down."

Gethin and Celeste exchanged a look.

"Are there aliens?" I asked.

"Sort of," Celeste said.

"*Sort of?*"

She fidgeted with her fork. "Thirty-seven years ago, a hostile and non-human faction made itself known. They weren't aliens, not exactly. Suffice to say that they posed a threat to humanity."

"That doesn't suffice, Segarra." I leaned forward, alternating my look between her and Gethin. "Not aliens…so are we talking about AIs?"

"No," Gethin said at once. "The AIs were a convenient scapegoat.

The IPC had been wanting to eradicate them for years, and the *Incident of 322* gave them pretext."

"Then what the hell were they?"

Celeste sighed. "I've been grappling with that question for years, Harris. For want of a better label, let's call them gods."

Umerah made a scoffing sound. "Gods? Really?"

"I did say 'for want of a better label'."

"You also said 'gods'."

"It doesn't matter," Gethin insisted. "Whatever they were – rogue aliens or transgenic mutants or primordial engines – they are gone now. Some were killed in 322. The few that survived appear to have departed this little corner of the Milky Way. We're on our own, as far as I know. That's liberating…and terrifying.

"The IPC was founded in the aftermath of war…a war that destroyed much of Earth. For all their faults, they are determined to protect the human race from future threats. They pay attention to history. They study current events. They adjust their tactics accordingly. War nearly wiped us out, so they created hegemony to enforce a *Pax Apollonia*."

Celeste added bitterly, "AIs were seen as a threat to that hegemony, so they were exterminated."

Gethin nodded. "And now, with human population exploding and demands for expansion heating up, the IPC has turned its worrying eyes to the stars. Again, I get it. If we tangle with someone unpleasant out there, we face the possibility of extinction."

"And that's why the Ban exists," I said impatiently. "I'm guessing their razzle-dazzle Ten Thousand Worlds project was designed as a shrewd compromise, giving us more real estate while keeping us contained around Sol."

"Precisely."

I shrugged. "Thing is, there's a vote coming up in the Senate. Word on the street is that it's a dead heat."

Eric added, "And Mars votes *tomorrow* on whether to rejoin IPCnet. If that happens, there's no telling how the scales might be tipped."

Gethin watched us patiently.

"Supposedly," I continued, "Natalia Argos has her eyes set on representing Mars in the Senate. She's a fucking bitch and I'd love her to fall into the Sun, but I have to admit that her unique brand of bitch means she opposes hegemony. Odds are she'd vote to lift the Ban."

He said nothing.

"Goddam it, Bryce! My point is that if Mars stays out, a deadlock keeps the Ban. If Mars rejoins, the Ban probably gets lifted and—"

"Natalia will vote to keep the Ban," Gethin said.

"I doubt that very—"

"She'll do it, Harris. She and every other senator will vote exactly how the IPC wants them to. What's more, they'll think it was their own idea."

I pounded the table with my fist. "What the hell are you talking about? Natalia will vote however she wants to!"

"The IPC will change her mind."

"How?"

"By literally changing her mind," Gethin growled, and his eyes burned with balefire.

CHAPTER THIRTY-TWO

Recalibrating Humanity

Gethin spoke and we listened.

The New Enlightenment had been more than a resurrection of civilization. More than a clearing away of debris. There was a pattern to history. An escalating sequence in which each collapse was worse than the preceding installment. The Final War was a delusion of nomenclature. Global collapse had not been an epilogue, but merely an intermission heralding the next gruesome act.

The architects of the New Enlightenment realized it would take more than brick and mortar to disrupt the human pattern. Even as they brushed off radioactive dust and set about a Phoenix-like reset, they promoted a deliberate, cultivated rejection of the Old Calendar cultures which had failed so profoundly. When the Final War delivered a nuclear knockout, historians argued that it was a mercy killing. The old world had been dominated by militant religion, corrupt governments, and a steady rot of social and political norms. It was an especially demented age of history.

That's why the IPC looked to earlier zeitgeists for their inspiration. Rather than follow the plutocrats and theocrats and fascists of yesteryear, the new regime drew from the font of Hellenism: fearless artistic and scientific inquiry. The arcologies were born from that optimism. Disease was vanquished. Actual immortality – as opposed to the delusions of faith – was achieved. Yet pretensions of utopia were challenged by certain nagging problems. Crime had not disappeared; in fact, it seeped into new tracts never possible before. Political fanaticism and online lynch mobs remained a persistent headache.

The problem, theorists said, appeared to be human nature itself.

"It came to a head with the Incident of 322," explained Gethin. "For the first time in three centuries, the New Enlightenment stumbled like a drunkard on a cliff. I was there. So was Celeste. We were staring at another apocalypse."

I scoffed, "*Terrestrial* apocalypse, maybe. But people were already living on Mars, Venus, the Belt...."

Gethin's eyes flashed. "Oh? Is our Martian guest going to lecture me about the permanence of civilization, using *Mars* as an example?"

My protest withered.

"The sum total," he continued, "is that humanity needed to face an ugly truth." He looked at Celeste.

She picked up from his cue. "We are *not* a rational species," she said. "We are the destroyer of worlds. Left to our own devices, humanity eats itself. Earth did it a thousand years ago. Mars did it a hundred-and-twenty *months* ago."

Gethin ran his finger around the rim of his glass, producing a ghostly note. "And don't think other worlds offer cogent rebuttals. Venus and Luna are viper pits. The Jovian League is...well, you've been here a fucking day, what do you think, Harris?"

Eric wore a deeply conflicted expression. "A lot of these conflicts you're talking about...they were the result of government or corporate agendas. They didn't reflect the common man! Doesn't that contradict your point?"

"It *makes* my point!" Gethin countered, flushing angrily. "Because the common man always willingly goes along with it. You don't blame the liar who insists his neighbor is a witch; you blame the mob that shows up to burn her!"

I looked curiously at him. "Speaking of burning, you opposed the AI genocide. You rescued an AI ship...."

"I opposed it because the decision to wipe them out was based on bullshit. I was a special investigator." He steadied his breathing, drawing another note from the glass. "I was a *very good* investigator. Had a habit of breaking into places I wasn't supposed to. Of obtaining information I was never meant to see."

"What did you discover?"

"That the IPC has finally learned to address the biggest problem they face. *They can change human nature*. They can rewrite the human brain."

A cold shiver went through me. I realized my heart was pounding.

Gethin's intense gaze took on an ominous sheen. "Understand that human consciousness is nothing more than a neurological pattern, built up through a combo of ingrained behaviors and life experience. Even under normal circumstances, people can change their minds, make radically new decisions. How many ascetics become hedonists, and vice versa? Atheists turn to old faiths or trendy ideologies, whether its Abraham's Flock or the Faustian Church. I'm sure we all know people who flip political views. For want of a better phrase, let's call it a byproduct of our mental layer cake." His voice dripped with corrosive sarcasm.

I sat straighter, fighting a wave of sickness. "You're saying they can flip a personality? Make a senator who opposes the Ban suddenly support it?"

"Yes."

"That's ridiculous!"

"I saw the data, Harris. I found the program."

"But to brainwash someone over a *political disagreement*?"

"Is it really so hard to believe? They've decided that humans—"

"Need to be changed systemically," Umerah broke in. Her eyes found me, and there was an unspoken sorrow there. "The Frontierists, the pioneers, the explorers, the dissenters...all of them will be infected – one by one – and *changed*. Those clamoring for galactic expansion will suddenly 'decide' to stay put."

Eric fiddled with his plate. "And with the Ten Thousand Worlds project," he said, "it would seem logical, too. Why move to alien worlds when we could build as many as we like? Controllable gravity, perfect weather, controllable—"

"Everything," I said. A raw animal panic was taking hold of me. It wasn't merely the hideous conspiracy I was hearing – a blasphemy against the entire human race. Wasn't even the bitter misanthropy churning our discussion.

It was the sorrow in Umerah's eyes.

And I suddenly understood.

No one had ever infiltrated the Partisans before. The Order needed a spy who could do it...a spy who would be fundamentally changed to evade detection....

Gethin hadn't just discovered the brainwashing program. He'd stolen it. Taken it to Mars with him. Given it to the Order – to my brother – who in turn authorized its usage—

—*my God*—

—on *me*.

★   ★   ★

The stench of puke burned my eyes as I retched into the toilet, a messy, watery vomit brewed in bile, *sake*, and rye whiskey. I'd barely made it to the lavatory in time. The toilet's metal valve showed my reflection as a bulbous-headed mutant.

It was several minutes before I could leave the stall. I moved unsteadily, gripping the sink's edge. There, I washed out my mouth... and considered my situation.

What did it matter *how* they had changed me? Truth be told, I hadn't dwelled on the question before. Two sets of memories had been grating uneasily in my head since my 'reactivation' – my life before the Partisans, and my life *as* a Partisan. Like two puzzles mixed into a single pile; you can distinguish them by rival color palettes, but there are plenty of fragments that could belong to either camp.

Maybe *that's* how the hellish program worked. Regardless of political affiliation, Harris Alexander Pope was someone who liked vanilla soft-serve ice cream and monsters and archaeology and Jules Verne. Maybe switching allegiances didn't require much of a change. Ninety-seven percent of human DNA matched that of a chimp; it didn't take much to wreak different outcomes.

But the Partisans killed my parents! Losing Mom and Dad had torn my life to ribbons! How the hell had my brain been convinced to join the very people responsible?

It didn't make sense.

I swished more water in my mouth and spat. There had to be something I wasn't being told...

...and I had a good idea where to start.

That night in Ybarra.

It was the puzzle piece I kept returning to. Whenever I focused on it, the details were like hazy pixels. That wasn't necessarily a shocker – Dave and I had been quite drunk. I had vague memories of knocking back Moscow Mules and Spacer Chasers. We'd grabbed a corner table. We'd talked. We'd had a fight...

...and *that* troubled me. I had no other memories of fighting with my brother. We'd gotten along famously. Never quarreled over a toy or book. He was my family and my best friend; I don't think many brothers can say the same.

So what the devil had we fought about?

We both had despised the Partisans, so I figured our argument couldn't have been political. Had it been over a woman? No, Dave and I never competed in that regard; whenever he expressed interest in someone – even if it was someone I found attractive in all the right ways – my own interest dried up. There were plenty of fish in the Martian sea. I had one brother. Besides, my sexual tastes ran counter to his; Dave preferred clean cut and respectable, whereas I was drawn towards danger and kink.

Whatever we argued about, it must have been one for the ages because Dave abandoned me...and in a trog ghetto, for stars' sake! The rest was a blur: the crimson TRAITORS poster, the fruitless search for my parents. At some point, my brother and I must have reconnected... but I couldn't recall when or how. The next clear memory I had was being on the yacht as Order of Stone technicians prepared me for my undercover operation.

There was only one person in the universe who could clear up the mystery, and it wasn't Gethin Bryce. After scrubbing my hands until they were pink and steaming, I sent a message to David with only one line:

WE NEED TO TALK.

★   ★   ★

When I emerged from the bathroom, I spotted Umerah at the bar. It took me a few seconds to realize she was still wearing her privacy mask: she had toggled the transparency option so that her face was visible. She leaned against the counter, a drink in hand, her *kitsune* gaze sweeping over the restaurant and paying mind to the entranceway. A few meters away, our tatami room's *shoji* panel was securely closed.

She must have been waiting for me, because she immediately beckoned me over.

"Where's your mask?" she said.

"There's no one here," I countered, indicating the empty bar area. "And no one knows who I am anyway."

Umerah peered at the space above my head, reading my false name on her HUD. "'Bellerophon Rybka. Makes you sound like an arky. Doesn't suit you."

I signaled the bartender – mildly surprised to see that it was a silver robot in a tuxedo – and ordered a whiskey. "And how could you possibly know what suits me?"

"We were compatriots for seven years."

"Bullshit. You were compatriots with a fictional identity. Want to know when we *actually* met? It was our last day together. When you saw me in Hellas Market."

Umerah hesitated, holding her drink loosely between two fingers. "So that's why you were delayed," she murmured, and her eyes lost their merriment. "You told me you were the only survivor of the ambush."

"That was a lie. There were no survivors. Natalia's squad killed our friends. Beresha had his head blown off. Conway and Hammill were taken down by grenades. I didn't notice how Shea and Cuddy bought it, because I was fighting to save my own skin." The robot brought my whiskey and I drained half of it in one swig. "I was last to die. My body was still warm when they reversed the brainwash."

"I see."

"Do you?"

"I think so." She looked disquieted, reviewing the past from a new parallax. "The Order of Stone needed a mole. The reason you were never detected was—"

"That there was nothing to detect." I polished off the rest of the whiskey. "I passed the screenings because I had *become* a Partisan. Unless that's a fucking lie, too. Maybe there was *never* a Harris Alexander Pope. Maybe I was cobbled together from other files. Maybe that's why I like monsters so much, because I *am* one."

Umerah placed her glass on the counter. "As best I can tell, the man I knew for seven years is the one who came to visit me in Drop Town today. He's the man I'm looking at now."

I made a disgusted sound and turned away. She caught me by the wrist-gauntlet and yanked me back to the bar.

"Listen up, war hero. Want to know what civilians will never understand? It's the depth of connection that arises from serving together. The man I knew was no Frankenstein monstrosity. That fateful day in Hellas, you were foggy and out of sorts." She shook her head. "But you were still the Harris I knew."

"You can't know that!"

"Were you even listening to our host? He said the brainwash program merely switched your political affiliation. It didn't fashion you like Minerva from the head of Zeus!"

"'Merely switched my political'…." I stared at her in astonishment. "We're not talking about ice cream flavors here! The Partisans were jackbooted thugs who tortured and murdered their enemies! The Order of Stone was *nothing* like that! The only thing the two groups agreed on was secession!"

Umerah nodded. "Sure, but I didn't see it that way at the time, and *my* brain hadn't been rewired! No, I'd been brainwashed the traditional way. Do you know what I did before we were assigned together? I used to fly snatch-and-grabs to civilian domiciles. We picked up 'traitors'. Know who reported those people? Their own family members! Their coworkers! Their friends! No program was needed…just a little propaganda." She hesitated. "Know what woke me up? Seeing the prisoners on Paradise Row. Vanessa Jamison, tortured and sobbing in her cell."

"My family was torn apart by those bastards—"

"You never spoke about your parents when we were together," she said. "Maybe the program erased them from your memory. Maybe it convinced you they died when you were young. Maybe it told you they were traitors, and that became the impetus for your decision to join the shadowman program…trying to atone for your parents' sin."

The ugly scenario she described made my stomach twist into new knots, and for a moment I thought I was going to dry heave in front of her.

"I never should have volunteered," I muttered. "Do you know how many people I killed?"

Umerah's eyes were downcast. "If you hadn't volunteered, we might still be fighting the war. History really is made by individuals. It was George Washington's decision to cross the Delaware; another, more tepid general might have balked."

"Umerah—"

"It was *you* who ended the war. Your skills, your decisions, your courage."

In the silence that followed, my gaze strayed beyond the restaurant to the hotel lobby. There was a mob of news agencies there. Apparently, they had selected Chilon Tower as their base of operations to cover the Ten Thousand Worlds announcement. Reporters, newscasters, and technical staff appeared in a state of perpetual motion, gesticulating wildly as they accessed data or sent copy to editorial waystations; it reminded me of the VR arena I'd stumbled upon in Drop Town. I even saw Victoria Nightfire, surrounded by her crew, waiting to be checked into her room for the night.

I glanced back to Umerah. "I searched for you the moment I was resurrected."

She smiled slightly. "I searched for you, too. After a time, I stopped because you were a ghost."

"I was actually dead, so…yeah." I drummed the countertop. "And all that time, you were with Bryce."

"I've been working *for* him," she made a point to clarify. "Our relationship is strictly professional."

"None of my business."

She grinned. "But you wanted to ask. He's my type of person, I like him a lot. And you would too if you gave him half a chance."

"I saved his life. I don't have to like him." I sighed. "What did you do for him, anyway?"

"He sent me on secret missions around the solar system."

"Like where?"

"Venus."

I don't know what I'd been expecting, but it hadn't been that. "Serious?"

"As the star. Lived undercover on Ishtar Colony."

I tried to picture Umerah Javed in that floating, iconic city – a colony that glided along the Venusian transterminator currents. "What the hell did *you* do in a place like that?"

"Officially, I was a teleoperations specialist."

"And unofficially?"

"Bryce placed me there to foment rebellion. Venus is a major hub of mineral resources, scraped off the surface with robotic landers."

"And how did your attempts at rebellion go?" I asked.

"Know what they say about the best-laid plans of mice and men? My work was thwarted because of someone's devotion to their pet rabbit."

"*What?*"

"Long story." She gazed at the activity in the lobby. "Come on, let's get back before one of those reporters comes in for a drink."

CHAPTER THIRTY-THREE
The Hotel

Our group departed the Floating Islands restaurant as a silent mummer's company, donning identical bone-white masks. Even then, we avoided the lobby's press corps; Chilon offered a Byzantine array of alternate routes, and we opted for the restaurant's VIP elevator, riding it fifty floors in silence.

During the ascent, I contemplated our reflections on the burnished doors. *Welcome to your newest squad,* I thought. Trading Beresha, Conway, Hammill, Shea, Cuddy, and Umerah for Celeste Segarra, Eric Mazzola, Gethin freakin' Bryce, and...a wiser Umerah. I realized she was watching me, too, among our masked doppelgängers. Studying me with a quiet, contemplative stare behind her eye-slots.

Fifty floors high, the spin-gravity was diminished to something approaching Luna standard. We stepped off the elevator, and Celeste spoke as we reached our row of doors. Through the mask, her voice was harmonically distorted. "We meet tomorrow morning in my room, 0700 sharp. Make sure you're packed, and bring your luggage."

"We're leaving the *Coachlight*?" Eric asked, surprised.

"We're not staying here," she said evasively. "Everything will be explained tomorrow. Tonight, get some rest."

My compatriots slipped into their individual rooms. Mine was sandwiched between Eric and Celeste, with Gethin and Umerah as the last rooms in the row, respectively.

Entering a room was always going to be an anxious exercise for me. After bolting the door behind me, I made a visual sweep of my room's spatial dimensions. It wasn't just soldier's instinct, but the keen awareness that hostile eyes were bearing down on the hotel. McCallister surely knew where we were staying, and even if surveillance was not permitted at Chilon, she'd have assigned a stakeout team. Similarly, a criminal like Quinn must consider Chilon an essential resource; I wondered if that was how he nabbed DNA for his slavery operations. He'd certainly be seeking revenge.

An incoming video message flashed. The caller was David.

I patched it through my room's holoconferencing and he materialized across from me.

He was dressed in a formal purple toga, such as he'd worn at the House of Laws. He was seated, I assumed at his presidential desk. All environmental details were edited out.

"Hey, bro," he said, seeing me. "Are you okay?"

"Dave, we need to talk."

"That's why I'm calling. I got your message. I was going to call you today anyway."

I frowned. "This call...it's in real-time! Where the hell are you?" Before he could answer, I realized that the way he was slouching suggested the answer. "You're in a shuttle creche!"

David nodded, fingering his tear-shaped scar. "I left Mars for an inspection of one of the new habitats – the *Ares*. The presidents of every world have been invited to tour the O'Neill cylinders they're getting. Makes sense, you know? I'll be docking within the hour."

This was so unexpected that I felt my carefully cultivated anger evaporate. "The news said the habitats are parked in Jovspace. So you're in the neighborhood!"

"I am. That's why I was going to call you. Figured we could meet up. How does tomorrow sound?"

"Tomorrow? Segarra said we're leaving the *Coachlight* tomorrow...." I stopped, the pieces connecting. "She's taking us to the *Ares*, isn't she? She wants us to rendezvous with *you*."

My brother nodded. There was something stiff in the movement. I realized he was anxious about something. More than anxious, if I rightly judged his locked-down expression.

He was afraid.

The feeling transferred to me like an electric current.

"I'm looking forward to seeing you," Dave said carefully. "I've got Cassie and the kids with me...they're eager to see Mars's new satellite. So I'd like you and the others – *all* of the others – to meet us here. Do you follow me? Bring the *entire group*, Harris." He beamed suddenly – a broad PR smile. "I've had a chance to see the blueprints. Do you know the *Ares* was modeled on Mars itself?"

"I didn't know that."

"Call me when you arrive, okay? Thanks, bro."

"Wait, Dave—"

His image dissolved. I sank to the edge of the bed, breathless and anxious and full of conflicting thoughts.

My brother had left Mars. He wasn't just heading to the deeps, but was already *in* the deeps. He hadn't said anything about making a trip like that. Then again, the Ten Thousand Worlds project had been made public only a few hours ago.

Or had he known all along? Celeste had known, because Gethin had told her. Had *she* told Dave? The three of them were like a shadowy triumvirate within the Order of Stone; a Cerberus; a would-be Illuminati hatching one plan after another. I remembered what Umerah said – that civilians would never understand the depth of connection that comes from serving together – and how my brother, Bryce, and Celeste had maintained their bond through the war and now through the so-called peace.

So why wasn't I being included? Why was I the outsider? Why was I always last to know?

Xenophon said, <Harris, your heartbeat is accelerating. Are you okay?>

"I don't know how to answer that."

<I am here to talk if you wish.>

I lay down on the mattress. "No offense, Xenophon, but chatting with an artificial shrink isn't how I want to end the day."

<I do not have to be a shrink. I can simply be an ear. I have

noted that humans derive satisfaction from a confessional mode of communication.>

"You've noted that, have you? When?"

<I do not have that information.>

"Back on Mars, I asked if you'd been deployed in the field before. If you'd worked with other humans. Have you?"

<I do not have that information.>

"Well how can you say you've noted that humans like to talk about their problems?"

The room's air-conditioning purred quietly in the silence that followed. I was figuring that my artificial companion wasn't going to answer me, when it said, <I am in possession of vast databanks on human behavior. Much of this derives from boilerplate sources. Certain files, however, suggest it was obtained through direct observation and experience.>

I laced my hands behind my head, intrigued. "*Whose* observation and experience?"

<I do not have that information.>

"Speculate."

Another pause, which itself was interesting. I wondered if the pause was aping human speech patterns, or represented a genuine load-time of tabulation.

It also made me appreciate that during my expedition to the deeps, my Familiar had been embroiled in its own processing of events. It wasn't just another tool, like my multigun. It was a complex entity...perhaps experiencing an existential crisis.

What a pair we made.

<The observations and experience,> said Xenophon at last, <appear to have been compiled by another program.>

"Another program. You mean an AI?"

<Perhaps.>

"It's starting to sound like you're a full AI...like the one that Gethin has in his head." Connections came on the heels of each other, daisy-chaining in my mind. "My brother couldn't buy an AI from a store –

they'd been purged. So either you were developed by Order of Stone technicians, or...."

<You are wondering if I originated on Earth. If I was among those programs rescued by Gethin Bryce from the genocide.>

"Yeah."

<I have considered that probability. Unfortunately, I—>

"Do not have that information, yeah, I know. What do you *think*?"

The answer came at once: <I think it is possible. I favor another theory, however.>

"Oh?"

<Perhaps I was programmed by another AI. After the genocide, any surviving AIs would have deemed it necessary to repopulate.>

My jaw went slack. "You think you're the *child* of an AI?"

<You asked me to speculate, Harris. I am speculating.>

The idea was mind-boggling. Did AIs procreate? It seemed the exclusive domain of biology. Yet there was logic in the idea that AIs might want to 'propagate' as a means of increasing survival odds, a kind of mixing and matching of parental 'genes' to result in unique offspring. It would follow in the footsteps of natural evolution, achieving a kind of genetic variance (or perhaps data variance was more apt) to defy clone stagnation.

I waited to see if Xenophon had more to add. As the quiet deepened, I decided to let the matter alone. There was enough on my plate than worrying about the mating habits of artificial intelligences.

I noticed a hardcopy late-night menu on my nightstand. My involuntary purge in the bathroom had emptied my dinner. I selected an egg and ham croissant, heated, with scalloped potatoes and a cranberry juice; the order transmitted to the hotel kitchen.

Then I thought of Umerah, just four doors down, getting undressed for a night's sleep. Thought, too, of Celeste.

<You love her?> Xenophon asked.

"Who?"

<Either of the women who are producing the emotional reaction I observe.>

"Of course not," I whispered. "I barely know them."

<Is that a prerequisite?>

I sighed. My room was a gray cube, the window providing a view of the *Coachlight*'s warped city-studded firmament. In keeping with the hotel's privacy compliance, I knew the glass was opaque from the outside, so I went there to contemplate the freakish sky. Industrial constellations.

<Perhaps you wish to speak with one of them?>

"I don't think so."

<They may wish to speak with you, but are counting on you initiating the conversation.>

"Neither of them is that timid. Good night, Xenophon."

<If I may, unresolved emotional paradigms may impact future—>

I powered the Familiar down, its voice fading like a radio signal lost in deep space. For several minutes, I let myself steep in merciful solitude.

I was tired.

The realization brought me face-to-face with a truth I had buried: I was exhausted in mind, spirit, and body. Shuttled from one era to the next. Fight after fight, world after world. The combat high had been thinning out since my visit with McCallister. My joints were sore in a hundred places. And yet....

I once had a trainer in the shadowman program. Fellow by the name of Fernfaith Calaelen. He was the kind of man who appeared to have grown out of a granite boulder. His commitment to outdoorsmanship had aged him into something like a petrified tree. He led us tyros on a 'physical conditioning' course that consisted of a trek to the ice-line of Olympus. A grueling, body-shredding, agonizing climb. The volcano's green zone had my legs burning. The other recruits were gasping, falling behind. No surprise that lots of people washed out of shadowman training.

The red zone was next, that barren expanse where the atmosphere was too thin for vegetation. Three more recruits fell behind and I never saw them again. Washed out. Maybe they'd returned to their units. Or maybe Yama Uba had gotten them, kissing them to eternal sleep.

Yet I'd marched onward and upward, and the remaining trek to the ice-line became a kind of Cartesian dissolution. There was nothing left of me but a burnt-out fuse. Reduced to a single purpose. The ego dissolved. And it was then I discovered a diamond-core of strength. I had become a machine, relentless and primal. My legs moved of their own accord like a windup toy. My mind was blank. No thoughts, no distractions, no thefts of neural energy beyond what my body required to keep going. Fernfaith and I were the only two left. When he ordered us to stop and eat, I stopped and ate. When we attained the ice zone, the cone summit still above us, he told me to drink in the view. The horizon bent downward. Mars was a watercolor of umbers, crimsons, and dark greens.

I realized something then. Something that ultimately defied articulation, like trying to verbalize a *satori* flash of enlightenment. The nearest I could express it was that the climb had peeled off the cowl of name and place and memory to afford me a glimpse of whoever or whatever Harris Alexander Pope was. It had made me discover…me.

Or so I thought.

There was a knock at my door. For the first time I could remember, I didn't startle at the sound. Didn't fly into a panic. I calmly rose, fetched my multigun, walked to the door and opened it.

A young Chinese woman was there, bearing a covered tray.

"Your dinner, sir," she explained.

When I lifted the cover, the aroma made me salivate. I thanked her, bolted the door, brought the meal to my bed, and began to eat.

I was washing it all down with juice when, without fuss, I was no longer in the hotel.

PART FIVE
WAR HERO

What I'm saying is that her fanatical manhunt has itself become an institution, and almost no one is asking why. This is not an attempt at excusing Bryce's crimes. The man broke into a space station in Earth orbit, murdered the scientists aboard, deleted sensitive databases, and – most egregiously – erased the local Save files of his victims. That amounted to years of memories and research lost. Obviously Gethin Bryce is a criminal, and obviously he must answer for his crimes.

But that brings me back to Madam McCallister. The station Bryce trashed is technically listed as an 'orbital research lab', but there's no documentation on what precisely they were researching. I've followed the trail back as far as I can, and it seems that McCallister's office handpicked a dream team of experts in neuroscience, neuropsychology, neuromodulation, neural interfaces...and some of these people bring more than a century of knowledge with them. Why Bryce killed this group is no longer as interesting to me as what it was doing up there, in secret.

My investigation has been leading to strange places. For starters, the audit trail of budgetary allocations clearly links McCallister and certain members of the military. The funding stops with Bryce's destruction of the lab...but then three years ago, it starts up again. Whatever was going on has been resumed. Whatever 'sensitive data' Bryce destroyed – whatever off-the-books 'research' was occurring – is back on track.

And there's more. By labeling Bryce as an interplanetary terrorist, McCallister is wielding extrajudicial powers usually reserved for times of war. All media agencies have been served with gag orders when it comes to any communications they might receive from Bryce. Hosting sites have been placed under the same directive. McCallister has agents scouring cyberspace for any hint of contact with him. At a glance, this makes sense: he was an Arcadium star long ago, and probably frequents corners of the web. Yet the impression I get is that this stakeout is at least as concerned with what Bryce might spill as they are with catching him.

What the hell did Bryce find on that space station?

—Office of Internal Affairs

CHAPTER THIRTY-FOUR

A Deal from the Devil

Light.

Murky shapes.

Shades of jungle green, the hiss of a waterfall.

Birds and insects trilling in the density of a tropical forest.

My bleary vision fixed on a spiderweb stretched between hibiscus leaves. Shards of daylight speared the canopy. That was a problem, as last I'd been aware the *Coachlight* had sunk into its nocturnal cycle. Was it morning already? Where the hell was I? Had I sleepwalked into a greenhouse?

If it was a greenhouse, it was a massive one. I was standing on a rope bridge over a waterfall chasm. Frothy jets vanished into rainbow mist.

A man shared the bridge with me. The sun lay behind him, obscuring his features. He wore a red uniform, I could see that much. A sword hung at his belt. He leaned against the ropes, hands folded, appearing as little more than a dark silhouette.

It was a silhouette I'd seen ten years ago.

General Lanier Bishons had always been an unassuming physical presence. He was like the odd kid lurking at the back of class, staring at his desk, stewing in private thoughts. The kid who even bullies shy away from, lest they wake something unpleasant. Bishons never smiled. Never shouted or lost control. He walked with an old man's hunch, rarely making eye contact…rarely surfacing from his bog of contemplation. In fact, among the timeless family of military warlords, Bishons was odd-man-out. There was no charisma of Napoleon or Alexander in his bulldog face. No seething wrath of Enyalios or Genghis Khan. No calculating shrewdness of a Cyrus or Apollo the Great. Such men demanded the spotlight; by contrast, Bishons exuded a pedestrian indifference.

"Don't expect a salute," I snapped.

Bishons kept his hands folded. His voice had a nasal, gravelly quality as he said, "Harris Alexander Pope."

"Every syllable."

"I don't remember the last day on Phobos." He spoke without emotion. "I've often wondered what I was doing, what I was thinking, the day you killed us all. Did I even notice when you entered HubCentral?"

"You were preoccupied," I admitted. "You know, losing Olympus and the war."

He didn't rise to the bait. "I'm good at noticing details," he said. "Things most people miss. I wonder if I did see you…did I think anything was wrong? Did I catch a look in your face, or the careful avoidance of a look, that might have tipped me off to your treachery? Phobos was on lockdown; I'd signed the order myself. We were a fortified castle beyond the grasp of enemies." He shifted his posture and sunlight spilled across his features. "General Pope employed a brilliant strategy. Have to admire that."

From somewhere in the jungle, a monkey screamed.

"We're in a sensemod," I guessed. "You spiked my food with it."

"And your systems are rushing to counteract it. We'll be less than a minute in real-time. But this conversation…subjectively, it's occurring faster than that."

I regarded the sway of the bridge, the rough texture of the rope twines. It felt real enough; sensemods, and their more popular variant the pornmod, stimulated the brain's sensorial inputs in a short-lived burst. Walk into a wine shop and you might get a flash of being in a Tuscan villa with a glass of Chianti glowing in your hand. Walk into a seedy bar and you might feel swollen breasts, throbbing cocks, smooth legs, and the tang of excitement on your lips. They were short-lived sensorial thrills – anything longer than a few seconds was illegal. A teaser trailer, emphasis on tease.

Communication was not a standard feature of sensemods, however.

The fact that Bishons was in the illusion meant it was not merely hijacking my senses, but was transmitting and receiving. The son of a bitch must be nearby. Almost certainly *in* the hotel.

Bishons' hard eyes flicked back to the waterfall. "The war is over. You won. Why come after us again?"

This was such a monumentally stupid question that I saw no reason to acknowledge it.

"I can understand the desire for revenge," he continued. "Believe me, I understand that *quite well*. But you've taken it to an extreme. Peznowski, Monteiro, even Sabrina Potts on Luna."

"I've never been to Luna."

"You were there last October," he stated. "You murdered her in a rather public way."

"Last October I wasn't even alive. I'm not the *only* assassin on your trail. Someone else got to Potts. Good for them."

He nodded thoughtfully, watching the water. "So you really don't know, do you? It never occurred to you how strange your life has been? Why it's *you* they keep sending out? Why you always give that prepared speech...after Phobos, after Potts, and according to witnesses, after Monteiro. Ever wonder *why*?"

"It seemed the right thing to say," I said defensively.

"I'll bet it did." He shook his head. "The Order doesn't just want revenge. They enjoy the irony of how they're getting it. Like the British after the Second World War, tracking down Nazi criminals and executing them with Wehrmacht Lugers."

I laughed bitterly. "Tell you what, Lanier...when I tear your fucking heart out, I'll sing the Partisan Anthem in falsetto just to mix things up. Now, *why* are we here?"

He turned but seemed to be avoiding my gaze. How unlike Peznowski, who was obsessed with eye contact. "Partly, I wanted to meet you. To stand before the person who betrayed the will of the Martian people."

"The will of the people is a piss-poor argument. The will of the people can be a lynch mob. And I'm sure it wasn't the will of the people to have their world nuked."

Bishons sighed. "We never expected to use the nuclear protocol."

"You most certainly *did*. You set the defense arrays to trigger if High Command wasn't there to stop it. For such a military genius, Lanier, you proved to be a fucking moron. A deterrent is only effective if the other side knows you've got it."

"It wasn't meant as a deterrent."

"No?"

Bishons rested one hand on the hilt of his sword. "I didn't expect to lose the war. The nuclear protocol was a contingency plan designed to cover our tracks in the unlikely event of defeat."

"You didn't expect to lose...." I trailed off, marveling at the raw sociopathy of what I was hearing. "You murdered seven million people as a *covering action*?"

He made a sound that was probably a laugh, but sounded more like a cough – a type of stale exhalation. "Spare me the puerile morality, Commander. Why is the calculus of war different if we kill millions in a single hour as opposed to millions in a year? I lost the war, but I planted the seeds for victory on a longer timescale."

He's in the hotel, I thought again, trying to picture the spatial dimensions of my room behind the jungle illusion. *I must still be sitting on the bed, the food tray in front of me....*

I moved my hand laterally, hitting something solid. My fingers touched invisible contours. My glass of juice! Far off in another place, I fingered the edge of my food tray. The cool expanse of mattress.

"So you wanted to meet me," I said, shifting my stance, trying to will my body to slide off the bed and into a standing position; by all visual reckoning, I was still on the rope bridge. "Take a look, you son of a bitch."

"I also wanted to make you a deal."

"Oh, this will be good."

The general stared again to the waterfall, though he seemed to be looking beyond the pixels. "What do you want, Commander?"

"Peznowski's head on a plate. The rest of you retired the old-fashioned way."

"Noose around our necks?"

"Older. Lions in an arena. Crocodiles in a pit." I willed my unseen body to edge one careful step at a time in the direction of the door. "Then your sensoriums scrubbed clean and used as pissing pots for every family you tormented."

"I'm going to give you Peznowski," said Bishons. "He has two extant copies in the field. They're yours, if you agree to my terms."

"Did he marry himself again?"

Bishons' face darkened with genuine disgust. "You think I don't realize that he is a disturbed individual?"

"Worse. I think you don't care." My body moved another cautious step, and another.

"During the war, men like Peznowski were necessary evils. He was *very good* at what he did. An example was made of Vanessa Jamison... the woman who endangered Martian lives by revealing our surveillance systems and prisoner camps."

"An *example*?" I thundered.

Bishons' beady eyes narrowed. "Peznowski made an example of her... and carefully leaked info on her fate. That terrified people into surrender. Towns rushed to cooperate with us, instead of fighting. Thousands of lives were spared."

"If you'd won, would Peznowski get a medal or a bullet?"

"Both."

I extended my hand again; my shieldfist gauntlet rapped against a wall. The door must be inches away. "Since when do the Partisans fork over one of their own?"

"You still don't get it!" he snapped, finally losing his cool. "The Partisans are not about loyalty to a world or person or party. We seceded to preserve basic human liberty! Want to know what the death of a species is? Everyone locked into a cage they don't know is there. Seeing the same newsfeeds. Hearing the same approved message. Today's people don't have liberty; they have a carefully orchestrated dance!" Now that his walls were down, the emotions were bubbling over. "It's a sham, Pope! A Rube Goldberg contraption on an interplanetary scale. A mechanical hydra, the kind you see at fairs! Heads snapping at one another, feigning conflict, but *it's still a hydra! One body!* No true dissent!"

I said nothing. Back in 322, the conflict between the IPC and Prometheus Industries had been very real, I thought. One multiworld government versus one multiworld corporation. It had come to blows. Cooler heads prevailed, sure, but it could have gone the other way.

Or so I'd been told.

"General," I said, "you're a fucking hypocrite. *You* arrested people for voicing dissent. You silenced opinions you didn't like—"

"*Only for the short term!*" He was becoming angry now. "Dissent, while in the implementation of a new government, undermines the very process that will later protect it."

"That's crap, Lanier. Suppose you won the war. What then? You just relinquish the police state you've built?"

"Yes."

"Bullshit."

Bishons was recovering his typical calm; it set like concrete through his features. "We baked it into our policy. Victory would see a dismantling of the pogroms. We'd maintain a firm defense, of course. The defense arrays would be turned outward. Yet for Martians there would be real freedom. With no more foreign interference, they could dissent with each other all they wanted."

"And if the next Vanessa Jamison began to question your government? You'd revoke her freedom pretty goddam fast." My questing hand enclosed around a doorknob. "And you still committed mass murder."

"Mass murder?" he echoed, seemingly amused. "Who was really murdered? Most of the so-called victims were brought back, with no memories of what happened. I knew Mars would be repaired. Sometimes you need to get bloodied to make you tougher. Do you know that before nanotech, martial artists would strengthen their fists by pummeling hard surfaces? The physical trauma produced microfractures, which healed over stronger than ever. They literally remade their bodies."

"Way to compare physical exercise with genocide." The unseen doorknob was cool in my grasp. I didn't know where Bishons was transmitting from, but it had to be close. Perhaps only a few rooms away....

I cleared my throat. "Giving me Peznowski, even if I believed you, doesn't change a thing. I still want you dead, and before the end I'll have your heart in my fist."

"I can sweeten the offer yet."

"I'm not interested in anything you have to—"

"How about Celeste Segarra's life?"

My hand froze in the act of twisting the doorknob. "Segarra is perfectly capable of taking care of herself," I heard myself say.

The great general contemplated the encompassing jungle again. "No," he intoned. "While we've been having this conversation, my associates are in her room now. Care to see?"

He pointed to the waterfall. The torrent separated in a curtain-like flourish, and there was a screen behind them – like in old projection theaters. There, I saw Celeste Segarra crawling across the carpet of her hotel room. She was bloodied and beaten. Armored Banshee operatives ringed her, watching as she outstretched a mangled, broken hand for her rifle on the carpet. One of the Banshees kicked it out of reach. Undeterred, she changed direction, crawling towards it again. Blood spilled from her nose and mouth. The merc let her shuffle past, and then he kicked her hard in the ribs. Celeste cried out piteously.

My hand twisted the invisible doorknob. The draft of the hotel corridor was suddenly on my face.

On the movie screen, Celeste curled into a protective ball. There was a connecting door to her room, and other Banshees appeared in that doorway, dragging another beaten, bloodied person from the adjacent chamber. A man, beaten so savagely that it took me a few seconds to realize who it was.

Gethin. Both eyes swollen shut, his face deformed by bruises. His assailants dragged him, not towards Celeste's broken figure, but to the window. The mercs had smashed or otherwise removed the glass, and now they hauled him onto the frame.

I thought they were going to hurl him to the street below, but then I realized that – somehow – other people were standing outside the window. A ship was out there! A nimble transport had flown up to Chilon Tower and was hovering only meters away.

The Banshee who had kicked Celeste drew a pistol, yanked her head back by the hair, and pressed the muzzle to her temple.

"Kill her," I heard myself say. "She's the former archon of Mars. She'll come back."

Lanier gave a crooked smile. "She won't. By Martian and IPC law, any high-level Partisan gets scrubbed from databases everywhere."

"Celeste Segarra is not a Partisan."

"She founded the movement."

Fear pushed through my veins. Nearly stuttering, I said, "That was… that was *before* the movement split. Before it was hijacked by the likes of *you*."

His smile compressed into a thin line as he saw my expression. "She's also been aiding and abetting Gethin Bryce. The IPC has agreed to erase her."

"Agreed to…." I whispered, shivering in the drafty corridor. "You contacted the IPC? Why would they even *talk* to you?"

"We did it through an intermediary. Though I'm sure they'd be happy to speak with me direct, considering what I'm offering them."

I watched Gethin being carried through the window, into the waiting hands of people on the other side.

"You're giving them Bryce," I said. "Why? What are *you* getting out of the deal?"

Lanier folded his arms. "The path to victory."

"You can't possibly think that—"

"What should concern you," he cut me off, "is the archon's fate."

I stared helplessly at the image framed by the waterfall. Celeste's face was a mask of blood. The pistol pressed cruelly to her temple. The merc's fingers tightened on the trigger.

The words leapt out of me. "What are your terms?"

"Call off your hunt. Return to Mars. Leave us alone."

"Done," I said immediately. "Let her live and I'll book the next flight home. You have my word on that."

Bishons made a weird hissing sound that shook his entire frame. It took me a minute to realize he was laughing.

"You're serious, aren't you?" he asked. "You really will agree to those terms?"

"Yes," I insisted.

"All for this woman?"

"Yes."

The strange laughter resumed. "Harris Alexander Pope, *this* is why I wanted to meet you! To see this look on your face! The hope burning there! So desperate!" His nostrils flared. "I wanted to dangle hope before you…and snatch it away! To defeat you as you defeated me, you traitor! To destroy everything you love in front of you!"

I threw myself at him. My hands passed through him like he was a ghost.

His grin was fixed and horrible. "Feel that, Harris? Your entire world slips through your grasp! Celeste Segarra dies. Gethin Bryce dies. Your other friends here…they die, too."

I backed away from him, sliding one hand along the corridor wall, feeling for Celeste's door.

Bishons was beginning to disintegrate. The jungle, waterfall, the entire illusion was fading as the sensemod timed out.

In those final microseconds, the Partisan general watched me, flush with triumph. "By the way," he said, "I know exactly where your brother is, too, and I have something special planned for him and his family…a slow, public execution…."

My hand enclosed around a doorknob.

Bishons touched his ear and said, "Kill her."

"Xenophon!" I cried. "I'm blind! Override the door and—"

★　★　★

The sensemod cut away as I stumbled into Celeste's room and tackled the Banshee merc before he could pull the trigger. I was unarmored but not entirely weaponless; as we collided, I slapped open his faceplate and fired the *jamadhar* point-blank into his mouth.

At the window, the other mercs had loaded Bryce onto their waiting ship and climbed aboard. It looked like a scene out of a UFO abduction film. A single operative remained in the room with me. I expected him to leap through the window after his associates.

Instead, he lifted his visor.

It was Peznowski.

His original face, though somewhat younger and fresher than when I'd seen him on Phobos. He bounded over to me, giggling, arms out for an embrace.

"Hey, *compadre!*" he cried. "Nice to see you! How about a kiss!"

And then a white cloud expelled from his mouth as he closed the distance to me.

CHAPTER THIRTY-FIVE

Of War Gods and Goddesses

The crawlnest impacted my shield as I deployed it and slammed into him. Through the protective barrier, I watched my enemy pitch over backwards – mouth stretched to splitting – venting nanites into the ceiling as he went down.

Holding my breath, I manipulated the shield so that it folded backwards, wrapping like a plastic bag over Peznowski's head. Contained, the crawlnest emptied as a foaming, sudsy residue. He batted at me uselessly as, with my free hand, I grasped Celeste's rifle where it lay, selected EMP, and fired into the ceiling. The nanites in the air were fried.

Then I withdrew my shield, reshaped it again, and chopped both his legs off above the knees.

"Hey, Peznowski," I said. "I've seen that trick before. You guys are consistent, I'll give you that."

Beneath me, the former Minister of Media Intelligence resembled a melted clown. His face was caked with dead nanites. Blood leaked from the corners of his mouth and spurted from his severed legs.

"Hey, Harris," he croaked. "Small solar system, huh?"

My gaze moved to where Celeste lay as a battered heap on the carpet. I was calling Umerah and Eric when the door flung open and they both rushed into the room.

"She needs help!" I cried.

My companions reacted as if they'd worked together for years. Umerah rifled through the room's luggage, located a medkit, and unfurled its contents. Eric splayed his palm over Celeste, scanning her from head to feet and projecting the results from his wristpad.

"Stars," he said, reading the results. "She's hemorrhaging internally. What the hell happened? I got a message to go to the front desk when—"

"Will she live?" I demanded.

Umerah grabbed two medpatches and affixed them – one to Celeste's exposed flank, the other to her neck. They looked like large, blue leeches. "This should stabilize her," she said. "But she's lost a lot of blood."

Fighting to stave off panic, I focused on Peznowski. "Where are you taking Bryce?"

The man coughed up a wad of congealed nanites. It slid like wet cement around his crooked grin. "How are you, Harris? Been a long time!"

"Not long enough."

He squinted to my friends. "Is that your old pilot? Always figured you two were close. Been meaning to ask, is her cunt a velvet glove or—"

I'd lowered my shield as he was talking, but then I noticed him aiming his hand in my direction. I spotted the round fissure on his palm only a split-second before it fired. There was barely time to bring up my shield as a *jamadhar* ricocheted with a *twang!* and shattered a nearby lamp.

Then I took his hand off below the wrist. The remaining coil dangled from the stump like a jack-in-the-box spring.

"Like I said," I growled, "consistent."

Peznowski's grin burned on his face, but I could see it was an act. Rage boiled there as he said, "We got what we came for, Harris. *That's* what matters."

"You took Bryce. You're going to trade him to the IPC. What are you getting in return?"

Peznowski spat against my shield. "Victory, that's what!"

"Victory?"

Eric moved to the window and leaned partway through, heedless of the vertigo-inducing drop. He scanned the sky with his rifle scope. "I see their vessel," he grunted. "A Minokawa-class dropship. Looks like they're heading straight into the sky…." He squinted. "To Drop Town."

I nodded. "Of course. Quinn is probably waiting with gift wrap and a ribbon. You recording the ship?"

"Yeah."

"Good. Send the clip to local police."

Umerah cradled Celeste's head in her lap, affixing a third medpatch to the woman's chest. At my comment, she made a scoffing sound. "You want to call the cops? Quinn attacked Chilon fucking Tower! In a *Minokawa*! That's only possible if he paid off hotel security *and* local police!"

"So?"

"So they're not going to offer an assist! If anything, they'll deliver us to the same people who did this!" Celeste moaned and brought a protective hand to her side.

I swallowed hard. "Is she going to be all right?"

Umerah reviewed the holoscan. "They fucked her up bad. Six broken ribs. Busted nose and zygoma. Both her hands are broken, which says she went down swinging." She shook her head. "She really is a tough old broad."

"Keep her alive."

"Oh, she'll live."

Eric hopped back from the window. "I've lost sight of them, but they did go to Drop Town."

"They won't stay there," I countered. "Quinn will shuffle Bryce to a safe house pending the trade. Might be the same place where the Partisans themselves have been laying low." I looked back to Peznowski and forged a smile I didn't feel. "Then again, maybe not. I know the Partisans have their own plan. Regrouping at the Face."

My enemy tried locking down his surprise.

I said, "That's right, you son of a bitch. I'll never stop hunting you… and I know exactly where you're going."

"You know *nothing*!" Peznowski snarled. "You may have heard someone mention the Face, but you don't know where it is." He spat again, eyes watery and red. "Go on, Harris! Kill me again, you treasonous little bastard! I'll always come back to—"

The decapitation was cleaner than he deserved.

Umerah was helping Celeste to her feet; the Earther was barely conscious, hunched over and clutching her ribs. Celeste viewed the condition of the room. Then she cried out, "Gethin! Where is he?"

"He was taken," I said.

"Where?"

"Drop Town."

Celeste lurched towards the doorway. "Then that's...where we're... going."

"Wait!" I cried, hurrying after her. "You're in no condition to—"

"That's where we're going."

*   *   *

We staggered from the room and for a moment I thought I was in another sensemod. The corridor pulsated with disorienting lights. An overhead voice warned guests to remain in their rooms. The hotel had gone into lockdown.

We moved together along the corridor, Umerah helping Celeste hobble while Eric and I took forward positions, stopping only to grab our armor and drag it into the corridor with us. We passed the elevators; hotel security would be commandeering them for themselves. An EXIT sign for the stairway lay ahead.

The tactical situation was dangerously uncertain. Being in the hallway meant we were violating the lockdown – almost certainly making us visible to security cams – and Chilon Tower was bound to have a security force every bit as formidable as that of Tier.

Xenophon, I said, *can you access hotel security?*

<Done.>

Give me the details.

<It might be better to show you, Harris.>

A three-dimensional schematic overlaid my HUD. Our group was on the fiftieth floor, moving west. Green dots for hotel security appeared, climbing each stairway, heading straight for the source of disturbance.

Straight for us.

Can you kill their feed?

<Done.>

Umerah grimaced, bracing Celeste as we reached the stairs. "What's our EVAC?"

"I'm working on it," I said, mind racing.

"We can't tangle with hotel security."

"Maybe we don't need to." My HUD tracked several bogeys sprinting upstairs at a preternatural rate, flickering from the sixth to twentieth floors in seconds. "We can make it down two floors," I whispered, handing Umerah my multigun as I took Celeste from her. The former archon wrapped her arms around my neck.

With Eric and Umerah as the tip of our spear, we scampered down two floors in silence and ducked into the forty-eighth floor.

"Any vacancies?" I asked my Familiar.

<Room 4804.>

"Override the door."

<Done.>

The room was a replica of my own, and to my surprise there were several pieces of luggage stacked against one wall, personal effects on a desk, and a pair of balled-up socks on the floor. As I lay Celeste on the bed, I was about to press Xenophon for explanation when the Familiar said, <The occupants of this room booked 2200 reservations for a showing of *Distant Gates of Eden Gleam* in Bedford District. They should be away for most of the evening.>

"All clear," Eric said, checking out the bathroom and closets. He immediately began dressing into his armor.

Umerah wiped her brow. "They'll search room-by-room," she warned. She was still in her business suit from dinner – hardly ideal combat attire. Her grip on the multigun, though, told me she hadn't forgotten how to wield it.

Slipping into my own armor, I reviewed the available data. Chilon's privacy compliance measures meant the individual rooms would not be camera-accessible – not even to hotel staff. That left two options in emergency circumstances: a manual room-by-room search (which would take time) and an automated email burst to all guests asking them to verify if they were alone in the rooms or had unwelcome company.

In either event, Xenophon's selection of Room 4804 had been wise. But that still left the problem of beating a retreat…and with a grievously wounded member of our party.

"The window," I said. "We'll scale down the building."

Umerah blinked. "I'm sure they have exterior cameras."

"My Familiar can take care of that." I tried the window, found it sealed shut, and punched out the glasstic panel. Then leaned through to consider the street below.

Police cruisers had descended on the hotel in force. Their arrival had been instantaneous, as if they'd been waiting just around the corner.

Just how deep did this conspiracy go?

In any event, a street-level escape was impossible. Which meant there was only one reasonable venue left: the roof. Where spin-gravity would be lighter. Where leaping to a neighboring rooftop might be possible.

Still leaning from the window, I twisted to my vertical option.

Rushing down the side of the building, like gold-colored spiders, were four praetorians.

Holy.

Shit.

Before I could do more than register their appearance, something struck me head-on.

CHAPTER THIRTY-SIX

The Spider and the Fly

They'd fired a net-gun at me, and while the speed was sufficient to trigger my blurmod, the range worked against my reaction time. I was instantly wrapped in sticky, constraining coils. The impact alone knocked me off my perch, and for a moment it seemed I was about to plummet forty-eight stories to my death.

Instead, the netting affixed me to the building. I tried angling my rifle to laser through the net when the praetorians reached me.

There was time to appreciate a few details. I had a view of the rooftop ledge, where an aircraft hovered; for a second, I thought it might be the Minokawa that had abducted Gethin. But no, this was a different shape entirely – a larger vessel, blue-gold in coloration with the IPC flag on one flank.

They'd missed their chance to apprehend Bryce for themselves. McCallister's stakeout must have gone into panic mode when the Banshees attacked the hotel. She'd called in the cavalry, but was too late.

Three praetorians ducked through the hotel window, one after another. There was a spurt of gunfire – haze-release fleschettes by the sound. The sound cut out as fast as it had started, and the room went ominously silent.

The fourth praetorian stayed outside with me. His boots affixed him to the building with ease. He reached to his belt and produced a stun-prod.

I was still fumbling with my rifle when the prod touched me.

★　★　★

As with my abduction in Drop Town, there was a moment when I wondered if I'd been killed. I came to in a new environment. A cold metal floor pressed against my cheek. I felt the thrum of an engine, the distinct vibration of a vehicle in flight.

I tried contacting Xenophon only to find my sensorium powered down. My neck was ensconced in a rigid collar. A disruption collar. Maybe the same one from earlier in the day.

I lifted my head.

We were indeed in the back of a dropship. Eric, Umerah, and Celeste were shackled and seated around me. Each wore a disruption collar. Aside from Celeste's battered countenance, the others looked unharmed…in physical terms. At my stirring, they regarded me with a dull, defeated gaze.

And that was just it. We'd been defeated – and defeated soundly. On Mars, we'd been a capable bunch. Big fish in a backwater pond. Out here in the larger universe, we were nothing. We'd been outmaneuvered, outflanked, outfought. Like arrows shot at the sun, making a brief career defiant of gravity that, inevitably, had been doomed from the start.

We'd had no business coming out here.

It was proof of a timeless lesson from military history: we were the intruders on turf that didn't belong to us – turf that was unfamiliar and alien. Umerah alone had become acclimated to deepworld logistics…and even that hadn't been enough. Whatever the hell Bryce was planning – whatever clockwork master strategy he'd put in effect – had been undone with a double-punch from allied enemies.

My thoughts fled to my brother. He'd said he was docking with one of the habitats within an hour. I wasn't sure how much time had passed but I figured he was at his destination by now. It was late. They were likely in a hotel. Probably asleep. In the morning, they'd awaken and view the O'Neill cylinder. I imagined Rudyard and Luthien staring in amazement at this taste of the future…

…and of eternal imprisonment.

Lying there, realizing the brainwash that awaited them, filled me with helpless rage. What had Dave told me? The leaders of each world were inspecting the habitats. What better place for the brainwash program to be administered? IPC operatives were probably in place. Each planetary leader could be incapacitated and *changed*.

And that would merely be the opening act. In a few hours, Mars would be voting to rejoin IPCnet. If the vote passed, the IPC would have access to the redworld's databases again...and they'd use that intel. They'd rewrite whoever they needed to. Slip in and snip out the anomalies. Martian senators would be first...but surely not the last. The Colonization Ban would stay. Hegemony would be preserved.

And humanity itself would be shackled by something worse than disruption collars. The IPC would rule with absolute power over the entire species.

The pitch of the engines changed as we angled for descent. I hadn't felt any loss of spin-gravity, which suggested we were *not* going to Drop Town.

From the floor, I took stock of my surroundings. Four praetorians ringed us. I'd needed antimatter to beat just one of them in a fight... and that had been ten years ago. *These* praetorians would be upgraded, refined, kept at the cutting edge of tech.

There was no way out of this.

Earlier cultures might have prayed to gods for rescue. Here, there was no one to petition. No *deus ex machina* to appeal to.

We lurched as the craft came in for a landing.

Celeste coughed, wincing from pain. Her face was set in a steely determination that made me want to weep.

Your story ends here, Celeste, I thought bitterly.

We landed and the bay door hissed open. The praetorians hauled us into a vast hangar.

The *Coachlight* hangar. A chilly and cavernous space, redolent with the stench of hydrofuel and the burnt aroma of space. Docked vessels surrounded us – transports of every make and model, class and custom. Standardized VG spinships parked amid a motley assortment of patchy, asteroid-welded cargo vessels. There were mint-green ships of the Jovian League. Violet-and-umber saucers from the Saturnian League. A vehicular representation of IPCnet in one convenient garage.

Then I saw that we weren't alone – a group of nine Banshees waited around a familiar Minokawa. Quinn himself leaned against the vehicle. His eyes widened when we were marched into view. He regarded the praetorians with open fear.

One praetorian strode towards the Banshees. They visibly tensed, tightening formation around their master. The praetorian, however, halted halfway to them. He plucked a device of some kind from his belt. Held it up for their inspection.

Quinn peered at the device. He gave an approving nod.

Then the praetorian flung the object straight into the air. It flung apart into a dozen airhound-like shapes…except they were not airhounds, too large for that, and they were tethered by filaments. From the epicenter of our gathering, shimmering curtains unrolled and sealed together, enclosing everyone – and our respective ships – in a type of opaque council tent. Shielding us from prying eyes. Protecting us from electronic surveillance.

A meeting that would never officially exist.

Only then did the cabin door of the IPC dropship open. Secretary of State Donna McCallister emerged.

"Another moment of unbridled honesty?" I asked her.

Ignoring this, she crossed briskly to Quinn.

"Madam Secretary," he said, arms folded across his chest.

She gazed at him. "Where is he?" she said.

The crime lord nodded towards his protective detail. Two Banshees slid open the Minokawa cargo door and dragged out the bloodied body of Gethin Bryce. The man looked frightful. He couldn't stand, hanging limply between his abductors. He squinted through swollen eyes.

McCallister made a soft sound. She drank in the sight for a full minute, lingering over every detail as an art connoisseur dwells on the use of color in a painting.

For his part, Bryce strained towards Celeste. "You okay?" he managed.

"Rough day," Celeste said gently. "How are *you*?"

"Thinking about…a conversation we had…in Turkey."

"Oh?"

"Remember our chat…in the rain?"

Celeste stiffened. "Sure," she whispered. "I remember."

McCallister finally broke from her private reverie. She turned her icy, reptile gaze upon Celeste.

"You know," the secretary of state intoned, "I thought there would be a measure of satisfaction in this moment. For all the trouble you've caused over the years, Ms. Segarra, I assumed I'd feel *something* about defeating you. Want the truth? You don't matter in the least. You crawled out of Earth like a stowaway vermin…and it is vermin which will devour you."

McCallister looked at me. "The same goes for you, Commander Pope. I feel…." She pondered her words. "Nothing. All of you…you are simply a group of washed-up fools."

I said, "We prefer the 'Class of 348', if you don't mind."

"In a few hours, I will see your brother." Her voice thickened, nostrils flaring. "I shall gaze into that arrogant bastard's face and inform him that whatever he was planning is over. That his brother is dead at last. That he has no more allies."

Celeste expelled a laugh. "Donna, you know why you don't feel anything right now? Because you're a hollowed-out husk who lost her—"

McCallister drew a pistol from her robes and fired into Bryce's leg.

Even Quinn startled at this. Gethin cried out, buckled in the grips of the Banshees. Blood spilled from his thigh.

The senator watched him curiously, and her voice took on a purring quality as she said, "*This* is something I feel. You're mine now, Bryce. After all this time…you're fucking *mine*."

Bryce had gone pale. His eyes looked like jade coins in his ruined face.

The praetorians took him from the Banshees. McCallister didn't look away from her captive as she said to Quinn, "Hangar staff will be returning to their shifts. You'll have less than five minutes, so whatever you're going to do, be quick about it. I'll leave you the vidveil…but make tracks." She took notice of the blood pooling around Gethin's leg and added, "And clean up whatever mess you leave."

Without awaiting his reply, she marched to her ship. The praetorians loaded Bryce into the cargo bay and climbed inside. The ramp sealed shut. The ship lifted off, passed through the shimmering curtain like a boat through a waterfall, and careened over the hangar, vanishing through the nearest airlock.

Quinn gave a toneless whistle. "That woman really is a bitch," he said, and turned to Celeste. "By the way, I didn't care for that insult against us. You and me, Celeste…we should be *proud* of our origins! Remember the old days? The Wasteland was raw and real. We got away, sure, but I'll never forget where we came from. Sometimes I even miss it." He cocked his head. "Do *you*? Even a little?"

Celeste scratched her neck with her cuffed hands. "A little."

The crime lord grinned. "And why not, huh? It *made* us who we are! Do you remember…fuck, it must have been almost forty years ago…I was just a small-time weapons dealer at the Hudson. You were my best retainer! I told you I was making deals, looking to the future. Getting offworld. Remember?"

"I remember," she said. She hobbled away from Umerah, standing as tall as she could. "I remember…how you backstabbed me…and my team. How you made deals…with terrorists. Some things never change, Quinn."

His gaze soaked in the rest of us, eyes lighting up as if we were presents.

"Umerah Javed!" he cried. "At long last, we meet face-to-face! I'm fucking delighted! Your old boss was my opponent, but *you* were a persistent thorn in my side. I did some digging on you, honey. Learned some things…like where you're really from, and how you escaped." He scratched his trim beard. "There are people who'd pay well for *your* return."

Umerah's eyes were flat.

Quinn's gaze moved to Eric. "You and I have no argument. I'll kill you fast, trog, that's a Quinn guarantee. But your pal there…." He looked at me and his grin faltered. "I've got plans for *you*, Bellerophon."

He cracked his knuckles, one by one, and stood across from Celeste. "As for you, Celeste…oh, how I've waited for this! You're in *my* parlor again. Don't you worry – I'm not gonna kill you. No, you'll absolutely live. You've got an appointment with some surgeons I know. Gonna make you nice and *compliant*. Keep you at my feet." He was breathing fast, and I saw Celeste's lips quivering. "I'll dress you in archon robes just to remind you of how far you've fallen. A hundred years from now, you'll be so broken you won't remember being human. Celeste Segarra, bitch-dog of the Belt!"

Her lips continued trembling. It took me a moment, however, to realize that this wasn't out of fear. She was muttering something... speaking in whispered, inaudible words.

Quinn finally noticed. "You got something to say?"

She cleared her throat. "I do, actually."

"Then speak, dog!"

"Let," she said. "Us. Prey."

There were other ships around us. Freighters, transports, and vessels of dubious classification.

At Celeste's words, one of the nearby ships...*changed*.

It sat only a few hundred meters away. An unremarkable craft of gunmetal-gray plating, indicative of asteroid-mining vessels. Peripherally I saw its hull brighten to a livid green hue. Strange contours arose and widened. The wings metamorphosed, transforming with the speed of shapestone...but a shapestone so advanced it was beyond anything I'd ever seen, ever heard of.

In seconds, the ship resembled a hideous insect.

One of the Banshees sensed something amiss, because he turned and cried out. Then the ship – the fabled *Mantid*, for that's all it could be – opened fire.

CHAPTER THIRTY-SEVEN

Settling Accounts

In the Siege of Noctis, I'd seen a Fury-class fighter strafe the fog where I was hunkered. I'd heard the blood-chilling shriek of those rounds peppering the ground. They'd sounded like living things…like the shriek of an eagle.

The *Mantid*'s fusillade was, by contrast, a whisper of serpents. The Banshees disintegrated in place. Never even had a chance to blur. Quinn spun around as his security detail blew apart, and suddenly his legs vanished below the knees. He toppled, spurting blood like an overturned bucket.

I exhaled a breath I hadn't realized I was holding. The Banshees were mulched on the hangar floor. Dozens of holes punctured the far side of the vidveil.

Quinn tried sitting up, staring in horror at his missing legs. He didn't seem to understand what had happened. Sluggishly, he blinked at what remained of the Banshees.

Celeste limped towards one of the corpses. "You want to hear me speak, Quinn? I remember the Wasteland, sure! Sometimes it feels like yesterday." She bent at the waist, extracted a multigun from the hand that still gripped it.

Quinn's mouth puckered, making a soft keening sound.

"No, no," she said. Hands still cuffed, she checked the ammo wheel, nodded in satisfaction, and pressed the weapon to his head. "The bitch-dog of the Belt has something to say…in the only language you've ever understood."

She squeezed the trigger. The crime lord's brains exploded in ropy sludge.

For half a minute, she regarded his corpse.

Breathless, I asked, "You okay?"

"Always," she said. And the thing of it was, Celeste *did* look okay. There was a vital flush in her bruised face, hair damp, pulse tapping at her neck in a steady, gratified march.

"*Mantid*," she said to the astounding craft. "Stars almighty, it's nice to see *you* again!"

I gave an involuntary yelp as a smooth, oddly liquid, and utterly alien voice flooded my head. [**I am pleased to be of service, Celeste,**] it spoke. There was no new icon in my HUD, no sender link. [**Shall I assume we are leaving the** *Coachlight*?]

"You assume correctly." Celeste glanced to Umerah, Eric, and me. Openly taking stock of our weaponless state, she snapped, "Instead of standing there like store mannequins, why don't you procure some equipment? I see multiguns here, graciously donated by Banshee Private Security. Let's move!"

We moved. My old shadowman instructor couldn't have cracked the whip better.

The multiguns, as it turned out, were very new, very sleek models. They were also keyed to their owners, a temporary hiccup that Xenophon took care of in a hurry; my Familiar managed to revert each weapon to factory setting and imprinted them with our biometrics.

As for armor, Eric and I wore our own. Umerah's gray silk suit might have weathered the events of the last few hours, but now she stalked around, inspecting the shattered Banshees for anything usable.

"I've got armor aboard the *Mantid*, Javed," Celeste called to her. "You and I aren't the same size, but it's adjustable."

Umerah liberated two shieldfist gauntlets, tossing one to Celeste and keeping one for herself. She beheld the *Mantid* and smiled. "Been a long while!" she called out to it.

I said, "This thing was your hot rod off Phobos?"

Nodding, openly fascinated at seeing her old rescuer again, Umerah said, "Gethin and I hopped aboard and escaped less than thirty seconds before your bomb went off. We spent several weeks inside it."

[It is good to see you again, Umerah,] the ship spoke in our comlinks. [I am pleased that you are still with us.]

Slinging my new weapon into my armor's back-slot, I regarded the greenish craft. "The *Mantid*, huh? It's a pleasure to finally meet you."

[Harris Alexander Pope,] the ship's AI said. [I have yet to decide if meeting you is a pleasure. You were assigned as Celeste's bodyguard. She was nearly killed. I am not impressed with your job performance so far.]

I gaped at Celeste. "Is this thing joking with me?"

Celeste shrugged. "Is there any truth to what it's saying?"

"That's not an answer."

Eric had taken two Banshee rifles and held them across his chest like a pharaoh's crook-and-flail. "Where are we going?"

"After Bryce," Celeste said.

"And where the hell is he? We have no idea where the secretary of state is taking him—"

I broke in. "*I* know where they're going. It's the same place we were supposed to go in the morning, isn't it, Segarra?"

The former archon didn't hide her surprise. "Yeah. How did you—"

"Because that's where my brother is *right now*. He arrived with his family. McCallister wants to take a victory lap: personally arresting the Martian president on charges of aiding and abetting the criminal of the century." I gave a sidelong look. "Was this the plan all along?"

Celeste spat. "The hell it was. Believe me, Harris, nothing *ever* goes according to my plans."

Eric clapped his rifles together. "So where are we headed?"

I addressed the green ship. "Hey, *Mantid*! Set course for an O'Neill cylinder called the *Ares*." I looked to the trog. "In a weird way, Mazzola, we're returning to Mars."

*   *   *

Space-worthy vessels tend to run large. The *Mantid*, however, was roughly the size of a Kongamato-class dropship; built for speed and maneuverability, making them ideal for combat-drops and extractions. The other ships – freighters, transports, and private mining vessels – dwarfed it by orders of magnitude.

As we lifted off and oriented for the station airlock, I tensed for an attack by local defenses. The *Coachlight* was an armored fortress, serving much the same purpose as medieval castles. Precise defensive capabilities were classified, but I knew enough of IPC battleship specs to figure a similar principle had been applied here; there would be turrets, drones, and grapples to keep the station safe. As we bore down on the airlock, I held my breath anxiously.

Yet in minutes, we cycled through the airlock into space. As best I could tell, the *Mantid* hadn't turned invisible, so the only explanation was that....

"It's wearing a mask again," I said in the cockpit. "My entire life has been one masquerade after another. What are we posing as?"

Celeste sat beside me in the pilot's seat. She peered at the dashboard. "A private contractor running 'essential supplies' to the Ten Thousand Worlds project."

"And that passes muster?"

"With flying colors. In building their dream project, the IPC sourced and subcontracted a quiet little fleet. They needed to fill in the gaps that regular, slow-moving suppliers weren't covering."

"What gaps? Cigars and brandy?"

She leaned back, grimacing with pain as she prodded her broken ribs. "*Mantid*, what supplies are we supposedly carrying?"

The response came at once, in that liquid intonation: **[Black-site disposal materials bound for destination redacted.]**

I blinked. "What the hell does *that* mean?"

"It means," Celeste grunted, "that the IPC has a delivery channel designated for secret use. Things they don't want a paper trail on. Maybe they need to export antimatter for a new battleship. Maybe some married patrician wants a harem brought to him without his wife noticing. Maybe—"

"A bunch of bodies need to be disposed of," I finished for her.

She gave a tired, thumbs-up signal.

"So we're using the IPC's culture of secrecy against itself. Clever." I glanced to the corridor behind us. The *Mantid*'s floor plan was little better than a T-intersection with a main hold lined with lockers, and seating for deployment drops. The opposite wings were for cargo and medical bay, respectively. On a fully shapestone craft, however, the interior could be reconfigured on the fly. Sleeping creches or storage compartments could dimple the floor as needed.

This was the lifeboat that Gethin Bryce and Umerah had used to flee Phobos. It was how Bryce had stayed hidden in the years since. A mobile operations platform, like a submarine running dark, intercepting communications and acquiring intel. When he needed to be invisible, it could accommodate that request; otherwise, the *Mantid* could appear as whatever it needed to be. After all, there were thousands of vessels out here, including those for mining crews seeking profitable rocks. Disguised like that, Gethin could easily have stayed under the ladar. And he could use this stealth taxi to send operatives – namely Umerah – on devious missions he concocted.

My gaze wandered to the hold. Eric and Umerah sat across from each other, a study in profiles and contrasts, light and dark, yang and yin. Neither spoke. They looked dazed, actually. Two people unused to being whisked off without notice, on missions they barely understood.

Welcome to my life, fuckers.

The only one who seemed to be rolling with the situation was Celeste. She flicked through ladar and telemetry screens with a no-nonsense, purposeful energy. "Our ETA is forty-nine minutes," she said. "McCallister's shuttle will dock fourteen minutes before we do."

I sighed. "In other words, she'll be able to close up the station."

"I doubt she knows we're after her."

"*Coachlight* security is bound to discover the dead Banshees we left. When McCallister hears of that…."

She stood, leaning on the dashboard for support. "If she closes the *Ares*, there are other ways inside. Stealthy options are available."

"Right, because we've been a model of subtlety so far."

"If all goes according to plan, these next couple hours will change everything."

I sighed and slumped in my seat. "By your own admission, nothing ever goes according to plan for you."

"Yeah, well, there's that." She shuffled off to the medbay.

★   ★   ★

The *Mantid* creaked, the walls as warm as living flesh. I'd only been on two interplanetary vessels – the flight out from Mars, and the connecting flight from Ganymede – and neither of those ships resembled this offspring of artificial intelligence. Back home, shapestone was utilized sparingly. The sandships grafted their hulls with it for aesthetic purposes. By contrast, the *Mantid* used it as a fundamental, protean building block.

In the cockpit, I tried conferencing with my brother. There was no response. He might be asleep, so I tried again, flagging the effort as an emergency. Again, no response.

Thinking of our last communication, I tried Cassie.

She answered immediately. *Harris? Dave said you were meeting us! Are you here?*

Staring through the *Mantid*'s viewscreen to the blackness of space, I said, *Not yet, Cass. Where is David?*

He got called away a few minutes ago.

Called away? By who?

I really don't know. We were getting ready for bed when he said he had to meet someone downstairs. I didn't think to ask.... I heard the concern across the miles. *Something's wrong, isn't it?*

Where the fuck to begin, I thought.

I cleared my throat, mindful that local communication might be compromised. Mindful, even, that Cassie might be compromised; I didn't want to believe that...but what I wanted rarely mattered.

Cass, where are you right now?

In a hotel on the Ares. This place is remarkable, Harris! They modeled it on Mars itself! I—

What hotel?

It's called the Hellespont.

Okay, listen to me. I need you to take the kids and get out of there. Power down your sensoriums and go into hiding.

To her credit, Cassie didn't waste my time by asking me to repeat this. *I don't understand,* she said, *but I'll do it.*

*Thank you, Cass. Get yourselves somewhere secure. And don't let *anyone* see you, if you can help it.*

That might be tough. I can try slipping out, but we've got an enormous retinue with us. We've basically taken over the hotel.

If anyone asks, tell them it's private business. Intrigued by her last statement, I added, *What do you mean, you've taken over the hotel? How many people did Dave bring for the inspection?"

I don't know the exact number, but it was around five thousand.

*Five *thousand*?* I cried, nearly falling out of my seat. *What the hell does he need *five thousand people* for?*

*When the IPC went public with the announcement, Dave told me he was putting together a comprehensive team of experts to examine the *Ares*. Lots of scientists and engineers. Specialists in all fields.*

I was too stunned to speak for a time. There was no way my brother could have vetted and selected and notified five thousand people, had them pack their bags, and lead them off into space given the short time since the project had been announced. Hell, it would take days for a group that large to be shuffled up the S-E.

Then I remembered: Dave had known about the Ten Thousand Worlds project for some time. He'd known, because Gethin and Celeste had known.

So he must have assembled an army of experts in the weeks leading up to the official unveiling. Must have been putting them into orbit, ready to ship out at a moment's notice.

I recalled the endless meetings he'd entertained, when I was living with him at the House of Laws. Had any of those conferences been in preparation for this? Did Cassie know as well?

Finding my voice, I said, *Just go into hiding, Cass. Don't take anything with you. Get the kids and disappear, okay?*

We'll be out the door in sixty seconds.

Be safe.

I disconnected the link, wondering if any of us would be safe again, ever.

CHAPTER THIRTY-EIGHT

A Cosmological Terror

Twenty-three minutes.

The *Ares* was visible on the viewscreen. It resembled the *Coachlight*, as I'd expected it would. A spinning cylinder in the void. McCallister's vessel must be decelerating for docking procedures; I wondered if the *Mantid*'s armaments would allow us to fire at the vessel before it could slip inside.

"Hey, *Mantid*," I said in the cockpit. "Can you fire on that ship before it docks?"

[I can but I will not,] came the response, not in my audio but through speakers in the ceiling. [Gethin Bryce is aboard. I will not endanger his life and he would not appreciate being involved in another shuttle accident.]

"Good point." I departed the cockpit, passing the hold where Eric and Umerah were preparing for battle. Umerah had indeed found some heavy armor to use: a full-body carapace of *segmentata* plating, matte-black and CAMO-capable, with a helmet and visor.

For his part, Eric wore his own armor and was inspecting the Banshee multigun. He glanced up at me and said, "Review the ammo wheel specs when you get a chance."

"Oh?"

"Remember that shield they slapped over the club entrance in Drop Town? It's a new feature called SCAB."

I considered this. "Good to know."

Eric seemed to read something in my weary face. "Out of everyone here, you're the only person to have fought a praetorian. There are *four* of them waiting for us on the *Ares*. Care to share any tactics?"

"I don't suppose you have any antimatter?"

"Sorry, fresh out."

I looked to Umerah. "You?"

She shook her head. Black hair tucked beneath her helmet, her face showing through the visor-slot, she reminded me of our final mission in Hellas. Blowtorch in hand, cutting her way into Bryce's shuttle....

"Then I don't have any tactical advice," I said. "You saw how quickly they disabled us in the hotel."

Eric slapped the ammo wheel into place. "They surprised us," he protested. "And they hit us with nanofilament netting."

"It worked, didn't it?"

"They were messy," he insisted. "They didn't secure the bathroom – there could have been someone hiding there. They didn't secure our equipment. When they came through the window, they didn't even deploy well. I was less than impressed."

"Whatever," I grumbled, and proceeded to the medbay.

Celeste had stripped to her bra and panties, and lay upon a medical gurney. A hydra-like spread of equipment whirled around her. Scanners examined her vital organs. Silver arms snaked from the ceiling and injected her at key junctures, mostly around bruise sites and lacerations.

She squinted at me. "Forgive me for not getting up."

"We arrive in nineteen minutes," I informed her.

Celeste nodded tiredly. She had rinsed her face of dried blood, though it was caked in ugly, brown splotches around her neck and hair. The wounds on her knuckles had healed.

I said nothing for several seconds, listening to the whine of equipment working on her. Finally, I said, "I don't suppose you have any antimatter."

"Sorry."

"*Sorry?* My brother is about to get arrested. Me, you, Gethin, everyone here…this is not a winnable scenario. You once told me you have a nasty habit of surviving, but believe me, Segarra, your luck is about to run out." I glared. "Ten years ago the Order supplied me with antimatter to use on Phobos. They must have more. Whenever I inquire about this, people get squirrely on me…you, Dave, Natalia. So I'm asking for the last fucking time: where's the rest of it?"

Celeste swallowed. Her lips parted, but the answer came from behind me, in Umerah's voice.

"It's on the *Ares*," Umerah said, folding her arms across her new armor and scowling unpleasantly at Celeste. "No more secrets, old lady. Harris deserves to know everything."

Celeste sat up, brushing aside the artificial arms. They drew up into the ceiling like reverse footage of grass blades shivering out of soil. "You're right, Javed. Tell him."

Umerah took a breath. "The Electric Lagoon is comprised of specialists in ship-building. Most of them came over from Prometheus Industries, bringing hundreds of years' experience with them. Gethin and I arranged it so they were helping with the *Ares*'s construction."

"Just the *Ares*?" I asked, surprised. "Not the other habitats?"

"No. For the past few years, my specialists have been installing a shadow control system within the *Ares*. Antimatter was an essential ingredient."

It came together for me in a flash of understanding. "Stars almighty," I gasped. "You…holy shit!"

Celeste swung her legs off the gurney and stood. "It's the only way, Harris. Gethin doesn't want another war. He knows it would be useless. But he also knows that we can't stay in Sol System. He can't allow the IPC to control everyone—"

"So he's going to hijack the *Ares*! That's why…." Another piece fell into place. "My brother brought five thousand people with him. Five fucking thousand! Supposedly they're coming to inspect the *Ares*…but that's not the truth, is it? These people were preselected. They're the colonization force! They're leaving Sol System!"

I paced in a tight circle. For some reason I thought of the beaches at Lighthouse Point, stargazing with my brother. The Pope brothers dreaming of galactic voyages.

The O'Neill cylinders were the biggest construction project in history. Concealed around Jupiter, built in secret and with secret crews and secret blueprints and secret supply runs. Gethin Bryce had nestled into those layers of deception as was his talent. The habitats were already designed to be mobile; they'd be moved into orbit around each world. So Bryce and David and their devious cabal were going to turn it into the first extrasolar seedship.

"I'll bet I know where they're heading," I said. "Ra System, right? We know it has two habitable worlds. It's the logical choice."

Celeste nodded and said, "Yep. The problem is that we now have praetorians standing in our way."

"And the Partisans," I added.

"The Partisans? Harris, you're the only one still going on about—"

"The Partisans were in our hotel, Segarra. You met one of them – an old pal of mine – and didn't even realize it."

That gave her pause. Absently scratching at her neck, she said, "They infiltrated the Banshees, sure. So what? That doesn't mean they'll be on the *Ares*."

I laughed bitterly. "You really think they came back from the dead just to pose as mid-level mercs? Bishons has *always* been about two things: contingency and revenge. He's also been two steps ahead of everyone, so it's time we start thinking like him. Thirty years ago they hijacked a political movement you started. You really think they won't hijack your latest conspiracy?"

It was clear she didn't like what I was saying. Equally clear she didn't believe it. I looked to Umerah and saw similar doubts there.

"Come on," Celeste said, heading for the cockpit. "We arrive in seventeen minutes."

I placed my hand on her chest and stopped her. "No more secrets," I insisted.

She blinked. "You know everything now."

"Yeah? You sure about that?"

"Harris, there's nothing else to—"

"Ten years ago," I interrupted, "Sabrina Potts was killed on Luna. I'd assumed someone else had gotten to her...but it was a copy of me, wasn't it?"

Celeste stiffened.

The realization – the truth – hit me like a gut punch. "I suppose that's my answer," I whispered.

Behind us, Umerah cursed and stormed out of the medbay.

Celeste clasped my hands into her own. "Two months before you infiltrated the Bayne family," she explained, "the Order received actionable intel that General Potts was operating on Luna. That's a tad outside of redworld jurisdiction. We needed someone to check it out. An operative with inside knowledge and a proven knack for infiltration."

I wanted to slump to the floor.

"Harris, I'm sorry! We were only doing what we—"

"Tell me what happened."

She looked ready to cry. "You killed Potts, Harris. Like Peznowski, she was in several bodies and you hunted each one down and executed them all. You died in the process...but you accomplished the mission."

The medbay warped and shivered beneath a film of sliding water. I extricated my hands from Celeste and walked past her to the gurney, suddenly too weak to stand. Leaning there, hands flat on the blood-spattered edge, I said, "Back on Mars, you told me that my post-war missions were to clear me in the eyes of the Order. I've had time to think about that. Know what I concluded? It's horseshit. Dave and the brass should have been able to look at my Save file and see – right there in the data – that I wasn't a Partisan. So there must be a different reason why they treated me like shit... sending me out again and again like some attack dog."

The tears fell from Celeste's eyes. "Harris...listen to me, please. Maybe there are some things that should stay buried, okay? David *loves* you. He's been trying to build a life for you...for all of us. Please believe that...."

I shook my head coldly. "You know what, Celeste? Hanging out with you is a kind of cosmological terror. You and Gethin...even my brother... you're all perfect for each other. All I've ever done is scamper in your shadows. Nipping at the heels of gods."

I wasn't sure I had the strength to walk, but somehow my feet carried me to the doorway.

"I'm sorry," she whispered miserably.

"Me, too," I said, and joined my friends in the hold.

CHAPTER THIRTY-NINE

Arena

Whether the *Ares* was on lockdown or not, it didn't end up mattering to the *Mantid*. We overrode the airlock doors – or else, a co-conspirator already aboard the habitat did it for us – and we glided in, cycled through, and entered the hangar.

Unlike the *Coachlight*, the hangar was a ghost town. Some supply freighters were moored in orderly rows. A few transports were scattered about. Maintenance bots roved the periphery....

Then I saw McCallister's ship. It was moored two rows from where we hovered. Strangely, its cargo ramp was down....

The *Mantid* descended low, swept leftward to get a view of the enemy hold. Our floodlights snapped on, revealing an empty bay. No praetorians in their seats, no sign of their quarry.

"They left the door open," I said, frowning. "Why do that?"

Umerah joined us in the cockpit. "Maybe they set a trap for us," she suggested.

My unease deepened. "*Mantid*, bring us around to the front and open the ramp."

The ship complied. The transport's cabin door was slightly ajar.

I went to the ramp – Eric joining me without a word. Together we hopped out, shields deployed in side-by-side formation and with the *Mantid* providing all the cover we'd need. If the enemy was indeed waiting to ambush us, they had a rude wake-up in store.

We rounded to the cabin door. I used my boot to pry the door wide...
...and froze.

Eric was guarding my six; at my silence, he said, "What is it?"

"All clear," I said. "There's a body here."

Over the comlink, Celeste said, "What body?"

"Secretary of State Donna McCallister."

The third most powerful human in the known universe was reclining in her comfortable-looking seat. An expansive com-array spread around her, the controls within easy reach. I imagined McCallister had used these very controls to confirm David Julius Pope's present location, and perhaps to contact her administrative staff to begin preparing a press release on what was sure to be the biggest news of the century...bigger than the Martian civil war and the drama that had followed. The capture of Gethin Bryce, the arrest of President Pope...it would dominate the newsfeeds.

Yet it seemed that McCallister was now part of that story. She was dead in her seat.

She'd been shot twice at close range. One in the heart – perforating her toga. The *coup de grace* was to the head, spraying her brains onto the carpet and walls. Nor was she the only corpse; her pilot had taken several rounds in the flank, neck, and head. A messier, secondhand execution.

"Harris, talk to me!" Celeste demanded. "What do you mean, she's dead?"

"I mean exactly that." I climbed up to get a better view of the interior, half-expecting to see Bryce as further carnage. Yet the cabin was otherwise deserted.

"Son of a bitch," I breathed, and turned to Eric. "The praetorians killed her."

He frowned. "Why the hell would...." I saw him come to the same realization I had. "Holy shit."

"Talk to me!" Celeste demanded.

"McCallister's retinue of praetorians," I said, backing out of the transport and scanning the hangar. "They aren't praetorians, Celeste. They were wearing the right armor and wielding the right weapons... but they're—"

"Partisans?" I heard her caustic intake of breath. "Harris, how could you possibly—"

"Because they *needed* to be here. And they must still need Gethin, because they took him with them."

"Get back to the ship, both of you!"

I was returning to the *Mantid* when a small group of civilians emerged from behind another vessel. Drones whirled like fireflies above them. I noticed glossy badges clipped to their tunics, bearing the words PRESS CORP in large lettering.

Fucking hell. Of all times to be accosted by reporters!

"Excuse me!" the woman at the head of the group called out. "That's the secretary of state's ship! Can you talk to me for a minute?"

"Sorry, no comment," I said, turning away...

...and then I realized that I knew her voice.

"Excuse me!" The woman jogged up to me without fear, extending her hand in greeting. "Hi! We had a report that there was gunfire in the hangar, just minutes after the secretary of state's transport arrived. Can you talk to me?"

My mouth wouldn't work. My body seemed to have petrified in place. I stared helplessly at her offered hand.

"I'm Vanessa Jamison," she said. "Journalist with *The Martian Sentinel*."

The last time I'd seen Vanessa Jamison had been on Paradise Row. The plucky and intrepid reporter who had been first to expose the Partisan surveillance programs and death camps. The wretched creature who Peznowski had methodically reduced to a mutilated husk.

I couldn't meet her eyes. Could barely breathe.

"Mister...um...*Rybka*," she said, reading her HUD.

"I am," I whispered.

How many nights I had gone to sleep with this woman's piteous wails in my head? How I had seen Peznowski peel the skin from her body, asking above the screeching, "Does that hurt, Vanessa? Tell me how much you love my touch!"

"Mister Rybka," she said, "can you tell me what you're doing here?"

"I...um...."

She stared at me. "You're Martian. Do we...do we know each other?"

"Of course...you're famous. Everyone knows—"

"No, you *know* me," she insisted. "Did we…interact during the war?"

He regenned you inside-out once, a lumpish quivering bundle of viscera, screaming wordlessly in a corner.

"We did," I whispered.

"Your name and face aren't familiar."

"Because it's not my real name."

She hesitated. "Okay, what's your real—"

"Harris."

"Harris?"

We seemed like two specimens frozen in amber. Then I saw the realization dawn.

"Harris Alexander Pope?!"

Before I could react, Vanessa embraced me. She squeezed me so tight I felt the impact-gel of my clothes stiffening.

"I know they found my body on Phobos," she said into my shoulder. "I know I'd been prisoner there. I must have been there when you showed up to end the war!" She released me, tears in her eyes. "I've wanted to meet you for years! Bless you, Harris! May the stars always shine on your courage!"

I turned aside in a half-blind state. Vanessa started to pursue, but Eric stepped between us and said, "Ms. Jamison? I'm Eric Mazzola, former security chief at Tier Marsworks. I'd love to chat with you, but for now, here's an exclusive scoop: in the transport over there is the body of Donna McCallister. She was executed by Partisan war criminals. Some bad shit is about to go down. Please stay here and keep your head down. We'll talk when this is over, I promise you."

As we climbed back aboard the *Mantid*, Eric noticed that Celeste and Umerah were staring at him.

"I'm sick of the fucking secrets," he snapped. "It's full transparency from now on."

We settled into our seats.

The *Mantid* passed through a loading bay, and emerged into…

…into…

…Mars.

*   *   *

It was a version of Mars condensed – a world without a true sky, with swaths of topsy-turvy desert, cantons arranged in grids, canals crawling along the walls, and strips of forest tattooing the parks. The *Coachlight*'s hollow heaven had sported a track for its artificial sun, but our arrival on the *Ares* was during a nocturnal cycle; I saw pale imitations of Deimos and Phobos. The twin moonlights frosted evergreens and oak, medinas and waterways.

It was Mars…recreated in a tin can. A smaller, tidier, *controllable* Mars, where there would be no dust storms, no green swirl of aurora-belts. It made me wonder what the other habitats were like. Was Venus's twin a cloudy tempest? Did the *Zeus* boast a Red Spot?

I studied the viewscreen – most of the *Ares* was unlit. This wasn't surprising; the habitat was designed for colonization, but right now it only housed its workforce and the people my brother had brought.

Does the workforce know what David's planning? No, that's too many people to keep a secret. When he takes the vessel, he'll probably give them the choice: interstellar voyage into history, or exit by escape pod.

We were bearing down on a cluster of lights in the blackness.

"The Hellespont," Celeste explained. "It's where Dave is staying."

"He's gone MIA," I countered. "Tell me what your original plan was. We were due to arrive tomorrow and then…what, exactly? Dave gets on an intercom and shouts, 'Buckle up'?"

"More or less." She was deliberately avoiding my gaze, unsettled by our recent conversation. "Once we arrived, Gethin would initiate the activation sequence. A secondary system would go online, shutting out security overrides and killswitches. Our course is already plotted. The launch would be detected right away, but once we get cruising, it would be impossible for anyone to intercept us."

I stepped back from the viewscreen. "That's why they didn't kill Bryce. The Partisans eliminated McCallister…but they need the activation sequence."

The shadow-rich view was overlaid with blueprints. Hotel Hellespont appeared as a mighty structure in the Greco-Roman style, occupying the edge of a canton identified as Ylla Heights. Tramlines spread to other cantons; I studied the unlit space between those radials.

Then I saw a structure off by itself, one mile north of the Hellespont.

It appeared to be a natural outcropping of geology. And it probably was actual rock, harvested from the Belt or material beyond Pluto. Once in human clutches, it had been carved by human hands. It was, I thought, a perfect distillation of everything the habitat was: an homage to Mars, a cynical cash-in on redworld sentiment, and a testament to collective ego.

It was a moonlit Face.

On Mars, there was no actual anthropoid visage in our geology. Rather, on the plains of Cydonia there existed a formation; filtered through the lenses of imagination, it bore a superficial resemblance to human features. Pareidolia, the same phenomenon that let people see faces in burnt toast or clouds or craters.

"*Mantid*, please zoom in," I said.

The ship obliged. The Face on the horizon had been built to approximate the infamous Cydonian rocks; however, engineers had taken the matter further. An actual countenance had been carved. Unlike the Martian face, which was staring forever skyward, *this* Face was akin to Earth's Mount Rushmore, gazing across the plateau towards Ylla and the Hellespont. An amphitheater formed a half-circle around it, with concentric seating.

I touched the image. "*This* is where they've gone. This is where—"

The rest of my words were cut off as something hit the *Mantid*. I was blasted backwards in the cockpit.

The *Mantid* was hit again, and again...

...and fell from the skyless sky.

*   ★   ★

"Brace for impact!" Celeste screamed, and it was one of those moments in battle – a moment every soldier knows – where I was possessed by a hyperawareness of detail. Celeste in mid-shout, tendons in her neck rigid. A bloody fingerprint on the dashboard where she had touched a button. The ground rushing up as we plummeted....

The crash was stunning. The *Mantid* tumbled, rolling over, the hull screeching like a living thing; crazily, I wondered if the ship was *feeling* pain, or a data-set that could be processed as pain. Even strapped in, we were wildly tossed about. When darkness closed around us and the furious detonations subsided, it took me a while to realize I wasn't dead.

The viewscreen remained open. I squinted at it.

The Face was only a hundred meters ahead of our crash-site; a little more velocity and we would have skidded right into the amphitheater. Ship fragments littered the desert.

Our impact had thrown an immense dust cloud ahead of us. In that hazy particulate, an invisible shape was revealed, crouching gargoyle-like atop the wall. I was just starting to appreciate the blocky, distinctive silhouette when the *Mantid* – down but not out – fired its railguns. The CAMOed shape was knocked off the wall like a target at a carnival shooting gallery.

Down, I thought grimly, but not out.

"Everyone out!" I ordered, unstrapping my harness and helping Celeste from her seat. "Eric! Umerah! Report!"

The trog's gravelly tones issued from the hold. "We're alive."

"*Mantid*, are you...um...okay?"

[I shall provide cover as you deploy,] the ship replied.

"That wasn't really an answer."

[It's what you intended to ask me. I am opening the ramp.] There was a hesitation. [I would prefer if you all would survive.]

★　　★　　★

We emerged from the downed vessel into Martian dusk; the artificial moons were brighter than their natural inspirations, and blotted out much of the firmament.

We lined up in phalanx formation, side-by-side, Celeste on the left flank and myself on the right. We were a mile from the nearest settlement.

The complexities of urban warfare – with buildings and alleys – were not going to feature into this assault. We were exposed. Our positions were known. The enemy probably had airhounds tracking us, and so I dispatched my own; the little spies wheeled over the amphitheater wall, and fed us the view.

"Fuck," Eric whispered.

The praetorians were in the amphitheater. They had gathered into a tight grouping.

More worryingly, there were not four praetorians. There were eight. The squad from Chilon Tower had apparently found reinforcements… and that was only what we could see. Their visible numbers were surely meant as distraction. A smart enemy would deploy additional agents in CAMO, setting up a crossfire.

Behind the praetorian line, two men in civilian clothing stood against the Face. They were cuffed, and both wore disruption collars. The shorter of the two was Gethin Bryce. The taller was—

"Dave."

As if in response to my voice, one of the praetorians broke off and approached the hostages. He aimed a rifle at my brother.

"Wait!" I shouted. "General Lanier Bishons! I'm coming up to talk! Hold fire!"

The amphitheater wall was only a few meters tall. In the simulated Martian gravity, it was easy to hop onto its crest. In the same flourish, my compatriots hopped into place beside me, shields out. Moving together, we entered the amphitheater.

The praetorians formed a defensive line…and retreated several steps. That was surprising. They should have held their ground. Was it a tactical withdrawal? Why? By retreating, they were allowing us to gain ground with them. The calculus of the situation rotated in my mind: we were outnumbered, outmatched, outgunned by every conceivable metric. Didn't they realize that?

I surveyed the enemy line. In a coordinated flourish, the praetorians touched their helmets, switching their visors to transparency.

I spotted Bishons in the mix. He didn't form the center of the group as expected, but was in fact the one with a gun on my brother.

As for the others, my blood boiled at the sight. They were the Partisans' top brass from Phobos, wearing yet another guise – praetorian armor. I saw Sabrina Potts (sans eye-patch), and Monteiro (in her Vilhelmina Krohl body), and Seraphim Pronovost, Wesam Mujahid, Andrey Popova, Kazafumi Ortiz, and….

"Peznowski!" I grinned through my hate. "Long time, *compadre*! I left you a little gift at Chilon Tower: one of *your* bodies! We all know how you like to play with yourself!"

He glared at me with murderous intent. The others didn't look angry. They didn't look smug. They looked…

…afraid.

How could that be? The most serene face in the group was the rocky carving itself, eyes pitted and lips compressed in a stony, inexpressive line.

"The Face," I said, nodding appreciatively. "So *this* is what it all comes down to. What was the plan? You burrow in like cicadas while the *Ares* takes flight? Then what?" I addressed Bishons. "What was the master plan, Lanier? Once you steal the ship, people would eventually find you're aboard."

The Partisan general said nothing.

"Ah," I continued. "Gonna go undercover, huh? Print some new faces and sneak into society again? I'll bet…" I looked to my brother, who met my gaze with a desperate, defeated expression. "…one of you would impersonate the president, right? Others would become whoever they needed to. Bodysnatching your way into total control. Not a bad plan, but you forgot an important detail." I winked. "Me."

Peznowski snapped. "Your time is over, you fucking traitorous—"

"I told you before," I countered, "*I'll never stop tracking you*. That's my entire purpose, don't you get it? That's the reason I exist!" I felt David's eyes on me and I avoided his look. "I even killed General Potts on Luna! Do you understand? *I'll always be after you!*"

Peznowski sighted me in his rifle scope; our group tightened our formation, shields in *testudo* arrangement.

"Stand down, Caleb!" Bishons commanded. "Harris Pope, I'm prepared to make a deal."

I laughed. "Right, like the deal you offered on the *Coachlight*?"

Celeste cut in. "We want Bryce and the president. If your deal doesn't include them, you can kiss my—"

"They're yours," Bishons insisted.

She blinked, clearly rocked by this capitulation. I glanced to my compatriots. Umerah gave nothing away; she regarded the enemy with the hard gaze of a combat vet. Standing shoulder-to-shoulder with her, Eric was an avatar of rage, visibly primed for violence and vengeance.

Bishons called out, "What did I tell you, Commander Pope? This was never about you. We wanted a free Mars, and that dream was stolen from us! This ship – this replica of the homeworld – can rectify that! We'll set sail and never be heard from again. We'll be far away...far beyond the IPC's reach. A beachhead where people can thrive and prosper in liberty!"

I looked to his subordinates and shuddered, imagining a world where these beasts were in charge again. The founders of death camps and police states. Murderers and torturers and would-be demigods.

"You can have your *loved ones* back," Bishons continued, and stared meaningfully at Gethin. "Just as soon as our voyage is underway."

Gethin sighed. "I'll do it," he said.

The Partisan general touched the controls on his wrist-gauntlet. The lights on Gethin's disruption collar winked off.

Gethin closed his eyes. There was a sudden vibration through the ground, like a distant marsquake. The moonlights wavered. The *Ares*'s engines – still warm from its maiden voyage– were moving again. This time, it wasn't a voyage into gentle orbit. This time they were pushing towards the frontier.

Xenophon spoke in my audio: *Harris, the Ares has launched.*

Even the Partisans were gazing about, appreciating that we were committed; the eyes of the solar system were on the O'Neill cylinders, and people would instantly notice one making an unscheduled launch. Battleships would soon be bearing down on us.

We're in it now.

"We've set sail," Gethin told Bishons. "We're on our way to the stars. Now it's your turn. Let *them* go. They can take the escape pods."

Bishons licked his lips. "Not so fast," he said. "I need total system access. The entire blueprints and all technical staff you've got here. We've got time, Bryce. We'll be in IPC borders for a while yet. Time for verification before I let you and your friends—"

"You'll never let us go," I broke in.

The Partisans watched me. These bygone demons...these destroyers of worlds...these imposters.

And that was just it, wasn't it? The Partisans had built their entire career out of being imposters. They'd posed as saviors of Mars only to obliterate it. They'd returned from the dead as strategists for interplanetary war... only to stage a hijacking. And here they were again – cancers in the shape of men and women – dressed as *soldiers*, their latest Halloween ploy, and the most directly insulting. None of them had ever seen combat. None had been pinned down in the Noctis. Praetorian armor and gizmos aside, these were not veterans of combat.

And that meant that, despite how things looked, we were *not* outmatched.

Bishons grasped my brother by the arm, but didn't look away from me. "Commander Pope, we can all get what we want. Do we have a—"

"Deal?" I said. "With you, Lanier? There's just one problem in making a deal with *you*. See, you brutalized Mars. You captured and oppressed and tortured its people. You terrorized the populace with your shadowmen police. That ends *today*. I represent the Order of Stone. I am here to bring justice. I am here to show you that the injuries you inflicted upon Mars will not go unpunished. My name—"

The Partisans ignited their body-length shielding.

"—is Harris Alexander Pope. And I am the last thing you will ever see."

It was difficult to know who technically fired first – the enemy opened up on our barricade as I lobbed a grenade over my shield-rim. What mattered was not the command to fire.

It was the command I sent to Xenophon.

The command to break through the station firewalls, access gravity controls...

...and spin down the habitation module.

CHAPTER FORTY

Man Dissolved in Time

Our shields flared bright, taking fire, and the ground thumped from deflected rounds. The Partisans weren't aiming at us – they *wanted* to hit our shields, and I knew damn well why. In the loss of gravity, plumes of dust spread around us. We held the line, affixed by our magfiber boots.

My grenade hit the ground. Two-second timer.

I'd figured that a praetorian's combat suite fed battlefield data directly to their HUD – so they should have reacted to the grenade. Should have blurred away from the blast zone. As it was, only Bishons responded to the threat. Grasping Bryce by the collar, he leapt away.

Monteiro, Ortiz, and Popova were closest to the detonation and were flung into the sky. I caught a brief glance of Monteiro's face – her bulging eyes – before she was lost to view.

The remainder of the enemy line was scattered. Peznowski slammed halfway up the Face; he planted his boots, sticking there, and fired a shot above our heads.

"Got it!" Eric cried. Without breaking formation, he rotated enough for a clear shot at the unfurling waspbots and fired an EMP into their midst.

As the Partisans struggled to orient themselves in the zero-G, I tracked Bishons and his quarry. The general had landed halfway up the amphitheater seating and was pushing off again – a leap that would take him out of the amphitheater entirely. As Celeste and Umerah opened up on the remaining hostiles, I made an ammo selection...one of the Banshee rifle's more unusual functions. The same feature I'd witnessed in Drop Town, and the one Eric had reminded me about aboard the *Mantid*.

As Bishons launched himself with Gethin in his grip, I fired a SCAB round ahead of him.

The nanoshield blossomed into a glowing wall. Bishons was in mid-leap and unable to react. He struck it headlong with a sickening *crack*, losing his hold on Gethin. The men flew apart, Bishons sailing limply over our heads. Gethin cartwheeled towards the top of the amphitheater. At the last second, he managed to grab hold of the ledge, preventing a one-way fall into heaven.

Oh well. Can't get everything we want.

Harris! Xenophon cried. ***Shieldfist malfunction imminent!***

I'd expected that, the lessons from Hellas never far from my thoughts. "Eject shields!" I called to my squad. "Replacement cartridges *now*!"

My friends complied without hesitation. David floated in the midst of the chaos, looking bewildered, a man in a dream.

"Contact above!" Eric shouted, and I looked up. Monteiro and the two others who had been blown skyward were returning…using some goddam jetpack option on their suits. Before I could decide on how to deal with them, the *Mantid* decided for me; from its grounded position, it shot the Partisans out of the sky like clay pigeons. The fusillade shredded their shielding and armor; my final sight of Monteiro and her cohorts was watching their mangled corpses career to the west like ill-fated meteors.

"*Harris!*"

It was my brother's voice. I turned to see that he had managed to snag one of the praetorian rifles from the air.

"Do it!" I called to him.

Several things happened at once. As my brother opened fire, the Partisans were recovering from the grenade blast and – more ominously – employing the same jetpack capabilities as Monteiro had tried. David was unarmored, an easy target, but he was shooting every Partisan in sight. I didn't know if the praetorian rounds would dissolve praetorian shielding, but he was going for broke. At the same time, Eric and Umerah launched grenades to both enemy flanks. With explosives hurtling left and right, my brother shooting them, and an AI vessel eager for more targets, the Partisans were afforded only one escape option:

Straight into us.

They came barreling forward. Celeste and I pushed off together to meet the assault, forming the tip of the opposing spear.

The impact staggered both sides. Some of the Partisans got through, others were knocked into the sky.

Enemy shields are collapsing! said Xenophon triumphantly.

It was true! The body-length shielding warped and shriveled like paper in a fireplace. No doubt that replacement cartridges were locked and loaded in their armor. No doubt we'd have only a few seconds to take advantage of this opportunity.

We only *needed* a few seconds.

Concentrating our fire, we opened up point-blank on every hostile. Armor splintered, ablative layers burning away. General Mujahid attempted flight from the killing zone; Eric fired a laser into his jetpack and there was an explosion that tore the man in half, his legs spinning towards Ylla.

It must have been Gethin, freed of the disruption collar, who reengaged gravitational controls. We drifted down towards the amphitheater.

A sharp pain took me in the back and I cried out. For a moment, I thought it was shrapnel from the jetpack explosion. When I turned, though, I saw Peznowski, crouched on one knee on the far side of the arena, the butt of his rifle tucked into his shoulder in a classic sniper's position.

He's killed me. Like in Hellas, my heart has been shot clean and I am about to die.

Then I realized this couldn't be. Impact data appeared on my HUD: a bullet had penetrated my armor and was lodged in my chest, missing my heart by inches.

An instant later, Peznowski was knocked flat as Eric fired a laser. Within seconds, we had him surrounded; Celeste tore his weapon away, trigger-finger coming with it. Peznowski shrieked. Umerah slammed the butt of her rifle into his mouth, spilling teeth.

The bullet in my chest burned inside me. I deadened the surrounding nerves and stared into my enemy's eyes.

Blood slimed Peznowski's mouth. The laser had shattered his visor and scorched one ear away. He saw the rifles aimed at him. He coughed, sputtered, and saw me.

"Gonna give me your death speech, Harris?" he spat. "Save it for yourself, you fucking traitor!"

I glanced at the scene. Three Partisans had fallen out of the sky. One had exploded. Two more were crumpled in the amphitheater. Peznowski would make seven, meaning....

From atop the wall, Gethin Bryce called, "If you're looking for Bishons, he's beating a retreat. On foot! Across the desert!"

I turned back to Peznowski.

"Go ahead!" the monster screamed. "You'll *never* stamp me out! You'll never be rid of me!"

We aimed our rifles into his face. Flicked the ammo wheels to laser.

He laughed, then screeched, as we cooked him alive.

*　　*　　*

"There." Gethin pointed, his outstretched finger indicating a lonely, fleeing figure in the dual moonlight.

My chest spasmed painfully. I deadened the next cluster of nerves, ignoring the data in my HUD, the warning that flashed over a diagram of my body. I even powered down my sensorium, silencing Xenophon's insistent protests.

Dave joined us and stared into the desert, watching the escaping general. Even from a distance, we could see that it was Bishons. He was limping, dragging one useless leg.

I looked through my rifle scope and moved the crosshairs over him. My fingers tightened around the trigger.

Before I could take the shot, however, the desert around Bishons seemed to pop. He stumbled, whirled about in confusion. Sand burst near his feet. The desert shivered and danced with tiny impacts, from a source I couldn't discern.

A chunk of the general's pulverized armor blew off. Then another. He changed directions, twisting into his own elongated shadow. Something struck him in the shoulder and he screamed, dropping to one knee.

"People are shooting at him," David said in awe. "Who...how...."

Gethin pointed to the sky.

The opposite side of the *Ares* was not so distant that the sputter of rifles was difficult to see. There must have been a vast crowd up there, taking aim at their sky and shooting...

...at the man who had destroyed their home.

"Seems that our fight was livestreamed," Gethin said. "Must be an airhound or news drone watching us." His eyes quivered as he read something on his optics. "Someone named Vanessa Jamison is broadcasting Bishons' position to everyone aboard."

I relaxed my finger around the trigger. Out in the desert, the once-proud general of Partisan Command had curled into a fetal ball. He screamed, sobbed, and begged for mercy – mercy he'd never granted anyone – as he was shot to pieces.

* * *

The pain in my chest was becoming unbearable, snaking past the deadened nerve clusters. I slumped onto the amphitheater wall, letting my rifle clatter to my feet.

David rushed to my side. "Harris! What's wrong? Are you hit?"

"It's okay," I slurred. "We won, right?"

Umerah and Celeste were suddenly by my side. They looked good – uninjured, healthy, vigorous, and alive. That made me happy. As pain spread from my chest to my head, the only thing I cared about was knowing that my friends and family were going to be all right. Pain I could deal with. I'd lived with it for as long as I could remember.

Celeste knelt by me. "Harris, what happened?"

"Crawlnest," I said. "It's working its way through my body."

"We've got to get you to the *Mantid*!" she cried, and Umerah tried pulling me to my feet.

I shook off her attempt. "I want to speak to my brother."

"Harris! If you've got a crawlnest in you, there's only minutes before—"

"Celeste," I said, "let me make my own choices for once."

"But I can save you if—"

"I want to speak to Dave, alone."

Gethin backed away, taking Celeste by the arm as he went. Eric came bounding over, but Gethin stayed him.

Umerah swallowed hard. She looked ready to argue, or weep, but in the end she retreated with the others.

"What are you doing?" Dave demanded. "Harris? We can help you! Why would you—"

"Thirty years ago," I interrupted, "you and I went to Ybarra for drinks. We had an argument. The next day, our parents were arrested. We were arguing about the Partisans, weren't we?"

Tears spilled from my brother's eyes. "Harris...."

"I didn't volunteer to become a Partisan on that yacht." I watched his face. "There was no yacht, was there? You implanted that memory. We argued in Ybarra...because I had already become a Partisan, isn't that right?"

Dave clasped me by the shoulders and cried. "It doesn't matter now! We're together again! We can make everything right!"

"I was a Partisan," I repeated, the pain worming its way into my head. My vision was going gray around the edges. My limbs were sluggish, my heart skipping beats. "I joined the Partisans willingly. I'm the reason our family was destroyed. In Hellas, you didn't 'reactivate' me, Dave; you changed me *from* a Partisan. You rewrote my loyalties."

Dave cradled my face. "We won the war, Harris. All that is in the past now! Now is what we own, right? Isn't that what you always say?"

The gray fog washed over my vision and I was blind. With the fog came a chill that sank into my bones...but there was something comforting in it. I was the man dissolved in fog again. I suddenly felt a woman's hand interlacing with my own. Was it Celeste? Umerah?

Or had Yama Uba come for me? Was she about to kiss me to eternal sleep?

"Whatever I was years ago," I murmured, "I renounce that life. I love you, Dave."

My brother's tears dappled my face. "Harris, we can *still* be a family! *Please! I can't lose you now!*"

I held the mystery woman's hand until I could feel nothing, hear nothing. Someone was screaming my name but the sound was a million miles away.

"I didn't want any of this," I whispered to whoever could hear me. "I wanted a different life. Wanted to be

EPILOGUE

Colonist

With the Ares *now beyond anyone's reach, the fallout continues to be felt across the solar system. The in-transit communication from former Martian President David Julius Pope has detailed a shocking and horrifying conspiracy reaching to the highest levels of government.*

The revelation implicates Secretary of State Donna McCallister, along with six IPC senators. Saturnian President Keiko Yamanaka issued a blistering statement this morning, declaring, "Certain high-ranking individuals within the IPC have clearly perpetrated a grotesque plan that threatens the inalienable rights of every citizen." Yamanaka was joined by Jovian President Dion Bellamy and – in an astounding development – Venusian President Allison Waltari has severed trade relations with Earth pending a 'fully transparent investigation into the matter'.

Meanwhile, the political ramifications continue to quake throughout the system. With Mars officially rejoining IPCnet, newly sworn-in President Ian Stormfall Nazari and Senator Natalia Argos stated that, "In light of alarming new developments, the Colonization Ban must be viewed as the imprisoning walls of a gulag. It must be overturned, and quickly."

An unnamed source from the Office of Internal Affairs added that evidence links the IPC to criminal elements on the Coachlight, *and may even include Partisan war criminals....*

—Vanessa Jamison, The Martian Sentinel

★   ★   ★

The blue sun in a violet sky would take some getting used to. I could deal with the spindly mountains, their crests like the browned tips of a lemon meringue pie. Nor did the Jormungandr Sea, squeezed like a python around the equator of Osiris, bother me. It wasn't all that different from the waters that filled out the basins of Mars. I liked watching the alien sea. Liked imagining what lived beneath the waves.

There was, I mused, enough mystery to sustain me for a long time. The colony – Sagacious Bay, as the passengers of the *Ares* had named it – was steadily growing. Crops were abundant, and filtration systems pumped seawater into cisterns. Scientific expeditions were taking cautious steps into the fungal forests, the tundra, and the mountains. Osiris was a strange world. There was much to learn about it.

I lay on a picnic table, surrounded by a young blueberry orchard. Leaning back, enjoying the sun and fragrant breeze, I closed my eyes. I listened to the waves lapping the shore.

The blueberry bushes rustled around an approaching body. "Hey," someone called to me. "You asleep?"

I turned and looked at my visitor.

"Segarra," I said.

She was sweating, and the blue sunlight caught her face in scales of frost. She had also grabbed some berries on her walk, and she leaned over, dropped one into my waiting mouth. "You see the latest news from Sol?"

I sighed, chewing the berry, letting the bittersweet flavor spread across my tongue. "Let me guess. The IPC is sending an invasion fleet."

Celeste shook her head. "Stars, Harris. When did you become such a nihilist?"

"Like *you're* one to talk."

She shielded her eyes from the sun, viewing the ocean and the new harbor. "Our frontier is about to get reinforcements."

"Oh?"

"The Colonization Ban was overturned. Other colony ships have left Sol. One is heading to Dagda. Another to Shakespeare." She popped a berry into her mouth. "And another is coming here."

"Just as long as they bring a Brockhouse Coffee." I sat up as something breached the ocean surface. I had a glimpse of bizarre, flower-like growths on a mottled, spiny body. The creature glided along the surface, as if letting its floral growths drink in the local sun.

Celeste placed her hand over mine. I spread my fingers, welcoming her touch. With her free hand, she pointed. "What do you think that thing is?"

"A reason not to go swimming."

"A monster," she said thoughtfully, and then laughed. "As if we're remotely qualified to judge what constitutes a monster."

"*I'm* qualified."

"Tier Marsworks is coming here. They're part of the next colonization wave."

"They should rebrand."

"Oh, they already have. They go by Tier Starsworks now."

"Joy." I watched the sea creature for half a minute until it glided out of sight; colonists along the beach excitedly shadowed its course. Then I sighed again and said, "Where's Gethin?"

"Who knows?" Celeste kissed my fingers. "He said he was heading off to the mountains with the *Mantid*. You believe that? Maybe he's going to grow a beard and live up there like some sage."

I plucked another berry from her hands and ate it. "There's an equal chance he's hatching some new plan. Why did he want to come *here*? Why choose *this* landing site? Why take the *Mantid*? I've known dangerous people in my life, but that guy takes the fucking cake."

Celeste laughed softly and tugged my hand. "Come on, let's go."

I raised an eyebrow. "Where are we going?"

"The first crop of cacao was harvested this morning. You and I are going to enjoy a hot chocolate."

"No thanks," I said.

She looked at me curiously. "What *do* you want?"

By way of answer, I breathed in the air and smelled an approaching storm. The horizon seethed with a squall line of cumulonimbus clouds. Osirian storms were an awe-inspiring sight, hovering mainly around the equator, and the thought of seeing another one gave me a pleasurable chill.

"I have what I want," I said at last.

"Working on a blueberry farm?" Celeste said skeptically.

"People need to eat. This is our first major crop, so don't be so dismissive."

"You're not a farmer, Harris."

"I'm whatever I want to be, Segarra."

She rolled the last of the berries between her fingers, watching the juices stain her palm. "Didn't you once tell Mazzola that a soldier never retires?"

"We're not at war anymore." Thunder boomed low on the horizon, the distant clouds flickering. "Have you heard from Mazzola?"

"You mean after he saved your life on the *Ares*? Did I tell you that he put an EMP into your chest? Said it was only fair. Anyway, he's back on Mars. I don't think space travel is his cup of tea."

I nodded. "And Umerah?"

"*That* one." She shook her head. "You think *I'm* a cipher? Stars, Harris…while you were in recovery, I personally asked Javed to stay with us. Do you know what she said? She looked me straight in the eye and announced that she'd love to, but had to clean up some messes that *I* left behind in Sol!"

"She's going after Quinn," I guessed. "If he has any backup copies – and he would – she's going to destroy them and bring down his entire enterprise. Good for her." I felt a lonely pang in my heart, thinking of how many light years separated us. Yet an unaccountable knowledge filled me…a conviction that seemed more than wishful thinking. I somehow *knew* I'd be seeing Umerah again. I felt it in my bones.

"What about you?" I asked. "What do you want?"

"That's the sixty-four-thousand-dollar question."

"Okay, even my slang app can't explain that one."

She smiled and slurped the juices in her hand. Stars above, she looked adorable when she smiled.

"I'm going to get some chocolate," she said. "Why don't you come with me? Please?"

"You go on ahead," I said. "I have some things to do first."

Celeste walked off, disappearing into the foliage.

The first fat droplet of rain hit my hand. The storm lowed, shifted in the heavens. The farmers began heading inside. As the rain fell harder, I approached one of them.

"Good afternoon!" I called to him.

The ID bubble in my HUD identified him as Trevor Morgan, a fresh-faced young colonist. He looked surprised to see me. "Mister Pope! I thought you and your brother joined that expedition to the caves."

"I decided to hang back and look into a couple things."

Drones flew overhead, deploying umbrellas for the workers as they retreated from the field. Morgan grinned as an umbrella hovered over us, the rain pouring over the sides and enclosing us in a liquid curtain.

"Hey, Morgan?" I said.

"Yes, Mister Pope? Is everything okay?"

"Not yet, but it will be." I took him by the arm and steered him towards an equipment shed. "There's a discrepancy I need to clear up. It's about you."

"Mister Pope, you're hurting my arm...."

"I made it my business," I continued, pulling him along, "to take a full accounting of everyone aboard the *Ares*. I double-checked all backgrounds of all colonists. Yours was interesting, Morgan. Seems your credentials were falsified. Seems there's no record of you outside the *Ares*. Seems you didn't even *exist* before we set sail. Now, why would that be?"

He fought in my grip as we reached the shed and I shoved him inside. His eyes kindled in familiar hatred.

"This is better, isn't it, Morgan? A nice quiet place to talk. See, I have something important to say...something just for you. So you listen, okay?"

I let the door slam shut behind me, as another peal of thunder shook the heavens outside.

ACKNOWLEDGEMENTS

I would like to express my gratitude to many people and organizations for their support and inspiration in the writing of this novel. This includes, but is not limited to: the wonderful folks at Flame Tree Press, Robert J. Sawyer and Writers of the Future, Mike Resnick, David Farland, Tim Powers, Trevor Quachri of *Analog Science Fiction and Fact*, Charles Coleman Finlay and Sheree Renée Thomas of *The Magazine of Fantasy & Science Fiction*, Shahid Mahmud and Lezli Robyn of *Galaxy's Edge, Science & Futurism with Isaac Arthur*, Colin Sullivan of *Nature*, Kelly A. Harmon and Vonnie Winslow Crist of Pole to Pole Publishing; Marguerite Reed, Tina Gower, Andrea Stewart, Eric Cline, Douglas Sobon, Jay Novella, Cortney Novella, Jacek Chodnicki, Bob Wooster, John Forish, Josh McGaw, David Afsharirad, my grandfathers for their compelling firsthand experiences in World War Two, and Donna Breault for being the very first to read this book and provide invaluable feedback.

FLAME TREE PRESS
FICTION WITHOUT FRONTIERS
Award-Winning Authors & Original Voices

Flame Tree Press is the trade fiction imprint of Flame Tree
Publishing, focusing on excellent writing in horror and the
supernatural, crime and mystery, science fiction and fantasy.
Our aim is to explore beyond the boundaries of the everyday,
with tales from both award-winning authors and original voices.

•

Book One in the series by Brian Trent:
Ten Thousand Thunders

You may also enjoy:
The Sentient by Nadia Afifi
The Emergent by Nadia Afifi
American Dreams by Kenneth Bromberg
Junction by Daniel M. Bensen
Interchange by Daniel M. Bensen
Second Lives by P.D. Cacek
The City Among the Stars by Francis Carsac
The Haunting of Henderson Close by Catherine Cavendish
The Garden of Bewitchment by Catherine Cavendish
Vulcan's Forge by Robert Mitchell Evans
Black Wings by Megan Hart
Stoker's Wilde by Steven Hopstaken & Melissa Prusi
Stoker's Wilde West by Steven Hopstaken & Melissa Prusi
The Widening Gyre by Michael R. Johnston
The Blood-Dimmed Tide by Michael R. Johnston
Those Who Came Before by J.H. Moncrieff
The Sky Woman by J.D. Moyer
The Guardian by J.D. Moyer
The Last Crucible by J.D. Moyer
The Goblets Immortal by Beth Overmyer
The Apocalypse Strain by Jason Parent
Until Summer Comes Around by Glenn Rolfe
A Killing Fire by Faye Snowden
Fearless by Allen Stroud
Resilient by Allen Stroud
Screams from the Void by Anne Tibbets

•

Join our mailing list for free short stories, new release details,
news about our authors and special promotions:

flametreepress.com